Fran Brady is a native of Dundee and a graduate of St. Andrews University. After a varied career in the voluntary sector, she turned from charity management to writing novels, short stories and the occasional poem. She has lived and worked all over Scotland and now lives in a village in West Lothian.

She writes wherever and whenever she can – *have laptop, will travel* – but her favourite time is very early in the morning when the rest of the world seems to be asleep. She is a member of a writing group that meets weekly in an old pub in Edinburgh.

She has one other published novel, *The Ball Game,* (www.franbrady.com) plus a collection of short stories, *Tales to Dip Into,* and a children's story, *The Honeysuckle Bird Café.*

Fran has three daughters, a stepson, six grandchildren, a husband and a dog.

A Good Time for Miracles is also available as an e-book from www.booksanctuary.co.uk or from the Amazon Kindle store

This book is dedicated to
the memory of my father,
Jack Brady, who gave me the
childhood memories this book
is based on.

A GOOD TIME FOR MIRACLES

by Fran Brady

Published in 2012 by FeedARead.com Publishing – Arts Council funded

PROLOGUE

1949

She awoke slowly, still in thrall to the dream. Then it receded, yielding to the brutal reality of this morning. They were gone, gone at last. She could no longer deny, pretend or hope.

The dream had been so real: she was a little girl again, watching her granny cleaning the dog's teeth. Granny cleaned her own teeth by taking them out and putting them in a jar of water overnight but the process with the slack-mouthed, slobbery dog was very different. Granny used an old toothbrush, worn to stubby spikes, like the one Kate's mother used for rubbing the Brasso off their candlesticks. She brushed the back molars first, four rows, close-together, good for gnawing; then she did the front teeth, hard and blunt, good for nipping; and finally the four incisors, good for snapping. The dog allowed Granny to manipulate his loose, dripping lips, eyes rolling towards his reward - the handful of cake crumbs on the table.

She pictured the dog's mouth: gnawing, nipping, snapping. She thought of the past year of her life: the arguments and the pleading, the false reassurances hiding secret progress; then birth certificates, passports, letters from recently-emigrated friends who would accommodate them till they found work and housing, forms to apply for assisted passages, savings lifted from post office accounts, new clothes and luggage bought; and finally, the date for sailing, the farewell party, the plans for transport to Southampton docks. Gnawing, nipping and snapping, like a dog tearing up an old slipper, the process had demolished her pathetic attempts to turn back the tide. She lay watching the summer dawn teasing the edges of the curtains, its brightness mocking her misery as she thought back over the year…

She hummed softly as she worked her way slowly round her sitting-room: Tuesday was always sitting-room day in her weekly housework programme and she lovingly lifted, dusted and replaced the

5

dozens of ornaments and photo-frames. Her hands shook a little as she dusted the crystal goblets and decanter in the cabinet. Imagine if she ever broke or even chipped one! They had belonged to Johnnie's great-aunt and were worth, he said, serious-money. They had been his mother's pride and joy and she had given them to her son on his marriage with meticulous instructions for their care. She moved on in relief to the welter of trashy souvenirs on top of the piano, swirling the feather duster among them. She fetched up in the bay window. To her delight, a young, pretty girl emerged from the shop on the opposite corner of the crossroads, chatting to an exiting customer. She drummed her fingers on the window-sill impatiently until the girl briefly looked across and up. She waved frantically; the girl gave her a jaunty 'thumbs-up' then disappeared back into the shop.

　　She smiled to herself as she moved through to her small kitchen to begin cooking the midday meal. She shook her head, a fond smile tempering disapproval. 'Maureen and her thumbs-up,' she thought. 'American nonsense.' All the fault of those GI Joes the girls had been dazzled by during the war. Good job they had all gone home now. There was altogether too much stuff about those faraway lands across the Atlantic Ocean: people talking of emigrating; advertisements offering passages on huge ships; young folks imagining streets paved with gold. 'Why, only the other night,' she thought, 'Maureen and Robbie were mooning over a book about Canada. As if the grass would be any greener. They'd never go and leave me…'

　　'Och Ma, it'll no matter if ye're bubbling. A' the mithers'll be greetin'.'

　　She shook her head. 'Ah jist cannae, hen.' Her voice, reed-thin, piped from her tight throat. 'Ah'll say ma guid-byes here and yer faither'll go wi ye tae the station.'

　　The girl acknowledged a lost cause and turned back to her ironing though whether they would get any more clothes in the case was doubtful.

　　The boy breezed in. 'A' set!' he announced. 'Ma case is closed. Dad an me're aff fur wee farewell dram.' He was quite the man now, old enough to go to the pub at last.

　　'Ma's no comin' tae see us aff,' Maureen was struggling to push the last frock into the case. 'She'd be better tae. She'll jist sit here greetin' on her ain. She'd be better among a' the ither mithers and *faithers at the station. They can a' comfort each ither. Tell her, Robbie.'*

He paused on his way out, jingling the dram-money in his pocket. Then he dropped down on one knee in front of her. She kneaded her fingers in his black curly hair as she always did. Tears – where had she found more? – fell on her hands and his hair. He reached up and wiped her cheeks with his own rough fingers. 'Jist you dae whit ye want, Ma,' he said.

As he moved back towards the door, she raised her head and showed her ravaged face. He winked cheerily and the outside door banged as he went off to meet his father at the miners' welfare club for that last drink...

But wait! The dream had its ending: the dog had its reward for submission. She turned her head and considered her sleeping husband. He might, could, *must* be persuaded.

Waiting in the butcher's queue, the warm summer morning intensifying the blood and sawdust stench, the women chatted. Except for Kate: she was frowning, looking intently at the ground, lips moving on a whispered monologue, then head jerking up as the queue shifted and she could gain a better view of the counter and its wares. The women glanced at her and then at each other.

'She's no hersel yet, puir lass. She's awfy doon,' thought Senga, Kate's next door neighbour.

'She's fair makin' a mountain oot o' a molehill. Anybody wad think they were deid. Kate's aye got tae dae the big drama!' thought Aggie, Kate's sister.

But Kate was neither despairing nor dramatising: Kate was planning, her eyes screwed up, her lips moving.

'There's gigot chops the day. That's his favourite. But last time they were a bit tough so Ah need to cook them awfy slow. An Ah'll pit some barley in wi them, he fair likes that. Ah'll start them aff richt awa when Ah get hame and let them hae twa hoors at the lowest gas. Oh, but Ah hae tae brown them first in the big pan wi some dripping, that keeps the flavour in an maks them look bonny. Ah winnae need ony mair tatties, there's plenty left. Ah'll mash them wi the top o' the milk – but wait, he had that on his porridge this mornin'. Ah'll need tae use

7

a wee drap evaporated milk instead. And Ah must remember he's decided he likes his carrots no quite cooked these days – he read in the papers that they're better fur ye, though Ah cannae see how, they gie me heartburn . . . '

It was her turn at last. The butcher beamed at Kate, admiring, as he always did, her soft wavy hair and wonderful dark eyes. He chose two of the biggest lamb chops, so big that the price he announced once they were on the scales, caused a gasp among those women near enough to hear.

'He's chancin' his airm. Half of that weight's bone and fat. The daftie'll surely no fa fur that,' thought Aggie.

'Kate'll tell him whaur tae get aff. Does he think her heid's buttoned up the back?' wondered Senga.

Kate barely registered the price and opened her purse. 'Is it a wee special occasion, then?' smirked the delighted butcher.

'Och, aye! Ye could say that.' Kate raised her voice 'Ye see, we're gaun tae Canada oorsels, tae live oot there with Maureen and Robbie.' She handed over a half-crown then sailed out the door, not waiting for her change, carving a swathe through the queuing women.

'Whit a show-aff! She'll get her come-uppance. Gaun tae Canada? Fat chance she's got,' muttered Aggie.

'Oh, Kate, my puir lassie,' mourned Senga, 'ye niver see whit's under yer nose, dae ye? Ye've mair chance o' gaein tae the moon.'

Fat Annie from the corner draper shop summed up all their feelings: 'Is she no jist a great ane fur kiddin' hersel?' She turned to her neighbour in the queue. 'Ah mind Ah telt Maureen that day…'

Maureen came back into the shop. Annie, behind the counter, looked up and grinned. 'That yer mither happy?'

'Aye, a wee thumbs-up'll keep her going till denner-time!'

'Whit is she gaun tae dae when ye've gaun tae Canada?'

'Wheest! Ah've no even begun tae tell he…well, Ah've dropped a few hints, mind ye, but she disnae seem tae hiv picked up on them at a' sae far.'

'She'll no likely be wantin' tae hear ony stuff like that. Kate's a great ane fur kiddin' hersel. She jist sees whit she wants tae. Ye'll hiv tae spell it out in big letters fur her.'

'Aye, ye're richt.'

Kate watched from her bay window until she saw him crossing the road. Her eyes lingered briefly on Maureen's old shop but today she could almost bear the pain. She hurried through to the kitchen to put a light under the potatoes. The twenty minutes they would take to boil was just enough time for him to wash the pit-grime off and change. The lamb and barley smelt wonderful. She was full of hope.

She heard their outside door slam and his feet racing up the short, carpeted stair. The inside door was flung back to bounce off the rubber door-stop on the wall. Her heart sank. He had had a row with someone; he was furious about something. Had he quarrelled again with his brother-in-law, Eck, the union shop steward? Last time, Eck had called him a scab and there had been an ugly fight at the pit-head. She and Aggie had been awkward with each other for weeks after it. Her hands shook as she turned down the gas under the potatoes.

She gasped in shock as his arms came round her waist from behind and she felt his breath on the back of her neck. What was this? Her quivering nostrils gave her no news of alcohol on his hot breath. Confused, she turned in his arms and looked up at him. He was beaming, chuckling, as if hugging some delightful secret to himself.

'He's decided himsel that we hiv tae go,' she thought dizzily. 'Ah didnae need tae spend a' that money on the biggest chops. They're half bone an fat onyway.'

'Ah've got grand news, lass,' he declared. 'My, that smells awfy guid. Git it ready while Ah hae ma wash. Ah'll tell ye a' aboot it while we eat.'

Kate frowned as she set the carrots to cook – well, half-cook. News? What could he mean? What could have happened? Then, draining the potatoes, it came to her: He must have already started finding out about sailings. Maybe even had a wee word with someone, been encouraged, reassured, helped to make up his mind. It was an effort to contain her excitement as she poured boiling water from the kettle on to his plate – he liked it very clean and nicely warm – then carefully dished up. Her hands shook so that she almost splashed the gravy. That sobered her: he hated a messy plate.

At last, they were sitting at the table, facing each other across the steaming food. *Tell me*, her eyes pleaded, though her lips were silent.

'Ah ken ye've been a wee bit doon since the lass and the laddie went awa,' he began. She thought of the secret bouts of weeping, the hideous dog-teeth dream.

'A wee bit, aye.'

'Weel,' he reached across the table and took her hand. 'Ah've got news that'll fair cheer ye up.'

Kate felt as if she was in one of those dewy-eyed scenes at the pictures when the hero finally makes all his lady-love's dreams come true. 'Tell me,' she breathed, making her eyes huge and beguiling, parting her lips a little as the leading lady always did in this scene.

He began to talk. She could see his lips moving but she heard no words. She had already moved into a parallel world...

She was ironing his last two shirts and worrying if there would be room for them in their already bulging case.

'Och Aggie,' she was brisk. 'It'll no matter if ye're bubbling. A' the familes'll be greetin'.'

Aggie shook her head. 'Ah jist cannae, Kate. Ah'll say ma guid-byes here.'

Kate turned back to her ironing. Just time to finish it then get his tea ready in time for him coming home from the club where he was having a last dram with his old pit-mates. 'All set!' she announced. 'That's the case closed. Will we have a wee farewell sherry?'

She paused on her way through to the kitchen to look at her sister's ravaged face. She hesitated, then dropped to one knee beside Aggie, reaching up with a work-worn hand to brush the tears off her cheek. 'Jist you dae whit ye want, Aggie,' she murmured. 'Jist you dae whit ye want.' Then she laughed breezily and went through to get the sherry for that last wee drink together...

'So, Ah start on the first of August,' he concluded 'Whit dae ye think o' that, eh?' He smacked his lips as much in appreciation of himself as of the lamb chop.

Start what? What on earth was he talking about?

'It's a grand chance, Katy. Chic Carswell - he'll be ma boss noo - says, if Ah gie it five years, Ah'll be in a great position tae move on. Ah'll have managerial experience as well as kennin' the coal face work and understannin' the men and a' the union stuff as well. He says we're the new breed o' managers... An the money! It's near double whit Ah'm earnin' at the moment. Ye can start shoppin', lass. Ye'll be the best dressed lassie in this street! An speakin' o' dressin', Ah'm goin' tae need some new shirts – ye ken, the anes wi *white* collars!'

Laughing uproariously at his own wit, he threw down his knife and fork on to his plate. 'That wis grand. Ah'll bet they chops wis some price. Pity we cannae eat the bones since ye hae tae pay fur them an a'. Still, ye're richt. It's a special occasion.' On his way out, he turned to her on a sudden thought: 'Hoo did ye ken we wid be celebratin' the nicht? Ye're a great lassie!'

When he had gone off to the club to celebrate his promotion and indulge in drunken dreams of a glorious white-collar future in the Fife mining industry, she sat for a long time among the dirty dishes, toying with the remains of her congealed food. At last, she arose and went through to begin washing up.

'Five years...an he'll get a much better job in Canada wi...wi...managerial experience.' She rolled the words thoughtfully round her tongue. Five years wasn't long. They'd been married twenty-five. Her thoughts drifted back...

'He fancies ye, Katy. Ah'm sure o' it.'

Her mother slapped the wet sheet on to the stool beside the mangle and began to feed it through the rollers. 'Gie's a haun, hen.'

Twenty-year-old Kate cast off her summer raincoat and moved through the wash-house steam to the other side of the mangle.

'Hoo can ye tell?' she asked as she received the mangled sheet on her side. 'Ah mean . . . he only asked ye if Ah liked caramel chews.'

'Aye, then Ah sees him buying a quarter in the sweety shop. He'll likely be roon wi them the nicht, ye'll see. He's a gran catch, Katy, see ye dinnae let this ane slip through yer fingers. Ye're no gettin' ony younger!'

Walking home with her mother, the heavy, laden washing basket carried between them, she fantasised a white dress, flower-girls, wedding presents, a home of her own...

It wouldn't maybe matter, if he wasn't exactly - what was it the agony column in Woman's Weekly called it? . . . a... a soul mate? What did they know about life in this miserable mining village? What did they know about her growing desperation?

'Ah can gie it a try, mither,' she promised. Ye're richt. He's a gran catch.'

CHAPTER ONE

KATE

1954

Senga came to a decision. Thirty-six hours to go until the weigh-in at the slimming class. If she didn't eat anything else *at all* until then, she could have just one more of Kate's feather-light scones.

'Only about six months to go, Senga.' Kate was full of suppressed excitement.

Through a mouthful of thickly buttered scone, Senga demurred. 'Ye mean six *weeks*, Kate – no, less. Tomorrow's the 20th November. I hope that stuff I ordered frae the catalogue disnae come too soon. It's the devil o' a job hiding it frae my lot. They're aye ferretin' and feelin' parcels and guessin'. Then they've the cheek tae complain on Christmas mornin' that they didnae get ony surprises!' She laughed, spraying scone crumbs over her ample bosom.

'Och, Ah didnae mean Christmas. Ah meant it'll soon be only six months afore his five years are up. He said it would tak five years fur him tae get enough *managerial experience* before he could mak a move. So Ah can ask him aboot emigratin' tae Canada soon…maybe start hintin' in the spring, then by the time the five years are up in July, we could be ready tae go.'

Senga eyed her uncertainly. 'Weel, Kate, hen… Ah widnae be too sure…'

She stopped as Kate fixed her with a hostile stare. 'Ah mean, it'll maybe no be *exactly* five years. He's awfy fond o' that job an he's makin' quite an impression. My Jim wis jist sayin' the other day that a' the men really look up tae him and he has the bosses' ears tae. He's

12

done awfy weel…' She tailed off. 'But, ye ken him best, hen… Ah didnae realise you twa were still thinking o' it. Whit does he say when ye talk aboot it?'

Still thinking about it? Kate had thought of little else for five years but what did Johnnie say? She shied away from the thought that she had never *actually*…

'He jist says, '*wait and see*',' she fabricated.

Senga considered the possibility of a fourth scone. If she was going to fast for thirty-six hours, she should stock up now. But there was only one scone left. She had been brought up that it was rude to take the last one off the plate.

'Of coorse, noo that we've a *grandchild* out there, he'll have tae see that we *need* tae go.' Kate dwelt fondly on the word. 'Children need grandparents.' It was something she had heard in a programme on the wireless one night.

Senga thought of her own grandmother: *crabbit, auld bitch.* She thought of Jim's grandmother, now thankfully dead. She had been a vicious gossip with a special line in emotional blackmail due to her senile disability at the end.

'Mmm…' she murmured. 'Weel…'

Then, catching Kate's eye: 'Och, aye, Ah'm sure ye're richt'… She covered her confusion… 'Is it a' richt if I have that last scone?'

Greedy pig. Ah wis hopin' tae keep that fur his afternoon piece. She's fair wastin' her time going tae slimmin' classes.

'Of coorse, Senga. They're there fur eatin'.'

Kate watched anxiously as the woman in the queue in front of her pointed to the last strawberry cream cake. It was his favourite and tonight she *must* have it for him. Aggie looked over the head of the woman she was serving in her little bakery shop. She caught Kate's eye and winked. 'That strawberry cream cake?' she responded to her customer. 'Richt ye are.'

She put it carefully into a white cardboard box and tied it with brown, hairy string, knotting it tightly and cutting the string with small, sharp scissors. 'That's three-an-fourpence.'

The woman flinched. 'Ah thocht…Ah thocht…they were twa-an-ninepence?'

'Naw! They've no been that fur a while. When did ye last buy ane o' them?'

The woman peered in her worn purse although she already knew its contents well. 'Ah dinnae hae enough…weel…' she salvaged a little pride. 'Ah *hae* enough but Ah hae ither roads fur the money.' If she spent this much on the cake she would not have enough for the bottle of milk that would be needed for tomorrow's breakfast porridge.

'Ah, weel. Ye ken best yersel.' Aggie laid the white box aside and the woman slunk out of the shop.

'Now then, Katy. Can I get ye onything? Maybe a wee special treat? Like a strawberry cream cake!' Aggie was enjoying her own joke.

'Aggie,' Kate was stern, 'whaur do ye get aff chargin' prices like that? They cakes wis twa-an-nine last week. Hoo come they've shot up like that? I hope ye dinnae think *Ah'm* goin' tae be payin' that sort of price?'

'Naw, naw,' Aggie winked at her sister. 'Family prices, ye ken. Discount fur freends! Besides. Ah kent by the look on yer face ye were after that cake an ye were fair wettin' yersel when Bessie asked fur it.'

'Ye never telt her it wis three-an-four jist tae pit her aff and keep it fur me? Och, Ah feel richt bad! She looked that sad and disappointed.'

'She'll live! Ye're ower soft-hearted. Now, whit's yer game? Whit are ye tryin' tae wheedle oot o' Johnnie this time?'

'Weel, Aggie, in three months' time, it'll be five years since he said he wanted tae work in this managerial job fur that length o' time. It taks at least three months and mair tae organise the passage tae Canada and a' the forms and passports an things so I've decided tonight's the night tae…ye ken…broach the subject!'

'An ye think he'll be interested?'

'Of coorse.' She *had* to believe it. 'We've a grandchild oot there and…' - she paused for dramatic emphasis – 'I got a letter this mornin'. There's anither on the wiy. Robbie's Janet's expectin'!'

'Fancy *you* wi twa grandweans!' To Aggie, Kate was still the spoilt, dreamy, irritating little sister whose arrival had turned her own childhood world upside down.

'Aye, an it's high time I wis ower there helping tae look after them, so, gie me that cake and Ah'm awa hame tae mak him the best dinner he's had in months. Then he'll no be able tae say no!'

14

'An hoo is his auld mither these days? Ah heard she's no managin' sae weel. She's been a widow that lang ye jist think she'll be able tae manage on her own fur ever. But she's getting auld and Jeannie that lives in her street says she's aye furgettin' things. Nearly set the hoose on fire the ither week. Went oot and left the guard aff and a big lump of coal fell oot and set the rug on fire. Lucky Jeannie smelt something and saw smoke startin' tae come oot the windae. Her man, Bob, had tae run in and throw a bucket o' water on it.'

'Ach, she's fine.' Old Maggie Cruikshanks was the last person Kate wanted to think about. She had never liked her mother-in-law who made no secret of the fact that she thought Kate was 'no near good enough for my Johnnie'. Kate had spent her married life avoiding Maggie and skirting round any discussions about her that Johnnie initiated. Contact had been formalised into set routines and seasons. 'Maggie'll see us a' oot.'

Kate hurried off to start her culinary offensive, dismissing Aggie's remarks about her mother-in-law.

'Aye kiddin' herself...' Aggie murmured derisively as she began to wipe down the empty shelf where the contentious cake had been.

Kate looked with sweaty satisfaction at the results of her labours. An hour ago she had decided that, rather than setting their usual places at the kitchen table for tea, she would use the visitors' table in the sitting-room, complete with table cloth and good china. 'He's goin' tae be bowled ower!' she decided happily.

The visitors' table, used on infrequent occasions when they had other people in for meals, was an antique gate-leg inherited from the same aunt who had bequeathed them all the serious-money crystal. It normally stood, slim and self-effacing behind the couch, until called forth to be erected in the middle of the floor when chairs from all parts of the house would be pressed into service around it. She had dragged it out and put it up but immediately seen that it was ridiculously big for the two of them. She had collapsed one side and put the table cloth on it. It had looked strangely forlorn and lacking, like a man with one arm. If it was to have only one side up, it needed to be against a wall.

She had puffed and heaved for half-an-hour, pulling out armchairs, pouffees and occasional tables, dismantling and reassembling displays of photos and ornaments, pushing the piano and

15

almost doing herself an injury. Words that never crossed her lips had flown through her fevered mind. But, at last, it was done and she had set the snowy-covered half-moon with dainty, wedding-present cutlery and china, adding a little vase with a single red rose snipped from the artificial posy which had been Aggie's silver wedding present to them.

From the oven came the aroma of steak-and-kidney stew. She would take it out fifteen minutes before serving and top it with the puff pastry she had made and put out on the window-sill to stay cool. That way the pastry would be light and not at all soggy – he hated that. She glanced at the clock. About forty minutes till pastry time. She thought of a *Housekeeping Monthly* article she had read recently, entitled *The Good Wife's Guide* - a sixteen point summary of how to greet a husband on his arrival home from work. Apart from having the house spotless, the dinner ready and any messy, noisy children under control, it emphasised the importance of the wife being totally attentive to his needs and delightfully *fresh-looking*. After her labours, she smelt anything but fresh: but there was time for a quick bath and change. She would use some of those lovely bath salts that Senga had given her last Christmas and put on Saturday's clean underwear now, even though it was only Thursday.

Kate sang as she poured the bright pink crystals into the gushing jet. She almost lost count of time as she wallowed in the fragrant steam and slipped into her favourite day-dream: she was on the big ship just about to land, all of *them* waving welcomes from the dock. Now what would she wear for that occasion…?

With a start, she remembered the pastry and the time. 'Ye're a dozy dolly' she chided herself. 'That wid be a fine thing if he cam' hame and you no even dressed and the pastry still sittin' oot on the windae-sill!'

She dressed quickly, dexterously manipulating the multiple hooks and eyes on her underwear, allowing herself a moment's preen in the mirror, admiring the new soft-wave perm (and only Mina, the hairdresser, and she herself knew about the discreet little tint).

She had set the pastry on top of the stew and the water to boil for the carrots (they must have only three minutes to be crunchy as he liked them) when she heard his key in the outside door. She listened, as she always did for his footsteps on the short, carpeted stair up to their inside door.

His tread was her early warning system. Springy bounds meant he'd had a good day. Dragging steps meant he was tired or possibly

16

unwell with a cold or in pain from the chronic backache that plagued his tall, rangy body. A slammed door followed by stamping feet meant he'd had a quarrel with someone at work: Eck, perhaps, with his sneering remarks and uncompromising union principles; or *that namby-pamby*, the mine-owner's son, who held a position far beyond his capabilities.

She was praying for a good omen as she strained her ears. There was a strange silence once he had quietly shut the outside door. He was not coming up the stairs, must be still standing at the bottom of them. He never did that! Had he been taken ill? She began to move anxiously towards the lobby. Then she heard a tread on the stairs that she did not recognise and could not decode. It was hesitant, thoughtful. He paused again, at the inside door. She could see his face distorted through the frosted glass porthole. She went back into the sitting-room uneasily. Were all her efforts going to be wasted?

As he came into the sitting-room, she greeted him with a warm smile but he did not look at her, or at the re-arranged furniture, the beautiful half-moon. He was looking at the floor and seemed at a loss how to greet her. *There's something wrong...*

She was about to slither into a soothing offer of a bottle of beer when he shook himself, straightened his shoulders and lifted his head. He looked round the room and laughed. 'Katy, I've always said it and I always will. Ye've the second sight! How did ye ken this was a special night for us? Ye've done it again. I mind the night I told ye about me gettin' the management job and ye had second-guessed me and cooked a special meal. Now ye've done it again!'

To her amazement, he held out his arms and beamed at her, encouraging her to come into them. This was not at all his usual homecoming ritual. She stared, unsure. But, as he went on beaming and laughing, arms out-flung, she moved into his embrace and snuggled her head under his chin (how long was it since she had done that?)

'My, you smell awfy guid,' he murmured, his long bony fingers moving involuntarily to cup one of her ample breasts. She lifted her head and they rubbed noses, an almost-forgotten part of their early-marriage foreplay. *'Milk the moment'*, said a wily, womanly voice.

She broke away from his embrace, wagging her finger playfully. 'Now, now...there's a good steak-and-kidney pie in the oven and we wouldn't want to spoil it, would we? There's always later...' She had forgotten she could be so arch and she was giggling as she went into the kitchen to put the carrots on.

The meal was a triumph. The steak-and-kidney were the very best from *Smirk The Butcher*, as Kate had privately dubbed him. The pastry was feather-light; even the carrots were perfect and he dribbled gravy down his long chin as he crunched them.

Throughout the meal, he kept up a flow of cheerful chatter: stories of colleagues at work, both underlings and overlords; revelations of his plans for future victories over Eck; speculations about gossip and rumour in the company; even a few jokes, edited from their crude original form. She maintained a bright, interested expression without listening. She was waiting for her moment, sure that this was the perfect time.

They were sauntering through their second helping of strawberry cream cake, having fairly walloped their way through the first, when he suddenly laid down his spoon and reached across the table to take her free hand in both of his.

'This meal's been a fair wonder,' he said. 'And so are you, Katy. How did you ken we needed to make tonight special? I've said it before and I'll say it again: Ye've the second sight!' He beamed at her. 'This'll be our last evening just the two o' us for a while, so it was a grand idea to make it so special.'

What on earth was he talking about?

'It'll no be forever, though,' he was saying. 'She's an old woman, we have to face that. She'll no live forever. But it'll seem strange at first havin' her here, I know, and it'll put extra work on you, Katy, I'm no denyin' that, an maybe make it more difficult for you to get out and about as freely as ye do at the moment. Still, I'm sure Agnes or Senga'll help out an come and sit wi her to let ye get out to the shops and so forth…'

He was talking faster and faster and then he ran out of words and ground to a halt as he saw the blank expression on her face.

'What're ye talking aboot?' breathed Katy. Deep inside, she heard the drumbeat of impending disaster. Her mouth went dry. She dropped her fork in the ruins of her second helping of strawberry cake and reached for the remains of his beer, gulping it down. Neither of them noticed this unprecedented behaviour.

He lit a cigarette and smoked messily, dropping ash on to his own cake ruins. They did not notice *this* unprecedented behaviour either. He began to speak again, jerkily, then gathering speed: 'I went round

18

to see mother on my way home.' She nodded acceptance of this everyday event. 'The doctor was there when I went in.'

'Is she no weel, then?'

'She's...she's...jist no copin' ony mair, no at a'.' He was lapsing into the broad dialect that he had carefully ironed out over the past five years. He caught himself. 'The doctor says she can't live alone any more. She's fallin' every day, sometimes more than once a day. She's aye hurtin' hersel... I mean, always hurting herself.' Hanging on to his posh pronunciation like a talisman.

'And then...' - he screwed himself up through an agony of embarrassment - '...she's no managing the toilet so well any more, doesn't always get there in time. She slipped and hit her head on the pan the other day and Jeannie-down-the-road found her in an awful mess, lyin' greetin'... I mean *crying*...on the floor. She's needin' lookin' after now.' He ran down at last, almost gibbering with embarrassment, a note of pleading in his voice.

Moanin' Maggie's ready fur the auld folks' hame at last! Thank God! That'll mak it easier fur us tae get awa, kennin' the auld...the old crow's bein' looked after.

'So, I knew you would want me to tell her to stop worryin' an just come and live with us. She was greetin' at the thought o' havin' to go into an old folks home but I told her we've plenty room now that Robbie and Maureen have left. And they're well settled. It's safe to say they're no comin' back.'

The words struck her like bolts of electricity. Her brain began to replay all he had said, beginning to grasp the reality. Her will shied away in terror but her mind ruthlessly laid it all out before her.

'And don't worry too much about the toilet thing. Dr Kenny said he'd get the district nurse to come in and explain about...about...' he was on shaky ground here as his mind refused to grapple with his old mother's toileting problems. 'Well, there's things you can get for her to wear...like...like the bairns had their nappies,' he finished triumphantly, on a note of inspiration.

'Incontinence pads,' said Kate, calmly, but her voice seemed to her to be coming from outside the window. She and Senga had giggled over a po-faced advertisement for these very necessities in *The Sunday Post* a few weeks ago.

'Aye, that's it. Och, Katy, ye're a good lassie. I knew I could count on you. What else could I do? That hoity-toity brother o' mine would be no use. I can't see that stuck-up wife o' his dirtyin' her hands with….with …well, what ye said.'

'Incontinence pads,' said Kate again and stared in surprise at the window. *Who was that outside on the sill?*

'We'll need to get the house sorted out tonight,' he was saying. 'She'll be here tomorrow. Dr Kenny is organising a wee ambulance thing for her and the men'll carry her upstairs in her chair. We'll really need to give her our bedroom as it's the biggest and she's got her commode and her walkin' frame and her chair and all that. We'll move our stuff into Maureen's old room, lucky there's a double-bed in there already, though it's a wee one, I ken, but it'll do us until we get ourselves organised to buy a new one, maybe get one off our dividend at The Store in their January sale next year…' Again he ground to a halt, willing her to respond. But she only stared at the cake-and-ash mess on his plate.

'I'll give ye a hand, Katy,' he appeased. 'I'll no go out to the club tonight – no until we've got everything sorted.' He stood awkwardly behind her chair, his hands hovering above her shoulders. She arose at once and began gathering up the debris of their meal, moving briskly towards the kitchen.

'It's a good job Ah had a' that practice at furniture removal this afternoon,' she thought, as she scraped the mess from his plate into the bin under the sink.

The voice of 'incontinence pads' seemed to have moved round the house to the kitchen window. It sneered as she began the washing up, hearing him start to shift furniture.

The boy and girl walked home from the pictures as quickly as they could, anxious to escape from the raw cold. As usual he had sat through the film with his heavy-as-wood arm weighing on her shoulders. As usual, they had exchanged only the barest scraps of conversation, mostly related to why she had been five minutes late at the cinema, what kind of sweets she would like to eat during the film, what time she had to be home for. Clip-clopping at his pace in her high heels, she tried to engage him in speculation about what other kind of ending the film might have had. He did not answer as she prattled breathlessly on, dissecting the plot and characters, exploring alternative possibilities. When they had to stop at a crossroads, waiting for a tram to whizz by, she persisted for a reply. He stared down at her blankly. 'Whit's the use o' that sort o' talk,' he wondered. 'We ken whit happened; we saw the end.'

When they reached her door, he bent down and planted the usual dry kiss on her cheek. 'Good night,' he said formally and she turned to go into the dirty little miner's cottage.

Then he spoke again: 'Katy, Ah was wondering...' She whirled round at the sudden change in routine, daring to hope he did have an opinion about the film after all. He shifted from one foot to the other, seeming nervous, unsure of himself, and she suddenly felt sorry for him. 'He's like a caged bird,' she thought, 'tryin' tae get oot.'

'My cousin, Alan, is gettin' married, a week on Saturday. He says Ah can bring a partner to the reception. Will you come wi me?'

She knew immediately what this meant: invited to a formal Cruikshanks family gathering; proclaimed as his girlfriend; accepted into the bosom of his family. There would be no going back: next stop the jeweller's shop.

She watched her breath turn to white vapour in the frosty air and two rivulets of water run down amidst the condensation on the inside of the kitchen window: her mother was making soup again. She thought of the crowded, mean, little kitchen that always smelled of soup; of the tiny attic almost filled by the sagging, frowsty, old double-bed she shared with her sister, Aggie; of her dreary, boring job in the cold factory; then of his parents' smart bungalow with its pretty garden and inside toilet – no, inside bathroom even - with a pile of fluffy white towels, the kind she had only ever seen in shop windows before.

'Well,' he stamped his feet impatiently. 'Will you come wi me?'
'Aye, Ah will,' she said, 'Ah will.'

Angus Smillie, *Smirk The Butcher*, was fed up. It had been a slow Monday morning, drizzly and cold for June. To make matters worse, his stomach – an appendage of generous proportions - was giving him hell. Normally, it was a good friend and he would pat it affectionately as he poured the eighth pint of beer into it in the pub of an evening. 'My hump' he called it. 'Like a camel,' he would explain, winking solemnly, 'I'll be glad o' it when I'm next stranded in the Sahara.'

But today it was definitely not happy. From time to time it emitted a low, threatening grumble, like the subterranean warnings of a building about to collapse. This was followed by a rising tide of griping pain which reached an excruciating peak before subsiding, leaving Smirk feeling sick and shaky. Worst of all, some of these subsidings were accompanied by noisy, pungent emissions from his backside. The last one had been so foul that he had rushed to the front door of the shop and wafted it to and fro vigorously until the smell abated. '*Thank God there are no customers in the noo,*' he had thought.

Sitting disconsolately on a stool in the back-shop, he contemplated various chores. Tidy up the paperwork? Make some more mince and sausages? Order more sawdust for the floor? Sharpen the knives? He half rose, still undecided, when a low rumble intimated another bout of pain and embarrassment. He sank back onto the stool muttering. 'Geez, Ah'm like a wumman in labour.'

The worst was over – thankfully unaccompanied this time by too much noise or smell – when the shop door bell tinkled. Smirk hesitated, peering through the curtain.

It was that bonny lass, Kate. He groaned. She was the last person he wanted to see him (or – perish the thought – *smell* him) this morning. He always admired her beautiful dark eyes, her abundant wavy hair, her voluptuous figure and her lovely smile.

Mind, she's no been smilin' sae much lately. Maybe she's got a touch o' the bellyache as weel.

Kate looked vaguely at the butcher meat displayed under the glass frame of the counter. She appeared not to have noticed the absence of Smirk. Feeling relatively safe at last, Smirk ventured through the curtain, composing his features into their usual unctuous smile though he couldn't quite manage the suggestive twinkle he reserved for Kate and some of his younger customers.

She continued to stare at the meat for sale and he waited a few seconds before prompting, as breezily as his aching innards allowed, 'And what would ma bonnie lassie be wantin' the day?'

When she raised her eyes he was shocked by her appearance. The dark eyes were red and sore-looking, her hair was lank, her skin reminded Smirk of the yellowy fat on the carcases he butchered. From force of habit, he ran his eyes down to her waist. This was usually one of the more pleasant moments of his day. But today, her body seemed shapeless and saggy, bundled up in an old crossover apron. Other

22

women frequently came running into his shop in such dirty old aprons, spattered with fire-soot and baby-sick. But, in all the years he had served her daily in the shop, he had never seen Kate anything other than freshly dressed and well corseted. '*She must really be no weel,*' he thought anxiously, forgetting his own troubles for the moment.

'Is there something wrang, lass?' he murmured, sounding so genuine in his concern that Kate was startled out of her self-absorption. She looked sharply at him.

'Ah'm no wantin' any o' yer over-priced fripperies the day,' she snapped. 'Ye've ripped me aff often enough in the past but Ah'm wise tae ye noo. Besides...' - her face seemed to crumple – '... whit's the point noo? We never get peace tae enjoy a meal thegither noo wi that auld biddie there. A' she can eat wi *her* gums is saps so jist gie me a pound of mince – an the cheap stuff'll dae fine.'

Smirk opened his mouth to protest the slur on his good name. Then a vicious bolt of pain shot through his insides and he felt his bowels turning to water. 'Mother o' God!' he yelped and, spinning round, he fled through to the lavatory behind the back-shop.

Kate blinked. There had been great satisfaction in claiming the day she had been promising herself for a long time. Smirk had cheated her, sniggering and simpering, for years and was well due his come-uppance. Letting fly at him like that, for a brief moment, had been an oasis in her desert. He had made a lovely whipping boy. But he had taken it so badly, yowling like a wounded animal and rushing off.

'*Maybe Ah've got the man a' wrang,*' she thought guiltily. '*Maybe he's never meant tae be such a sleaze-bag a' these years. Maybe he cannae help himsel. Maybe Ah wis ower cruel.*'

Tentatively she ventured through to the back-shop calling apologetically: 'Mr Smirk... Ah mean Mr Smillie... Are ye a' richt? Ah wis jist jokin'. Dinnae mind me. Whaur *are* ye, Mr Smillie?'

She stood nonplussed amidst the clutter in the small back-shop. *Whaur the devil's he gone tae? He's jist vanished.* Her repentance soured into irritation. *Is he hidin'? Playin' games wi me?* Then she jumped in alarm as a sudden loud blast came from the corner of the room. *Whit in hell is goin' on?* Her eyes picked out a small door in the corner and, when she heard the sounds of a chain being pulled, water gushing and pipes wheezing, she understood at last.

She began to laugh, just tittering at first, then, gathering momentum, rollicking into a full-throated skirl. Tears ran down her cheeks. At last, she crept out, keeping her head down, not looking at the two women who had come into the shop-front and had been standing, amazed, listening to her wild laughter.

'Wis that no Kate?' said Jeannie to the other woman. 'Ah've no seen her fur ages. Ah've been wunnerin' hoo Maggie, my auld neighbour, is gettin' on. Ah wis goin' tae cry roon an see her but… Weel, ye ken whit Kate's like, keeps herself tae herself these days.'

'Ach, she's a stuck-up piece,' said the other woman sourly. 'Thinks she's Archie! Jist because that lassie o' hers has married a posh fella in Canada and has a big hoose and her Robbie's got himself a grand job 'in the retail trade', if ye please. So *she* says! Likely jist serving behind a coonter. An speakin' o' servin' and coonters, whaur's that damn butcher this mornin'? Does he think Ah've a' day tae stand here waitin' fur him? Ah've a good mind tae jist go and get some fish instead. Och, at last, here he comes. God Almichty, whit's that awfy stink? Geez, he's awa again? Whaur's he goin' noo?'

Kate let herself back into the house slowly, creeping up the carpeted stairs and easing herself silently into the lobby. She tiptoed past the bedroom door holding her breath. If she was quick, there would be time for a cup of tea and a large slice of fruit cake before *the auld yin* woke up.

She slumped down at the kitchen table slurping the tea and stuffing the cake into her mouth as if she was blocking a dam. She was contemplating a second slice when the querulous call came: 'Kate, where are ye? Is it dinner-time yet? I think I need my bed changed and I've no had my pink pills yet the day.'

As Kate went into the foul-smelling bedroom, the old woman demanded. 'Where have ye been? I heard ye comin' back a while ago. Did ye get something nice for oor dinner? Is it mince an tatties?'

'No, mother,' Kate turned back the bedclothes and surveyed the mess. 'It's egg and chips, the day. Ye can dip yer chips in the egg yolk and suck them. Ye'll like that.'

'I'm no sure, Kate. Eggs sometimes gie me awfy wind…' She broke off. 'What have I said that's so funny?'

Kate was laughing hysterically, the tears running down her face and dripping on to the fruitcake crumbs on her bosom.

Kate worked her way slowly round her crowded sitting-room. Once upon a time, Tuesday - sitting-room day in her weekly housework programme - had been her favourite. Now she was all too aware of the heavy invalid chair dominating the room, the clutter of medicines jostling with her ornaments and photo-frames, the pale pink carpet stained by unmentionable accidents. She glanced at the clock. Only half-past-nine: still so much of the morning to go. She ignored the crystal goblets and decanter in the cabinet. Too much bother and, since they never used them anyway, what was the point of dusting them? Let them wait till he noticed that his serious-money treasures were filthy.

She lingered over the welter of trashy souvenirs on top of the piano, recalling carefree trips to Blackpool Illuminations and Llamas Fair at Kirkcaldy, letting the feather duster trail over the piano keys with a ghostly tinkle.

All too soon, she fetched up in the bay window. She watched Fat Annie swilling the doorstep of the drapery shop on the corner. She still harboured a suspicion from years back that the woman had encouraged Maureen's ideas of emigrating to Canada.

Down the road, Old Smirk's shop was still 'closed due to illness'. No-one seemed to know what was wrong with the butcher or when he would be back in his shop. He had been in hospital for weeks now – some stomach thing, it was whispered. Kate remembered that morning two months ago and blushed, half with embarrassment, half with guilt. She had laughed at him unmercifully and now the poor soul was really ill.

'Ah should go an see him in the hospital,' she thought suddenly. *'Ah could tak him grapes, or sweeties, or a fancy magazine aboot cars, or horses, or... '* She realised that she had no idea what he was interested in. She didn't suppose there were magazines about butchery meat, were there? *Likely, he'd be wantin' ane o' those wi pictures o' half-naked lassies.* But she couldn't see herself asking for such a thing in the newsagents which was two shops down from Smirk's and where she had bought her *Woman's Weekly* and *Housekeeping Monthly* for the past twenty years. *Maybe a wee bunch o' flooers.*

The demanding tap of Old Maggie's stick penetrated her musings. 'That you wool-gathering again, Kate? How long does it take you to clean that room? And me sitting in my mess here waitin' for you to find time for a poor old woman what cannae help herself. Aye, it's awfy to be auld and naebody wants ye!'

Kate moved through to the kitchen to don rubber gloves and collect cleaning equipment. 'Comin', mither. We'll soon mak ye comfy again.'

'I suppose ye were looking oot that window again? What are ye expectin' to see? Ye'd think ye'd never seen the view before!' Old Maggie's curiosity sounded like a jeer to Kate.

'What's it to you?' she snapped. 'It's nothin'. Ah'd no tell *you* onyway if there wis a reason...' She began the distasteful task of cleaning up the old woman and changing the sheets, avoiding Maggie's eye, not acknowledging her grudging gratitude.

The bed set to rights and the evidence disposed of (thank goodness for that washing machine Johnnie had bought her), Kate brought Maggie her porridge and toast. As always, she sat on the end of the bed and had a cup of tea herself. Not that she wanted to, but Maggie had insisted from the first day that she needed some company as she ate her breakfast.

'Is there any news o' Mr Smillie?' Maggie slurped the milky porridge. It ran in grey lumps down the large cloth napkin tucked into the front of her nightgown. 'Is he gettin' any better?'

Kate averted her eyes and stared into her teacup. 'No, Ah've no heard onythin'.' It's a richt pest havin' tae wait fur that van tae come roon to buy oor meat. An that's only twice a week. We've never eaten sae much fish and eggs in oor lives! Still, they're supposed tae be good fur ye so we'll no starve, Ah dare say.'

She moved back to her small kitchen to begin cooking the midday meal. *Old Smirk and his awfy wind. Whit a laugh – a laugh that turned oot no tae be a laugh at a'. What if Ah did go tae see him?*

'Mmm,' Henry Simpson looked down his long, aristocratic nose at the notes and charts in his hand. Then he looked down from his great skinny height at plump Sister Connie who was in charge of Men's Surgical. He continued to read and she noticed, as she always did, how the bony tip of his nose twitched, the nostrils flaring. '*Like a prize greyhound lowering itself to sniff a mongrel's bum,*' she thought, not for the first time, but her expression of rapt respect did not waver. The gaggle of medical students shuffled and whispered, subsiding into queasy silence at a quick frown from his bushy, silver eyebrows.

Mister Simpson took the handsome meerschaum pipe – always in his mouth but never lit during ward rounds – and tapped the notes with its stem. He sucked in his breath and his courtiers held theirs, waiting.

Angus Smillie (*Family Butchers since 1910 – only quality meat sold*) looked at the consultant's impressive, ascetic figure and especially at the slim, elegant hands, long tapering fingers and perfectly shaped nails. *'Funny,'* he thought. *'You couldn't really imagine him doing the work of a surgeon.'* Hands covered in blood, up to his elbows inside a patient's guts, sweat dripping from his brow under the big operating-theatre lights. Surgery and butchery came out of the same stable, in his book, so he had a sense of fellow feeling with the man who had sliced open his ample stomach and removed the insidious tumour which had been the cause of all his woes.

As the little court around the bed waited upon the great man's pronouncement, Angus's thoughts drifted back to his childhood. He had been only four years old the first time he had seen a butcher at work…

His mother was confined to bed after the birth of his little sister, Martha, and he was in the care of his Granny and Grandpa Smillie, in their big, draughty, old tenement house. 'Mind you be a good boy,' his mum had abjured him, so he was trying hard. But everything was wrong that morning. Granny, usually so cheerful and gentle, was sniffing her way through her breakfast. Keeping his little golden head bent over his porridge, Angus caught: 'She's been that a good doggie…had her since she was a wee pup… can't bear to see her suffer any longer…need to take her down to the PDSA this mornin'…can't put us through another night like that.'

Granny rose, her porridge hardly touched. 'Ah cannae tak the wee man wi me. Ye'll have to tak him wi you.'

Earlier on, Angus had been thinking that the three of them, sitting round the table eating their porridge, were like the characters in one of Mum's bedtime stories: Daddy Bear, Mummy Bear and Baby Bear. But something had told him that this observation would not get the usual indulgent reception, and he had wisely stowed this fanciful comparison away for another day. He darted a look at his thin-faced Grandpa. He knew that Grandpa owned a shop and went there everyday. He had never seen his Grandpa anything other than formally dressed with stiff collar, sober tie and dark waistcoat, the gold watch-chain dangling across it. Angus had never really speculated on what kind of shop it was.

Grandpa was a man of few words, and those usually uttered with some pomposity and expectation of a respectful audience. As the two males, young and old, ate up their porridge, the silence in the kitchen amplified and the old clock on the mantelpiece above the range ticked ever more loudly. He tried desperately to eat without making any noise at all, slipping the porridge gingerly off the spoon into his mouth, sliding it round his teeth and tongue carefully and swallowing it very slowly. His plate was only half-empty at this painstaking rate when Grandpa rose and, without a look at him, said; 'Best be getting along then, Angus. Get your coat and boots.'

Abandoning his breakfast, he went with Grandpa to the lobby press where the coats, boots and shoes were kept. The coats hung neatly on a rack of hooks along one wall; the boots and shoes marched in shining rows along slatted shelves rising from the floor. It was quite different from the jumble of muddy boots, holey socks, hairy shawls and coats-with-their-arms-turned-inside-out that was the lobby press in Angus's home.

Walking through the damp early morning, they exchanged no word. On arrival at the shop, he was consigned to the care of Miss Mathieson, in the smoky little cubicle, where she took the money and gave change to the customers through a small glass window.

The shop was bitterly cold, quite empty. He formed a vague impression of gleaming white tiles everywhere and yellow, gritty, dusty stuff on the floor before being whisked into Miss M's den which was over-heated by a paraffin stove and smelt of hundreds of cigarettes left to burn out in their ashtray.

He was almost asleep in the stuffy heat, as Miss M went off to wash the step outside in preparation for the first customers of the morning. Desperate for some air, he stumbled out of the cubicle and, hearing men's voices, followed the sound, fetching up at a half-open door to a large, very cold room. Angus's horrified eyes took in enormous hooks with skinned, headless, dead animals hanging upside around the walls and three white-clad figures around a huge central table on which lay a large carcase, with limbs severed, oozing blood. One of the men, very tall and thin with a long nose, had a huge knife in one hand and what looked like a heart, dripping blood, in the other. His white apron was spattered with the red, red blood – it was the stuff of nightmares and Angus fled, whimpering, back to the sanctuary of Miss M's hot little cubicle.

He was set to the job of tearing up old newspapers – whole pages for wrapping the meat in and small squares to hang on the nail in the lavatory. His little fingers proved adept at this task but his mind was racing, full of the Bluebeard experience he had just had. It was much later when he thought of connecting the bloody butcher, the fearsome knife and the dripping heart with his silent, scrupulously clean Grandpa. But the two images seemed irreconcilable to his childish imagination and he dismissed the idea.

'On the mend. Very satisfactory progress. He may begin getting up for a few minutes each day. He may try a little solid food as well. Now, sister…' The retinue shuffled in his wake as he sailed off, without a glance at Angus.

'And thank *you* for a grand wee blether. Ye're a richt friendly lad,' muttered Angus.

Grandpa'll never be dead as long as your kind's around. Must go wi the job! Maybe I should start behaving high-an-mighty as well. Maybe my bonnie Kate would take more interest in me if I did, rather than the way I've aye been trying to get her attention. It's an idea… Tired now, he slipped down in his bed and, through half-closed eyes, watched Consultant Simpson continue on his ward round.

Jim Kenny closed the door of the bedroom with a sigh of relief. Thirty years of being a family doctor had, to some extent, inured him to frowsty beds, stale, cluttered bedrooms and the regrettable emissions of the human body, especially when old or ill. But he always rejoiced briefly in the moment of escape.

Not that the daughter-in-law wasn't doing her best. The rest of the house seemed as spotlessly clean as ever; although possibly lacking some of its…? He pondered this as he moved down the lobby. Yes, lacking the air of *joyful prettiness* he remembered from past visits to measly or mumpy children. But, then, with a demanding and incontinent old woman to care for, that was hardly surprising.

A sudden, tremendous noise erupted, shaking the whole flat and escalating to a howling shriek. *What in hell was that?* He followed the sound into the kitchen where he found Kate standing in one corner, looking fearfully across to where a white metal drum was waltzing wildly, hitting the cooker on one side and another, larger, white drum on the other. *This* drum also had a life of its own and was emitting a cloud of steam. If it was making any noise, however, it was completely drowned out by the smaller drum.

Dr Kenny and Kate remained in their respective stations, both transfixed by the din and unable to communicate above it, until at last it abated and mercifully tapered into comparative silence, giving a few death-rattle jerks before finally lapsing into stillness.

'What in the name of Almighty God is that, m'dear?' he asked.

'It's ca'd a Spin Drier,' she replied shakily. 'Ah jist got it yesterday. Tae help wi a' the washin'. It's instead o' puttin' the sheets and clothes through the wringer. It's supposed tae mak them a lot easier tae dry – gets more o' the water oot o' them. Some noise though, is it no? Ah'll be deef as well as daft usin' that thing every day!'

He advanced gingerly into the room, keeping a wary eye on the drier. 'Well, it's certainly good you've got the latest inventions to help you. That's a washing machine I see too, isn't it? Ye're a lucky lass. That husband of yours is a good man.'

Kate tried to remember how it felt to be 'lucky'. When her babies had been born, both perfect, and when she had been a busy, happy young mum, watching them grow up, she had often thanked God for these blessings and – yes – she would have answered to 'lucky'. It seemed a long time ago.

'Now…' Dr Kenny was talking again and she forced her tired brain to engage with his words: 'I think we'll increase the dose at bedtime and see if that will help her to get more sleep. And you too,' he added in an unaccustomed flash of insight. He had survived doctoring in this mining community through the depression-then-war-then-austerity years by dint of treating symptoms and ailments, firmly avoiding the personal problems and emotional miseries of his patients. The trials and tribulations of the relatives caring for his patients he considered totally outside his province. But he was not without compassion and Kate's hollow, haunted eyes disturbed him.

'I hope you are still managing to get out and about yourself, m'dear. It's important to keep your own morale up. Now, don't worry. Your mother-in-law does have a fair bit of pain and her incontinence is bothersome, I know. But her heart and lungs are still sound – we'll have her with us for a few years yet!'

'That's awfy good news.' He barely noticed her faint, ironic reply as he bustled out the front door. Kate watched from the bay window as he briskly threw his bag into the smart black car, then walked round to

30

the driver's side. He looked up, saw her, and gave her a cheery wave, before driving off with a belch of exhaust fumes.

'Must be grand,' she thought, *'tae jist drop into folks' troubles, hand oot a few pills and bit o' guid advice, then swan aff tae the next hoose. That's a lot easier than livin' in among it twenty-four hoors a day.'*

'Kate, Kate, where are ye? I'm needin' ye. Quick lass... Where *is* that damned lassie? Ach, ye're too late, as usual. What a work ye give yerself. If ye'd come when I shout...'

Kate wearily collected the ever-ready bucket, rubber gloves, strong soap and roll of cotton-wool wadding (the 'shit-kit,' she and Senga called it).

Only eleven o' clock and two lots o' sheets a' ready. Mair work fur the twa steam engines in the kitchen.

Twenty minutes later, Maggie slipped into the fresh bed with a happy sigh. 'That's fine now,' she said. 'Ye're getting real good at it,' she added grudgingly. At first, Kate had been inept, sometimes getting into a bigger mess trying to clean up than there had been at the start. And she had tutted, sniffed, even retched, once even rushing out of the room, leaving the old woman sitting in the half-cleaned mess for several minutes before returning, red-eyed, to finish the job.

'Ah'm jist runnin' doon tae Aggie's tae get some pies fur denner.'

About to doze off, Maggie started awake as the front door slammed. She heard Kate's feet on the inside stairs then the second slam. *Shop-bought pies again. Can that lassie no get herself organised and mak us a nice pot o' soup? And if she suggests one more time that I put on those bloody great pads the nurse brought round... What dae they think I am? A bairn in nappies?*

Johnnie ate the grey, greasy pies without comment. He seemed preoccupied, a little smile on his face, as if contemplating some secret source of satisfaction. Kate barely touched hers as she ran back and forward between the kitchen and Maggie's calls from the bedroom. She was not hungry anyway. She had finished off the fruit cake standing dejectedly at the kitchen window after Dr Kenny's visit and now it lay heavy in her stomach.

'What do you think, Katy?' he was saying now as she came back into the kitchen for the third time. 'I'm going to a conference.'

31

Kate puzzled. What was a *conference*? She raked in her memory and came up with something she had heard on the wireless about politicians from different countries all meeting in some foreign town she had never heard of.

'Whaur-aboot?' she asked.

'St Andrews.'

St Andrews. She wondered which far-flung country had a place with the same name as the lovely old town near them.

'Whaur is that?'

'For ony's sake, Katy. What's wrong wi ye? Ye ken fine where St Andrews is! Did we no take the bairns there often enough to the beach when they were wee? Never mind that, the important thing is...' But she had gone, running down the lobby to answer the urgent 'Katy, quick, lass, I need ye!'

Desperate to avoid a third laundry session with the two machines (*steamie and screamie*, she had christened them), she manhandled the old woman roughly out of bed and on to the commode. And praise be! She was in time.

Old Maggie grumbled as she settled back into bed, 'I'm no a sack of tatties. The way you lug me about, ye'll do me a mischief one o' these times. And, where's my cup of tea? I'll have a slice of that nice fruitcake with it too.'

'Ye're oot o' luck!' thought Kate with some satisfaction, though she knew it would be cause for more grumbling. Still, no use giving the old moaner two opportunities. She'd just wait and give her an unwelcome surprise when she saw the meagre Blue Riband biscuit rather than the delicious cake which had been this week's mercy-parcel from Senga, bless her.

It had been Fat Annie from Maureen's old shop who had given Kate that tip, along with several others, when Kate had called in to buy stockings one day. Annie was a veteran survivor of caring for Old Moaners, having nursed her own parents for a total of twelve years. She had survived by a marathon of comfort eating, emerging too fat and too old for the marriage market, glad to take over the draper's shop on the corner and thus become a lynchpin of the gossip network and something of a local wise woman. She had, during her years of enslavement, invented a number of survival strategies, which she freely passed on to Kate. *Pick yer battles. Dinnae waste yer time and energy arguing wi them. Ignore ninety percent o' whit they say. Tell them as little as possible and only whit they want tae hear.*

To these wise maxims Kate had added one of her own. *Always have a fantasy ready to slip into when it gets too much to bear.* She was currently working her way through one in which she was taking her three-year-old granddaughter for a trip to the park. She had no idea what children's play-parks were like in Canada, or what the walk there would be like, indeed anything at all about the place beyond brief descriptions from sparse letters, so she simply imagined them going to the park where she had taken her own children. What mattered was the feel of the little hand in hers, the chatter, the tugs on her arm as the child broke into skipping and hopping at the sight of the swings and slide. The best bit was the shiver that went through her each time the little one said 'Granny'.

As she was pouring his tea, he tried again. 'This conference . . . ' he began.

'Oh, yes...' Kate was vague. She had been on the point of slipping off to the playpark. Then, catching his rising irritation, 'Aye...tell me...'

'Katy, Katy, Katy...where *is* my tea? And don't forget the fruit cake!'

She weighed up her priorities. She moved through to the sitting-room and shut its door to the lobby. Then she came back into the kitchen and closed *its* door to the sitting-room. Two whole doors between them and the banshee wailing. 'Now,' she leaned on the kitchen door. 'Whit is it ye want tae tell me?'

He finished his biscuit and lit a cigarette, savouring her undivided attention at last.

'You know how I've been asked to take hold of the reins in the office while young Mark's away?'

'Young Mark?' Katy groped in her tired, cluttered brain.

'He's the boss's son, you ken that fine. Bloody little runt, struts about like he's Mr Brainbox, thinks he knows it all, just because he was born wi a silver spoon in his mouth. An he's pig-ignorant half the time. If it wasn't for me, and the times I've kept him right, stopped him creatin' another disaster, cleaned up his messes...' Then, catching sight of the clock, 'Well, anyway, the runt is gettin' married – poor lassie! And he's to be away from the mine for three months' honeymoon – Paris, Rome, and all that pretentious nonsense. So I've been asked to do his work and *act up* – that's what they call it. As if I'm no doin' it most o' the time as it is. So, *I* get to go to the

33

conference for mine-owners and mine managers in St Andrews!' He finished on a triumphant note.

'That's…that's…grand for ye.' Kate was already turning to open the door. She had thought it was something that affected her but now she saw it was just *his* stuff as usual.

'It's a great opportunity, Katy. I'll be rubbin' shoulders with the high-ups in the industry – makin' important contacts and…' Smarting at her indifference, he cast around for a route to her attention ' . . . and I'll be gone all day, not home at dinner-time. Ye'll have no dinner to make. Ye'll get the day all to yourself.'

Maggie's calls intensified to angry yelps and penetrated through the two doors. 'Well….' He considered possibilities, one eye on the clock. 'Ye can get Senga or Aggie to come in and sit with mother, for a wee while. If you leave her dinner ready, they might even feed her an let ye have a good long while out. Ach, go on!' He had a sudden burst of generosity. 'Ye deserve a wee break. Why no?'

'Why no indeed?' She thought to herself as she settled down for her precious half-hour of peace in the mid-afternoon. Maggie had been changed into what passed for day-clothes for her - a loose-fitting wrap-around frock, long woollen socks and a voluminous cardigan – then successfully hauled and pulled off the bed and into her wheelchair. This was pushed with some huffing and puffing by Kate, and much scraping of the skirting boards and door-jambs, into the sitting-room bay window so that Maggie could look out. She always started by delivering a venomous running commentary on each passer-by spotted in the street, or, if the street was quiet, on the hidden shopkeepers. However, the effort of getting up and being brought through always tired her out and, as usual, she had lapsed into snoring within five or ten minutes, her grizzled head sunk on her chest, saliva drooling on to the cardigan. Kate had learned to have the room especially warm, banking up the fire or resorting to a quick blast of the electric fire. Once Maggie was asleep, Kate would stretch herself out on the couch and, ignoring the competing claims of washing, ironing and cooking, would give herself over to day-dreaming. She had a whole library of dreams she was half-way through and she picked them up as the mood took her. Maggie would start awake after half-an-hour and assume, on

seeing Katy stretched out, that she too had been asleep. 'A young lassie like you! When I was your age…'

But Kate never wasted this precious oasis in sleep. Her secret world across the Atlantic was much more alluring, however tired she was.

But today, she could not settle. His parting words echoed in her head. *Why no? Ye deserve it.* And her thoughts turned to her own *'what if?'* of a few days ago. Go to the hospital in Leven? She had not been there since Robbie's birth twenty-odd years ago. How would she get there without anyone knowing? They would all misunderstand, not knowing how guilty she felt about having laughed at poor old Smirk when he was seriously ill. She knew how much he admired her. She felt a sudden fierce need for one of his admiring glances or cheeky compliments.

By the time Maggie snorted awake, plans were well in hand and she had reached the *what will I wear?* stage.

Senga pursed her lips doubtfully. 'But what if she…ye ken…if Ah dinnae get her on the commode soon enough? Ah'd no ken what tae dae wi the 'shit-kit'. Naw, Kate, Ah wid come in for a wee while but no for a' that time. Whit on earth are ye goin' tae dae a' that time onyway? Naw, sorry, hen.' She handed Kate one of her famous lemon drizzle cakes apologetically.

Aggie shook her head. 'Nae chance,' she declared roundly. 'Ye'll no get onybody willin' tae dae that. A wee while maybe…but three or four hoors, an feed the messy auld bag as weel, and maybe hae tae wipe her bum and clean up her…'

'Ach, furget it!' On the point of angry tears, Kate blundered out of the bakery shop, narrowly avoiding knocking over Fat Annie who was coming in for her morning's supply of jammy doughnuts. Only Annie's solid bulk prevented her from sprawling on to the shop's front step.

'Whit's wrang wi oor Kate the day?' she asked Aggie, breathing heavily from Kate's punishing tackle.

'She only wants me tae look after Auld Moaning Minnie fur three or four hoors next Wednesday, if ye please. *He*'s goin' tae some fancy meetin' in St Andrews so she disnae hae tae be in fur denner-time and she's got some daft notion aboot 'having some time to myself'.' Aggie

35

pretended a posh accent, quite alien to Kate. 'Ah cannae think whaur she thinks she's goin' tae go, a' by hersel fur hoors.'

Annie looked thoughtful as she dipped into the large sugary bag and began on the first doughnut.

'Kate, Kate! Hang on a minute, lass!' Annie puffed, almost jogging to catch up with the striding figure ahead. 'Ah've something tae say tae ye.'

'Whit is it, then?' Kate snapped. She was not in the mood for one of Annie's gossipy yarns. Seduced like all of them from time to time by Annie's stories about her neighbours, she knew that her own private life was fair game as well and would likely form the basis of the story for the next customer. As Aggie said, 'Yer ears should be ringin' louder than the shop door bell when ye go oot of *her* shop.'

'Ah heard ye were trying tae get someone tae look after yer mither-in-law next week.'

So that'll be the day's bit o' gossip in the draper's shop. Sod Aggie fur tellin' her!

'Weel, Ah thocht...fur peety's sake slow doon, will ye? Ah cannae keep up wi ye! Ah thocht Ah wid offer ma services. Ah mind fine whit it was like, never gettin' a day aff, ne'er a meenit tae yersel, up twa or three times in the nicht.'

Kate stopped and surveyed her. Hardly daring to believe the promise opening up before her, she challenged: 'Whit aboot cleaning up her bed, gettin' her on and aff the commode – *if* ye mak it in time. Clearin' up the mess she maks eatin'. Listenin' tae her shoutin' a' the time?'

'Ach, Kate, lassie,' interrupted Annie comfortably. 'Did Ah no dae it for twa o' them fur years? Ah've no forgotten whit tae dae. It's like ridin' a bike! Ah couldnae be there till twelve o'clock when the shop shuts fur half-day but Ah can stay as lang as ye like after that. Ach, dinnae start greetin', hen. Here...'

She pulled Kate into the draper's shop as they reached its door, shutting and locking it quickly behind them, leaving the *closed for a wee minute* sign in place. Ten minutes later, Kate fairly skipped across the road and up the stairs into her house.

'Aye, aye, auld yin!' she called cheekily to Maggie's instant litany of complaints and demands. 'Dinnae fash yersel! Ah've got yer favourite Belgian biscuits and there's lemon cake frae Senga so ye can mak a gran pig o' yersel wi them!'

'Impudent bitch!' muttered the old woman. 'I'll learn her.' She eyed the commode. 'I'll take the smile off her face!'

'Come along, Mr Smillie. Put that cigarette out now and get yourself into bed ready for visiting time.'

Angus sighed. It felt good to be out of bed and sitting on a chair, good to be allowed to walk – well, shuffle - up the long ward with its green-curtained cubicles, to the toilets at the end, rather than skittering about with bedpans any more. He was beginning to believe he might actually return to the real world again one day. But these dratted visiting hours on three afternoons a week were the bane of his existence.

Sister Connie, normally quite easy-going, turned into a stickler. It was almost as bad as the morning Consultant's Round. All patients to be sitting up in their beds, pillows propped perfectly, counterpanes spotlessly smooth. A couple of the very old, frail patients, who were never sat up at any other time, looked, Angus thought, like drunks propped up against lampposts. Invariably they listed to one side within minutes and only the fearsome tightness of the tucked-in bedcovers saved them from sliding out onto the floor.

With the help of the buxom nurse, he got into bed and submitted to its starchy constraints. Sister Connie cast a final piercing glance round the ward then nodded to the junior nurse at the door. As the first of the visitors began to surge in, Angus closed his eyes. He preferred not to see the pitying glances of his fellow inmates or, worse still, risk being adopted by someone else's well-meaning visitor.

His tactic, finely honed after five weeks, was to feign sleep for the first ten minutes; then, when he felt sure no-one was looking at him any more, to slide his book from his locker and begin nonchalantly to read, conveying – he hoped - how sorry he was for other patients who had to put up with boring visitors whilst he had the luxury of curling up with a good book.

It was not that he had not had any visitors at all. The very first week, only two days after his operation in fact, a woman had appeared. She was, he learned later, one Ethel Morrison, a distant cousin who had been over from Canada on holiday and was 'searching for her roots'. She had emigrated with her mother and father in her early twenties to escape the war and they had lost touch with 'the folks in the old country'. The Smillies and Morrisons were both families of short lives and few children and she had been having little luck until someone directed her to Angus's butcher shop. Finding it 'closed due to illness' she had made enquiries at the newsagent's two doors down and then had made her determined way to the hospital. But Angus had proved unsatisfactory, sunk in a post-operative haze of nausea, pain and drugged sleep. To her questions, he had managed only mumbles and groans and she had left sadly after twenty minutes. Whether she simply felt he was a complete wash-out or whether she had to sail off back to her adopted country, he did not know. When he was feeling better a few weeks later, he regretted not having had the chance to talk with her. He could have pumped her for details about life over there and that would have given him fodder for chats with Bonnie Kate, who seemed to be obsessed with the place.

The nursing staff had been very impressed with his exotic visitor. Indeed, it was largely from them that he knew about it, having retained only the haziest memory of her himself. His subsequent dearth of visitors had disappointed them but they doggedly maintained the fiction that he just never knew who might come and so must be sitting at attention throughout each visiting time.

He had managed to slide his book out of the locker without attracting a nurse's attention and was settling down to lose himself in it, when he became aware of light, clicking footsteps coming down the ward

Somebody's wife, a wee bit late. He did not look up. Then he realised that the clicking had stopped at the end of his bed. He waited for it to move on but it did not. After several seconds, he raised his eyes cautiously. That was some size of a bunch of flowers. Who, in God's name, could be hiding behind it?

'Hello, Mr Smirk,' said Kate.

CHAPTER TWO

AGGIE

'That's us all agreed then.'

Johnnie Cruikshanks flicked a glance round the table then shuffled together the papers that lay in front of him. His outward demeanour was calm, hands steady, voice neutral, but inside he was churning.

This was the first union negotiation he had been in charge of, though, heavens knows, he had sat through enough of them watching young Mark, the boss's son, flounder and bluster, yapping like the over-priced pedigree poodle he was and having to be rescued from conceding to excessive demands from hard-faced union officials.

Johnnie had come up through the ranks. He knew how union men operated and he often had a fair level with sympathy with their demands. But he was management now and, in the temporary absence of the young whippersnapper, he was in charge. He had to think and act like management. *'Fair but firm,'* he told himself. *'Give and get respect.'* These were the mantras he had brought back with him from the St Andrews mine-owners' conference last month.

The four men confronted each other across the littered table.

On one side, Johnnie and Chic Carswell, a well-educated but unambitious man who took some pride in Johnnie's rise to stardom since it had been he who had talent-spotted him and encouraged him five years ago.

On the union side, Bob Gilhooley, a heavy-set, slow-witted fellow, who had been neighbour to Johnnie's mother for the past twenty years. It was a mystery to Bob how 'Auld Maggie's laddie' had ended up in the manager's chair, though he dimly felt it should be a good thing to have one of their own there.

Beside Bob, sat Eck Fairweather who regarded Johnnie as a traitor, a bloody fifth columnist who had sold his soul to the enemy. The family connection of wives who were sisters only made the treachery all the more contemptible. He despised Johnnie but continued to think the world of his beautiful wife, Kate. Not given to flights of fancy, Eck had only one day-dream that he indulged in occasionally. He was well aware that he had gone after the wrong sister.

Now he had the infuriating feeling that Johnnie had stitched them up. The agreed deal sounded plausible but Eck *knew* that management had come off best again. But he was no match for Johnnie's rhetoric and Chic's smooth parrying, which seemed to accept, even agree with, the union demands and then somehow turn them round so that the miners ended up having gained only a few inches of ground instead of the yards they sought.

The thinly-rolled cigarette between his yellow fingers met a violent end in the overflowing ashtray. He rose, pushing his chair back impatiently.

'Ach, come on, Bob. We've wasted enough time this mornin'.'

Bob moved out ahead of Eck; Chic slipped past him in search of a much-needed cup of tea; Eck and Johnnie were left alone in the office.

In the month that it had been Johnnie's domain, it had changed from the cluttered, inefficient mess that young Mark liked to loll about in to a tidy, productive working environment.

Eck thought of the hot, noisy, filthy pit that awaited him as he looked round the neat, clean, sunshiney office, plants on the sill of a window ajar to counteract the cigarette smoke.

But he would not have it any other way, he told himself. He did a man's job underground and he was proud of it. Not for him the namby-pamby pen-pushing that Johnnie seemed to love so much. It only galled him that Johnnie was the one going home with the fat pay-packet whilst he and his fellow miners struggled to scrape a living.

He thought of the wife that Johnnie went home to: Kate with her nicely furnished, immaculate, well-stocked house, not like Aggie's shabby, messy, badly-managed domain; Kate with her big dark eyes and lovely hair, still a glossy black, not like Aggie's tired eyes and pepper-and-salt frizz; Kate with her kitchen always smelling of delicious food and her pretty china on snowy tablecloths, not like the badly-cooked or shop-bought muck that Aggie served up on their dirty, cluttered kitchen table.

His lips curled and he turned on his heel, unable to contain the angry *'puh!'* that escaped his lips.

'Hang on, Eck.' Johnnie had known Eck for twenty-odd years; he had weathered many of his beetle-browed frowns and harsh, rapped-out retorts. Johnnie knew that, over the years, Eck had raised his hand viciously and often to his wife and daughters but he admired how Aggie had faced up to the bully and had gradually gained, if not the upper hand, at least a measure of parity.

But he had also seen how this diminishing power-base had fuelled the stew of Eck's simmering irritation. He knew Eck for the not-quite-extinct volcano he was.

'How's things at home? How's Aggie doin' in the shop? Have you heard from your lassies recently?'

Eck looked at him scornfully. What made this managers' toady think he wanted to exchange small talk? He particularly objected to Johnnie playing the family connection card when he had just stitched him up at the monthly union-management meeting. *Does he think ma heid's buttoned up the back? Thinks Ah cannae see through him? Soft-soaping me wi pussy-footin' enquiries aboot Aggie and the lassies – as if he gies a damn!*

'We had a letter from Robbie and Janet last week with a photo o' their new bairn. She looks a right sonsy wee thing. And they're going to call her Kate. That's fair pleased my wee wife, as you can imagine.' Johnnie warmed to his task, essaying a man-to-man chuckle, which brought absolutely no response from the stony-faced Eck. 'What about young Agnes and Maisie? How are they gettin' on? Did I hear that Maisie is engaged? And Agnes doing so well with her singing on the stage out there! We'll likely be hearing she's famous one of these days. Then we can all enjoy some reflected glory from having kent her since she was born...'

Johnnie ground to a halt in the face of Eck's unyielding stare. For a moment roles were reversed and Eck held the power, withholding from Johnnie the reaction he sought. Eck savoured the sweetness of that moment, rolling it round his tongue like good tobacco. Then he threw back his head and laughed. It was a harsh, grating sound and it surged out the open window towards the group of men who were crossing the yard towards the pit-head and the cage waiting to take them down for their shift.

'It's no went weel,' they said to each other, 'we'll no be gettin' the Christmas bonus we want. That's Eck soundin' richt cheesed aff.'

'Ye should be lookin' tae yer ain wife, Johnnie,' was Eck's parting shot. 'She's lookin' like a drudge these days, runnin' after that auld bitch. But then, ye're a dab hand at getting the maist work oot o' folk - we a' ken that. An gettin' yer ain wiy, walkin' ower folk. Ah hope ye rot in hell!'

His footsteps echoed down the short lobby and out into the yard as he strode off to join his fellow shift-workers.

'Nice talking to you, Eck, as usual,' said Johnnie to the empty room, grimacing at his failure to make any impression on Eck's rigid dislike and mistrust of him. *All very well for Kate to tell me no to rile the bugger. She should try it sometime. And what did he mean saying she's looking like a drudge. Bloody cheek, poking his nose in. The way he treats Aggie, he's got no room to speak. Not that she puts up wi his bloody bad-temper. She's got him pegged and she doesn't let him bully her.*

He liked his sister-in-law: a fine woman and a grand singer; he must make a point of going in to see her in her bakery shop one day soon. It had been months…not since last Hogmanay, in fact. What was that song she had sung so beautifully?

He hummed as he gathered up the papers from the union meeting and took them through to the front office to the filing clerks.

Eck ran a long bony finger round his gums, extracting a few lurking strands of grey, gristly meat. He inspected these over the top of his spectacles then held his finger out to the hovering old dog.

Aggie ignored this familiar performance: twenty-seven years of marriage had inured her to her husband's less attractive habits. It meant she could dispense with camouflaging her own. Theirs was now a partnership of open mutual distaste but it did have the saving grace of candour. Aggie often marvelled at how Kate's marriage appeared to be built on subterfuge and manipulation – well, *attempted* manipulation. Kate seemed to devote a great deal of time to spectacularly unsuccessful schemes to soften her Johnnie up and persuade him to do what she wanted. *Silly bitch.*

Eck rose from the table without comment. Their middle-of-the-day dinner was always two greasy pies from Aggie's bakery and a spoonful of baked beans in tomato sauce. He ate with resigned speed, careless of the red grease dripping down his pouchy chin and settling in the stubbly cleft. Aggie had never been much of a cook and, now that she had cheap access to so much ready-made food, she saw no point in trying any more.

He stomped through to the back porch off the kitchen where his work boots and miner's hat were kept. It was time for him to head off to the mine for back-shift, one o'clock in the afternoon till eight o'clock at night. She took his piece-tin through to him.

He would eat the two thick corned beef sandwiches and drink the bottle of cold tea. The three little fancy cakes, left over from the morning rush in the shop, he would *not* eat. 'Sweetie rubbish' he called them, to which she would reply: 'Ye'll no be needing ony o' that then, will ye? You bein' sae sweet a' ready!'

Once upon a time, such a remark would have had him 'taking his hand off her jaw', his shorthand for the sudden, vicious blows to the side of the head that Aggie and their two daughters had lived with for years.

Aggie despised women who crept around with black eyes and bruised bodies, terrified to stand up to their violent men. She had fought back with words and glances every bit as vicious as his blows. In time, he had begun to hesitate; then to alternate between lashing out and refraining; then finally to cease the violence.

She couldn't pinpoint the exact day when she knew he would never hit her or the lassies again. It had been a slow tapering-off, replaced nowadays by festering irritation, harsh, rapped-out words and menacing looks. Aggie met these with supreme disdain. *Water aff a duck's back,* she would shrug. *Happy Harry*, she called him sarcastically to other people and even, occasionally, to his face. His reply usually touched upon her scrawny figure, wispy, greying hair and thick ankles.

She knew the cakes would be handed out to other men on the shift at piece-time. She knew this because when she met the men in the street there would be courteous gratitude from some and suggestive allusions to *bonnie wee tarts* from others.

Washing the dishes at the sink, she judged her timing.

When he barked 'That's me aff, then,' she shouted 'Just a meenit, Ah need tae tell ye something.'

His miner's-hatted head appeared round the kitchen door. 'Aye, whit?'

'Ah'll no be here when ye get hame at half-eight. Ah'm goin' tae Senga's tae gie her a perm.' She did not turn round as she spoke; her angular back like a fortress wall. 'Ah'll leave yer supper in the oven.'

There was a short silence, so heavy that she could hear the dog breathing. She counted slowly inside herself as she always did when facing him down. She sensed him looking furiously at the clock. She heard the door slam and his angry footsteps on the path and she relaxed, slumping against the sink, cursing as she felt the water seeping through her apron on to her skirt waistband.

Then the excitement of what she had planned for that evening surged inside her. She had seen the advertisement in the local paper. A new amateur operatic company was being formed in Leven – only a short bus-ride away – and it was auditioning for a revue of the songs of Ivor Novello, whose untimely death a few years ago had left his fans bereft.

Aggie's heart had leapt when she had seen the item in the paper and she had known immediately that nothing would stop her from going to Leven tonight.

People often commented on the startling difference between the two sisters' voices: Kate, who was all frilly curves, with a light speaking voice, delivered a deep, throbbing contralto; Aggie, who was all plain-clothes angles, with a harsh speaking voice, delivered a meltingly sweet soprano. Folk said it was like a case of mistaken identity but on one thing they were all agreed: those Kelly sisters were beautiful singers and not even the hard years of the depression, the war and post-war austerity, followed by losing all four of their children to the yawning maw of New World emigration, had diminished their glorious voices. If anything, they had taken on an even greater beauty, enriched by suffering and yearning.

The more Aggie thought about being able to sing the songs of her favourite composer to a *real* audience, to dress up and strut about a stage, acting out the wonderful romantic stories which had burned within her for years, the stronger became her conviction that the show was meant for her.

Her singing ability was not in question; she never even considered that she would not be head-and-shoulders above anyone else in the audition. Her only difficulty lay in getting to the audition; beyond that, she did not think.

Once she had been chosen for the show, nothing could stop her; of that she was sure. She had turned over various strategies for escaping from the routines and demands of her life. In the end, she had simply decided on an outright lie.

To tell Eck the real reason would have meant scorn and obstruction. How he hated her succeeding at anything! Hadn't he raised endless objections and cast dour predictions of disaster over her plan to take on the bakery five years ago when young Agnes and her sister Maisie had left for Canada? He had had to eat his words, along with the endless pies, over the succeeding years as the shop thrived and brought in a tidy little income, often as much as he was earning at the coal face. She knew that galled him – that her 'plesterin' aboot wi cakes and buns' could bring in as much as his back-breaking, dangerous job.

She hummed *We'll Gather Lilacs in the Spring Again* all afternoon in the bakery, dancing through the clearing up at the end of the day, hurrying home to bank up the fire so she could have enough hot water for a bath before changing into her best skirt and blouse and heading off to catch the half-past-six bus to Leven.

Of her promise to leave Eck's tea in the oven she remembered nothing so that when he came in at half-past-eight, tired, filthy and hungry, it was to a fire almost out, no coal in the fireside scuttle, no food on offer.

Blast the bloody wumman. He threw together a meagre supper of yesterday's stale baps with a smear of mouldy jam. *She's no much o' a wife these days.* His thoughts drifted back…

It was his seventeenth birthday. For three long years since leaving school, he had pestered his mother to be allowed to go down the pit with his father. She had held out as long as possible, hating to think of her 'wee laddie' being swallowed up by that life. It wasn't just the dirt, the danger and the toil she had resisted for him. It was what it did to the men's souls: a combination of hating and fearing the work yet taking a fierce pride in it; the raw camaraderie of men who sweated and strained together, almost naked and caked with coal-dust, in the bowels of the earth; an exclusive club, forever unknown to the womenfolk. She knew she would lose him once he joined.

His father had stayed out of the argument. Jim Fairweather believed in parents presenting a united front to their children and would never have openly contradicted his wife in front of young Sandy

45

and his sister Peggy. In his heart, he knew that Sandy (or Eck as the lad had begun to style himself, thinking it sounded more manly and miner-like) had been born to be a miner. It had only ever been a matter of time.

Cathie had finally given in a month before Eck's seventeenth birthday, running out of strength to battle any more. His disdain for the nice, safe, clean job she had procured for him in the local Co-operative shop – with a view to 'becoming a real grocer one day' – had escalated into revolt and he had threatened to hand in his notice and take to hanging about on street corners with the other unemployed lads. She had imagined him turning into a layabout, getting into bad company, maybe caught up in feckless crime.

And so there he was, striding up the street with his father, pit-blackened, exhausted, his mind a jumble of frightening, exhilarating impressions from his first day underground.

Part of him was hardly able to contemplate the thought of going back down again tomorrow – let alone the next day and the next – so great had been the relief when the shift was over and the cage had brought them back up to daylight and safe, sweet air again. But part of him was already eager to be back down there, a real man among men, his heart racing with the ever-present sense of danger and the sheer, unbelievable horror of it all. He had watched the other men, marvelling that none of them commented on the hideous conditions, trying desperately to ape their casual acceptance and jocularity in what seemed to him like the mouth of hell.

At the crossroads, the knot of men broke up and there were calls of 'See ye the nicht' and 'It your turn, Jimmy – ye owe me a pint, mind.'

Terry Kelly, a wiry middle-aged man, slapped Eck on the back. 'Weel done, lad,' he said. 'You come doon tae the club the nicht wi yer dad an enjoy yersel. Ye deserve it. The first day's aye hard but ye'll get used tae it – nothing else fur it! My Aggie is singing at the club the nicht –raisin' money fur the bairns' Christmas Party. She's a grand singer, though Ah say it masel.'

Cathie's red eyes bore testimony to how her feelings had raged inside her all day but she said nothing as she filled up the tin bath with hot water by the fire and scrubbed pit-grime off two strong, muscled backs instead of one. They wolfed down her tripe and onion stew.

Copying his father, Eck slumped in a fireside chair and snored for half-an-hour (though Cathie knew fine that he was wide awake and *only pretending). Then both men leapt up, shook themselves like wet dogs and set off for the club, laughing and jingling their money in their trouser pockets.*

The club was a noisy fug. Steam from wet jackets mingled with smoke from gritty, old pipes and meanly-rolled cigarettes. Through watering eyes, Eck saw a tall slender girl, dressed in a green frock with a black sash, standing beside the piano on the stage. He thought, with a rare flash of poetic insight, that the girl looked like a willow tree in her green dress, bending over, long dark hair sweeping down to the piano keys as she conferred with her accompanist. The piano struck up an introduction and slowly the rowdy throng quietened, the sssshhh working its way from front to back and reaching even the bar staff, so that they ceased clattering tumblers and ringing the cash register.

When the girl began to sing, a real hush fell. The clarity of the high sweet voice held them all in thrall. She sang with obvious, almost shameless, delight in her own power. The slight bow she took in acknowledgement of their whistling, stomping applause was cursory, mocking.

'And why wouldn't you be bowled over?' she seemed to be saying. 'I'm the best! And wasted on you lot.'

Eck was captivated: not so much by her singing – it was well enough, he supposed, he was no judge of such things and cared very little for music - but by her attitude. He wanted to make the acquaintance immediately of this feisty, high-handed lassie.

Seeing his face, his father laughed. 'She's a wee bit oot o' your league, lad,' he said, not without sympathy. 'An she's four or five years older than ye, anyway.'

But Eck barely heard. He had his new crusade. Now that the battle to become a miner was won, he needed another. He would win this singing, taunting lass and he would start right now.

He pushed through the crowded room towards the stage in time to accost Aggie coming down its steps. Her bold, derisive stare as he spoke to her quickened his pulses and launched him on the long path to conquest and domination.

The bus lurched through the misty October night. Upstairs, the smoking passengers suffered especially from the heavy handed driving and incautious braking, some tutting, a few cursing, as the double-decker swayed round each corner. Aggie puffed angrily on her woodbine.

'The nerve o' the wee shit!' she muttered, fury and disbelief staving off the moment of acceptance. *A looovely voice:* in her head she mimicked the affected tones of the director. *But just a little toooo mature for us, dearie. Novello's heroines are young and beyoootiful...*

For years, the romance and the power of the music had been the secret track in her mind. However grim the realities of her life and her marriage, she had always been able to slip away from them at a moment's notice.

Mammy! Mammy! the bairns would cry, tugging at her sooty, smelly old pinafore. *Good God, wumman,* Eck would thunder, shoving her aside as he strode off to another drunken night at the Miners' Welfare Club. *Can ye no get yersel organised? Keep the hoose clean and put some decent food on the table?* And she had simply closed her eyes and drifted away to where romance and lilacs were always in bloom.

She remembered the first night she had sung Novello.

It was a benefit concert at the Welfare Club. She often sang there but, up till then, had stuck to melodramatic Scottish ballads like *Rothesay Bay* or cloying Irish immigrant stuff like *I'll take you home again, Kathleen*. But, that night, she had resolved to try something new, having recently discovered the wonderful music of Ivor Novello from an old school friend who took singing lessons.

Aggie privately considered the lassie was wasting her time with her mediocre voice and railed at the unfairness of fate. She milked the friend for tips and ideas, borrowing the sheet music to learn the words, listening intently as her friend complied with requests to sing new songs enough times to let Aggie learn them.

She had a new frock that night too, she recalled. Kate, handy with a needle and with an eye for style, had made it for her out of a green chenille bedspread that had frayed at the edges but still had some useable material in the middle. The heavy stuff hung well on her slender figure, which was accentuated by the old black velvet sash which she and Kate used with all their dresses, sharing and occasionally squabbling over it if their needs clashed. The sash had been their grandmother's - or so said their father gravely every time he saw them wearing it. It was worn and threadbare but, at a distance, still looked impressive. Kate and she had grown up loving it, playing 'dressy-ups' with it whilst hobbling in their mother's old shoes, then graduating to using it for real once womanly curves began to swell.

Not that *her* curves had come to much. Kate had cornered the market there, just as she had appropriated most of their parents' attention and affection, being forever the bonnie baby of the family.

But that night, on the stage at the Welfare Club, in her new green dress and with this wonderful song thrilling inside her, she felt like a princess. Only in the realm of singing was Aggie ever confident of her superiority over Kate. Kate's voice was fine enough, with the perfect pitch that was nature's gift to them both. But it was low-pitched, a natural contralto, so there were fewer pieces that suited it and people paid less attention to it. When Aggie sang, people immediately stopped what they were doing or saying. It was as if she threw open a door for them, flooding them with light, drawing them on through the door whilst she retreated ever further away, luring them deeper into her world, until she brought the song - and their adventure – to a close, leaving them gasping and clamouring for more.

That night, she delivered her new song without introduction, after a few opening bars to call the crowd to order. Their stunned faces at the end confirmed her choice. *Rothesay Bay* and good old *Kathleen* had had their day. Novello – and his enchanting, lyrical musicality - had arrived.

What a night that was – the beginning of a lifetime love affair. Not with the pimply-faced, swaggering youth who accosted her as she came down from the stage, but with that musical world of romance, tenderness and elegance.

Somehow it didn't matter that she didn't love him, as he pursued her over the next eighteen months, finally wearing her down to the point of consent. She had to marry someone. She had had precious few offers - and there was bloody Kate, three years younger than her and already engaged, rubbing her nose in it. '*As well to get it over with*,' she had thought. '*He's no worse than a' the rest o' them.*'

The bus swung into the village and along her road. She rose reluctantly and swayed down the narrow stairs, swearing, grabbing a rail, as the vehicle reared to a stop. Her footsteps dragged as she drew near the house.

She began to hum one of her Novello favourites, *Someday my heart will awake*, trying to conjure up her secret world as a buttress against sordid reality, but tonight it eluded her. When she came to the lines, *Maybe this gentle refrain - Some day will echo again*, she began to cry, stopping to lean against a lamppost, snuffling and struggling for breath in the foggy night air.

He opened the door to let the old dog out for a last pee in the street and saw her. *She's greetin'.* A compassionate urge eddied weakly in him then he remembered the cold house and his miserable supper. *Whit's she got tae greet aboot? It's me wis doon the pit a' day and cam' hame tae nae supper.*

Let her get over whatever was bothering her. He was going to bed. He whistled to the dog and they went back in, slamming the door.

Aggie sloshed the slimy mop over the bakery floor. Outside the October morning was misty, long-shadowed, with a blue-purple tinge that gave the grey rows of council house roofs an undeserved beauty. She leant on the mop and stared past the cakes in the window at the skyline, neither seeing nor appreciating it. Unbidden, a line from a song – one more suited to Kate's voice - came into her mind: *When a lovely flame dies, Smoke gets in your eyes.*

Her flame had indeed died and her love affair with the glorious Ivor was over. He had rejected her because she was too old. He, on the other hand, was ageless and timeless and, like some pagan deity, would always demand only beautiful young virgins. She had lost not simply her youth and the chance to enter into his magic world, but she had lost her refuge, the secret identity that at times had seemed more real to her than Aggie Fairweather, Eck's wife. Without it, she was not sure she could go on. Not if this was all there was, all there would ever be.

The shop door bell jangled as the first customer of the day came in.

'Mind ye dinnae slip on the floor. Ah've jist washed it,' she said automatically. The sound of her speaking voice, ordinary and business-like, surprised her. It was the first time she had heard it since the blow had fallen at the audition.

She had left the hall immediately after her turn; she had crawled in beside a snoring Eck and wept herself to sleep; then she had risen in the grey morning, leaving him asleep to slip along the road and open up for the early morning rolls delivery. Her voice seemed to be functioning separately; indeed a separate person altogether seemed to be taking its place behind the counter, listening to the customer, collecting the rolls and scones being asked for, putting them into bags, taking money, giving change. The broken-hearted, bereaved Aggie watched aghast, horrified at such callousness. '*Unfeeling bitch,*' she thought. '*It's no richt, no decent.*' It was like watching the widow laughing and joking at the funeral.

By the end of the morning, she was exhausted: being two people at the same time was very hard work. Thank God it was Wednesday, early closing.

She swept the remaining pies and cakes into a box to take home, not caring that iced fancies rubbed shoulders with onion bridies. They would do for his dinner and supper. For herself, she was too weary and heartsick to care about food. She would go back to bed this afternoon with a hot water bottle and a toddy made with some whisky filched from his meagre supply in the sideboard. She might even pretend to be sick, tell him she had been vomiting and skittering in the toilet during his shift. Then he would curse, give her a wide berth for fear of catching something and make up a bed in the cold, dusty, empty room that had belonged to their daughters. She would get a blissful night to herself, without his snoring and grunting and even – worst of all – his occasional, groping demands.

The fine morning had given way to a blustery, wet day and she swore as she juggled umbrella and bakery box. Every buffet from the wind, every drip down the back of her neck when the umbrella swooped out of control seemed like an insult. She felt like nothing good would ever happen to her again.

She decided she would have two toddies and to hell with what he would say when he saw the level of the whisky bottle. She could put some cold tea in it to bring it back up to the mark he had made on the bottle. As she came to this decision, she rounded the corner past the draper's shop, noting that it was already closed. '*She's quick aff the mark,*' she thought. '*It's only jist gone twelve.*'

Then she spied the bulky figure of Fat Annie shuffling diagonally over the crossroads. *Whaur's that auld gossip goin' in sich a hurry?* She watched in some surprise, jolted out of her self-absorbed misery, as the fat one hurried through her sister's gate and up the side of the block to let herself in through Kate's outside door.

Aggie was intrigued. She knew that Annie had 'sat' for Kate a few weeks ago one Wednesday afternoon when Johnnie was at his swanky St Andrews conference, letting Kate have several hours off from the care of Old Maggie. Aggie had thought Annie daft to do it: one day off

51

would only whet Kate's appetite and Annie would find herself in
regular demand. Indeed, this had been partly why she herself had
refused to accede to Kate's request for help. Kate had had a damn soft
life up till now, compared with the rest of them, and it was her turn to
suffer a wee bit. Letting her off the hook, even for a short time, would
only make her discontented. No, she had to take what fate was dishing
out to her for the moment and get on with it. Maybe now she'd
appreciate what other folk had had to put up with while she lived in the
lap of luxury and spent her days dusting ornaments and dyeing her
hair.

Aggie took shelter in the doorway of Annie's shop, watching
curiously. So Annie had a key to Kate's house, did she? It looked like
this Wednesday afternoon thing was becoming a habit. But where was
Johnnie? He would be on his way home for his midday dinner, surely?
Aggie cursed as she remembered that her own husband was waiting
for his dinner before going off to work at ten-to-one. The dinner-time
pies lay in the bottom of her box – she could feel their warm grease
soaking through onto her hands.

She was about to give up and run home when Kate emerged. She
was smartly-dressed in a navy blue jacket and skirt. Her freshly waved
hair blew in the damp breeze and she hastily took the bright red scarf
from the neck of the jacket and put it over her head, tying it in a
fetching bow under her chin. High heeled shoes clicked out into the
street and up to the nearby bus stop.

Aggie watched in bewilderment as a bus drew up and Kate
hopped up into it. Aggie started out of her trance just in time to sprint
ahead of it and see its destination, displayed on the front window:
Windygates, a village some ten miles away. Now, why, in the name of
God, was Kate going there? And where was Johnnie? And what was
Fat Annie doing with a key to Kate's house? If only she had time to go
over and find out… But it was now twenty-past-twelve and it would be
half-past by the time she got home. The pies would be cold and Eck
would be furious.

It was a rushed, unappetising dinner of congealing grease and
half-heated beans, the pies not enhanced by the flecks of pink icing
and smears of artificial cream.

Aggie had thought to cry herself to sleep again after the toddies.
But, as she drifted off at half-past-two, she found she was dwelling as
much on her sister's behaviour today as on yesterday's crushing
disappointment, so that her dreams were of Kate up on the stage,

transformed into a twenty-year-old soprano, whilst she, Aggie, sat in the back row of the theatre, a shrivelled old woman.

'It's yersel then, wee Katy.' Aggie had watched her sister crossing the road to the bakery shop and was poised to inveigle her into a friendly conversation designed to lower Kate's guard. 'How are ye, these days? Ah've no seen ye for a wee while. Is Auld Moanin' Maggie still keepin' ye on the trot?'

Kate was looking well, she thought. Much better, certainly, than she had the last time Aggie had seen her. That would be the day Kate had been desperately asking around for someone to come and sit with the auld tyrant. She seemed to have recouped some of her old bloom, the sheen of optimism that always annoyed Aggie. '*What's she got tae look sae happy aboot,*' thought Aggie sourly. But she reined in her resentment, remembering her fact-finding mission.

'Ah'm no sae bad, Aggie. The auld yin is jist the auld yin.' Kate made a *moue* of her pretty lips and shrugged. 'Ah jist ignore her the best Ah can. She cannae last furever - that's whit Ah tell masel. Ah jist try tae think o' ither things an pay nae attention tae her mumpin'. Have ye ony shortbread the day. Ah want stuff that looks home-made, mind.'

Aggie laughed. 'Goin' tae pass it aff as yer ain, are ye? Well, Ah'll no blow the gaff on ye – no if ye mak it worth ma while!' She winked and the sisters shared a rare moment of complicity.

As she carefully put a dozen squares of the crumbly shortbread into a paper bag, Aggie seized the moment of warmth between them.

'Ah hear Fat Annie's been obligin' ye wi some granny-sittin'. That's richt guid o' her. Ah suppose it's like auld times fur her. She had that mony years o' it wi her ain auld folk. Geez, Ah remember them, tae. A richt pair o' targers. They had Annie run ragged fur years.'

Kate said nothing, bending her glossy, dark head (*Noo when dis she get time fur dyein' her hair these days?*) as she gently laid the bag of shortbread to lie flat in the bottom of her shopping basket. She took rather a long time to complete this manoeuvre.

Aggie watched her suspiciously. *Was that a blush? Were her hands shaking just a little?* Aggie circled her prey.

'So whit are ye daein wi Johnnie at denner-times on a Wednesday?'

'Ma Johnnie's busy on Wednesdays at denner-time the noo. He's got…' Kate struggled to remember the phrase '…oh, aye, *working lunches* in St Andrews. He got asked tae join a committee or something after that conference-thing an it meets every Wednesday an they have denner thegither an chew the fat. Well…' she giggled. 'Ah hope it isnae jist fat they get fur their denner!' She gave a merry peal of laughter but, to Aggie, it sounded forced, a shade *too* merry.

'So that gies ye every Wednesday aff noo, does it? An Fat Annie standin' by tae tak ower wi Auld Maggie. Very handy! Ye've landed on yer feet again, ye wee minx.' Aggie tried to make her voice light and playful but she was finding it hard to disguise her disgust. *Somebody aye bales her oot. She aye gets the sympathy vote.* She felt a wave of jealous self-pity.

Kate paid for the shortbread and was moving quickly out of the shop when Aggie moved in for the kill. 'An whit are ye goin' tae *Windygates* fur?'

Aggie walked slowly home, the bag of leftover bakeries bumping against her leg. As she rounded the corner into Burns Avenue, suddenly the thought of the miserable house repelled her.

Usually she liked when Eck was back-shift, enjoying the three hours to herself before he returned at half-past-eight. She would make herself a pot of tea, light a woodbine, and sit down to look through the paper or listen to the wireless.

Sometimes, there was a letter from Agnes or Maisie to read and, occasionally, she would make the effort to write back. But she was no writer and, in any case, what on earth was there to write about? She said the same things every time whereas their letters were always full of news and change. She barely recognised the tentative girls who had left five years ago in the confident women who signed these letters. She was glad for them, of course, but it all seemed to have very little to do with *her* life now. Of their father, they only ever made the same perfunctory enquiry – *hope Father is well* - and sent the same equally perfunctory message – *give Father my love.*

Aggie always snorted when she read that. '*What wid he do wi that,*' she wondered. '*He'd nae interest in it when they were here.*'

Tonight, however, the tea-and-woodbine hour had lost its charm. She was unsettled, in need of someone to share her thoughts with.

Since Kate had shot out of the shop this afternoon – *like a scalded cat* – Aggie had been turning over in her mind the garbled explanation her sister had given about her trip to Windygates. The shop had been steadily busy for the rest of the afternoon and she had had no time to consider the story with anything like the care it deserved. She cast around in her mind for a confidante - tricky at this time of day. Many of the women she knew would be busy getting food on the table for men and children. She needed another back-shift wife. Eck had only recently started this shift so she hadn't heard him mention any of the other men yet, had she?

Then she grinned. Of course! One day last week he had gone to the pit in the late morning for a union-management meeting before his shift. He had been particularly grim-faced that night and she had regretted giving him an opening by asking idly if he'd seen much of Johnnie Cruikshanks recently. The ensuing tirade had lasted half-an-hour.

It had been a couple of days before the audition and she had been spending more time than usual in her secret world of romantic songs so his ranting about Johnnie's defection from miners' ranks to managers' toady and his particularly odious behaviour that morning had simply washed around her as background noise. But, like someone who absorbs information whilst asleep, she could dredge up quite a lot of what had been said if she concentrated. She felt sure he had mentioned one of the other men on the shift with him . . .

Yes! She had it! Bob Gilhooley, Auld Moanin' Maggie's neighbour. *Now, wis that no perfect?* Jeannie Gilhooley was a woman who always had time for tales and a warm welcome for their bearer.

She veered her lopsided steps towards the other side of the road and crossed quickly, heading for the cul-de-sac at the end of the long avenue, where a row of miners' cottages formed a guard of honour up to the pretentious bungalow in the far corner.

Johnnie Cruikshank's father had been in the building trade, indeed had risen to be an under-manager. With a small inheritance from his grandmother, he had purchased in 1924 the feu on the piece of vacant land at the end of the cottages and with his contacts in the trade had been able to build the house for his wife, Maggie, and their two sons. In itself a simple enough, four-roomed house, it borrowed its grand air solely from the contrast with the miserable cottages, although these had at least been grudgingly modernised by the mine-owners, put to shame by the wave of post-war building. They now sported lean-to additions at the back which housed sculleries with running water and toilets that flushed.

Outside Jeannie's gate, she was assailed by misgivings. The gossip grapevine was a healthy strain in their small community. The women could be staunchly loyal to each other, they often rallied round to protect and support each other in times of crisis or disaster, but, when all was said and done, there was nothing like a good blether, spiced with a wee bit of scandal, to brighten up a dreary life.

Aggie knew that a nod would be as good as a wink to Jeannie and the pebble once cast into the pool would spread its ripples fast. And once cast, it could not be recalled. She hesitated. Kate had had it hard of late, it was true. No-one envied her the daily grind of caring for the auld moaner and all the women knew of her longing to emigrate to be with daughter Maureen and son Robbie in Canada.

'It's a mean thing ye're daein, Aggie Fairweather,' she sternly told herself. She looked along the end of the row of cottages to the empty bungalow. It would be sold when Maggie died and Johnnie and his cocky wee brother would get the money. G*eez, she'll no even need the assisted passage, she'll be able tae go tae Canada first class on the boat.*

She pictured Kate, beautifully dressed, with expensive matching luggage, setting off, waving goodbye like departing royalty from the first class deck to her poor sister on the quayside. She felt her heart beginning to harden. Matters were taken out of her hands at that very moment as Jeannie opened her front door and, with one step, was down the tiny path to the gate.

'Ah thocht it wis you, Aggie! Ah saw ye oot o' the windae. Are ye comin' tae see me? Ye're no goin' up tae the bungalow, are ye? Has Kate sent ye? Is it something aboot Auld Maggie? How are they a' gettin' on? How is the auld yin? How is Kate managin'? What...' Jeannie was a curious woman whose encyclopaedic knowledge of the affairs of the community was the result of meticulous research.

'Hiv ye given up breathin', Jeannie?' laughed Aggie. 'Ah cannae remember yer first question noo, let alone a' the ones that cam' after it. Onyway, Ah'm jist havin' a wee walk before goin' hame and Ah kent Bob wis back-shift same as Eck so Ah thocht Ah'd jist cry in and see hoo ye're daein yersel.'

Jeannie caught her drift immediately. Aggie never went for walks and she had never, except for first-footing on Hogmanay, simply 'cried in' anywhere. It was not her style at all, though the other women indulged daily in such liberties, some of them spending half their lives in and out of each other's houses.

Aggie had purpose, Jeannie knew well, and she simmered with anticipation at the thought.

'Come awa in, Aggie,' she said warmly. 'Ah'll mak us a fresh pot o' tea.'

'An Ah've got some pineapples tarts here.' Aggie waved her bag, her earlier scruples forgotten. Jeannie exuded the seductive lure of a good gossip session and promised the balm of diversion and compensation to Aggie's sad heart.

'Tak yer coat aff and mak yersel at hame. Ah'll pit the kettle on.' Jeannie hurried through to the tiny scullery. As she emptied the tea-leaves from the last brew on to the straggling geranium on the window-sill, she mused on what Aggie was here to tell her.

It would probably be to do with Kate, Johnnie and Old Maggie. Were they going to put the auld lass in a home and emigrate at last? Were they goin' tae sell the bungalow? Had Johnnie finally over-reached himself with the bosses and been sacked for cheek? Had Eck finally burst his banks and murdered Johnnie? It must be something big to have driven Aggie to seek out a confidante. She usually poured scorn on the rumour-mongering and endless picking over of details that many of the women indulged in. Her caustic tongue had strangled many a good story at birth.

The whistle of the kettle pierced Jeannie's conjectures.

'God, Aggie, that's some mess ye've got there,' she exclaimed looking doubtfully into the battered cake-box. 'Wait till Ah get a couple o' teaspoons. We'll jist hae tae pick oot wee bitties at a time. Cannae waste ony, no at the price they are.' Then, remembering to whom she was talking: 'They're smashin', though, and worth every penny.'

The two women settled down, alternately sipping their tea and poking into the mess of yellow icing, smashed pastry, tinned pineapple pieces and sticky, fake cream. When only a few smeary yellow blobs remained in the box, both women's bosoms were liberally sprinkled with pastry crumbs, second cups of tea had been poured and woodbine lit, Jeannie leaned back in her chair and eyed Aggie speculatively. She was itching to prompt but instinct told her to wait.

Her patience was soon rewarded. On her third draw of the cigarette, Aggie began to talk. Jeannie sighed with pleasure as she listened. It had been well worth waiting for.

Jeannie would have loved to keep Aggie longer, pumping her for more detail and leading her in juicy speculation, but, frustratingly, her twenty-year-old twin sons came clumping in at six o'clock, pushing and shoving each other, brawling and horsing throughout the house, demanding what was for tea and could they have it quick because they were 'goin' winchin'' that evening.

Looking at their heavy-set bodies and rather vacant faces – they definitely favoured their father in looks – Aggie pitied the poor lassies. Yielding to their ill-mannered interest in her bakeries bag, she left empty-handed but light-hearted. The gossip with Jeannie had been even more delicious than the pineapple tarts. She felt infinitely better than she had for days, ever since that damned audition, in fact.

She barely noticed the light rain that was beginning to fall and, unburdened now, both physically and mentally, she felt she could walk for miles. It did occur to her, however, that she had ceded the sausage rolls for Eck's supper to the twins' rapacity.

Ah'll better gang back tae the shop and get some more, she decided. Bored with the thought of retracing her steps, and still full of new-found energy, she took a more circuitous route.

And so it was –fate, or the hand of God, perhaps – that Aggie came to pass by the Methodist Church and see outside a poster inviting 'keen singers' to come to a 'try-out' for Handel's *Messiah* on Sunday afternoon.

She almost walked by without noticing it. Brought up a Roman Catholic, like all the Irish-descent families in the area, she was rarely in church these days. Eck had 'converted' to marry her and it was only old Terry Kelly's admiration for the lad's strength and endurance at the coal face and the two men's shared, fanatical love for their miners' union that had enabled him to agree to a 'mixed marriage'. Attendance at mass had always been for Aggie a boring duty, inescapable whilst under her father's roof, but quickly and thankfully sloughed off once out from under it. Eck had lapsed rapidly too and the baptisms of their daughters had been mere sops to Terry.

Old habits die hard, though, and Aggie, if pressed, would have said she was a Catholic, and it was a sin to cross the threshold of a Protestant Church, even for a wedding or funeral. The two sects rubbed along tolerably well in the small community by dint of tightly-observed rules and boundaries. They might be friendly, but the line was drawn when it came to attending each other's services. One Catholic family had recently caused weeks of debate by not only going to the wedding reception after the service (this was just allowable and no more) but by actually turning up at the Protestant Church door and throwing confetti when the newly-weds emerged. Some people said this was all right; they hadn't actually *gone in* to the building. Others said it was tantamount to joining in the service and the errant pair should hot-foot it to Father O'Malley's confessional box at once.

Thus Aggie barely registered the Methodist Church as she passed it, so little did she think it would ever have to do with her life. But the words 'keen singers' and 'try-out' flicked into her newly-charged brain causing her to slew to a halt several paces past the church steps then walk slowly backwards.

She had heard of the *Messiah*, even heard snatches of it on the wireless sometimes and had once caught a soprano solo which had played over in her head for a few days afterwards. But the lyrics, which had been about a 'redeemer living,' if she remembered it right, hadn't seemed nearly as romantic and enthralling as Novello's stuff and she had soon forgotten it. It hadn't been that bad, though, she thought, and, if it gave her a chance to sing with people listening and applauding (maybe they were even allowed to clap in a proddy kirk?), then it had to be worth a go.

'Geez, this is definitely my lucky day!' she thought. *'First Ah get oor Katy on the end o' a hook, then Ah get Jeannie the Mooth on ma side and a' set tae dae the bizness, then Ah see this try-oot – that'll be a kirky word fur audition, Ah suppose. This ca's fur a celebration!'*

She breezed into the darkening shop and cast around for something for supper. Then she remembered the half-cooked steak-and-kidney pies that had been delivered in the late afternoon and put in the cold store for sale tomorrow. They were an expensive luxury and she only ever got three or four in at once, except for the New Year's Day dinners when they were standard traditional fare for everyone. Three were already ordered but the fourth she had bought on spec, hoping to tempt someone with more money than sense. Someone like Kate, maybe.

59

On impulse, she seized one and put it, with more care than usual, into a big cardboard box, using brown string to make a carrying parcel of it. *Ye're in fur a treat the nicht, Ecky, ma lad,* she laughed as she locked up and left for home again.

Now what would she sing for the try-out? Something solemn and churchy but better not be any of the Catholic hymns – that would put them off for sure. She trawled through her collection, lingering regretfully on some unsuitable favourites, finally settling on a number from the 1920's musical *Bless the Bride.*

She began to practise it as she peeled the potatoes and heated the oven. *This is My Lovely Day*, she sang with all the solemnity she could muster, visualising a beautiful white bride floating reverently down a church aisle, *This is the day I shall remember the day I'm dying...*

Bob and Eck trudged wearily round the corner into Burns Avenue. The fine soaking drizzle mingled with the coal dust on their jackets and ran down their tired faces in gritty streaks.

There were baths available for the men nowadays at the pit-head but both men were in unspoken agreement of rejecting the bawdy, locker-room atmosphere of the bath-house. It was used mainly by the younger men. *Cock-strutters*, Eck mentally dismissed them, reluctant to dwell upon his own forlorn specimen, these days seldom called into service.

They had talked about pit and union matters with some animation on the way to the shift early that afternoon – or, at least, Eck had talked and Bob had listened and endorsed everything Eck had said. Bossed all his life by his mother and his wife, Bob knew no other role in a relationship. Opinions were things other people had. It had never really occurred to him that *he* might have one. For Eck, nagged by his mother as a youth and now defied by his wife, Bob was the perfect companion.

Now they were too tired and uncomfortable in filthy wet clothes to talk or think. Reaching Number 22, Eck and Aggie's home, they parted with little more than a nod and a muttered 'See ye the morn.'

Eck clumped round the house to the back door, took off his heavy, wet jacket, shook it out and threw it into the back porch. Then he sat on the step and eased off his boots, banging them together to knock the worst of the dirt off them. As he hung up the jacket and threw the boots into a corner, a wonderful smell assaulted his nostrils and hunger reared up inside him like lust.

'*Whit the hell?*' he thought. '*We're no haein visitors the nicht, are we? Aggie never telt me.*'

Late supper after back-shift was usually something cold with chips. Aggie was not good at chips. The happy synergy between size of potato chip, temperature of fat in the chip-pan and time both should spend together was not an art she was ever going to master. Either the chips were too big and the fat not hot enough, resulting in half-cooked, greasy chunks, or the chips were too meagre and the fat too hot, resulting in blackened, hard sticks. On the rare occasion when both size and temperature were correct, she invariably left them in too short or too long a time. Eck was inured to it though he frequently sought solace in the local fish-and-chip shop.

Tonight the kitchen was warm and fragrant. The table was neatly set but with only two places he saw with relief. Two pots bubbled on the hob but the aroma was coming from the oven. He prized open the grimy oven door: A large steak pie was cooking, the puffy topping just beginning to turn golden and the gravy to bubble round the edges. Hearing movement upstairs, he went out into the lobby and was assailed by a very different smell – fruity, tangy, with a soapy undertow. *Whit the hell's goin' on?*

Aggie appeared at the top of the stairs and he saw at once that she was not still wearing the baggy skirt and old black jumper that she always wore under her shop overall. She looked fresher, brighter than usual.

'Ah've jist run yer bath,' she said as she descended. Eck blinked and blinked again.

'Is it jist the twa o' us the nicht fur supper?' he demanded, dealing with his primary concern first. Then, as she nodded, 'Whit in God's name is that smell upstairs. It's like the washin' and makin' jam a' rolled intae ane.'

Aggie turned from the kitchen door. 'It's new stuff ca'd 'bubble-bath'. It says on the bottle that it's good fur aches and pains. Ah thocht it might dae ye guid on a damp nicht like this.'

She closed the kitchen door and the bath smell began to triumph over the steak pie. Bewildered, he hesitated but his stomach rumbled, bidding him be mindful of priorities, so he hurried upstairs to the new experience of scented ablution.

Aggie smiled as she drained the potatoes and turned out the oven. She realised that, for the first time for days, she too was hungry. When she heard his step on the stairs she began to dish out. Coming into the kitchen, freshly bathed and slavering in anticipation, Eck experienced a moment of long-forgotten pleasure.

His wife was singing one of the few songs in her repertoire that he had ever been able to remember, reminding him sharply of their courtship days: *This is My Lovely Day*.

Perhaps tonight his forlorn specimen would see some service at last.

CHAPTER THREE

JEANNIE

Bob clumped heavily round to the back of the cottage. He could already smell the mince-and-tatties and his heavy jowls drooled as he tugged off his boots and coat, dumping them on the coal bunker outside.

One of his sons had the job of brushing down his coat and cleaning his boots each morning. One of the consolations of being dominated by Jeannie was that she effortlessly did likewise to their two boisterous sons. They might swagger in front of the lassies and horse about boastfully, kidding themselves they were their own men. Bob knew otherwise and often chuckled to himself to see them squirm when Jeannie sharpened her tongue on them for skimping one of their designated chores or leaving the toilet pan in a shitty mess.

The hip-bath in the lean-to toilet was already half-full of hot water and he stripped off quickly and plunged into it with a sigh of content, applying the long-handled brush briskly to back and shoulders, sloshing the water over head and neck, then stepping out of the blackened water to wrap himself in the old grey towel provided for his purposes. Jeannie kept the newer, white towels for herself.

He emerged into the living room then popped his head into the other lean–to which was the tiny scullery where Jeannie miraculously managed to prepare and cook food for four adults, as well as wash the dishes and pots.

'By, that smells grand, darlin',' he greeted his wife. Her neat little rump was on full view as she bent over to check on an apple crumble in the oven. He enjoyed the view for several seconds then hastily re-arranged his features as she straightened up and turned to face him.

'What are ye hanging aboot there fur?' she demanded. 'Gang through and get dressed. Ah'm servin' oot ony minute.'

She seemed excited, flustered, '*like someone in a hurry,*' he thought, and, recognising the signs, wondered what new piece of juicy gossip she had come by that day. Like a sleuth newshound, she was always fit to burst when a new story was breaking. *Ah jist hope she lets me get some of that grub down first before she maks me join in wi the gossipin'.*

Jeannie's own meal was untouched and almost cold before she ran out of steam which suited Bob fine as he had little to do beyond grunting and giving the odd sharp intake of breath for good measure. In between these responses, he easily managed to down two large helpings of mince-and-tatties and one of the apple crumble, which he fetched himself from the kitchen when she paused for breath. She finally ran down and, beginning to stab testily at her dinner with a fork, demanded: 'Well, what dae ye think o' that, then?'

Bob licked his plate clean and gave a comfortable belch. 'Let me see, noo, hen,' he began ponderously. 'Aggie saw Kate gettin' the bus tae Windygates one Wednesday afternoon when Fat Annie wis lookin' after Auld Maggie tae gie Kate a break…?'

This was how they always did it. She vomited out the full story and then he fed it back to her bit by bit, giving her the chance to correct, confirm, amplify and embroider on the details. The resulting product of this well-practised process usually bore little resemblance to the ingredients that Jeannie had swallowed from her original source.

Tonight, the process took a good hour and was much enjoyed by both. Though not naturally a gossip himself, Bob always enjoyed seeing his Jeannie so animated. He was well aware that this process of preparing the latest scandal for full publication acted like an aphrodisiac tonic upon her and he willingly played his part *during* the process for the pleasure of playing it still more *afterwards*.

As she washed up the dishes, humming happily to herself, and he rustled through the newspaper in his fireside chair, he dwelt in happy expectation upon the earlier sight of her perky backside paying homage to the apple crumble in the oven.

'Have ye got yer winter gloves stock in yet, Annie?'

Jeannie was the first customer that day and Annie moved ponderously and a little resentfully from the back-shop where she had been enjoying a leisurely cup of tea and chocolate biscuit. Drapery and haberdashery were not usually the first things on shoppers' minds of a morning and she had felt safe until the unwelcome jangle of the shop door bell.

'Ah've had some in but no them a' yet,' she conceded reluctantly. 'It's early days yet, only October and still mild.'

'Ah like tae be prepared, though,' said Jeannie tranquilly and Annie, sighing, began to root about in the glass-fronted drawers that lined the wall behind the counter.

These were labelled tidily – handkerchiefs ladies, handkerchiefs gents, suspender belts ladies, braces gents, and so on. A legacy from the meticulous previous owner but not one that Annie had ever made much use of. She had her own haphazard system but it bore no resemblance to one where the contents of any drawer were likely to relate to the label on its glass front. Her brain, still a long way from being at full throttle for the day, grappled ineffectively with the mystery of where she was likely to have put the recent consignment of winter gloves.

Jeannie did not hurry her. She had her own preoccupations in which, if truth be known, gloves – winter or otherwise - featured very little. As Annie began to bang the drawers open and shut, she walked over to the shop's glass door and looked out over the crossroads.

'Ah'm thinkin',' she remarked inconsequentially, 'we've no seen much o' Kate Cruikshanks o' late. Ah wonder hoo she's gettin' on wi ma auld neighbour, Maggie. Maybe Ah'll cry in and see her some time. Do ye think that wid be a' richt? Ah widnae want tae mak a nuisance o' masel or stick ma nose intae other folk's bizness.'

'Perish the thought!' Annie muttered to herself. '*That wid no be like you at a', Jeannie Gilhooley.*'

The two women often enjoyed a good blether about other people's business, they being the acknowledged queens of the gossip scene in the community. The rest of the women alternately enjoyed and feared the web of scandal and intrigue which the two loved to create – Annie from the centre of the web in her corner shop with its commanding view of the crossroads and Jeannie from the outlying intricacies of the web as she crawled around its span. But, like conspiring thieves, they did not always agree. Occasionally loyalties conflicted. Usually the imperative of the web won out but, on rare occasions, one of them would have reason to resist the spinning process.

Such was one of these rare occasions now for Annie. Her Wednesday afternoons, looking after Old Maggie and giving Kate a few hours freedom, had quickly become something she looked forward to. It was a combination of Kate's gratitude, manifesting itself in interesting little presents – a rare treat for Annie - and then there was the pleasure of being in Kate's lovely house, so well furnished, so prettily decorated.

Even the time she spent with the old woman gave her satisfaction. She was so good at it, compared to Kate, said Maggie, and that gave Annie a rare glow of appreciation. Fancy her being better at anything than Kate Cruikshanks, whose face, figure, beautiful children, smart husband and well-ordered life had long been the envy of most of the women and especially of childless, husbandless Annie, whose mirror told her all she needed to know about other comparisons.

'Ah'm sure Kate will mak ye welcome,' she said primly.

'But maybe no *every* day o' the week?' Jeannie sensed Annie's resistance immediately and knew that a boundary was being drawn.

'She's no goin' tae play the game here. She must've her ain fish tae fry,' she mused.

'Well, ye'll hae tae ask *her* that,' said Annie. 'Ah'm sure Ah widnae ken. Now, are ye wantin' tae look at these gloves or no?'

Jeannie decided to give Annie one last chance to get on board. She played it straight down the middle. 'Ah heard ye were lookin' after Auld Maggie fur Kate on Wednesday afternoons.'

'Ye hear a lot o' things, Jeannie. It's one o' the things Ah admire aboot ye. Ye're a grand listener.'

'Ach, Annie! Stop yer cairry-on! Ye ken fine whit Ah mean. Is Kate goin' oot on Wednesday afternoons or no? And whaur is she goin' tae? And hoo often has she been? Is it true she gets a' dressed up tae go? How long does she go fur? And…'

The shop door bell jangled rudely, cutting across the rising tide of interrogation. *'Thank the Lord fur that!'* thought Annie.

'Which gloves wid ye like, Jeannie?' she said smoothly.

Jeannie glared at her. 'It's far too early in the year tae be thinkin' o' gloves,' she spat. 'Ah aye *knit* ma ain onyway. An Ah get a far better selection o' patterns an wool in Leven!'

She flounced out the door, pushing past and not seeing a surprised Aggie who was in sudden and desperate need of the secret supply of women's necessities which Annie kept discreetly hidden in a large floor-level drawer marked *knitting patterns.*

'Whit's got intae her the day? It's no like Jeannie tae be in a bad mood. She near knocked me on ma dowp – an me feelin' a mite fragile in that area the day, if ye get ma meanin'.'

'She's a wee bit fed up o' me, Ah think,' chuckled Annie. 'Ah didnae gie her whit she wis wantin'. But, ye ken me, Aggie, Ah cannae be doin' wi gossipin'…'

'You, Annie? Gossip? Never shid they three words be said in the same sentence!' Aggie grinned. Jeannie was about her business already.

Jeannie stomped along the road, buried in her own buzzing thoughts, frustrated at Annie's unhelpful attitude. She had been counting on Annie as a serious fifth columnist with ready access to Kate's secret life. But Annie was batting for the other side it would seem.

'Damn her!' thought Jeannie. *'Whit's she goin' all sanctimonious and secretive on me fur? Whit does she owe Kate Cruikshanks, Ah'd like tae ken? There's nae need fur it. Ah'm a better freend tae her than that Kate's ever been.'*

'Ach, wha needs her, onyway?' she concluded out loud, much to the surprise of two children who were haring past, late for school. 'Ah'll find it oot fur masel and the devil wi the fat yap!'

In her own mind – and helped by Bob's ponderous prompting last night – she was already constructing a number of likely, and unlikely, scenarios.

Only Jeannie knew that some of them would find their way into one of the jotters under her bed. Titbits of gossip acted as stimulation to her fertile storyteller's brain. She *would* ferret out the truth and circulate it – and usually a few ill-founded rumours along the way. That was her day job, as it were.

But Jeannie had another life: she had been born to weave stories and her head was always full of them. Rarely a day went by without her sneaking up to the bedroom, pulling out the latest jotter from under the bed, and sitting at the old, scratched dressing table in the window, writing in a fast, flowing script. She wrote about people's lives: births, deaths and marriages; fights, slaps and hugs; joys, sorrows, hopes and fears; loyalties and betrayals; grannies, children and pets; rises and falls in fortunes; parties, weddings and funerals; wins, losses and debts... It was all there and her characters were more real to her than her neighbours.

Only Bob knew that she wrote and he thought it 'just her funny wee way'. He never asked to read any of it. As a child, she had been fiercely discouraged to the point of prohibition by her parents who saw it, at best, as wasting time and, at worst, as opening her mind to the influence of Auld Nick himself. They had been strict Roman Catholics and much given to fear of the devil.

At school, there had been some half-hearted encouragement which had largely taken the form of trying to divert her talent into more worthy writing – saccharine poems, moral tales or lady-like homilies. Jeannie's propensity to create earthy characters and dialogue straight out of her own keen experience and sharp observation had found no admirers.

So she had become a *secret* spinner of tales, addicted to her 'scribblin', as Bob called it indulgently. Now some twenty-five years of scribbling filled dozens of jotters in tightly packed piles under the bed.

Her musings had taken her to the end of the road where the twice-weekly butcher's van stopped to serve the area. It was there now reminding her that she needed to get some meat for the noon-day dinner and late supper. She liked to give Bob good meals before and after back-shift.

A substantial queue had formed to be served from the back of the van and she joined it. The queue moved slowly and the women in it enjoyed ample chat time. However, even *their* blethering ability began to feel the strain as the customer in front of Jeannie lingered on, talking to the fresh-faced young man serving behind the small counter, long after her purchases were complete.

Jeannie had been half playing over possibilities for the Kate story in her mind and half listening in to a conversation behind her which confirmed her suspicions about another piece of currently circulating gossip. She became aware of restless mutterings in the queue:

'Does she think we've got a' day?'

'Is she buying up the hale van?'

'Are we stuck in this damned queue fur the duration?'

A slow, pushing tide swelled towards the van and fetched up against Jeannie's back, propelling her on to the first step up to the van. She half turned to issue a sharp reproof to the hapless woman behind her, who had been the involuntary spearhead of the surge, when she heard a word that riveted her to the spot.

'Aye,' the butcher-lad was saying. 'Ah'll likely call in again and see how Mr Smillie is progressin'. He wis jist hame frae hospital the first time Ah went and still pretty weak. But he'll likely be mair like his auld sel by noo. It depends when Ah have the van in Windygates.'

Windygates! Jeannie licked her lips and twitched her nose – a sure sign that she scented a lead.

Jeannie sighed with pleasure and laid her pencil down on the dressing table. '*Now that was a good one,*' she thought. She had hardly been able to contain herself throughout the day as she cooked, cleaned and paid her usual afternoon visit to Bob's old father, taking him some of their dinner-time sausage casserole for his tea.

The twins had been clumping around between the scullery and toilet, eating jammy pieces and sprucing themselves up for a darts match at the pub, when she had finally managed to slip upstairs, muttering 'Ah'm jist goin' tae hae a wee-lie doon. Ah've a bit o' a headache.'

Not that they noticed or cared. The twins bounded through life on a tide of noisy self-gratification and only Jeannie's iron control kept them from deteriorating into complete social embarrassments. They had not gone down the mine when they came of age. *A mug's game,* they had declared, with no regard for their father's feelings. Only in front of Eck Fairweather did they rein in this cavalier opinion, remembering several painful encounters over the years between their boyish bare legs and Eck's large, hard hand.

They had found work of a sort in the burgeoning second-hand car business and now coasted along its shadier edges, making money from deals struck with innocent first-time car buyers who subsequently – and usually very soon after - needed repairs and spare parts, which the twins then sourced from scrap yards and sold at inflated prices. They were smooth talkers and flashy dressers but people predicted they would one day get their come-uppance. 'They think they're Archie,' folk said derisively. 'But they're only a flea on Archie's dog's tail!'

Turning round, Jeannie realised with a start that it was almost dark in the bedroom. Catching the last of the late September evening's light at the window and with her eyes accustoming to the gathering gloom, she had not realised it.

The small house was now silent. The twins had gone off to their drinking and darts in the pub. Usually she would be waiting on the stairs for them when they finished their cavorting about and would send them straight back to clean up the mess she knew they had left in both scullery and toilet. It was, if anyone had been there to see it, a fine sight - two strapping jack-the-lads cowering into instant submission before the fierce small woman who stood, arms akimbo, blocking their way. They would creep back and perform the cleaning and tidying rituals instilled into them from boyhood and both tiny rooms would soon be immaculate. If, however, Jeannie was not there to accost them, they would, like well-trained dogs that will go feral at the scent of a rabbit, simply eschew all past obedience, giving – like the rabbiting dog – no thought to future retribution.

'Ach, they lads'll have left the place like a pig-sty,' she grimaced. Hurrying downstairs, she was appalled to see that the clock on the mantelpiece said twenty-to-eight.

Holy shit! Less than an hour till Bob would be home, nothing done about the supper, the kitchen like a battlefield and the toilet not fit for human habitation. The clock had belonged to Bob's granny, was over a hundred years old, and regularly claimed the right to a little elderly eccentricity, sometimes going slow, sometimes fast. This made it somewhat unreliable. Jeannie swore again and ran upstairs to check the cheap, tin alarm clock on Bob's side of the bed.

It said *five-to* and she screwed up her face in the effort to remember how fast he always kept it, liking to feel he didn't have to get up the minute it went off. Was it quarter-of-an-hour, twenty minutes, twenty-five? Good job her Bob wasn't like Eck Fairweather. Bob would sigh and make her feel guilty if he had to wait for his supper but he wouldn't raise even his voice, let alone his hands.

She glanced hungrily at the jotter containing her latest story which she had laid on her own bedside table. She always loved to read over what she had written shortly after it was finished. She was a voracious reader and kept the local library in brisk business but best of all was reading what she had written herself. It gave her such a thrill. She would need to make sure she was upstairs well before Bob so she had time for reading before he came to bed. For all his easy-going ways, Bob had one sticking point: he was a man who liked his conjugal rights nightly.

As she hastily lit the gas under the ever-ready chip-pan and peeled potatoes for chips, she reflected on the story she had just written. She had indulged her flight of fancy and created a work of pure fiction in which a character, remarkably like Kate Cruikshanks, had entered into a salacious liaison with a local shopkeeper who lived a short bus-ride away.

One of the benefits of being married to a man with a very healthy sexual appetite was that Jeannie had a working knowledge of some of the more interesting practices of bedroom life and, thanks to Bob's fevered murmurings during these practices, had developed a competent vocabulary for describing them. '*This story's a real cracker,*' she thought complacently. '*It's a pity Bob isnae interested in reading. He wid fair get a kick oot o' this ain! On the other hand, I'd likely get nae sleep at a' if he did read it and I'd be walking bow-legged the morn. And it widnae be the first time!*'

Jeannie smiled tolerantly as she complacently contemplated Bedroom Bob whom no-one else would have recognised in the big, slow, hen-pecked man they knew.

She was right. Bob *harrumphed* and sighed heavily as he waited for her to clean the hip-bath and pick the dirty wet towels up off the floor and he rustled the paper more noisily than was necessary as he waited for the pork chops to cook and the chips to fry. But he said nothing and was as complimentary as always about the food, demolishing half-an-hour's culinary work in five hungry minutes. She cheated and heated up one of Aggie's rhubarb tarts with tinned custard but, if he noticed a lack of wifely dedication in this dessert, he made no comment.

Perhaps the playful skelp to her backside as she passed him on the way to the scullery with the empty plates was a touch more enthusiastic than usual, verging on downright nippy, in fact. But that was probably just him warming up for high jinks later rather than a reproof. '*Ah'll definitely hae tae go upstairs early if Ah want tae get ma readin' done,*' she surmised.

Jeannie stirred the pan of white sauce with one hand and held her library book in the other. She screwed up her eyes to read the close text, frowning and moving the book this way and that to catch the light better.

She really did need spectacles but the unappetising range of frames available on the National Health had quickly discouraged her when she had ventured into the optician's. She had heard the twins' derisory comments about 'spekky lassies' and 'four-eyed monsters' and she had no wish to jeopardise her looks simply in order to read better. She valued Bob's slavish devotion too much and, despite his twenty years of fidelity, she had not forgotten that *one* time…

She had been six months pregnant with the twins. 'In full-bloom,' some said, kindly; 'Like bloody humpty-dumpty!' said others, less kindly.

Bob had dwelt loyally in the full-bloom camp up till then. Indeed her pregnancy was a source of pride and excitement for him. Her heavy breasts and swelling abdomen –everything about her pregnancy - only served to increase his desire for her and, as well as their usual nightly exercise routine, it became rare for her to be allowed out of bed in the morning either without being put through her paces. The day she found out it was twins he even chased her upstairs in the middle of the afternoon.

Although frequently rendered sore by such constant, vigorous attention, she nevertheless gloried in it, feeling every inch the complete woman and well aware of the growing power it gave her over him. It was the first year of their marriage and lines were being drawn that would circumscribe their relationship for life. She was satisfied with the shape these lines were taking. What was a little temporary discomfort compared to establishing lasting domination?

Then the doctor stuck his unwelcome oar in. At her monthly check-up, he noticed her wincing as she sat down and insisted on examining her fully up on the couch. He pursed his lips and sucked in his breath during the brief examination, which Jeannie suffered primly, not meeting his eye.

Once she was dressed and seated again, he asked her bluntly how often she was having 'full intercourse' with her husband. She was surprised, not aware that there was any other kind, and, distracted by the idea, laughed and told him that, if Bob had his way, it would probably be 'every half-hour, an as full as you like!'

'It's a mercy he has tae go doon the pit and earn us some money fur the babbies comin' or I'd never get anythin' else done,' she delared. 'My expectin' has fair fired him up. An Ah thocht he wis hot enough a'ready!' She chuckled proudly, delighted with her own allure and her husband's rapacity.

Dr Kenny was appalled. In the ten years he had been practising medicine in this mining community, he had seen often enough the result of brutal, demanding men but it had not occurred to him that gentle, slow-witted Bob Gilhooley, who was devoted to his little wife, would be treating her like this in the seventh month of her pregnancy with twins.

Jeannie was immediately made aware that what they were doing was endangering her own and her unborn babies' health and must stop forthwith.

She was appalled. 'Stop a'thegither?' she faltered. 'But…'

'It's only until a month or so after the birth,' Jim Kenny reassured, chuckling inside himself at her expression. *A pair of randy rabbits! Who would have thought it?* 'If all is well then, you can certainly resume marital relations. But I can't stress enough how important it is at the moment.'

Bob was incredulous. 'Ach, he disnae understand hoo it is fur us, Jeannie,' he cried. 'We're no like ither folk…we cannae…it's no richt…'

His limited vocabulary ran out, unable to cope with the enormity of the situation. Then, 'Aw, dinnae greet, lass. We cannae hurt the babbies. We'll jist hae tae…' He tailed off, quite unable to imagine what they were going to do.

Somehow they got through the next few weeks, barely speaking to each other, afraid to touch or rub up against each other, even – or especially - by accident in bed. It was reaching the intolerable stage and Jeannie was seriously contemplating simply taking the risk, not because of her own desires – these were at a low ebb at this stage in her pregnancy – but mainly because she could sense her power over Bob slipping. He had taken to staying out late at the pub of an evening and ignoring her requests even when they escalated into orders. Once she had even caught him looking at her with a glint of rebellion in his eyes when she had told him to pick up his dirty socks from the bedroom floor. He had been surly and resistant.

Then it all changed. Suddenly, she had her Bob back again, good-humoured, gentle, amenable and pliable. It was like a miracle, like winning the pools without doing the coupon.

Wrapped up in preparations for the impending births and preoccupied with negotiating her enormous bulk through the last weeks before them, she simply accepted it thankfully. *He's got over it,* she presumed. *He loves me enough tae ken it jist has tae be like this the noo.* And she was more than satisfied with this latest evidence of her power over him.

It was not until six weeks after the birth of the boys that she learned about Chrissie the barmaid who was well known to confer her favours liberally, earning her the nickname among the miners of 'buttery bum' *(it slides aroon a' ower the place).*

Chrissie had taken pity on Bob, quickly appraising his situation as he sat morosely over his pint in the pub on those endless evenings of Jeannie's last ten weeks of pregnancy. Chrissie had been a brisk, tidy worker and had been able to put a smile on his face in ten minutes down in the cellar among the beer-barrels and be back upstairs to serve the next queue of customers without a hair out of place. If any of the other men had noticed that Bob was always absent when she went down to change the barrel, they had either thought he was helping her or had simply connived at the other possibility. Many of them had had cause to be grateful to Chrissie for getting them through similar periods in their own lives in the past.

As the time for Jeannie to resume her bedroom duties approached, Bob felt less need for the nightly episodes in the cellar. The anticipation of resuming 'full intercourse' with his darling Jeannie was enough. He was in a high state of excitement the day she came home from the doctor's after her final post-natal examination.

So great was his delight in her and so close were they that night that it seemed only natural to tell her about Chrissie. Bob was not able to keep the secret any longer; it burdened his simple soul and he was anxious to be rid of it at last. Telling Jeannie was all part of the resumption of their wonderful sex life.

Jeannie listened in horror and her anger and disgust shocked and scared him. 'There'll be nae mair babbies,' she declared roundly, 'if that's the way ye cairry on. Ah'll see Dr Kenny the morn and see aboot gettin' sterilised. He'll understand. He disnae think it a guid idea fur me tae get pregnant again soon onyway. An ye'd be useless wi thae rubber things.'

Bob had never strayed again. There had never been any need. But Jeannie had never forgotten not only his infidelity, and the hurt of that, but also his total inability to see that what he had done was particularly wrong.

'But Ah didnae love her, Jeannie,' he said over and over again. 'You're ma lass and no-one else will ever…but, ye ken we couldnae…well no fur a' they weeks. Whit wis Ah tae dae?'

'*No,*' thought Jeannie as the sauce came to the boil and she deftly lifted the pan off the cooker with one hand. '*There'll be nae spekkies yet. He's never gettin' an excuse again.*'

The book which Jeannie had been reading one-handed whilst making white sauce and meandering down memory lane all at the same time, was a rather dubious detective novel, one of a series following the exploits of a 'private eye' whose seedy one-man business ostensibly dealt in divorce evidence but somehow always ended up in being involved in big-time murder investigations. As Jeannie put down the book later that night on her bedside table and prepared to give her attention to Bob, she was, however, less exercised by the unfolding murder plot than by the prying activities of the 'eye' in the earlier chapters as he secretly followed the adulterous spouse and gathered the necessary evidence for the cuckolded client.

Her mind was only half on the business in hand for the next hour or so and, by the time they put the light out and Bob lapsed contentedly into snuffling snores, his mouth still clamped wetly on one of her nipples, she was beginning to formulate an idea.

'Thanks, Aggie.' Jeannie put the bakeries in the basket on her arm and handed over a half-crown. As Aggie rooted in the till for her change, Jeannie cleared her throat and ventured 'Have ye seen ony mair o' Kate, then? Have ye spoken tae her? Has she been oot again this week? Wis Annie lookin' after Auld Maggie again on Wednesday? Is she still gaein tae Windygates?'

Aggie twinkled as she handed her a sixpence and four big pennies. 'That's a wheen o' questions, Jeannie! Here wis me hopin' *you* were goin' tae be telling *me* some interestin' news. Are you losin' yer touch? Ah thought ye'd hae solved the mystery by noo.'

Jeannie bridled at this slur on her competence. 'It's no that easy, Aggie,' she retorted. 'Ah thocht Annie wid shed some light on it but she's playin' silly buggers. Kiddin' on it's nothin' tae dae wi her. Ah could belt her ane.'

She smarted as she recalled her second abortive attempt yesterday to engage Annie in the *Wednesdays in Windygates* investigation (or WW, as Jeannie privately thought of it). Annie had been, if anything, even more maddeningly evasive – *the smug bitch!*

75

'Ach, Jeannie,' goaded Aggie, 'surely ye're no needin' that fat gossip. You've aye been better than *The Sunday Post* fur keepin' us up-tae-date wi a' the news aroon here. Ah've aye thocht Annie wis nae mair than yer second-in-command!' Aggie let out a mirthful skirl.

Jeannie eyed her suspiciously. Was Aggie having her on?

There was something about Aggie these past few days, she thought. Aggie was looking and sounding brighter than she had for years and there was an air of suppressed excitement about her, as if she was nursing a delightful secret or looking forward to some promised treat. Was it just the possibility of unmasking some nefarious goings-on in the Cruikshanks household – it was well known how little love was lost between the two sisters - or was there some other agenda here? Jeannie, briefly diverted from her focus on WW, stared intently at Aggie.

'Ye're lookin' richt weel, this mornin', Aggie,' she remarked inconsequentially. 'Soundin' like ye havnae a care in the world. Have ye lost a sixpence and found a shillin'? Ye were lookin' that doon in the mooth when ye cam' roon the ither day but no ony mair. Have ye won the pools? Is Eck takin' ye awa on a gran holiday?'

Aggie snorted at the idea that any mood change for the better could be attributed to Eck. But... *'Ah'd better watch oot, here,'* she thought. *'The last thing Ah want is Jeannie stickin' her nose intae whit Ah'm goin' tae be doin'. That wid pit the ba on the slates.'*

Attack being the best form of defence, she parried swiftly. 'Never you mind changin' the subject, Missus Jeannie Gilhooley! Are ye goin' tae find oot whit oor Kate's up tae, with or withoot Fat Annie's help?'

Stung by this broadside, Jeannie was hustled into revealing her secret weapon prematurely. 'Ah have it a' in hand,' she said grandly. 'Ah'm goin' tae get first hand evidence.'

Aggie blinked. 'Evidence? What o'?'

'Ah'm goin' tae catch her red-handed,' Jeannie was now well-launched into private-eye speak.

'Daein what?' demanded a bewildered Aggie. Things seemed to have moved forward at an alarming pace. Kate was now sounding like a criminal being staked out by a posse of policemen.

'Well, if we kent that, there'd be nae need tae *pit a tail on* her tae find oot, wid there?' Then, seeing Aggie's blank look of incomprehension, '*Follow* her, that's whit Ah mean.'

'Follow her!' Aggie was startled. She had no interest in detective stories so the jargon phrase had meant nothing to her. Then, as the idea took hold: 'Wha the hell are ye goin' tae get tae dae that? An how could they dae it? There's hardly onyone *but* Kate on that bus when she gets on it at that time o' day. She'd spot someone watchin' her richt awa.'

Jeannie was irritated. These were details she had yet to grapple with and she regretted having allowed Aggie to railroad her into revealing her strategy before it was ready for public scrutiny. But not for the world would she have let Aggie see her discomfort. She had her reputation to consider and it had had enough mud slung at it already this morning.

'Jist you leave that tae me, Aggie,' she said airily. 'They's jist details – jist minor details!' She swept grandly out of the shop, leaving Aggie staring after her with a bemused smile.

'She reads too many rubbishy library books, that ane,' she thought. *'That's a richt daft notion. Ah weel...'*

She turned her thoughts comfortably to contemplation of the first meeting of the *Messiah* singing group that evening. Forgetting both Jeannie and Kate, or Windygates and Wednesdays, she burst happily into a full-throated *Hallelujah!*

Bob stared at Jeannie across the top of his after-dinner cup of tea.

'But what guid wid that dae?' he asked in bewilderment. 'Whit guid wid pinnin' a tail on Kate Cruikshanks dae? Ye mean, like the bairns dae at the Christmas party tae the donkey on the wa? Ach, Kate'd never let ye onyway. Mind, a fine sicht she'd be!'

He thoughtfully contemplated Kate's well-padded backside, with a donkey's tail dangling from it. He chuckled. *An my Jeannie wid fair suit ane tae! Now, whit wid be best fur her? Maybe a wee white rabbit scut?*

'Are you *listenin'* tae me, Bob Gilhooley?' demanded Jeannie, well aware that he had gone off on some daft canter. 'Ah said nothin' aboot *pinnin'* tails. Ah'm talkin' aboot '*pittin'* a tail on someone'. It means settin' someone tae follow someone else tae find oot whit they are daein. But they dinnae *ken* they're being followed an watched.'

'Man, that's some idea,' marvelled Bob. 'Whaur did ye get it frae?'

'It's whit detectives dae, of course. Hoo else wid they ever get evidence and catch the criminals?'

'But I thocht it wis Kate Cruikshanks ye were tryin' tae find oot aboot,' protested Bob in alarm. 'Whit are ye wantin' tae get mixed up wi criminals fur?'

Jeannie ignored him. He would catch up eventually. He always did. Life was just too short, she had decided many years ago, to spend it laboriously explaining her quick-fire thought processes to Bob. Sometimes he got there in the end; more often he just gave up and accepted that it was all beyond him.

'The thing is,' Jeannie pursed her lips, 'It's got tae be somebody Kate disnae ken. Can *you* think o' someone Ah could get tae dae it?' She fixed him with a beady eye.

Bob squirmed. This sudden jump from passive sounding board to active participant was a promotion way beyond his level of competence. His eye roved desperately round the room in search of inspiration and fell on the clock.

'Geez, is that the time?' he exclaimed in relief. 'Eck'll be here ony meenit.'

He hurried out to the back door where his working boots stood gleaming on a fresh sheet of newspaper and his work jacket, neatly brushed, hung on the back of the scullery door. The twins had been made to expiate fully their ill-advised bid for freedom before they left that morning for another day of dodgy dealing. As he struggled into his boots, he dwelt happily on images of Jeannie's bare backside adorned by various types of tails.

As he was shrugging into his jacket, he suddenly remembered what he had to say to her and grimaced anxiously.

'Ah'll be late back the night, hen.' He stood half in, half out of the door, nervously shifting from one foot to the other. 'It's jist that…well, ye see…it's nothin' tae be botherin' yersel aboot…'

There was a sharp rap on the door and Eck's dry cough could be heard. Bob rushed his fences: 'It's Chrissie, the barmaid at The Auld Toll, she's retirin', like, an some o' us are goin' tae hae a farewell drink wi her…'

He faltered as Jeannie's head came up and her eyes flashed dangerously. 'Ach, Jeannie, ye ken that wis a' years an years ago, an it never meant onythin' and Chrissie kent that hersel an…'

Eck rapped impatiently again and Jeannie's eyes flickered towards the front door. Then her expression suddenly changed.

'So wha's takin' ower frae the auld slapper? Is it somebody new?'

'Oh aye,' Bob grabbed thankfully at this new direction. 'It's a young lad that the brewers are bringing in. He's been working in a pub ower in Dundee and daein sae weel that he's been promoted tae come an manage The Toll. Name's Graham Something. Seems like a fine lad.'

'So he's here a'ready? An he's new tae these parts? Like… nae-one kens him at a'? Is he single? Has he got a wife? Is he stayin' above the pub? Hoo lang has he been here, then?'

Bob, when faced with one of Jeannie's catalogues of questions, always simply answered the last one. 'He jist arrived a couple o' days ago. Chrissie's been showin' him the ropes, like, this week an then she leaves on Friday.'

'Weel, see if you can find oot mair aboot him the nicht,' Jeannie ordered. 'He might be jist whit we're needin'.'

'Oh aye, richt,' said Bob mystified but relieved that the Chrissie issue had passed over so painlessly. 'Comin', comin', Eck,' he called as another irritable volley of rapping accompanied a shout of 'Whaur the hell are ye, Bob? We're goin' tae be late!'

Jeannie poured herself another cup of tea and lit a woodbine. Someone completely new to the area was quite a rare phenomenon in their small, tight-knit community. He wouldn't stay unknown for long. She would have to strike while the iron was hot.

Now… if this was one of my stories…how would it happen? Her brow furrowed in concentration, she sat wreathed in smoke and then, stubbing the cigarette out abruptly in her saucer, she ran upstairs, tugged the jotter out from under the bed and began to scribble feverishly.

CHAPTER FOUR

KATE

Kate closed the outside door with a bang and stepped briskly on to the path. The icy air hit her like a slap in the face and she gasped.

Oh, hell. That's richt. The windaes were runnin' wi condensation this mornin'. The weather's changed. Ah clean forgot.

It was no wonder she had forgotten. Wednesday mornings flew by in flash of tending to 'the auld yin' and preparing food for Annie to give her for her dinner, getting herself smartened up for her weekly expedition and, most important of all, making sure that the house was in apple-pie order.

Kate was under no illusions about Fat Annie's mixed motives for her so-far perfect attendance record on a Wednesday afternoon. Sure, Annie understood better than most the grinding drudgery of caring for Old Maggie and the desperate need for an occasional time of respite, but Kate also knew that Annie would relish this opportunity to carry out a detailed inspection of the house and its cupboards and contents. Any interesting finds, or lurking evidence of slipshod housewifery, would form the basis of the next week's gossip in the draper's shop. This risk was the price she had to pay for her precious few hours of freedom. It meant that she had to clean the house like a whirling dervish, inside cupboards and all, and make sure anything of a remotely private nature was safely locked in the metal strongbox under her bed.

And, of course, all this had to be done without Maggie realising what she was doing and why. Maggie seemed to enjoy her afternoons with Annie but Kate knew that, if she guessed there was any danger of Annie 'getting to ken their business', she would cause a proper stink and complain to Johnnie. *Then the ba wid be well and truly on the slates.*

Johnnie had not enquired into what Kate was doing on Wednesdays or who was coming in to sit with his old mother. If he thought about it at all – which was doubtful as he was so wrapped up in the adventure of his mining management meetings in St. Andrews – he probably assumed it was Aggie or Senga obliging Kate for an hour or so. He rarely spoke to his mother beyond a perfunctory *All right, mither?* - then, without waiting for an answer, *That's grand!* He would not at all have liked the idea of gossipy Annie being given the run of their house but, Kate reasoned, *whit he disnae ken'll dae him nae harm.*

She turned irritably back to the house. The bus was due any minute and she ran up the stairs and burst into the house calling 'It's jist me back fur ma winter coat. It's awfy cauld oot there.'

Annie's enormous buttocks protruded from the lobby press where she was down on her hands and knees examining the floor-level contents and Kate chuckled as she resisted the temptation to apply a high-heeled shoe to the huge target. She flung open the door of the wardrobe and rifled impatiently through the frocks and blouses. The coat was right at the back, not having been needed for the past six months. Pulling it out roughly, Kate swore as she saw that it still had the dry-cleaning paper wrapper over the shoulders and half-a-dozen wee pink tickets fastened on to lapels and sleeves with safety pins. She tore off the wrapper and shrugged into the woollen embrace. The pink tickets would have to wait. She would deal with them on the bus.

The bus was thundering into sight as she let herself out the gate and she began to run towards it, waving her arms frantically. The driver spotted her – indeed he now looked forward to seeing the bonnie, smartly-dressed lady board his bus at this stop every Wednesday afternoon – and he allowed the bus to slow down and coast gracefully to a halt instead of playing his usual game of slam-on-the-brakes-and-see-how-many-passengers-you-can-throw-on-the-floor.

Kate collapsed panting on the first seat and busied herself getting out her fare for the conductor. That done and, with her breath coming back to her, she took off the coat and applied herself to the pink label task. She did not look round for or at any other passengers. Mostly the bus was empty downstairs when she got on it at this time but a couple of times there had been one or two other people. She had made a point of making no contact, however cursory, with them. She wanted no casual conversations, no getting drawn into explaining what she was doing, where she was going. The story she had fed Aggie, she knew well, was paper-thin: a *n old school friend writing out of the blue to tell Kate of a sad loss – a fisherman husband drowned off the coast at St Monans where the friend had lived since her marriage twenty-odd years ago; Kate was going to see her and comfort her, getting the bus to Windygates and changing there for another to the old fishing village.*

If Kate was unlucky enough to meet anyone who knew her on the bus and had to give this fragile alibi another airing, she would have then to be very careful that whoever she talked to would not observe what she actually did when she got off the bus in Windygates. She might even end up having to waste half her precious afternoon actually getting on a St Monans bus, then getting off and catching the next one back to Windygates. *An a richt bloody plester and waste o' time that wid be.*

So, with her back firmly turned to the rest of the bus, intent on the wee pink labels, there was no chance that she would spot the smartly-dressed young man hiding behind a broadsheet newspaper at the back of the bus.

Graham Currie was enjoying settling in to his new job as manager of The Auld Toll bar. The men who dropped in regularly for their nip-and-a-pint were friendly. The sixty-year-old barmaid who had run it for years while her much older husband, officially the manager, had quietly drunk himself to death upstairs, had left things in tidy order. Graham had picked up a few spicy references to old Chrissie from some of the regulars but, looking at the raddled features and sagging body, he had found them pretty incredible. *Just a joke,* he reckoned. *One of their wee folk tales, maybe.*

One of the men he was getting to know well was Bob Gilhooley. Bob was in the habit of dropping in at half-past-eleven in the morning for a wee dram before his dinner and was often the only man in for half-an-hour or so.

Graham liked the big, gentle man, soon working out that he liked a joke, especially if it had a wee bit of naughtiness to it. After ten years working behind a bar, Graham had a fund of jokes of all types and grades of naughtiness. With a skill born of years of dealing with drinking customers, Graham effortlessly chose the jokes that Bob's lumbering thought processes could cope with and which held just enough titillation to light up his craggy face without venturing into territory that would shock the simple soul.

Then, a couple of days ago, Bob had not been himself at all. He had sat brooding over his drink, watching Graham all the time in a way that unnerved him. Twice Bob had started to say something and stopped. Eventually, he had sidled up to the bar and muttered something to Graham which had sounded like 'Whit dae ye dae on Wednesday afternoons?'

Graham thought this a most unlikely conversational gambit and felt sure he had misheard. Bob persisted with a few other, similarly inconsequential, questions until Graham decided that either he, himself, needed a hearing aid or the man was having some kind of turn. Eventually, Graham poured himself a modest half-pint shandy and took it over to the corner table to which Bob had retreated after his last incomprehensible mumble.

'Now then, Bob,' he said firmly. 'What's on your mind? You've clearly got something bothering you. What is it? You know you can tell me.'

This was Graham's best counselling manner and had yielded him many a fine insight into his customers over the years. Not that he ever used it for scandal-mongering. He was the soul of discretion and this had led in turn to even more secrets being shared with him. He had a healthy interest in people and was an astute enough businessman to know that drinkers will more often frequent a pub where there is a sympathetic ear, especially if they can rely on the owner of that ear to keep his mouth shut.

Bob grasped at the opening thankfully. 'Ye're richt there, ma lad. If Ah dinnae get on wi it, Jeannie'll hae ma guts fur garters.'

'Jeannie's your wife, isn't she?' Graham checked a crucial fact before allowing Bob to proceed.

'Aye, she's a gran wee wife,' Bob nodded proudly. Then he became glum. 'But she'll no half pit salt on ma tail if Ah dinnae get her whit she needs.' He lapsed into worried silence and sought comfort in a healthy swig of his whisky.

'And what *does* she need?' Graham struggled to keep his face straight. He had seen little Jeannie Gilhooley and it was verging on ridiculous to see this giant of a man, with his enormous, calloused hands, clasped round his glass, shaking with fear at the thought of displeasing her.

'Well, ye see, lad…ma Jeannie likes tae… tae keep tabs on a'thing that goes on . . . an we've a wee bittie mystery in these parts at the moment.'

'*Oh, ho!*' Graham thought, '*So our wee Jeannie's the village gossip, is she?*'

Aloud he said, 'I see, Bob. And she's depending on you to find something out, is that it?'

'Aye, that's it exactly.' Bob was mightily relieved that the lad had cottoned on so easily. 'So, will ye help us, then?'

'Me? What can I do? You're forgetting I'm quite new here. I know nothing of what goes on here yet.'

'But that's jist it, man. She's needin' someone new tae the place. Someone that naebody kens.'

'Oh aye? How's that?'

Bob took a fortifying draught of his dram. He waved his large hand vaguely at the window which looked out on the crossroads. 'Ye ken Johnnie Cruikshanks that lives ower there?'

Graham had spoken briefly to Johnnie on his one visit to The Toll since its change of management and had picked up, from eavesdropping on several conversations, the mixture of respect and resentment that Johnnie's rise from the ranks had engendered in the miners.

'Mmm…' he said noncommittally, wondering where this was leading.

Bob ploughed manfully on, aware of time running out and knowing what he would get – or, worse still, *not* get - if he went home for a third day without the goods.

'It's Johnnie's wife, Kate, ye see. She goin' tae Windygates on a Wednesday afternoon…' He ran out of steam and gazed hopefully at Graham.

'Is that a problem?' Graham queried, beginning to feel that pulling teeth would be a dawdle compared to eliciting information from Bob.

'Naebody kens whit fur…an Jeannie *wants* tae ken. So will ye dae it?'

'Do what?' Graham was really baffled by this time and seriously doubting the wisdom of coming over to Bob's table in the first place.

'Jeannie's got ane o' her clever ideas, ye see. She gets them frae a' the books she reads. Ah mind ae time she…'

'Never mind that,' Graham interposed desperately, throwing counselling skills to the winds, afraid the pub would soon fill up with the usual midday crowd and they would never get to the bottom of this. 'Just tell me what you think *I've* got to do with it and hurry up!'

'She wants you tae follow her. You bein' new aroon here, she'd no maybe notice you, ye see.'

'Me – follow your wife? What in God's name for?' Graham was totally lost by this time and on the point of giving up.

'Naw, naw!' Bob burst out in frustration. 'Ye've tae follow *Kate*. Tae Windygates, man, an find oot whit she's up tae. Fur God's sake, jist dae it and get Jeannie aff ma back. Ah've heard damn all else oot o' her fur days.' He slurped the last of his whisky and fixed Graham with a pleading eye.

A noisy gang of miners had burst into the pub and Graham rose to serve them. Bob rose too, blocking his path. 'Can Ah tell her ye'll dae it?' he demanded frantically. 'Can Ah?'

Graham hesitated. Then, on impulse, he nodded. *'Why not?'* he thought. *'It'll be a bit of fun, playing detectives, and it'll get me right into Jeannie's good books - no bad thing if she's the queen bee around here.'*

'OK, pal,' he said easily, employing the American slang he had picked up as a young lad during the war. 'Just get some details about when this Kate goes to Windygates and what bus she gets. If it's early afternoon, I can spare a couple of hours while the pub's shut. Now, excuse me, I must see to my customers.'

Bob had walked home light of heart and step. *Wait till he told Jeannie! Man, he wid be in for a wee treat the nicht at bedtime!*

Kate puffed a little as she climbed the hill to the row of bungalows at the top. She was beginning to regret the woollen coat. It had been warm on the bus and now the exertion of the climb was making her sweat. She paused half-way up to take the coat off then toiled on with it over her arm.

Angus Smillie watched her from the bay window of his neat little bungalow. It was one of six built in this cul-de-sac between the wars, all identical, with two front bay windows and red-tiled roofs with a dormer window protruding out over the front door between the two bays. Angus's father had bought it new and it had been his mother's pride and joy with its modern bathroom and kitchen.

When both his parents had died within a few months of each other some five years ago, his sister, Martha, was already settled on a sheep farm in Australia with the Welshman she had met and married during the war. Angus had smoothly inherited the property and become a happy bachelor alone.

After living with years of constant bickering between his parents and watching the destructive effects, he had no desire to embark upon the married state and relished the peace and independence of living alone. He had renovated the bungalow, indulging his taste for modern décor and gadgetry. His mother would have turned in her grave, a fact he was well aware of and which gave him no small satisfaction.

He resisted the urge to go out to the front gate to meet her. She had shoo-ed him back in anxiously the first Wednesday. *Dae ye want the hale toun tae ken Ah'm here?* she had cried.

He had wanted to tell her the truth: *Aye! I'm tickled pink ye're here. I want the whole world to ken.* But he respected her reticence - it had always been a large part of her charm for him. Other women customers might give him back his bawdy cheek with interest or simper coyly when he teased them. Kate had always maintained an almost maidenly modesty which had kept him dangling for the past ten years.

So now he waited impatiently for her laborious progress to bring her to his door. He glanced with satisfaction at the tray of tea and gingerbread set neatly out on the small table in the centre of the comfortable sitting-room. A few weeks ago, he had liberated his mother's best wedding china from forty-odd years of captivity in the display cabinet and polished the silver teapot, matching milk jug, sugar basin and tongs. Kate had expressed approval of the dainty sugar lumps (*just twa, please, Angus)* and used the dainty bone-handled cake knife with due deference. He loved watching her delicately wipe her mouth with the damask napkins which he had also freed from years of disuse and sip her tea from the pretty fine china cups.

Although she was well aware he was watching her through the net curtains, she rang the bell decorously. He played the game and kept her waiting a respectable length of time before opening the front door. Their greeting was all that convention demanded: a few words exchanged on the doorstep; a moment standing together in the doorway admiring the roses still blooming in the garden; a gesture of invitation to the inside of the house; a moment's modest hesitation;

then she preceded him into the hall and he turned back to close the outside door.

Neither of them saw the young man strolling casually by and glancing just once up at the number plate on the door. Nor had Kate noticed him coming up the hill at a decent distance behind her. And she had no notion that he had also been on the bus and had waited till the upstairs passengers descended, half-smoked cigarettes dangling from their hands and lips, before slipping in behind them to get off at Windygates.

The room fell silent as the small talk petered out. The mild-for-the-time-of-year weather with this sudden cold snap today had been all but done to death; the state of Angus's health and the progress of his post-operative recovery had been analysed and approved; Kate's struggles with Old Maggie had been sighed over and sympathetic noises made; one or two little, completely non-scandalous, bits of local news had been conveyed about some of his customers.

One of the other things he had always admired was her lack of gossipy venom and the gentle, accepting way she always spoke about others. He knew that the other women, her ugly sister included, said she lived 'in another world' and they meant it disparagingly but for him it was one of her most attractive features. She was quite simply *different*.

He glanced at the clock.

'It's near time, ma dear,' he said gently. She shivered with excitement and he watched her swelling bosom quiver, dislodging a few stray gingerbread crumbs.

'Did ye manage tae get…?'

'Are you ready for…?' They spoke across each other clumsily, then laughed self-consciously.

'You first,' he said gallantly. She blushed, then, as the clock on the mantelpiece chimed three, blurted out: 'Hiv ye ta'en a' the…the *precautions* we talked aboot last time?'

He nodded solemnly and rose from the armchair. He crossed to the other side of the room, to a small, important-looking table which stood in the corner beside the window. He opened its slim, single drawer and contemplated the contents. Then he turned and held out his hand to her. 'Come, ma dear,' he said formally. 'Everything's ready. Let's hope we have success this time.'

Kate jumped off the bus and returned the driver's cheery wave before tripping blithely across the road. She let herself in through the front door humming one of her favourite songs, *Smoke gets in your eyes.* Then she wrinkled her nose in disgust as she went through the inside door at the top of the short carpeted stair.

'The dirty auld bugger's been at it again,' she thought. *'Thank God Ah missed that ane.'* She found Annie emptying the pan from the commode into the toilet.

'Ach, that's no sae bad then, Annie,' she said. 'Ye got her on it in time, then.'

'Aye, *this* time,' agreed Fat Annie equably. 'We werna quite sae lucky the last time – an that wis only an hoor ago. Ah've pit the sheets in yer machine-thingy but Ah dinnae dare tae try an pit it on, no after the last time.'

Annie's attempt to master the intricacies of 'steamie' had resulted in Kate being met by a soapy tide eddying over the kitchen floor on her return last Wednesday. Kate sighed as she went into the kitchen and began to fill up the machine, first opening the window to dispel some of the rank smell from the soiled sheets that lay in its drum.

Richt back tae reality wi a capital R, she grimaced. But the effects of her wonderful afternoon were still with her and she smiled happily as she hung the winter coat in the wardrobe – taking a small paper bag out of one of the pockets first - and went through to share a cup of tea with Annie.

'Ah'm richt gratefu tae ye, Annie,' she said as she handed over the bag.

Annie thanked her demurely and deferred opening the bag till she was alone. She loved the little luxuries Kate chose for these thank-yous - scented hand creams, fragrant soaps, pretty bookmarks and tiny photo-frames, always dainty, lady-like things that made Annie feel, for a brief moment, almost dainty and lady-like too. She liked to savour that rare moment in private.

The tea was poured and Annie performed her last service of the day by taking a cup through to Maggie.

'Gie her a slab o' that apple tart,' suggested Kate. 'It'll shut her up for ten meenits while we get oor ain cuppie. Ah got it oot o' Aggie's shop yesterday. It's still fresh.' Then, seeing Annie eyeing the tart hungrily as she cut a piece for the old woman, '…an hae a bit yersel, of coorse'.

As the two women settled down for their snack – *'Ah'm livin' aff tea and cake the day,'* thought Kate, who had had no time for dinner before leaving at one o'clock earlier that day – Annie apprised Kate of an unwelcome fact.

'We had a wee visitor the day,' she announced. 'Jeannie Gilhooley cried in at twa o'clock. Said she'd cam' tae see hoo her auld neibour's gettin' on. She wis fair surprised when it wis *me* that opened the door.'

This was, of course, a bare-faced lie. Annie knew that Jeannie knew Kate went out on Wednesday afternoons *and* that Jeannie knew all about the arrangements for the care of Old Maggie.

Kate felt her cheeks growing hot and rose to open the sitting-room window, turning her back on Annie, murmuring: 'It disnae seem sae cauld noo as it did this mornin'. Ye never ken whit the weather's goin' tae dae at this time o' year.'

The through-draught from the kitchen window caught the sitting-room one and almost snatched it out of Kate's hand. In the flurry to control and secure it, she had time to regain her composure and get her wits about her.

This farewell-and-thank-you cup of tea with Annie was always a minefield. Up to now, she had managed to skirt around Annie's thinly-veiled probing and send her off without any 'cuttings' – much to Annie's disgust. But, with Jeannie Gilhooley on board, it was bidding fair to become a veritable death-trap. She had a vision of the two gossips putting their heads together, spinning one of their pernicious webs about her, in her own sitting-room.

'An Jeannie wis jist sayin', as weel, that she'd had some news o' oor butcher, the bold Mr Smillie. He's been oot o' hospital fur a few weeks noo, it seems. The young lad that brings the butcher's van roon on Mondays an Thursdays these days has been tae visit him.'

Annie fixed Kate with a wide-open stare, feigned innocence barely masking rampant speculation. 'He lives in Windygates, ye ken.'

Then, as Kate said nothing but only appeared to be concentrating intently on balancing a large dollop of cream on the slice of apple tart she was conveying to her mouth, 'Maybe ye'll see him sometime when ye get aff the bus there? Ah, hell, Kate, whit are ye doin? Ye shid tak wee'er moothfus. Ye're goin' tae choke yersel!'

Kate was spluttering, purple-faced, spraying cream-flecked pastry crumbs over her best Fair-Isle cardigan.

By the time Kate had got her breath back, helped by a few hearty slaps on her back, administered with more enthusiasm than was strictly necessary by a frustrated Annie, Old Maggie was demanding attention:

'Katy, Katy, where are ye? Ye've been gallivantin' long enough. I'm needin' the window closed. It's gettin' cold.'

Dusting the crumbs from her front and patting her hair back into place, Kate went thankfully through to the old woman. *'Ah niver thocht Ah'd see the day Ah'd be glad o' the auld moaner but she's a wee blessin' in disguise the day,'* she thought.

'Thanks, again, Annie,' she called dismissively over her shoulder as she went out of the sitting-room. 'Ah'll see ye next week, if no afore.'

Annie curled her lip in disappointed disgust. After the half-hour with Jeannie when the two women had quite made up their differences of the past few days, Annie had abandoned her loyalties to Kate. Jeannie's startling revelation about Angus Smillie's whereabouts, and the irresistible conclusion to be drawn from the Windygates connection, had been just too delicious.

Besides, when Jeannie had come to the door, Annie had just spent an unrewarding hour searching the house for some likely material to fuel future gossip sessions and found nothing – not a letter, not a bill, *no sae much as a bloody messages-list* - and every cupboard in perfect order, pristine-clean. Red-faced, sweating and exhausted, she had finally fetched up on her hands and knees staring at the large, locked metal chest which reposed under the bed in Kate and Johnnie's room. *The sly wee minx is hidin' it a'. Ah'm wastin' ma time,* she had groaned as she hauled herself to her feet and lumbered through, wheezing, to attend to Maggie who was waking up from her early afternoon doze.

Then the door bell had rung and there had been her best gossiping partner, with just the kind of nice wee titbit she was craving. The two women had buried the hatchet in a matter of moments and, like two hippos sinking happily into squelching mud, had plunged juicily into a mire of speculation and assumption.

Ach, the hell wi Miss Fancy-breeks Kate, Annie concluded as she let herself out of the gate. *There's mair than ane wiy tae skin a cat. We'll get tae the bottom o' it yet.*

The hand she thrust into her pocket to avoid the damp chill that was blowing in on the late afternoon wind encountered the paper-bagged present that Kate had given her earlier and she felt a tiny stirring of compunction which she quickly suppressed.

Just before dawn came the dog-teeth dream again. So long since the last one but she came awake with the well-remembered sense of escalating, inescapable menace: the gnawing molars; the nipping front teeth; the snapping incisors.

She lay gasping, thinking of her persistent desires which ran side-by-side with the nagging fear of discovery; the questions, first from Aggie, then from Annie, and now the terrifying prospect of Jeannie's investigations getting underway; and, in the future, perhaps...discovery, exposure, retribution.

She lay watching the grey early light of the autumn morning begin to straggle round the edges of the curtains. She had barely slept all night. Each fitful doze had ended in her starting awake with a different conclusion.

First she had decided in terror that her visits to Angus must cease forthwith, Annie and Jeannie must be given no more ammunition; next time she had drifted into consciousness with a happy smile on her face, recalling the wonderful time she had had that afternoon – only a few brief minutes, for sure, but definitely the best yet – and had been unable even to contemplate giving it up; then, after hours of swinging between these two extremes, awaking time and again with variations, permutations and compromises (*maybe just one more visit? maybe go to Windygates by a different route? maybe get someone else to look after Maggie?*), she had fallen into a deep, pre-dawn sleep and into the clutches of the hideous dog-teeth dream.

She turned her throbbing head to look at her sleeping husband, listening to his breath whistling softly out of his long, aquiline nose. He would never understand; he would be angry, humiliated, unforgiving. Then she would never persuade him to make her dreams come true and take her away to Canada, away from this dreary, pointless existence, away from the wagging tongues and petty jealousies – *even after the auld yin's oot o' the wiy.*

He must never find out.

Bob slid a blackened, apologetic face round the scullery door. 'That's me hame, ma wee darlin',' he said unnecessarily. Jeannie had, of course, heard Eck's gruff farewell, heard Bob dropping his boots heavily on to the step at the back door, heard his nervous whistling as he slung his coal-dusty coat onto the bunker for the twins to deal with in the morning.

She did not turn round from the sink where she was washing up the utensils used to make a fish pie. 'Ye've no been at a',' was her throwaway, accusatory greeting. A statement not a question: Jeannie always read Bob like a child's primer.

'Ach, Jeannie, Ah couldnae think o' ony excuse tae gie Eck. He kens fine Ah niver gae tae the pub in ma dirty work claes. Ah aye cam' hame and wash and change first. An then there's nae time afore they shut at half-nine.'

She whirled round and glared at him. 'Ye ken we talked aboot that – aboot whit ye'd say tae Eck.'

'An Ah did say it,' he chimed in eagerly. 'Ah telt Eck Ah wis needin' fags and wis goin' tae the pub tae get them but he had half-a-dozen left in an auld packet, as weel as havin' a new packet no startit on, and he said Ah wis tae tak the auld packet and jist pay him back the morn. Ah couldnae think o' onythin' else tae say.'

'Weel, fancy that! You no bein' able tae hae an idea o' yer ain! There's a surprise!' Jeannie was withering and he slunk off ashamed though unclear what else she had expected of him.

Jeannie hung the clean utensils on the rack above the cooker and turned her attentions to icing a Victoria sponge for their pudding. She slapped the stringy, white goo on to the cake with short, stabbing movements which reflected her annoyance and impatience. She would have to wait till tomorrow now to find out if this Graham lad from the pub *had* followed Kate this afternoon and, if so, what he had seen and found out. Jeannie was in for a sleepless night and Bob was destined to be disappointed at the beginning of it. There would be *two* grumpy people in the small cottage the next morning.

'Naw, nae cuttin's at a'.' Annie was glum as she bagged up the day's takings prior to locking it away in the safe in the back-shop. 'Mind, she wis fair flustered when Ah telt her that *you*'d been at the door. Leapt up like she'd a poker up her bum and started fartin' aboot wi the windae. An when Ah mentioned the name *Angus Smillie*, she near choked tae death on a wee crumb o' apple tart. Then Auld Maggie cried her through and that wis that… But whit aboot you, though? Did Bob manage tae speak tae the lad at the pub? Did he follow her? Did he find oot onythin'?'

'Ach, it's a proper scunner, Annie. This Graham-lad-frae-the-pub wisnae there when Bob went in this mornin'. Seems he scarpered awa tae Dundee at the crack o' dawn. They're sayin' his granny's been took ill. Bloody pest!'

'Weel, Jeannie,' a flicker of fairness tempered Annie's thirst for news. 'Ah dinnae suppose the auld biddy could help gettin' no weel.' With a rare flash of dry humour, she added, 'Ah dinnae suppose she's took ill jist take spike *oor* guns!'

'If ye're no goin' tae tak it seriously, Ah'm aff,' Jeannie turned on her heel and stomped out of the shop. Annie sighed. Jeannie was a good pal, there was no-one like her for a good gossipy blether, but she was sometimes sadly lacking in the humour, especially when her bloodhound nose was glued to the ground as it certainly was at the moment.

Jeannie stood outside the draper shop and surveyed the crossroads. On the other corner was The Auld Toll pub, where the errant Graham ought to be. She clicked her tongue in frustration. On the diagonally facing corner was the Cruikshanks' house.

Jeannie glanced up at its bay window and saw Kate herself, standing immobile, framed by the heavy gold velvet curtains that were the envy of all the other housewives. The distance was much too great, of course, but Jeannie fancied that their eyes met and held, that she saw fear and pleading in Kate's eyes. But Jeannie had not risen to her powerful position in the community by showing mercy to potential victims. *Ye're up tae something, ma bonnie lass. But we'll get tae the bottom o' it, if it kills us.*

'Geez, Jeannie! Whit are ye doin' still here? Ah thocht ye were awa hame.' Annie, reversing out the shop to lock the door, cannoned into Jeannie's back and almost sent her sprawling.

Across the road, watching the pair of them, Kate allowed the first smile of that day to flicker over her worried face. *Peety they dinnae knock each ither ower and brain themsels on the pavement.*

The two gossip queens parted and Jeannie wandered fretfully towards home, not relishing another evening of stalemate in her investigations. *An whit if the auld granny gets worse - or dees, even! - an he has tae stay there langer? We'll never get tae hear whit he saw Kate doin'...*

As she turned into Burns Avenue, she spied Aggie striding briskly ahead of her. *Ah'll cry in tae see Ag. Tell her aboot gettin' Kate followed. Mak it sound really excitin'. Like Ah'm on the verge o'...* She raked in her mind for the phrase in the detective novel *....o' a... a crucial breakthrough. Aye, that's it.*

Quite cheered at this prospect, she quickened her steps heading for Number 22.

CHAPTER FIVE

AGGIE

Aggie was singing, the soaring notes of the soprano solo pouring out of the open bathroom window as she sluiced the greasy face-cloth under her armpits.

After her immediate triumph at the first Sunday afternoon try-out, these Thursday night practices at the Methodist Church had quickly become the leaven of her week. At first she had felt very out-of-place, like an impostor waiting to be discovered, and the stares and nudges of the group which had gathered that first Sunday afternoon had almost driven her away without so much as a note being sung.

But the combination of their acute need for a new leading soprano – their previous one having just married and been swallowed up in the metropolis of Edinburgh – and Aggie's unquenchable desire to sing had quickly overcome reservations on both sides.

Once she had delivered her audition piece, there had never been any doubt of her acceptance into the choir. Shared love of music and excited anticipation of performance had soon proved bonds strong enough to overcome sectarian suspicion. The choir members knew that she had Catholic roots, of course, and some of the older ones had vaguely known her parents but, as it quickly became clear that she set no store by the religion of her birth and had no interest in commenting on or deriding theirs, they soon forgave and ceased to remember her unfortunate antecedents and began to count her as one of them.

So much so, she thought, as she balanced on one leg to wash a foot in the cracked sink, that they sometimes even said 'See you on Sunday' to her as well as each other when the Thursday evening practice was over.

And so it was standing outside number 22 Burns Avenue that Jeannie first heard Handel's *I know that my redeemer liveth*. Though

95

no judge of music, and her tastes running to the Big Band - Glenn Miller sound rather than this classical stuff, she was nevertheless momentarily transfixed.

'Can that wumman sing or no?' she thought. *'She should be on the stage, no servin' pies and cakes a' day an puttin' up wi that soor-faced bugger, Eck.'* Then, as the golden aria ended and the bathroom window was abruptly snapped shut, another thought struck her: *'Whit on earth wis that she wis singin'? Whaur did she get that frae?'*

Something spoke to Jeannie's finely-honed instincts and she revised her plan of paying a surprise visit on Aggie. She hovered uncertainly in the shade of some evergreen bushes at the gate of number 20, analysing her growing hunch, watching number 22 intently.

Through the leafy screen she saw Aggie come into her sitting-room and go over to stand at her fireplace. Jeannie's eyes bulged as Aggie began to preen before the mirror above it, fluffing up her wispy, greying hair, smearing on lipstick, patting a powder-puff on her red nose. Jeannie watched as Aggie turned her head to one side, smiled and pouted at herself, then began to mouth extravagantly articulated words. Jeannie could not hear through the closed window but she had no doubt that Aggie was singing her heart out. *As if she's a' ready on a stage...there's something goin' on here.*

A few minutes later, Jeannie's eyes almost fell out of her head when Aggie emerged from her house, wearing her best coat, carrying an old leather music case, walking awkwardly on unaccustomed high-heels. Jeannie shrank into the bushes, her heart beating uncomfortably fast. Aggie was inches away from Jeannie when she stopped, made a sound of annoyance and turned back into the house, obviously having forgotten some important thing.

Whit is she up tae? There's somethin' awfy fishy goin' on here. Stalled for the moment in the WW investigation, Jeannie was delighted to have a new case to solve. With the putting-of-tails-upon-suspects very much on her frustrated mind, Jeannie decided to try her hand at it.

She removed herself to another clump of bushes on the other side of the street and waited. *If Ag rumbles me, Ah'll jist say Ah'm on ma wiy tae pay another visit tae Bob's auld father, that he wisnae lookin' sae weel earlier on the day...or that Ah'm goin' tae get him a bottle o' beer frae the pub tae cheer him up.*

Aggie reappeared, now carrying a cake-box as well, and the two women processed up Burns Avenue, the one blissfully unaware of her stalker, the other in a high state of fevered excitement, dodging skillfully from hide to hide – bushes, telegraph poles, billboards, sheds and old air-raid shelters.

Ah'm a natural at this. Jeannie Gilhooley was enjoying herself.

'From the top… *If* you please, ladies and gentlemen.'

The fussy little choirmaster rapped his baton on the lectern and the motley gathering of Presbyterians, Methodists, various other minor Protestant denominations and one solitary Catholic came to order.

As they began to sing, the sopranos, altos, tenors and basses all slipping melodiously into their stride, Aggie closed her eyes and waited for her cue. As the moment for the start of her solo approached, her heart swelled. The newly-discovered delight of singing with and being part of a group of like-minded others who loved to make music with their voices was eclipsed only by the thrill of being such a key member of the group and such a vital part of the performance.

Naturally a loner, the propensity to alienate herself from those around her had been exacerbated by years of sibling jealousy, marital misery and innate dislike of her community's intimate – sometimes rapacious - interest in each other's business. But now she was experiencing the pleasure of belonging and being accepted and appreciated.

And she had grown to love this music. At first it had been merely the chance to sing that mattered and the thrill of being immediately chosen as the leading soprano had been the icing on the cake. She had not expected to enjoy this 'kirky stuff' as much as the lush, sentimental ballads she had always favoured. But as she quickly learned the words and melodies, there had been born in her a deeply satisfying involvement in the score and even in its meaning. As she sang of this longed-for and glorious redeemer, a small flicker of interest trembled inside her. She began to sense that there might be more to Christianity than parroted rosaries, garbled, repetitive confessions and the fish-on-a-Friday, keep-away-from-the-proddies religion of her youth.

That evening, she sang especially well, her glorious voice soaring powerfully to the vaulted ceiling of the old church.

'Perfect phrasing and diction much improved,' praised the choirmaster.

'Just lovely,' said the other choristers.

'Our little jewel,' said a kindly, smiling fellow-soprano called Margot.

Aggie had never been called either little or anything remotely resembling a jewel in her life. However small she had been as a child, Kate had always been smaller and more winsome and certainly her jewel-like qualities had never been commented upon by her husband. She had a dim memory of one of her daughters hugging her once and crying 'Ye're a treasure, Ma!' but that had been mere cupboard love after Aggie had scrimped and saved for months to get the lassie the fancy frock she coveted. Aggie had known that fine.

This genuine and affectionate praise was a new experience. Aggie's arid soul drank it in and deep in its dry roots began to grow – ever so slowly – towards a blossoming.

As they tidied up the cups from their end-of-practice tea and cakes (usually it was just biscuits but Aggie had further endeared herself to them all that night by bringing a selection of 'wee fancies' from the shop), the choirmaster announced:

'We're booked for the second of January. We'll be performing in The Alhambra in Burntisland. Seven-thirty performance, two-thirty for final rehearsal on site with the orchestra. Leaving here at one-thirty, I'll book the bus.'

He nodded to them all and left the church hall with brisk, clip-clop steps. An excited buzz broke out. The Alhambra! A real orchestra! They had been expecting to perform in the church sometime in the next few months – or maybe in one of the community halls in the area – but this was beyond their wildest dreams.

'Do you know, I thought he was looking like the cat that got the cream tonight!' laughed the lady who had called Aggie a jewel. 'The sly old puss! Well, my dear,' turning to Aggie, who was standing transfixed by the sink where she had been washing up the teacups, 'you're going to be famous. And rightly so,' she added generously.

Aggie floated home in a dream. A jewel! Famous! Rightly so! Singing solo in The Alhambra! It was heady stuff. She walked twice up and down the length of Burns Avenue before she could bring herself to go home and cross the threshold of reality. She passed the end of the Gilhooleys' cul-de-sac four times in the process, a fact that was not lost on Jeannie who was waiting impatiently by her front window for Bob to come home and learn about the latest mystery requiring the Gilhooley treatment.

Eck pushed the blackened chips around his plate. The jelly from the small terrine of 'potted hough' which had been the only other occupant of the plate had melted into a sea of grey-brown liquid filmed with tiny strands of the shredded meat. He made a small dam of the inedible burnt chips to create a puddle, then idly began extracting a few from the bottom of the dam to let the muddy tide flow under it, turning it into a bridge of sorts.

Abruptly he lost interest in his creation and threw his knife and fork down on to the plate. Even by Aggie's standards, it was a spectacularly unappetising offering. Glancing over at Aggie's plate he saw she had not eaten her 'potted hough' and was merely nibbling on the less black ends of her chips.

'Are ye no wantin' that?' He pointed at what was left of her half-melted terrine.

Aggie started and looked vaguely at him, then at her plate. Mutely, she shoved it towards him and rose to clear his plate away, scraping the remains from it into the bucket by the sink.

Eck regarded her side view with narrowed eyes. Even by the standards of their uncommunicative, separate-worlds marriage, she was behaving in an unusually detached manner. He thought briefly of the steak-pie-and-bubble-bath night a few weeks ago. *A bloody flash-in-the-pan – Ah micht have kent.*

As he had hoped that night, there had been love-making after the pie. And it had been good – well, better than he had had for years. Aggie's interest in bedroom activities had always been minimal and her resigned and derisory attitude to his erectile inadequacies had been very much part of the mutual cruelty - physical on his side, mental on hers - that had formed the bedrock of their marriage. But that night she had been jovial and tolerant, even briefly lending a hand to encourage him to 'have another go'. When he had achieved his first climax in years, she had laughingly applauded and he had dropped off to sleep feeling very pleased with himself, unaware that she had risen soon after to sit by the dying fire embers, nursing new dreams along with the toddy she had decided to treat herself to.

The next day he had still been mellow. Casting around for some topic of conversation over their lunch-time pies and beans, and remembering his own recent observations to Johnnie, he had asked: 'An hoo's yer sister Kate managing wi lookin' after that auld mither o' Johnnie's? Ah telt him jist the ither day that he's a damned cheek expectin' it o' her. An her sich a dainty wee lass, the thocht o' *her* havin' tae…'

He had broken off at the look on Aggie's face. For a moment, at the mention of Kate's name, she had looked stricken, almost guilty, he would have said. Then, as he had ploughed on into expressions of sympathy and admiration for her sister, her face had hardened into its familiar sneering lines.

'Oh aye,' she had snapped sarcastically. 'Lets a' feel awfy sorry fur puir wee Katy! She's that hard done-by in her braw hoose wi her braw claes.'

She had risen abruptly and snatched a packet of woodbines from the mantelpiece, lighting one up with a shaky hand.

'Her wi her swanky man that comes hame clean at nichts and wi a decent wage packet at the end o' the week – no ane that only ever gets noticed fur troublemakin' wi bloody union shite!'

He had replied in kind, ruthlessly extolling the difference between shapely, gentle Kate and her scrawny, abrasive sister. Like two pegs that had been momentarily shaken out of their holes and rattled about together for a brief time making a cheerful sound, they had quickly subsided deep back into their holes and resumed their lifelong positions.

There had been no more happy times upstairs since then. He had not even tried, feeling that the usual disgusted sufferance, merciless jeering and open relief at the end of his efforts would be hard to bear after a brief glimpse of better things.

Now he finished her hough and, still hungry, pushed his chair back brusquely. 'That wis hellish,' he snarled. 'Ah'm awa tae the chippy fur some decent grub.'

She had her back to him now, standing at the sink, and a slight shrug of her shoulders was the only indication that she had heard. She was humming a tune as usual. He was used to that – *her* constant singing and humming and *his* frequent discontented sighs and menacing grunts formed the duet of their life together.

He slammed irritably out of the back door, passing the kitchen window as he rounded the house on the narrow path to the front gate. Her humming grew louder as he approached the open kitchen window then suddenly turned into singing, at first low volume then reaching full pitch by the time he was at the front gate.

He stopped to listen and frowned. Though he could not have named any of her songs and had long ago ceased to take notice of them, they had sunk into his subconscious over the years. He knew he had never heard this one. Not only that, he knew suddenly that he had never heard her sing anything even *like* this one. It had a solemnity he did not associate with her usual sentimental repertoire. But, most of all, the words perplexed him: they were like a hymn but not one *he* had ever heard before. '*Churchy stuff! Ah hope she's no goin' religious on me,*' he thought anxiously. '*That wid be the last bloody straw!*'

He decided to eat his fish supper on the way to the Welfare Club. They had a license to sell alcohol there till ten o'clock and, if he was quick, he would make it in time for last orders. He jingled the remains of that week's money in his pocket. *Ach, shite! It'll hae tae be jist a poke o' chips an nae fish if Ah want a pint at the club as weel.*

Aggie upended the basin full of lukewarm, dirty water into the sink and left it to its own devices. The sink would remain half full of the greasy, soupy water, as the drain failed to cope with the debris, and a crust of grey fat would solidify round its rim, trapping the upended basin left floating on top.

This would be the sight that would greet Eck when he came down for his breakfast tomorrow. She would head straight off to the shop at the crack of dawn without a glance at the unedifying sight. Eck's complaints about such slovenly practices had long ago ceased to register with her. Perhaps he had even stopped them?

He had expressed voluble scorn when she had first outlined her plan to take over and run the bakery. *Ye'll hae it like a pig-sty in nae time. The customers'll be boakin' no buyin'!*

But, surprising even herself, Aggie had proved that she had her head screwed on when it came to running the business and had understood that what he predicted could come true, though she would never have admitted it to him. She had, so far, somehow managed to maintain a level of cleanliness and presentation that satisfied her

101

customers. The effort to do so, however, completely exhausted her slim stock of interest in repetitive cleaning tasks so that even the slapdash modicum of housework she had previously done in her own home now seemed beyond her.

She was wise enough, however, to realise that the sight and smell of her unsavoury home might make customers wonder about the hidden side of the bakery shop and feel uneasy about patronising it. So she had simply stopped inviting anyone to their house. Not that this had been a big change. Eck's surly demeanour and unpredictable temper had always proved a powerful disincentive to people 'crying in' and, now that the need to reciprocate hospitality to her daughters' friends had gone, there were few people likely to expect an invitation.

She made herself a pot of tea and took two battered pieces of chocolate cake out of a paper bag lying on top of the welter of old letters, single gloves, broken dog-leads, bus tickets and other rubbish which lay on the kitchen cabinet. They had been all that remained of a very large cake she had cut up and sold in individual slices that afternoon – a new venture that had proved appealing to women looking for a wee treat but not able to afford a whole cake. Her original thought had been for them to have a piece each. But his cavalier treatment and summary condemnation of the dinner she had hastily thrown together had put any thoughts of a shared chocolate-cake moment out of her head.

Soor-faced bugger! He wis damned lucky tae get onythin'. It wis gone eight o'clock when Ah got in frae the practice.

Her restless perambulations up and down Burns Avenue had made her even later than usual and it had been a frantic rush to get the meal ready. However 'hellish' the food she produced, Eck still demanded that it be ready the moment he came downstairs from washing after his shift and was likely to turn extremely nasty if it was not. The fact that he was frequently unable to eat it was secondary to this basic demand. There had been many a bruising hand taken off Aggie's jaw or a brutal 'boot up the arse' in the past for failing to 'hae the denner on the table when *Ah'm* ready fur it an no when it suits *you*'.

As she poured the tea, her mind began to tease delightfully around the edges of her new secret, licking at its delicious corners. She saw herself on stage in the choir looking out at the large auditorium; she heard the audience clapping expectantly when the curtain went up; she saw herself walking forward to the front of the stage when the time came for her first solo; she heard the burst of spontaneous, excited applause when she finished it; she saw...

Abruptly the sliding tongue of her imagination came up against a jagged edge and she recoiled with a sharp intake of breath. *Oh ma God! The conductor mannie had said the **second of January!***

Aggie choked on the last mouthful of cake. In her excitement at the prospect of a real stage performance, she had not really registered the date.

The second of January was very much part of the extended New Year celebrations in their community. True, the men went back to work after the allotted one day off on the first, but, since the war, the second had become an important day in the female calendar.

During the dark days of wartime danger and deprivation, the woman in the community had drawn closer together as they battled on, many without their men folk who were away in the services, others virtually alone as their husbands had to work incredibly long hours to cover for those who had gone to the war. Women had borne the babies conceived in snatched moments on service leaves and then endured the pain of not knowing if these children would ever see their fathers, some through years of uncertainty, culminating in either joyful reunion, horrified acceptance of what remained of the man they had known or final acknowledgement of widowhood.

They had suffered the dreary, daily grind of rationing for years on end, long after victory had been declared, long after their inventiveness and patience had run out. And through it all, they had cared for and stood by each other in a way that simply didn't happen on the easy street of peace and plenty.

But one practice that *had* survived those years of fear and friendship was the annual party for all the women in the community on the second of January. Despite, perhaps because of, the hectic week of preparations, parties and mammoth clearing-up sessions that preceded the second, this day had become 'The Wummen's Get-thegither' and was always happily anticipated and very well-attended. Any woman missing from it was always noticed; her non-attendance, reasons and excuses would all be as public as apologies read out at the start of a formal committee meeting.

Aggie had never missed one, had even managed to host one in the days when her daughters could shame her into hospitality and even rally round to help tidy up the house, set tables and prepare the 'spread'.

Some of the women in the choir were 'members' of this annual get-together, of course, but they would simply and openly tell the truth about where they had to be that day. Others in the gathering would make sneering remarks about 'kirky types awa tae get their souls saved again' but it would be worth no more discussion than that and easily forgotten.

On the other hand, if Aggie did not go, many would express and explore a close interest. It was well known she had always chosen not to open the bakery that day. 'Ah'm aye buggered by the second,' she had said from the first year of her business venture. 'A guid laugh at the Get-thegither gets me goin' again.'

The other women understood this sentiment only too well. Preparations for *The New Year* began in September when all the local shops, Aggie's bakery included, began their Christmas Clubs, which meant the women paid into a savings scheme each week. A week before Christmas they would be issued with special vouchers to buy goods in that shop.

They should really have been called Hogmanay Clubs since in this community Christmas was of small significance, the men not even having the day off work, and the whole santa-and-sleighbells carry-on being considered by many to be suspiciously English in origin and nature. But Hogmanay and New Year - now they were a quite different matter.

Even the poorest families scrimped and saved to have their New Year bottle of whisky, their slab of 'black bun' and their tin of shortbread. The week between Christmas Day and Hogmanay was the busiest one of the year, for shopkeepers and for housewives. The former did their best business of the year: Aggie sold a mountain of black bun and 'shortie'; the butcher ran out of steak pies and sausages; and the off-license was queued round the corner at all times of the day. The housewives exhausted themselves vigorously cleaning often already spotless houses, anxious that 'the New Year disnae cam' into a dirty hoose', and buying and cooking enormous amounts of food.

There existed a pathological horror of running out of anything or of not having to hand something a first-footing visitor might express a wish for and this imperative had now escalated into a fierce competition which delighted the shopkeepers and put immense strain on family purses. As post-war rationing had gradually lost its grip, and perhaps as a reaction to those years of want and denial, the whole ridiculous race had begun to spiral out of control.

The men played their part too, getting into training for the drinking, smoking and singing marathon by having several not-so-dry runs in the pub and club the fortnight before. There were many pitched battles in homes in this fortnight as the men tried to wheedle or threaten carefully saved money from their wives for these practice runs.

This was, of course, one of the reasons that the Christmas Clubs were so popular. The men might demand or plunder the vouchers but, unless they only wanted food and eatable fancies, they were no good to them. The off-license also ran a vouchers scheme but it was only ever used by women who had well-behaved husbands (*jessies*, the other men called them) or tee-total ones (*couldnae haud their drink - had tae gie it up).*

Most women held off buying the New Year bottle for as long as possible but a few unwise ones fell for early offers of reduced prices, hoping to hide these bargains until New Year's Eve. These would be the bottles that 'never saw midnight', probably never even saw the morning of Hogmanay.

Unlucky or unwary wives, with particularly domineering or devious men, could find themselves with all their carefully hoarded money gone, already spent in the training period. Their club vouchers could buy the food they would need but they faced the unthinkable shame of being unable to offer their first-footers a drink. They would now be forced to court the lesser shame of borrowing from neighbours and friends. Kate, whose more ample income and self-controlled husband placed her beyond such worries, was always a soft and sympathetic touch and needy women especially valued her understanding assurances of discretion.

'Ye're a daft bitch,' Aggie would declare scornfully, if she did happen to find out. 'A'body kens that lad drinks every penny he can get his muckle hands on. Ye'll never see yer money again!' And she was often proved right but Kate simply wrote the loss off, absorbing it by some judicious savings in the January sales, and never mentioning it again to the debtor.

Hogmanay was always free-flow first-footing —an unpredictable affair with every house set up for a full scale party. It was a lottery as to which one would end up with the big crowd that would do justice to the groaning table of food and array of drinks on the sideboard. Much depended on how many people who had reached the same stage of inebriation happened to be in the same house at the same time.

105

Depending on how that stage took each person, there might then be a great party, a horrible fight, a great deal of vomiting or just a gaggle of maudlin mutterers and snorers. You just never knew.

The children who were trailed around the houses, the younger ones in carry-cots and piggy-backs on parents' shoulders, the older ones dragging increasingly weary feet through icy slush, soon became adept at recognising the kind of outcome that could be expected and knew when to exploit the situation for unlimited, unnoticed drinks of raspberry cordial, illicitly laced with a drop of the hard stuff by the adventurous older boys, and when to settle themselves in a corner and try to sleep through hours of singing and merry-making.

New Year's Day was quite different, having a formal structure. It did not begin until late afternoon, since no-one had gone to bed until nearly dawn once Hogmanay had been finally declared over, the Old Year officially seen out and the New Year thoroughly ushered in.

Whilst the men snored on, the women and children would be up just in time to catch the winter sunset. *Ye never see daylicht on Ne'erday* was considered a fitting accolade to a good Hogmanay.

Once the depredations of the night before had been put to right, empty beer, whisky and sherry bottles put out in the bin, food and drink spills, some fresh, some regurgitated, cleaned up and whole sinks full of glasses and plates washed, it was time, if yours was the chosen house that year, to start preparing *Ne'erday Denner*.

This was traditionally when as many of your extended family as you could squeeze round your table would be invited to share in Steak Pie and Trifle – the menu was the same in every house and was washed down by copious amounts of that well-known beverage, *the hair o' the dog*.

It was especially hard on a woman whose house had ended up as the Hogmanay party spot, fighting arena or vomiting doss-house, if she was also doing *Ne'erday Denner* for the family that year. A hang-over headache with nausea and over-tired, fractious children made it even more of a challenge.

At least very little cooking was involved as the steak pies were bought ready to heat up and eat and the trifles were sold in large glass bowls in 'The Store', as the Co-operative Society Shop was known. The women paid a small deposit for the glass bowls which were washed and returned as soon as possible to get the deposit back. But there were still tatties to peel and boil, tins of peas to open and – the worst bit – large amounts of crockery and cutlery to bring out. This often entailed bending down and reaching into rarely used cupboard recesses – a painful and risky process when your head is throbbing and your guts are churning.

The table had inevitably to be extended, turned around and hauled into the middle of the room. Chairs had to be found from every corner of the house and pressed into service; even the piano stool and the pouffee with a cushion on top might have to be used. By the time the guests arrived, the woman would be exhausted but triumphant, especially if she had managed all this without waking her man from his drunken stupor. Then the first guests would be encouraged to burst in on his foul-breathed snoring, upbraiding him, dragging him out of bed, declaring *That must hae been a richt skinfu ye had last nicht!* He would be thrown unceremoniously into the bathroom and told to *get yersel a wash an shave, man, an get yersel through here fur yer Ne'erday Denner!*

Once the meal was over, usually by mid-evening, the party would begin. Like the meal, this had a pre-ordained format, each person well aware of what was expected of him or her in terms of providing entertainment. No false modesty was allowed, in fact was seldom even essayed, and many would already have had a rehearsal in the serendipitous gatherings the night before and were therefore more than ready for this organised performance.

Songs, recitations, even short dramatic sketches made up the programme and these were repeated year in, year out with almost no variation. Indeed the very predictability of each person's contribution was an integral part of this traditional party: Kate always delivered a deeply contralto, doe-eyed version of *Dark Lochnagar;* Johnnie dressed up and acted out a hilarious rendition of *The Laird of Cockpen;* Eck rapped out *I'll take you home again, Kathleen,* managing to make the song's promise sound like a threat; Jeannie and Bob duetted *The Crookit Bawbee*; Fat Annie, whose singing voice was a tuneless screech, settled for a word-perfect rendering of Robert Burns' poem, *To a Mouse.*

Apart from the returning war heroes, who had proudly brought back their rousing, regimental choruses, Aggie was one of the few people who had ever managed to introduce new material and she was accorded this leeway partly because of her unrivalled voice – no-one wanted to run the risk of her taking the huff and depriving them – and partly because of her sharp tongue and forceful personality. Over the years she had introduced them to more and more of the sentimental

107

ballads and romantic songs from stage musicals that she so loved and now these mixed familiarly, if not quite comfortably, with the traditional Scottish and Irish stuff.

As more and more of the younger generation left to seek their fortune across the Atlantic or Down Under, a new poignancy had been added to the old emigrant laments and there was never a dry eye in the house when everyone joined in the yearning, homesick '*It's oh! But I'm longin' for my ain folk...*' Kate had openly wept at this point for the last five years and been beerily comforted by Johnnie or, if he was too drunk or too busy to notice, by others around her, the men especially keen to give her a consoling hug.

The party would once again last well into the early morning as people were persuaded to perform again and again, sometimes the same thing many times, sometimes an old number remembered from previous parties. As morning approached, those men on early shift, starting at six o'clock, would either try and snatch a wee nap in a chair or simply fortify themselves with a large plate of ham-an-eggs, stovies or tripe. The hostess, however weary or inebriated herself, had always to make the effort to get at least one of these dishes ready for the men who were going straight from the party down the pit for a seven hour shift. Big slabs of the remaining black bun would be wrapped in greaseproof paper for their piece-time.

Up until noon on the second, there were few windows with curtains open and an almost funereal pall would be lying over the village. But in one house, at least, all would be bustle and scurry as yet more food and the last of the drink - if indeed any remained – would be laid out.

Truth to tell, a very large pot of tea, constantly replenished, would be the most important beverage that day. Very few of the women had the stomach for any more alcohol, a few even declaring that *the verra sicht o' it maks ma belly heave.* By three o'clock they would begin straggling wearily towards the appointed venue, trailing sickly children after them (far too much rich food), and the *Get-thegither* would slowly crank into action.

At first there would be only sighs and groans, some over that unique physical discomfort brought on by a combination of too much alcohol and too little sleep, some over depleted purses, ruined carpets and fractured relationships resulting from drunken brawls. But at some point in the late afternoon, as the daylight faded and the lights went on, someone would recall a particularly outrageous moment from the past two days or begin sharing a particularly juicy bit of scandal that had become apparent when tongues were loosened and guards were down.

Then the tenour of the gathering would change, faces would brighten, memories would be jogged, humour would break through and the real business of the day would begin...

'Did ye see that frock she was wearin' – well more like no wearin'. Ah thocht she wis goin' tae fa oot o' it every time she bent ower tae pour oot mair drink.'

'Ah heard she did fa oot o' it when she wis leanin' doon tae poker the fire an ye can guess wha wis there tae see it. He's been sniffin' aroon fur months. Thocht a' his birthdays had cam' at aince! Mind, she wis that blootered she never even noticed.'

'Whit! Never noticed her boobies had fell oot?'

'Naw! Never noticed him standing slaverin' beside her. Jist stuffed them back into her brassiere and carried on wi the pairty.'

'That wis some stuff they were handin' oot at number 40. Ah bet he had it half- drunk before Hogmanay and she topped it up wi something – cauld tea, maybe.'

'Cauld lavvie cleaner, mair like. It near took the skin aff ma tongue.'

'Aye, richt enough, it wis awfy burnie. Maybe she thocht she's better no mak it ower weak or she'd be rumbled. Mind, half the folk there were past carin' from whit Ah could see.'

'Och, some folk wid sook it through a shitey cloth.'

'Aye – 'specially by fower o'clock in the mornin' on Hogmanay.'

'They Gilhooley lads cam' hame roarin' fu at nine o'clock last night. They'd been oot since seven o'clock in the evenin' on Hogmanay. The hale street heard them. Jeannie and Bob were awa oot tae their Ne'erday Denner at Bob's sister's hoose, the daft laddies couldnae find their door-keys, they were trying tae climb in the windae and it got stuck wi ane o' them half-in, half-oot, yowlin' like a stuck pig, and the other ane sittin' oot on the pavement bawlin' an singin' and laughin' an doin' nothin' tae help him.'

'Ach, they twa have never had the sense they were born wi. Jeannie wid be black affronted. Whit happened? Dinnae tell me he wis still stuck wi his dowp stickin' oot the windae when Bob and Jeannie got hame in the wee sma hoors?'

'Naw, that wis the best laugh. Big Eck heard them. He and Johnnie had had ane o' their barnies ower at Kate's hoose and Aggie had shoved him oot, telt him tae go an cool aff. He wis walkin' doon the Avenue when he heard the commotion. He went roon and helped the lad get back oot but he took the chance tae gie him a few damn good skelps on the bum first. That sobered him up richt enough.'

'He wid! He's aye been ower free wi his hands. Mind you, Ah dinnae blame him this time. Wha could resist it? An it would be nothin' tae whit Jeannie wid dae tae the pair o' them when she heard o' it...'

'Wheest! Here's the wumman hersel comin' ower...'

Aggie chuckled as she recalled choice snippets from past Getthegithers. Her own caustic wit was always highly prized and she grinned remembering some of her best cracks which had had the women pleading for mercy: *Fur ony sake, Aggie, stop! Ah'm goin' tae wet ma breeks.*

Then she frowned. She would be missed, her absence discussed and investigated. She could tell them the truth... She briefly considered this and immediately blenched at the thought of their condemnation: *Ye're never goin' wi a load o' proddies and singin' their sangs? Yer faither wid turn in his grave! Are ye turnin' intae ane o' thae religious maniacs?*

Eck would find out, pour scorn on her and put every obstacle in her path: *Whit are ye daein cairryin' on wi the likes o' them fur? Ye'll dae onythin' tae get up on a stage and show aff. Ye've mair need tae git this pig-sty o' a hoose cleaned and learn hoo tae cook a decent meal. Ah'll be damned if ye're goin' tae mak a fool o' me like this.*

But worst of all, her secret would no longer *be* hers, her lovely world where she was a little jewel, deserving of fame and praise, would be invaded and sullied by the constraint and denigration that was her everyday reality. No! A way would be found, *must* be found. She had three months to find it. Plenty time...

CHAPTER SIX

JEANNIE

The tall thin woman slipped silently into the empty church for her rendezvous with destiny. At last she was escaping from the clutches of the brutal husband who had cast such a pall over her young life and marred her beauty with his cruelty. The gnarled old priest was waiting at the altar with his big black bible in his hand. In his other hand he held a huge brass candlestick in which a thick yellow candle was flickering. On a small table nearby stood a matching brass hand bell. She closed her eyes as she knelt in front of the priest and prepared to undergo the ceremony that would free her from the dreadful curse that was blighting her life. Now the curse would be transferred to the man who was terrorising her and she would be free to pursue her dreams...

Jeannie threw down her pencil in irritation as the quiet cul-de-sac erupted. The noise swelled to a deafening level and climaxed in a screaming, throbbing roar before mercifully dying.

They've got that bloody motor bike again. Ah telt them Ah widnae hae it sittin' ootside ma door. Damn dangerous thing and maks a hellish racket! No tae mention the stink that cam's aff it.

She charged downstairs and straight out the front door to the gate. The neighbours were treated to the always popular spectacle of *those twa big 'hallicat' laddies* cowering before their mother, *wee Jeannie Gilhooley, no the size of tuppence.* After a few minutes, the bike roared off again with only one twin on it and the other was being chased indoors.

'That'll be that, then,' said across-the-road Nellie to her fourteen-year-old daughter who was lifting the baby out of the rickety old high chair. 'Nae mair motor bikes fur a wee while – until the next time. They aye try it on. Maybe they think Jeannie'll gie in ane o' these days. Fat chance!'

The girl set the baby down on the frayed fireside rug and turned to deal with the three other children who were half eating, half playing with their meal of bread-and-milk saps. 'Ah wish she'd let them hae the bike,' she said. 'They look that grand on it.'

She stealthily contemplated the swaggering twins and entertained a few girlish fantasies which her mother did her best to squash with a withering 'Grand big heids, mair like, wi nothin' much atween the ears. They twa wis ahent the door when the brains were bein' gied oot.'

Like everyone else, she was puzzled and exasperated that these feckless apron-strung lads seemed to do no real work – never broke sweat – but managed to swagger around in fancy suits and fancy cars with money jingling in their pockets. It was a sum that didn't add up in most people's experience and it left the bad taste of bewildered resentment in their mouths.

'Ye'll get it when yer faither cam's hame.'

Young Rab Gilhooley heaved a sigh of relief. This remark always signaled the end of Jeannie's tirade, being her belated, unconvincing acknowledgement that the man of the house *should* be the one laying down the law. The idea of Bob ever doing such a thing belonged in the realms of fantasy but Jeannie liked to maintain the fiction and insisted that her sons did so too.

'We'd better be awa oot again, then, when he gets hame,' said Rab with a mock tremble in his voice. He lifted the lid off the big black stew-pot on the cooker and poked the contents with a wooden spoon. 'Liver and onions,' he said approvingly. 'Is that left ower frae denner-time? Can we finish it up?'

The twins' eating habits and times were so erratic that Jeannie had long since given up trying to guess if or when they would want food. She usually made extra at midday in case, as tonight, they wanted to grace the table at some point with their presence. More often than not, she ended up handing the remains to next-door's dog.

The twins were great customers of fish-and-chip shops and great makers of enormous, messy, midnight sandwiches, creating some innovative, and frequently disgusting, fillings. Once, at this befuddled hour, they had spread tinned cat food liberally on hunks of bread, spicing the sandwich with crocus bulbs which they had mistaken for shallots. They had come to no harm and had not been at all put out when they discovered their mistake. *Tasted grand!* they had declared, grinning. *Maybe we've invented a new recipe.*

Jeannie tutted just once more, then succumbed. Like all mothers, she could be easily mollified by the opportunity to provide good food to strapping, hungry sons.

'Ah'll mak some chips tae gang wi it,' she offered. 'You go and get yersel changed.'

The twins wore flashy suits with wide trouser legs and double-breasted jackets during the day but in the evenings, to go to the pub for darts and dominoes or to the pictures with some lucky girl, they favoured grey flannels with navy blazers or Harris Tweed jackets.

'Did ye get me some mair Brylcream, Ma?' he demanded as he headed for the stairs.

By the time his younger (by half-an-hour) brother arrived back home from the car dealers where they were currently employed, having sorrowfully traded in the offending bike for a sedate Hillman saloon, the house was full of the appetising aroma of rich onion gravy and freshly-made, perfectly-cooked chips.

Dave stole up behind Jeannie as she dished out their food. He lifted the neat bun off her neck and planted a wet kiss on the nape. 'Ye're a wee star, Ma,' he enthused, 'We're starvin'.'

The twins frequently spoke in the plural as of one mind – *no even ane decent mind atween the twa o' them*, was actually what most people thought of them.

Jeannie shrugged him off impatiently, hiding her secret pleasure. 'Get awa wi ye! Ye're worse than yer faither.'

Dave shared a complicit grin with his brother who was just coming out of the tiny bathroom, his sleek hair testifying that his mother had not forgotten to buy the new jar of Brylcream. The twins were not as ignorant as their parents liked to think of the *cairry-on that those twa auld buggers get up tae.*

They occasionally discussed it with a mixture of admiration and embarrassment. They never mentioned it to their pals, of course, knowing it would simply be laughed out of court. They had once, when their adolescent minds and bodies were beginning to grope towards understanding, mentioned it to a friend a few years older than them.

'Ye're daft!' the friend had declared roundly. 'Mithers and faithers dinnae dae onythin' like that. They're a' past it a lang time ago.'

The twins knew different but, in this matter if in no other, they exercised a tiny grain of common sense and kept the knowledge to themselves.

As the lads wolfed down the food, she sat down by the fire and pensively lit up a woodbine. She was enjoying writing the rather gothic melodrama based on her detective work the other day but she knew that the truth of the matter *must* be very different.

She had watched Aggie walk confidently up to the Methodist Church then, equally confidently, tramp the path around it and disappear into the building through a side door. She had continued to watch as a few other people did the same. None of them were people she knew well enough to accost and ask what was going on. She had lingered without result until some time after the last person had gone in.

The notice board outside, which had lured Aggie in a few weeks ago, now only proclaimed the baleful, cryptic message: *Be not deceived; God is not mocked.*

She had caught one scrap of conversation from an enthusiastic, bright young man accompanying an older woman who looked like his mother: '. . . *heard about it at the prayer meeting...*'

Was Aggie going into this proddy kirk to *pray?* But, if she wanted to pray – and Jeannie did not immediately discount the possibility, knowing some of the circumstances of Aggie's life and marriage - why did she not go down to the Catholic Church and say her rosary, as Jeannie herself occasionally did when the going got tough? No, there was something else going on here and Jeannie was itching to get to grips with it. This called for some assiduous research.

She threw her half-smoked cigarette into the fire and rose briskly. 'Mind ye wash up yer plates and leave the kitchen tidy,' she abjured the twins. 'Ah'll be doon tae check afore ye go oot again. Peety help ye if ye leave the place in a mess.'

'Richt ye are, Ma.' But their facile, unconvincing reply fell on deaf ears. She was already mounting the stairs bent on finishing her melodrama before beginning to plan her investigation.

Jeannie set an enormous ham-and-egg pie down on the table. Bob eyed it hungrily admiring the golden pastry crust and the plentiful chunks of bacon poking up through the bubbling egg topping.

114

'Ah hope that's a' fur us, my wee darlin',' he said greedily. 'They daft laddies dinnae deserve ony. Ye niver ken when they're goin' tae be here or whit the hell they want tae eat.'

Jeannie paused with the knife in her hand, tantalising him unbearably.

'Tell me this,' she accosted him, 'Did Eck say onythin' aboot Aggie goin' oot last nicht? Did he ken whaur she wis goin'?'

Bob blinked. He was finding it extremely difficult to think about anything else other than the spell-binding sight and smell of the pie and the clamour of his rumbling stomach. 'Ah cannae mind, hen. Can we talk aboot it aifter...'

Jeannie laid down the knife and fixed him with a steely eye. 'Think, Bob!' she demanded. 'Think! Did he say onythin' when ye were walkin' tae the pit this afternoon?'

Then, seeing Bob's blank look, she quickly recapped on all she had told him the night before of her stalking of Aggie and what she had seen, ending, 'So? Does Eck ken onythin' or no?'

Bob groaned as he tried to force his tired, hungry mind to find an answer. It had been a particularly grueling shift with two of the men off sick. *Belly-ache and the runs as weel.* One of the men had begun to suggest that they must have had *ane of they dodgy pies oot o' that bakery shop* but a sharp nudge in his bare ribs from the man working alongside him at the coal face had warned him that big Eck's slit-eyed glare was upon him and his jocular aspersions had abruptly dried up.

There had been extra work for them all to do and the twenty minute break – their piece-time – had been curtailed. Bob was bone-weary and starving. He wanted nothing more than a good feed and an hour's snooze by the fire to give him enough second wind for his nightly hour of pleasure.

But he could see that his wife was in an implacable frame of mind. Any minute now, she was likely to cut the beautiful pie in half and put one piece away *fur the laddies' supper,* seriously reducing his own allocation. He cast around for a way to avert this disaster and his eye fell upon a framed sampler hanging on the wall at the side of the fire.

It had been done by Jeannie's mother when she was a girl and insisted that this was *Home Sweet Home*, a considerable feat of imagination for that long-ago young embroiderer who had grown up in a mean, overcrowded cottage long before the mine-owners had been shamed into improving and extending the miserable dwellings.

115

Desperation gave him a rare flash of inspiration.

'She's goin' tae an embroidery class. The church is runnin' it,' he improvised. 'Now, can Ah get ma supper or no? Whit dis a man hae tae dae aroon here tae get fed?'

As they demolished the pie, accompanied by potato salad which Bob loved – chunks of hot potato, well-salted and slathered in salad cream – Jeannie struck again. 'But, there wis men goin' in tae the place as weel. They wisnae after learnin' embroidery.'

Bob laid down his fork and knife with a long, contented sigh which ended in a juicy belch. Rather proud of the success of his previous tactic, he experimented with a little more fabrication. 'Ah think they dae carpentry there as weel,' he offered.

Jeannie snorted. 'Dinnae push yer luck,' she said obliquely as she rose to fetch the treacle sponge for their pudding.

Bob was lying, of course. The chances of his ever pulling the wool over Jeannie's eyes were so slim as to be invisible but she would let him off this time because he had given her something to think about…

Senga hovered happily over the embroidery threads, fondling their texture, lifting one out and turning it towards the daylight at the shop door, comparing two possible shades, setting contrasting ones together and standing back, lips pursed, to consider the effect.

Annie left her to it, subsiding on to - and generously overflowing - the small stool behind the counter, her morning bag of doughnuts already open in her fat hands. For several minutes there was a contented silence in the shop as each woman pursued a favourite occupation.

Senga loved to sew and her fussy, chintzy house bore testimony to this passion. Every chair or couch had embroidered sleeve covers, anti-macassars and cushions. Bedspreads, pillow-cases, table and tray cloths, even clothes for herself and her children, had all had the Senga treatment. But, almost as much as actually doing it, she loved choosing the coloured threads and often fell asleep at night happily planning a new colour combination. Annie's passions were less artistic, being largely limited to eating and gossiping.

'That'll hae tae dae fur noo.' Senga regretfully laid three skeins of thread from the green spectrum back in the drawer. 'Ah'll hae tae wait till next week tae get they anes. Dinnae ye sell them tae onybody else, mind. They'll be perfect fur the trees in the scene Ah'm workin' on.'

'Dinnae fash yersel, Senga. Ah'll pit them by fur ye. No that they're likely tae be a' sold in a week. The world's no fu o' folk daft on embroidery. Mair's the peety! Ah could be a rich woman if Ah had mair customers like you.'

Annie rose, sucking the sugar off her fingers and wiping them by kneading them into her large, spongy stomach. 'Whit are ye workin' on the noo?'

'It's a hieland scene on a table cloth. Ah'm at it every spare meenit, tryin' tae get it finished in time. It's fur Maureen oot in Canada, fur her Christmas. It'll hae tae be posted in a couple o' weeks tae get there in time. Ah promised Kate Ah'd dae it – weel, Ah offered, really, a wee while ago when she wis lookin' sae doon in the mooth. Ah thocht it would cheer her up a bit.'

Senga's kindly face creased in sympathy, remembering how Kate had been when her mother-in-law first came to stay. 'Mind,' she added, thoughtfully, 'Kate's lookin' a lot better these days, near back tae her auld sel. Likely, she's jist got used tae it. An the auld shit-the-bed cannae live furever, that's whit Ah keep tellin' her.'

'Ach, Auld Maggie's no that bad. Ah've had some really good blethers wi her. She kens a lot aboot folk aroon here and it's richt interessin'.'

Annie had gained a lot of useful background knowledge from these 'blethers' with Old Maggie Cruikshanks, stuff that might well come in handy in the future, and this had somewhat made up for her disappointment at being unable to ferret out any up-to-date material in the house.

'That's richt,' Senga recalled, 'Ye've been lookin' after the auld yin tae let Kate oot noo an then. It's guid o' ye, Annie, an it must be doin' the lassie guid. Maybe that's why she's lookin' better. Mind, Ah cannae think whaur she goes, on her own. Ah've seen her catching a bus a couple o' times, dressed up real smart... Ach, weel, that's her bizness an we're a' jist glad she's gettin' a wee while aff and it's doin' her sae much guid, are we no?'

Annie sniffed disparagingly. Senga, like all the women, could enjoy hearing a piece of gossip but, *un*like most of them, she rarely remembered it and almost never passed it on. She had, in Annie's opinion, an unhelpful tendency to think the best of people and feel

117

they had a right to a private life. As Kate's neighbour and friend, she could have been ideally placed to be an informant but Annie knew there would be no good trying to recruit her.

'Fur heaven's sake, leave they threads,' she said irritably, as Senga began ineffectually to try and restore some order to the muddle of colours and shades. 'Ah'll dae it masel when the shop's quiet.'

'Weel… if ye're sure.' Senga recoiled, puzzled by Annie's sharp tone, and applied herself to searching for her purse which had, as usual, worked its way to the bottom of her bulging handbag.

'Aye, Ah'm sure. Hae a do'nut.' Annie relented. Senga *was* one of her best customers. She held out the bag generously.

'Weel, Ah had lost a hale half-pound last nicht at the slimming class so Ah think Ah deserve a treat,' beamed Senga. The two munched happily as the sale was concluded.

Annie was absorbed in the task of re-sorting the embroidery drawer, creating a spectrum from pastel to deep in each colour, when the shop door bell tinkled. She did not immediately look up. When she did, it was to see Jeannie regarding her intently and with some amazement.

'It's yersel, Jeannie,' Annie greeted her. 'Whit are ye lookin' sae dumfoonered aboot? Ye've surely seen embroidery threads afore?'

Jeannie stared at the threads and at the paper bag, now empty, that lay on the counter beside them. The bag bore the legend *Aggie's Bakery: A Good Roll Does Satisfy.*

She licked her lips and twitched her nose. Surely she hadn't misjudged Bob for once? Could he possibly have been telling the truth about Aggie? Was she really going to embroidery classes in the Methodist Church? If so, why? And why had she clearly been singing at herself in the mirror and sprucing herself up so much? And taking a box of cakes with her? It was too much of a co-incidence, surely, that bag and that drawer of threads sitting together on Annie's counter? *Wis Aggie in here buyin' threads and brocht a bag of stuff in for Annie at the same time?*

Jeannie frequently made herself, as well as everyone else, dizzy with her lists of questions.

Truth to tell, she was sorely in need of a diversion. There had been very bad news yesterday. Bob had come home from the pub at dinner-time yesterday with a long tale about Graham, the new manager, the very lad she was pinning her hopes on for progress in the WW investigation.

118

There had been a new man behind the bar, reported Bob, an older lad. Graham's granny had indeed died and he was still in Dundee and likely to be for some time. The temporary manager, drafted in by the brewery, knew Graham well and was pleased to be the centre of attention as he explained it all.

Graham, it transpired, had been orphaned when a young lad, his mother having died in childbirth, along with the infant, and his father having succumbed to TB a couple of years later. Granny, a First World War widow, had taken over and become mother to the boy. Graham and Granny had been all-in-all to each other for the last twenty-five years, the rest of the family having either emigrated to New World countries, defected to England or been killed in the Second World War.

So Graham, as well as dealing with his grief, now found himself the main man in the situation, organising the funeral, clearing the house and arranging its sale. Granny had inherited a former shepherd's cottage in the Carse of Gowrie from her father and had moved there with Graham during the war, thinking it safer than staying in the city of Dundee, and the two had stayed on there after the bombs stopped.

'So he's no comin' hame fur a while, Ah'm afraid,' Bob had sympathised, knowing how much Jeannie was looking forward to his return. 'The brewery have gien him 'compassionate leave'.'

'Bloody hell,' Jeannie mourned, 'he'll likely have forgotten a' he had tae tell us onyway by then wi his heid fu o' grannies and funerals and hooses.'

'If he *dis* cam' back at a',' Bob rubbed salt in the wound. 'Some o' the men wis sayin' he micht decide jist tae stay in the Carse in the wee cottage. It'll be his noo. An it's his…his…' He struggled to remember the phrase that had been rippling around the pub '…it's his *childhood hame.*'

'Whit a load o' tripe,' Jeanie spat, venting her disappointment. 'Whit daftie cam' oot wi that?'

'It wis Johnnie Cruikshanks himself,' Bob was stung by her dismissal of his report. 'He's nae daftie.'

'Whit wis high-an-michty Cruikshanks doin' slummin' it in the pub wi you lot?'

'Ach, Johnnie's a' richt. He'd been at ane o' they meetin's that the managers pass the time wi – in Leven, Ah think – and he got back

119

a wee bittie early fur his denner. So he cried intae the pub fur a quick pint.'

Johnnie's observation about Graham's inheritance, and the choice he might make about it, had been taken up by the other men and the phrase, *childhood hame*, had been passed around with nods of understanding, despite big Eck's ill-natured, mincing caricature of it and his rider, 'Sentimental shite!'

Jeannie and Bob had eaten in glum silence. Casting around for a way to brighten her mood, Bob remembered her preoccupation with Aggie a few days ago. 'Ah'll hae a word wi Eck, darlin', and see if he kens whit Aggie is up tae, if ye like.'

'Ah thocht ye said she wis gaein tae embroidery classes?' Jeannie was suspicious. Bob, who was clearly not cut out for a life of crime and subterfuge and had completely forgotten his spur-of-the-moment fabrication, subsided, blustering and blushing under her scathing eye. Once again, he had been glad to escape at Eck's knock.

Now Jeannie was more than ready for the heady scent of breakthrough. 'Has Aggie been in here the day?' she demanded.

Annie carried on sorting the threads. Obviously Jeannie was in for a blether and not to buy so she felt justified in doing so. 'Aye, she wis in a wee while ago and brocht ma do'nuts ower at the same time, saved me haein tae close up and go fur them masel.'

Jeannie leaned forward, excited, and placed her small, white hand on Annie's large, red one, gaining Annie's full attention as she asked: 'An did ye get a good sale oot o' her?'

'Weel…' Annie said, considering, 'no sae much the day but she wis askin' me tae maybe try an get a few things fur her.'

Aggie had indeed been exploring the possibility of getting the clothes she would require for the big day. The ladies in the choir were all to be wearing navy blue pleated skirts and white blouses with frilled collars. Aggie possessed only one very old navy skirt and, although not renowned for her sartorial savvy, she did realise it would not cut the mustard for such an occasion and in such company. Blouses with frilled collars had never been her scene and she had briefly contemplated asking Kate for a loan of some such garment from her extensive wardrobe but had dismissed the idea at once – too close to home and, of course, too large for Aggie's meagre chest.

Nothing in the shop today had fitted the bill but Aggie had assured Annie that she would not be needing the new clothes till the end of the year. 'Ah've jist ta'en a real fancy fur an ootfit like that for

Hogmanay this year,' she had explained to Annie. 'Ah saw it on a wumman in a magazine an Ah thocht she looked smashin'.'

Annie had promised to see if she could procure the desired garments. 'Ah'll be puttin' ma Christmas order in soon tae ma clothes supplier. Ah'll see what Ah can dae.'

'Weel, weel,' she had thought, *'Aggie takin' an interest in claes. Wonders will never cease! The end o' rationin' must be goin' tae her heid.'*

'Is she wantin' ye tae order much?' Jeannie demanded excitedly. She could hardly believe her luck. This was really being in the right place at the right time.

'There was jist the twa things she mentioned the day but she said she micht need ither stuff nearer the time.' Annie replied absently; she had returned to her thread-sorting task.

'Time? Whit time? Whit did she mean?'

The shop door opened with a loud trill and a woman struggled in with a small, thumb-sucking child in a folding pram. The door's bell startled the child who woke and began to scream.

'Geez, Annie, can ye no dae somethin' aboot the bloody racket that door maks?' yelled the mother over the child's screams as she tried to calm her frightened toddler.

Clearly no further progress could be expected. Jeannie left them all to it and wandered thoughtfully in the direction of the bakery.

'That's six pies an a wee loaf: one-an-eleven-pence,' said Aggie. She took the florin the woman gave her and returned the penny change quickly. The shop was queued out the door and reverberated to the noise of the waiting women's chatter. Jeannie squeezed into the shop with some difficulty and fell easily into conversation with Nellie, one of her neighbours from the cul-de-sac.

Time passed; Aggie's store of teabread and tarts diminished; the women blethered; the queue moved slowly. Jeannie had attained third place in the queue when Nellie who was in front of her suddenly dived into her shopping basket and began checking the contents of her well-worn purse.

'The bugger's been at it again!' she announced to an unsurprised audience. ' A' he thinks aboot is getting himsel beer-money and his wife an bairns can starve for a' he cares.'

121

The queue's sympathetic murmur concurred with this assessment of Nellie's man's character and there were a few half-hearted offers of a short-term loan which Nellie regretfully declined knowing she would never be able to repay it and being already in enough debt as a result of her husband's inability to see beyond his next visit to the pub.

She stomped tearfully out and Jeannie realised with a start that the woman now in front of her being served was none other than Kate. Her frustrations over the stalemate in that particular investigation resurfaced, momentarily eclipsing her preoccupation with the Aggie mystery. She leaned forward a little and tuned in her ear.

Kate's business was being conducted briskly, partly because Aggie was feeling the pressure of the long queue, partly because sisterly small-talk had never really been much of a feature of this relationship.

'Sorry aboot the steak-and-kidney pie, Katy,' Aggie was saying as she finished toting up on a paper bag that was already covered in scribbled sums. 'That's twa-an-three, hen, thanks.' Then, as she handed Kate her three-pence change off the half-a-crown, 'Maybe ye'll get ane at the butcher's van later the day. We dinnae half miss Mr Smillie's shop. Ye hivnae heard if he's comin' back, hiv ye? Ah heard he wis near at death's door… Haivens, Katy, watch whit ye're daein! Tak yer time. Ye near knocked Jeannie ower.'

At the mention of the much-missed butcher, Kate had snatched her change and whirled round to rush out of the shop.

'That'll be her awa, then,' remarked Aggie drily. 'Sometimes, ye hiv tae wunner aboot that lassie. Ye niver ken whit's goin' on in her heid.'

'Interessin', very interessin',' thought Jeannie. She remembered Annie's report of Kate's reaction when the butcher's name had been mentioned: *near choked tae death on a wee crumb o' apple tart.* Was it possible that her story-writing speculations were nearer the mark than she had ever seriously considered? Could Kate possibly be having - Jeannie rolled the glamorous word round in her mind deliciously - an *affair* with the convalescent butcher in Windygates?

'Are ye buying onythin' or no, Jeannie?' demanded a harassed Aggie. 'Ah dinnae hae time fur chewing the fat the day, if that's a' ye're after.'

Jeannie started out of her reverie. 'Sorry, Aggie, Ah jist had ither things on ma mind fur a wee moment there. Ah'll tak fower cream cookies an a pan loaf.'

She did not forget to scrutinise Aggie for signs of a new-found passion for embroidery (whatever those were likely to be) but her previously strongly focused attention on Aggie was now diluted by intense revival of interest in Kate.

As she walked home, she dwelt for the hundredth time upon the bad luck that had - for the moment at least - frustrated the outcome of her Kate-stalking strategy. *Did the laddie's auld granny hae tae dee richt noo?* She railed inwardly, cursing fate.

She was almost home when an altogether novel thought suddenly put a new expression on her sharp little face. If she could tail Aggie so successfully, what was to stop her having a go with Kate? *Tricky stuff, though, nae lampposts or air-raid shelters tae hide behind on a bus.*

Clearly this would require some careful planning. She was so intent in her own thoughts as she prepared the cabbage and ham – 'bubble-and-squeak' – for their midday dinner that she did not hear Bob coming in from the pub and screeched as his big, fleshy fingers closed in a sudden hearty pinch of her left buttock.

'They're at it again,' thought Nellie-across-the-road wistfully as she scraped the mould off an elderly crust of bread then ran it under the tap and set it on the hearth to steam in an attempt to make it seem fresh. 'God kens hoo Jeannie dis it, keepin' him sae keen, at her age.'

Jeannie could hardly shove Bob out the door fast enough. 'Dinnae keep Eck waitin' ony mair.' She handed him his piece-tin and opened the front door.

Eck's dry, sneering cough was not lost on her as Bob leaned down for his usual farewell kiss. The moment the door was shut behind them, she raced upstairs, for once in her housewifely life, leaving the dirty dishes to wait till later.

Once upstairs, she dived under the bed and pulled out an old shopping bag, emptying its contents on to the candlewick bedspread. She surveyed them quickly: a thirties-style hat and coat, both dove grey; a small pair of rather thick-lens spectacles; a prim, black leather handbag with sturdy matching shoes. An old lady's outfit, quite a stylish one, but trapped in a sartorial time warp.

Would it be enough? It had looked quite convincing yesterday when she had had a trying-on session after bearing her spoils home from her father-in-law's house. Old Jasper, Bob's father, had been somewhat mystified when she had declared her intention of giving his little house a bit of a 'tidy-out'.

'Nae need fur that, lass,' he had protested from his chair by the fire where he spent his quiet, housebound, contented days. He had removed the ever-present pipe from his mouth long enough to elucidate: 'The home help's comin' the morn. She sees tae a'thing.'

But Jeannie had persisted, explaining that she felt that some of his cupboards and drawers needed clearing out, that she had meant to do it at spring cleaning time but hadn't got around to it.

Jasper had shrugged and gone back to dozing over the racing pages of the paper, mulling over a bet he was considering putting on – his next door neighbour was a man of the turf and understood the old man's need for a regular flutter so he called in on a daily basis to collect the modest bets and even occasionally, if luck had been a lady, to hand over winnings. Jasper listened avidly to his crackling old wireless to hear how his 'fillies' were doing and always checked the newspaper as well for results so there was no chance of anyone making any sort of 'skin' off him.

Half-an-hour of searching had given her what she needed and she had laid her late mother-in-law's old shopping bag, containing the results of her search, out at the front door before coming back in to say cheerio to her father-in-law. But he had been fast asleep, the newspaper over his face fluttering gently with each breath, the wireless softly intoning horse-racing results on the shelf beside him.

Jeannie had taken a small notebook from the shelf, torn off the top three pages, which were covered in horses' names, race times and bookies'odds, and had written in heavy dark pencil: *Will come tomorrow in the morning instead. Got something must do in afternoon.* That would be enough for him: he was the least inquisitive or intrusive of men.

Then she had checked that the small cottage pie she had brought him for his supper had a tea-towel over it to keep out dust or flies and that he had enough milk for his porridge in the morning in the cold box outside the kitchen window, noting with a smile the almost military neatness of the tiny scullery. *God bless the auld soul, he dis awfy weel.* Jeannie was fond of her father-in-law and was glad he had outlived his domineering wife to enjoy these years of complacent idleness, without the need to conceal his few simple pleasures or grovel repentantly when they were discovered.

'It wis a sad thing when a man that worked sae hard couldnae be boss in his ain hoose,' she had reflected as she walked home, quite unconscious of any ironic relevance to her own marriage.

Now she hastily donned the disguise, pulling the hat well down over her head and adding a scarf to the neck of the coat to hide most of her chin. The face and figure which confronted her in the wardrobe mirror gave her a strange, walking-over-my-grave sensation and, for a moment, she could almost hear her mother-in-law's shrewish voice and feel again her own resentment of Bob's submissiveness to his mother's interfering comments and persistent commands which had followed him into his married life.

Ella Gilhooley had resisted until the day she had died, five years ago, being relegated to second place in Bob's allegiance. In some ways, the pattern that Ella had set had made it easier for Jeannie to establish her own power over Bob since he knew no other role or status in a relationship with a woman and readily accepted it. In an ideal world, he would have simply swapped the mother's totalitarian rule for the wife's. It should have been a case of: *the queen is dead, long live the queen.* Unfortunately for all three of them, the queen did not know she was dead and simply refused to lie down.

Jeannie and Ella had declared war, with hapless Bob the disputed territory, and the skirmishes, border raids and occasional all-out battles had quickly become the warp and woof of their daily lives. Though neither of them would ever have voiced such a thought, Ella's sudden death had come as a relief to Bob and Jeannie – *and* to Jasper who had had to watch, listen and sympathise with all three parties, though only ever privately with each one. Indeed he thought, looking back on those sixteen years between Bob's marriage and his wife's death, that listening and shaking his head sadly had constituted pretty well *all* his part in conversations with his wife, his son and his daughter-in-law.

The unwelcome memories ran through Jeannie's head as she let herself out of her front gate and hurried up the avenue towards the bus stop. The old shoes though seldom worn - having been Ella's best for high days, holidays and Hogmanays - were rather large for her and made it difficult to establish an effective walking pace. As soon as she

125

got into a decent stride, one of her feet would almost walk out of its shoe and the thick, stacked heel would drop noisily on to the pavement. She had not thought to practice moving about in the outfit and she cursed freely as she clacked up the road. *Áh soond like a bairn playin' dressy-ups wi her mither's shoes.*

She glanced anxiously at the net-curtained windows in the street, hoping that the noise she was making would not cause them to twitch. She forced herself to walk more slowly and control the errant footwear. There was no sign of the bus yet: she had time. A wide-eyed-innocent word with Annie that morning had reassured her that Kate was planning another of her trips and there was only one bus each hour to Windygates.

It was time to progress the WW investigation.

CHAPTER SEVEN

KATE

It had been touch and go that morning on several counts: whether she would have enough clean, dry bed linen for yet another change; whether she would get the food for Maggie's and Annie's dinner ready in time; whether she would get the house completely ready for Annie's critical, prying eyes; whether she would keep her temper with the merciless old moaner and resist retaliating verbally or even physically – it would have been so easy to exercise just a bit too much force when manoeuvering the old woman in and out of bed or make the water too hot or too cold when cleaning her scraggy old backside several times a day.

As she had hared about the house, harried not only by Maggie's demanding whine but also by fear of running out of time, a small nagging pain had begun to throb behind her eyes and now it had escalated into a full-blown headache. As the bus passed the top of Burns Avenue and began to coast to the bus-stop, she leaned back in her seat and closed her hot, teary eyes.

Her head felt twice its usual weight and size and she longed to lay it down on a cool pillow and rest. The pain behind her eyes had spread and now her jaw and gums ached too; she could feel the back of her neck beginning to get in on the act as well.

Whit's wrang wi me? Ah should've ta'en an aspirin afore Ah cam' oot. Ah meant tae… It wis sich a beltin' rush tae get a'thing ready. Nae wunner ma heid's like tae blow aff. Maybe, if Ah jist hae a wee sleep the noo…

She closed her eyes thankfully, turning her head away from the nearby door of the bus and letting her aching forehead rest against the cool window. She was vaguely aware of someone getting on and heard the conductor moving up the bus behind the new passenger but she did not open her eyes to see the prim elderly lady in her dated clothes pass up the aisle and take her seat four rows behind.

It was the dog-dream again but this time not only were the teeth snapping and tearing. The animal was jumping up, its big, heavy paws on her shoulders, pushing her, rocking her…

'That's us at the terminus, hen.' The burly conductor was shaking her with increasing urgency that spoke of concern.

Over the past weeks he had become used to seeing this attractive, well-dressed lady every Wednesday afternoon and, although she never took the bait to engage in chit-chat as he liked to do with his regulars, he still felt a professional protectiveness towards her.

'That's us at Ain'ster.'

Kate surfaced slowly from the heavy, fevered sleep into which she had sunk more and more deeply as the bus had lurched through the string of villages. She stared fuzzily out the window. She could see a large harbour bustling with fishing boats and fishing business. She could see slanting rain rippling across large puddles, people hurrying with collars turned up and hats pulled down, umbrellas waving out of control and turning inside out in the buffeting wind.

The place was not completely unfamiliar to her: she groped for the memory… A summer fortnight before the war, she and Aggie with the four children in a boarding house near the sea, their men folk coming down at the weekend. Fish suppers sitting on the harbour wall, crab-hunting in shallow pools, cliff-top walks with the children chasing each other in and out of an old ruined tower. She drifted…

'Ye'll hae tae get aff, Ah'm afraid. Ye cannae stay here.' The conductor's courtesy was tinged with impatience now. He was looking forward to a cup of tea and a fag in the staff canteen before his next journey and this lady customer was eating into precious break-time.

He put his hand firmly under her elbow and began to exert some upward pressure. 'Come on.' He used his firm, no-nonsense voice, perfected by years of dealing with late night drunks.

Kate allowed herself to be helped to her feet. She leaned heavily on his arm as he led her down the aisle and almost lifted her bodily off the platform and down on to the pavement. When he finally removed all support, she swayed and he hastily took her arm and attached it to a nearby railing. He was beginning to wonder if she had been drinking but there was no smell of alcohol and she had seemed quite normal, if a little flustered, when she had first come on the bus at her usual stop.

'Go an get yersel oot o' the rain,' he advised her, pointing to a tearoom across the road. 'Ye look like ye could use a wee cup o' tea.'

As he hurried off to the canteen, he reflected that she had only had a ticket to Windygates but had stayed on to Anstruther, more than half-hour's journey further.

'Funny,' he mused. *'That wis the same wi that ither wee wumman, the funny auld ane wi the granny-mutchy hat.'* But *she* had primly approached him as she left the bus and offered to pay the difference, muttering something about having changed her mind.

The lady he had just manhandled off the bus had had almost twenty miles free ride. *Ach weel, it's no comin' oot o' ma pocket,* he concluded as he stood in the canteen queue, *it's comin' aff a broad back.* He felt confident that this one little discrepancy would not ruin his employers.

Sheltering in a shop doorway next to the tearoom, Jeannie was in a quandary.

Whit the hell is she doin'? had been the refrain in her head for the past forty minutes, ever since the bus had left Windygates.

She had been preparing herself to alight, noting with satisfaction that a large, fat man two rows in front was doing likewise. She had been all ready to slip discreetly in behind him and had been already appraising the street for good camouflage opportunities as the bus slowed towards the bus shelter.

But Kate had not moved; the fat man had risen and exited; Jeannie had hesitated on the edge of her seat, expecting Kate to suddenly start up, realise where she was and hurry out of the bus. The bus had waited for an agonising two minutes, during which Jeannie had strained like a greyhound in the traps, but Kate had not moved and they had journeyed on.

At each of the villages where the bus had stopped – Kennoway, Ceres, Pitscottie, Largoward, Crail - Jeannie's greyhound routine had been repeated. By the time the terminus at Anstruther was reached, she was quite baffled. For one thing she had not thought beyond Windygates, partly because her mind had been for so long fixated on the idea of the Smillie-the-butcher-connection, partly because the bus she had boarded had clearly proclaimed *Windygates* on its front as its destination. But it had continued gaily on and Kate with it.

She watched the troublesome bus now pull out of its stance in the small terminus and turn towards its next starting point. A new conductor got on and applied himself to changing the destination window but she caught a glimpse of the old one just before it changed: *Windygates* and *Anstruther*: that was it – because Windygates was a junction where you could change and catch buses to other places all over Fife, it had the star billing; Anstruther had to take second place. Neither she nor Aggie had noticed this when looking at it.

Jeannie recalled what Aggie had told her back at the very beginning when the Kate story had first broken. There was Kate's own story - something about that wee fishing place, St Monans, an old school friend recently widowed.

Jeannie screwed up her face as she tried to visualise the map of Fife. She was no traveller and the network of bus routes that had sprung up since wartime restrictions on fuel had been lifted were a mystery to her. This bus had not taken a coastal route but, perhaps there would be another one that *would* go from here along the coast to St Monans; maybe changing at Anstruther was a quite legitimate way to go to St Monans from Methil? But Kate had said she changed at *Windygates,* hadn't she? Indeed, the very mention of the word seemed to make her distinctly twitchy if both Annie and Aggie's accounts were to be believed. There had been no talk of Anstruther at all. Had Kate been putting up a very clever smokescreen, throwing them all off the scent with talk of Windygates when Anstruther was the key? But what was she going to do here, for heaven's sake? If she *was* simply changing to go to visit this bereaved old pal, why had she not been truthful and described her journey accurately?

As she indulged herself in a particularly tortuous string of questions, she observed Kate being assisted off the bus and watched as Kate continued to stand hanging on to the railing, not moving. The rain was heavier than ever and Kate's uncovered hair was plastered to her head in moments. Her head was bowed and long, sodden strands drooped, covering her face. A few people glanced curiously at her as they scurried past but mainly their concern was to get themselves out of the downpour as fast as possible.

Minutes passed; the rain did not lessen; the street became deserted; people sheltered in shops, doorways and closes; the luckier ones hurried to nearby homes. Kate did not move from her railing and Jeannie throbbed with indecision and impatience.

She began to wonder what on earth she, sensible Jeannie Gilhooley, was doing, dressed up like a dog's dinner with shoes that she could barely walk in, stranded in this strange place in such hellish weather. She had envisaged herself nimbly slipping off the bus at

Windygates, which she *had* been to before as it was only a few miles from Methil, and following a briskly walking, blissfully unaware Kate to some exciting rendezvous with the butcher. Perhaps a tearoom or a cinema, maybe a park if the weather stayed fair. That would have been good, plenty of bushes to hide behind. She had allowed her ever-vivid imagination to picture Kate and her illicit lover murmuring sweet nothings to each other on a park bench whilst she, Jeannie, was concealed in a bush behind them, hearing every word. Delicious!

But it had all gone horribly wrong and now Jeannie felt as if she had gone into a cinema to see one picture and found herself watching another completely different one, not at all to her taste. As she watched Kate crouching helplessly over the railing, she began to understand that the sleuth-detective role she had cast herself in that afternoon was not to be the one she would play after all.

That Kate was in trouble, in need of help, was plain. As the last few 'droukit' residents of *Ain'ster* melted away into their various refuges, it was as if a cold, white light came on in the little bus-terminus square, mercilessly illuminating the woman huddled over the railing in the relentless, soaking rain. Jeannie felt as if a taut wire stretched between her and Kate, as if there was no-one else in the world at that moment, or as if they were two characters on a stage with the audience holding its breath to see what would happen.

There's somethin' awfy wrang wi her. Ah'll hae tae go an help her. Ah cannae jist leave her tae strangers, no that they're botherin' wi her onyway. They're a' too busy savin' their ain skins. Some place this! Jeannie consigned the town of Anstruther and its residents to a place fit only for rats. *But, if she sees me close up, she'll ken it's me. Whit am Ah goin' tae say aboot this get-up Ah'm in. An she maybe saw me on the bus…*

As Jeannie wrestled with her conscience, a bus drew up invitingly, a bus that would take her home and out of this ridiculous, desperately uncomfortable situation. *And* her cover would not be blown; her investigation could proceed another day – though definitely with other shoes on. She could leave Kate to her fate; she could put the investigation first; maintain her position in the community as gossip queen.

Then, unbidden, a picture suddenly came into Jeannie's mind of a very different scenario, a very different Jeannie. Rather than the inquisitive, ruthless gossip she was known and feared as, she saw herself as someone people confided in and sought support from. She would know just as much as ever – indeed more – about the private lives of her neighbours, there would be as much or even more material for her secret stories, but instead of using what she learned to sow misery and encourage scandal-mongering, she would act as trusted listener and good friend. She would actually be invited to blethering sessions instead of having to elbow her way in to them, women would not stop talking when they saw her coming, she would be greeted with open friendly smiles rather than either nervous wariness or lip-smacking demands for tittle-tattle.

It was not a role she had ever considered or been attracted to but, as she stood irresolute in the damp doorway in this strange place, she was aware of a defining moment in her life. A kind of crossroads.

A particularly fierce gust of bitterly cold wind swept round the square and the rain intensified, battering pavements and puddles. Kate sagged lower, her head almost touching the railing but still she did not move.

'Ach, sod it!' Jeannie exclaimed aloud, much to the amazement of a portly elderly gentleman who had also chosen this doorway for shelter. He was even further surprised when the little old lady snatched off her little old lady's hat and shook out a shiny skein of long dark hair. She removed the spectacles, searched in her large handbag for the small umbrella she was never without, shook it out and marched across the square. The incessant drumming of the rain almost masked the loud click-clacking of her heels.

The tearoom was crowded. The normally modest pace of mid-afternoon business had been greatly accelerated by refugees from the inclement weather. As Jeannie entered with Kate tottering and leaning heavily on her arm, a harassed waitress rushed past them, calling discouragingly, 'There's a queue. Ye'll hae tae wait fur a table. We're rushed aff oor feet.'

Jeannie ignored her, dragged Kate towards a nearby table and accosted two commercial travellers who were trying, somewhat unsuccessfully in the noise generated by so many disgruntled, wet people, to have their usual weekly business meeting at their usual table.

'Excuse me,' she spoke formally but firmly. 'This lady has been ta'en quite ill. She must hae a seat at once.'

She looked meaningfully at the paraphernalia of their business discussion spread out on the table. After one glance at the sweating, swooning Kate, the men rose quickly and began sweeping the important-looking papers into important-looking brief cases.

Jeannie at once pushed Kate into one of their chairs. Kate's sodden, thick woollen coat made an audible squelching noise as she subsided heavily on to the chair. The men exchanged amused grins which said: *Some lady! Farting like that in public!*

Jeannie took Kate's handbag off her arm, undid her coat buttons and, moving behind her, pulled the coat off Kate's shoulders.

'That's better,' she spoke as if to a child. 'Now we'll gie yer hair a wee rub.' She took her handkerchief and did the best she could, although the small scrap of material was scarcely adequate for the masses of dripping hair tumbling around Kate's blotched face.

'Hot tea and some scones is whit we're needin',' she pronounced, signaling to the waitress, who looked briefly surprised to see them thus ensconced but was much too busy to care about or deal with such outrageous queue-jumping.

Kate sat slumped in her chair, breathing heavily, noisily.

'If she wisnae wide awake, Ah'd say she wis snorin'. Her chest sounds awfy bad. She cannae be weel at a',' thought Jeannie.

She raked once more in the large handbag. 'Tak these twa aspirin, hen,' she advised, placing two little white pills on Kate's plate beside her scone. 'An drink up yer tea. Get yersel warmed up.'

Then, as Kate began slowly to comply, her hand shaking so much the tea splashed onto the bunched-up coat round her waist, 'Now then, Kate Cruikshanks, whit's goin' on? Whit are ye doin' here on yer own? Whit...?' She suddenly remembered her crossroads moment in the shop doorway and the new Jeannie Gilhooley that had been invented there and then.

She stopped. 'Ach, never mind. Dinnae mind me. Ah'm an auld gossip sometimes, Ah ken, but...'

She met Kate's bleary eye and saw horrified recognition dawn in it. 'No, sit doon, fur haiven's sake...'

Kate was attempting to disentangle herself from the confines of the wet coat round her waist and to rise from her chair.

'Ye're no fit tae be goin' onywhere on yer own. Dinnae fash yersel. Ah'll mind my ain bizness.'

Jeannie stopped, struck quite dumb by the sound of this unprecedented declaration from her lips and Kate, sinking defeated back into the wet coat, stared at her. For the first time since she had looked up from her railing and seen Jeannie, she spoke, the voice rasping in her throat.

'Whit are ye doin' here? Can ye no leave me alane? Whit are ye wearin' they auld-wifey claes and clacketty shoes fur? Whaur the hell are we? Whit am Ah doin' here masel? Ah should be in Windygates. This wis the day we were goin' tae get it a' arranged. Angus'll be wonderin' whit the hell's happened tae me. We'll no be able tae dae it an it's took weeks tae set it up. God! If ma heid would jist stop bangin'…'

She tailed off and, laying the offending head down on the table among the scones and jam, began to sob.

'An Ah thocht Ah wis the ane wi a' the questions,' thought Jeannie.

Her mind raced as she processed Kate's indiscreet ramblings. Angus would be the bold Mr Smillie himself, for sure – she had been right all along! But what on earth was it they had been setting up and what was it they were going to arrange? Could Kate be going to *elope* with him?

This would be just the best gossip scoop ever. Annie and Aggie would be amazed and her rightful place as feared queen in the community would be assured. Then she remembered! *Ach, Ah've done it again. Ah'm nae much good at this.*

She leaned across the table and touched Kate's bowed head. 'Dinnae greet, lassie,' she said. 'Whitever's wrang we can maybe sort it oot. An Ah'll no breathe a word tae a soul, Ah promise.'

Kate lifted her head and looked disbelievingly at Jeannie. 'Dinnae try tae kid me, Jeannie Gilhooley. Ah dinnae ken hoo ye got here or wha telt ye aboot me but Ah ken fine whit ye're goin' tae dae next. Ye'll be wagging that wicked tongue o' yours a' ower Fife jist as soon as ye get hame and get they ridiculous claes aff.'

Jeannie winced. She saw herself, in that moment, as others saw her and she heard the disgust and dislike in Kate's hoarse, uneven voice.

'Naw, ye're wrang, Kate,' she said pleadingly.' Ah've…Ah've…' she sought for words to describe her epiphany. 'Ah've turned ower a new leaf. Aye, that's it.' She liked the phrase and felt all the better for it. 'That's it! Turned ower a new leaf!'

An hour later, during which Kate had been coaxed out of the wet coat altogether, her hair had dried to a mass of tangled curls, the aspirin had begun to take beneficial effect and another round of tea and scones had been consumed, the women were still talking together over the teacups.

From a place of hesitant suspicion, Kate had gradually been coaxed to belief in Jeannie's new role as trustworthy confidante and the relief she felt at being able to share what had been going on and what was being planned was immense.

Jeannie was thrilled, well in love with her new image, excited to be part of Kate's plans, only too glad to offer her help and promise her silence.

Angus Smillie thought that if he stared out the bay window any longer and any harder he would go blind. The two hours since Kate should have been here had dragged by. He had passed from mild irritation (the dainty, crustless date sandwiches he had so lovingly prepared had begun to curl at the edges) to disappointed bewilderment and finally to real anxiety.

Something's happened to her. There's somethin' wrong. An today was the day. We've finally got it a' organised. We cannae wait any longer or it'll be too late...

As the clock ticked unforgivingly on towards three-thirty, he began to panic. He looked at the small table beside the window, at the papers spread out on it, at the large black telephone that stood in the midst of them.

What am I goin' to do if she hasnae come by the time it rings? Will I just go ahead an dae it a' masel? Is that what she'd want? Or has she changed her mind? Is that why she's no here?

She had never been late. Regularly now for - what was it? - eight or nine weeks she had arrived about half-past-one and stayed till nearly four o'clock. There had never been so much as a mention of what it would mean if she didn't come.

He thought now that there were a hundred things that might intrude on their precious Wednesday afternoons: the old woman could be taken ill, or Kate herself, or her husband; there could be any kind of unforeseen emergency in the home or family that made it impossible for her to escape. Maybe that woman, Annie-from-the-draper's-shop, had not been able to oblige today, had let Kate down at the last minute. But they had never discussed these contingencies, blithely parting each time with a jaunty 'See ye next week!'

135

Angus had sensed and now he acknowledged openly to himself how much these weekly visits had come to mean to him. His convalescence was going wonderfully well. The snooty-nosed consultant had expressed as near to pleasure as he permitted himself at Angus's last check-up.

'You're looking very well, Mr Smillie.' His dry voice had rustled in a way that had made Angus want to clear his throat for him. 'In fact...' the consultant had cast his mind back to the overweight, pale-faced, frightened man he had first seen last spring and compared that image with the slimmer, bright-eyed, confident person sitting in front of him '...in fact, you look like a new man! I think we can say the operation has been a great success and you should make a full recovery with no complications.' He had permitted himself a little self-congratulatory smirk.

Angus did not entirely share Mr Self-Important Simpson's view of the situation. Glad as he was that his body was well again, he knew it was not this fact alone that was putting the spring in his step which the consultant had noticed and claimed credit for.

Kate's visits had quickly become the highlight of his week and given him a reason for living. Without the daily imperative of a business to run, without other people in his house or his life, he could well have sunk into a depression compounded of physical weakness, self-pity and fear.

Kate's gentle, compassionate encouragement, her courage in her own extremely trying circumstances, her modest acceptance of her lot, her remarkable optimism, her cheery wit – all these had worked a magic on his drooping spirit from that first day of her surprising visit to him in hospital.

From simply admiring and cheekily fancying her from a distance, he had come to know and appreciate the real woman. That he had been able, in turn, to help *her* was a source of great satisfaction to him and their tentative relationship had blossomed into friendship. What would become of this friendship, how, when or where it would end – or develop – he did not allow himself to think. He was still living in the day-to-day, self-centred limbo of convalescence.

True, he *had* begun to think about returning to the real world. A gentle phased return to work was being advised with no heavy lifting yet for several months and no getting over-tired. He was ahead of them here for he had already lined up an assistant for his return to the shop.

Terry, the young lad who had been running the butcher's van to Methil from a shop in Kirkcaldy during his long absence, had dropped in to see him soon after his return home from hospital and the two had struck up an easy, productive relationship. Terry told him stories about the customers and Angus filled in useful background knowledge for him about them. The two now often shared a good laugh, born of their individual experiences of these very customers. It had kept Angus in touch with his working world and he had grown to like and trust the young man.

When he had suggested to Terry that he give up his job with the Kirkcaldy butcher and come and work for Smillie's once the shop opened again, the lad had jumped at the chance. A blind man could see the possibilities here, Terry thought excitedly. Angus Smillie was a bachelor with no close family: in twenty years' time, when he was ready to retire, he would have no-one to leave the business to. The faraway nephew and niece out in Australia were unlikely to be much of a threat. Terry took the long view, being a young man with his head screwed on.

'Aye, it should work well wi the pair o' us,' thought Angus now as he ruminated on his planned return after the New Year. *'It'll be grand to have some company and a young pair o' legs to do the runnin'.'*

The telephone shrilled, cutting into his thoughts, and he was brought back sharply to his present dilemma. *Oh my God! What should I do? If I dinnae go ahead wi it, it'll be too late…but what if Kate has changed her mind and didnae want me to?*

He stared at the screaming instrument, its clamour seeming to intensify with each ring. Unable to bear it any longer, he snatched up the heavy receiver and held it to his ear.

'I have your trans-Atlantic call, sir,' said a plummy female voice. 'I'm putting you through now.' He listened mesmerised to the series of clicks and crackles, imagining a wire running all the way from his sitting-room under the ocean. He took a deep breath as a man's voice came on the line.

It was all over in less than ten minutes. *'Just as well, you wouldnae believe what they charge ye for these calls. An there's a' the other money we'll need. The sooner I get back behind the counter and get making some more money the better,'* he thought, although he was comfortably aware that his healthy bank balance would easily survive this attack on it.

Nothin' I'd rather spend it on, though. She's that worth it, ma lovely Kate… He was happily drifting into one of the delightful sleepy fantasies that had been so much a feature of his convalescence when his doorbell shrilled. He leapt up in relief. *She's here at last. Wait till I tell her we've started arrangin' it!*

He was totally unprepared for and completely dumbfounded by the apparition that stood on his doormat. A funny little old lady… Well, not so old, maybe. She seemed to have long dark hair hanging wetly down her back. Angus peered incredulously in the dismal gloom. Wasn't there something strangely familiar about her?

'Good God!' His astonished exclamation echoed round the darkening garden. 'Is that Mrs Gilhooley? What in the name o' heaven are *you* doin' here?'

For the past half-an-hour, Annie had been looking fretfully and frequently out of Kate's darkening bay window. The *dreich* weather was hastening the end of the November afternoon.

Whaur the hell is she the day? She's aye hame by half-fower an it's gone a quarter-tae-five. The auld yin'll be wantin' her tea soon.

Then, at last, she spotted Kate alighting from the bus across the road. *Aboot bloody time! She's no half pushin' her luck…*

She watched as Kate began to make her way up to the crossroads. *Tak yer time, nae hurry hen, Ah've nothin' else tae dae but sit here fur the duration.*

Kate was walking very slowly, head down and – Annie's gaze sharpened incredulously – weaving a little from side to side. *She's no been at the bottle, for peety's sake? That's no whit she's been doin' these afternoons? Gettin' hersel blootered? She's surely no turnin' intae a secret alkie!*

Annie watched as Kate stood at the crossroads, hanging on to the lamppost, whilst the traffic cleared several times and crossing would have been quite safe. *It's an awfy disgrace. If high-falutin' Johnnie Cruikshanks kent his wife wis makin' sich a drunken spectacle o' hersel…an richt ootside the hoose!*

Annie was on the point of getting her coat to go down and fetch the disgraceful Kate when she saw her set out to cross the road. Then she wished even more that she had gone down earlier to help.

Having missed several golden opportunities to cross the road in perfect safety, Kate now set out to stumble her uneven way across just as a brewer's dray, loaded with full barrels, rounded the corner and headed towards her. At the same time, a couple of cyclists, two-abreast, chatting unconcernedly to each other, were coming the other way.

Annie saw all this from her anxious vantage point: *Holy Mary, Mither o' God! She'll be killed!* Rushing to the rescue was not in Annie's elephantine repertoire so she could only watch in horror as the drayman, yelling angrily, yanked the horse sharply into the middle of the road, causing it to pass within inches of the cyclists.

For a few moments, while net curtains twitched all over the street and passers-by stopped to stare in shock, the air was thick and blue with the drayman's angry shouts, the horse's startled whinnying and the cyclists' horrified cries.

Kate checked and stood for a moment as if unsure how to proceed, watching the furious drayman rein the horse to a halt and dismount to retrieve one of his barrels which had broken free and rolled off in the fracas. Annie had no trouble lip-reading what he shouted to the dithering Kate and blushed at such words, rarely uttered in a woman's presence. Kate, however, seemed untouched by the episode for she simply raised a placatory hand to the man and continued her jagged progress to the other side of a now thankfully empty road.

Annie breathed a sigh of relief when she saw her reach the gate and, after some fumbling, open the catch and let herself in.

Ah'll need tae try an sober her up afore Johnnie gets hame. An keep her awa frae the auld yin. If she sees her half-cut, there'll be hell tae pay!

There came the classic sounds of a homecoming drunk attempting to fit key in lock and, tutting disgustedly, Annie lumbered down the short, carpeted inside stair and yanked open the front door. She reeled painfully against the bottom edge of the wooden banister as Kate fell into her arms.

'In the name o' the wee man, Kate,' she gasped. 'For ony's sake, get yersel in here afore the hale street kens the state ye're in.'

She was panting as, with a huge effort, she steadied them both upright in the small square at the bottom of the stairs. Their unavoidable proximity told her one thing immediately, however: Kate was certainly not drunk. There was no smell or sign of alcohol about her. Kate was, in fact, fevered and extremely unwell. This instant

139

impression was confirmed as Annie helped Kate toil up the stairs and heard her labouring, rasping breath.

Annie's next two hours were not at all as she had imagined they would be: no cosy cup of tea with Kate, trying to pry some 'cuttings' from her; no wee luxury thank-you present; no easy stroll home to her own silent, empty house.

Instead she found herself: helping Kate out of her clothes and into bed, administering aspirin and hot toddy; throwing together sardines-on-toast for a demanding Maggie and then changing a sodden bed that was the old woman's dissatisfied revenge for this poor substitute for her usual cooked tea; explaining it all to a surprised Johnnie when he came in from work at half-past-six; and, finally, at Johnnie's request, calling in at the doctor's house on her way home to ask him to come and see Kate as soon as possible.

Annie was exhausted when she eventually reached her own home though she did have Johnnie's courteous and sincere expressions of gratitude ringing in her ears and that, she concluded, as she subsided in her favourite armchair with a mountain of cheesy scrambled egg, tomato ketchup and chips, was even nicer than Kate's glitzy wee presents.

Wait till Ah tell Jeannie! Or will Ah? Johnnie wis that nice tae me, shakin' ma hand, thankin' me. He widnae want me tae be blabbin'. Whit wis it he said, in that posh voice he has noo? 'I'm in your debt, Annie. Thank God we had someone so trustworthy on hand.'

She preened as she thoughtfully licked a large chip, savouring, not only the tomato sauce on it, but also the unaccustomed sensation of being important and appreciated at the centre of a drama rather than marginalised and predatory.

It had been quite a day for changed hearts and momentous decisions but the woman who had been the catalyst for them all was quite unaware of the important role she had played. As she lay in a deep, delirious sleep, she was equally unaware of Dr Kenny's pronouncement later that evening: 'Influenza with pleurisy, I'm afraid. She'll need care and rest for a while.'

Johnnie gloomily absorbed Jim Kenny's diagnosis as they shared a dram in the sitting-room after the doctor's examination of Kate.

'But she'll be all right?' he asked anxiously. 'Soon?'

140

He frowned, trying to make sense of the idea of Kate as someone needing, rather than giving, care.

'I mean… What are we goin' to do?' His eyes flicked to the closed sitting-room door but they both knew that his thoughts were going through it, down the lobby and into his mother's room.

Jim Kenny sighed. '*Here we go again,*' he thought. '*What is it with men like this?*'

He had become accustomed and now rather enjoyed tackling men whose openly brutal abusiveness towards their wives resulted in the women needing medical care. He had developed a tongue-lashing technique that made such bullies cringe. But men like Johnnie, who loved their wives and would never have dreamt of showing physical brutality to them, could sometimes behave in ways that had effects just as damaging. '*It's like a kind of blindness,*' he reflected.

He was briefly reminded of an episode twenty years ago or more – *who had it been, now?* – when a very loving husband had nearly killed his wife and their unborn twins just by too much 'love'.

'Mr Cruikshanks,' he spoke gently but very firmly. 'You have to understand the situation. Mrs Cruikshanks is quite ill and will be for at least a fortnight. She is also contagious and should be kept away from other people as much as possible, especially frail, elderly people.'

'But she was all right this mornin'. She's no been complainin'. She's been perfectly healthy. Surely she can get better quicker than that?' There was an edge of panicky pleading in Johnnie's voice.

'This is a serious strain of influenza and there are the added complications of the pleurisy.' Dr Jim was inflexible. 'It's not helped' - he moved in for the kill - 'by the fact that your wife is exhausted. So much heavy lifting, so much back-breaking work and so many broken nights…' He spread his hands expressively and delivered the *coup de grace*: 'Your wife is not a machine!'

'But, she never said anythin'!' burst out Johnnie. 'She's been fine up till now . . . I think…' He tailed off and Dr Jim pressed the advantage.

'Are you quite sure about that? Have you been listening to what she has been saying? Have you been aware of how she has been looking?'

An unwelcome memory flitted into Johnnie's head: Eck, after the union meeting a few weeks ago, saying - *what was it?* - '…yer ain wife… lookin' like a drudge these days, runnin' after that auld bitch… gettin' yer ain wiy, walkin' ower folk…'

141

He stared at his untouched whisky as if he saw in it a picture that was both startling and horrifying. When he finally raised his eyes, Jim Kenny saw with relief that there was no need to say any more.

Kate, unconscious in the small bedroom, muttering miserably through frightening, fever-filled dreams, was unaware that she had wrought yet another sea-change.

But it was one thing for Johnnie to acknowledge the situation; it was quite another for him to cope with it. Already, that evening, he had had one distasteful and embarrassing episode involving his mother and the commode and he knew another was probably looming soon.

Kate herself would need care to ensure she took the medicine Dr Kenny had left her and perhaps she too would need help to go to the bathroom. The sodden, smelly sheets Annie had kindly stripped off the old woman's bed were still soaking in the washing machine drum and he had no idea what to do with them or it. There would be the through-the-night calls and demands that normally he was only dimly aware of Kate attending to.

And what about the morning? How on earth was he to cope with an invalid and a demanding, incontinent old woman and still get to his office by eight o'clock? And who would look after Maggie during the day? And what about…?

Overwhelmed, he put his head in his hands and groaned. Jim Kenny downed his whisky and rose. He had always made a point of not getting entangled in the manifold difficulties that illness can cause in a family. His job was medical, directed at the sick patient, and he did it to the best of his ability. Advising on, or helping with, the arrangements, sacrifices and restructuring of lives that his diagnoses frequently led to, was - he had always considered - out of his arena. It had been, for him, the only way to survive in this community through the last thirty years.

He almost made good his escape, but Johnnie leapt to his feet and barred his way. 'Do ye ken anythin' about washing machines?' he demanded.

Just why Johnnie chose to home in on this one aspect of his many problems was never to be known. Perhaps it seemed like one rock face he could begin to scale when the others seemed too mountainous to contemplate. He could not have picked a better. Unbeknown to him, Jim Kenny made a hobby of exploring how machines work, keeping up to date with the latest inventions and endlessly fiddling with – and sometimes even mending – broken ones. He was never able to resist the opportunity to see how a machine worked or, even better, explain to someone else how it worked.

'Yes, indeed,' he said proudly. 'We have one at home.'

In fact, his wife never used it, preferring to leave the charwoman to her washing board, but Jim himself occasionally switched it on and washed a few things for the pleasure of observing it at work. He already had plans to send a detailed critique, with suggested improvements, to the manufacturers.

He caught Johnnie's eye and his drift. 'Oh, come on then,' he said, good-humouredly. 'You pour us another drink and I'll show you how to do your washing!'

There is nothing like working side-by-side in the companionable satisfaction of shared achievement to loosen tongues (and the third round of whiskies also helped). By the time the two men had mastered not only the washing machine but also the spin-drier, hung the sheets up on the kitchen pulley, emptied the machine and tidied up the kitchen, a sort-of-plan had been hatched that might just get them all through the next two weeks.

So great was Johnnie's relief that he was able to deal with his mother's bedtime needs with some equanimity and even gentleness, surprising her into a rare word of motherly pride.

'Ye're a good laddie. Yer father would've been proud o' ye.' Unfortunately, she was unable to resist adding: 'Even if ye did marry that silly bitch. What is *she* doin' takin' to her bed?'

By the time he had given Kate a hot drink, helped her to the bathroom, settled her down for the night with reassurances that everything was 'in hand, ma dear, in hand' and finally made up a bed for himself on the sitting-room couch, he was so tired that he could no longer remember what the damned plan was.

He dreamed he was chasing Kate and she kept falling down but, whenever he was almost upon her, she rose up and ran still further away. He had to keep running after her, she needed his help. But how could he help her if she would not let him catch her?

CHAPTER EIGHT

AGGIE

Aggie was singing, the pure notes of Handel's lovely aria filling the little shop and mingling with the wonderful aroma of fresh, warm bread. Outside the bitter, pre-dawn chill was icing the pavements and only in houses where the men were on early shift were there any lights to be seen.

Aggie loved this solitary hour in her little shop and never minded tumbling out of bed, even in pitch-dark winter mornings to open up for the early deliveries. The bakery van came about five and she always opened up before six to catch the early-shift men on their way to the pit. Few could resist the smell of hot rolls and she always cunningly had a knife and a slab of good, white butter sitting out on the counter to make it even more tempting.

Those who had not risen early enough to have time for their breakfast porridge, or those whose homes held slovenly wives or too many clamouring children – or, worse still, both - were especially vulnerable to these wiles. Many had cause to rue the number of buttered rolls they wolfed down at six in the morning when they searched their pockets for enough money for 'a nip an a pint' after the shift.

Aggie rose at half-past-four and was in the shop by ten-to-five. She had perfected the technique of barely waking up, on very cold mornings simply pulling her outer clothes on top of her nightdress, and could be in the shop with the gas oven blasting out against the cold before she had lost her own bed-warmth.

She made herself a pot of tea and was usually enjoying her second cup by the time
the van arrived. Now, with the new bread and rolls steaming fragrantly on the shelves, she was happily setting out the cakes and buns under the glass counter, enjoying the peace and promise of another day.

144

For now her days *were* full of promise as the *Messiah* practices rolled by and the choir looked eagerly forward to its moment of glory on the second of January. Of course, she had still not solved the problem of how to get away that day. The women's Get-together was to be at Senga's house this year, already the women were talking eagerly of it and Senga was embroidering a spectacular new tablecloth for the event.

But every time her mind turned to the problem, she seemed unable to focus seriously upon it. Nothing was going to stop her, of that she was certain, and so, somehow, the tricky minor detail of her escape plan would simply drift away, lost in luxurious contemplation of the concert and her starring role.

She sang on, lost in music and anticipation. She did not immediately register the anxious rapping on the locked shop door.

Johnnie had also been awake since four-thirty. Twice during the night he had risen, foggy with sleep, to answer his mother's call. The second time he had been too slow and dealing with the resulting soaked bed, trying to master his irritation, find clean sheets, put the dirty ones to soak in the machine tub and settle the fractious old woman back into bed had left him so fraught that there was no hope of further sleep. He had thought of the dozens of times he had been only slightly aware of Kate rising quietly or slipping back into bed with a murmured apology for disturbing him.

Returning to the sitting-room just before five, he had looked through the curtains at the dark, empty street, experiencing for the first time in his life that self-pitying feeling of being the only person in the world awake. Then he had seen Aggie, rounding the corner and heading for her shop.

Muddled remnants of the plan he and Dr Jim had concocted the night before had tumbled through his tired brain. It had certainly involved Aggie – and Fat Annie, too, he thought – but he could not quite recall the details. Shaking himself to dispel the fogginess in his mind, he had forced himself into his clothes, which lay in a crumpled heap on an armchair, located his shoes and, after a quick check on Kate who was still sleeping heavily, her breath whistling shrilly in her constricted lungs, he had stumbled down the stairs and out into the cold morning air.

Aggie opened the shop door and stared in surprise at Johnnie. This was not the Johnnie Cruikshanks she, or anyone else, was accustomed to seeing. Gone was the suave, confident air, the well-groomed, well-set–up appearance. This man was haggard, unshaven and agitated.

Somethin's wrang. The auld yin? Deid, maybe? But whit does he want me tae dae aboot it?

'Come in, Johnnie,' she said, unnecessarily, for he was already thrusting his way into the shop. 'An whit can Ah dae fur ye this fine mornin'?'

Johnnie stopped short in front of the counter. Momentarily, every other thought and care were driven out of his mind by the smell in the little shop. He realised that he had not eaten since his working lunch in St. Andrews the day before. There had been no time and no food ready at home for him anyway. Three large whiskies with Dr Jim had been his only sustenance for some sixteen hours. His mouth watered and his belly rumbled.

'Give me some of yer rolls, Aggie,' he pleaded. 'I'm famished and that smell is goin' round ma heart.'

Aggie frowned as she tried to make sense of this. What on earth was he doing here at this time in the morning, demanding food? Why was he not at home in bed with every expectation of a satisfying bowl of porridge, followed by bacon-and-eggs, at half-past-seven?

'Ah dinnae really open till quarter-tae-six...' she began; then, seeing his look of wolfish despair, 'Och, a' richt, ye're family after a'.'

She fetched the butter and took two large, warm rolls from the shelf. As she sliced them open and spread the butter thickly, he watched in owlish concentration; then he gobbled them down, careless of crumbs and flecks of butter falling onto his jacket. She proffered a third and it was accepted eagerly and demolished in similar fashion.

'Man, that's better!' he declared, some of the tension going out of his face for a moment. 'Ye're a fine woman, Aggie. I've always said it, always admired ye.'

'That's as maybe,' she retorted drily. 'Ah'm thinkin' it's ma hot rolls and butter that ye're admirin' richt noo. Are ye goin' tae tell me whit the hell this is a' aboot? Is yer auld mither deid or whit?'

Her bluntness recalled him abruptly to the real reason for his visit. 'No, it's worse than that,' he groaned, subsiding on to a chair that Aggie kept by the door for some of her more elderly – or very pregnant - queuing customers.

'Is it oor Kate, then?' Her voice sharpened with sudden dread. *Ma wee sister – surely no?* The years of jealous animosity rose up in her mind and she felt a wave of bitter regret.

When he nodded his head miserably, she gasped and choked on the bile that rose in her throat. 'But what the hell happened tae her? Ah saw her only the ither day – she was a' richt. At least Ah *think* she was…'

Johnnie heard the echo of his own moment of truth the night before. Had no-one been aware of how Kate was really feeling or looking?

Eck did! The thought was like gall in his mouth. Was it really down to a bad-tempered, bullying brother-in-law to be the only one to notice? Husband and sister exchanged looks of shame and remorse. Aggie spoke hoarsely:

'How did it happen? When did she…' She could not say the word. She covered her face with her hands and a sob wrenched from her throat.

'She took ill yesterday afternoon when she was out. Annie-from-the-drapers was looking after my mother. Kate was barely able to stand when she got home. Annie put her to bed and we called the doctor. He said…' Johnnie paused, re-living the moment of diagnosis and his dawning realisation of its implications. 'I dinnae ken what I'm goin' to do,' he finished miserably.

Aggie knelt on the floor beside him, taking his hand in hers, compassion and shock stripping away inhibition. 'Ye puir, puir man. Ye'll miss her sore. She wis aye a guid wife tae ye but ye can comfort yersel that ye were aye a grand man tae her. Ye gave her a fine life an she's at peace noo…' She hardly knew what she was saying; the platitudes seemed to be saying themselves. 'We'll need tae get word tae the young folk in Canada. It's a sair heart fur them, stuck oot there. They'd never get hame in time fur the funeral…'

'*Funeral!*' the word echoed round the shop like a whip-crack. 'What the hell are ye talkin' about? Kate's no dead. I never said she was dead. She's ill - very ill, the doctor says. Pleurisy and a bad dose o' the flu. She's got to rest in bed, no go near anyone else - for a whole fortnight! It's a' very well for doctors to say those things, Aggie, but how am I goin' to manage without her? There's my mother…'

He broke off as Aggie rose to her feet. She stood looking at him, shaking her head, as if in disbelief.

'So it's jist the usual case o' *never miss the water till the well runs dry,* eh?' Relief and some residue of remorse made her want to lash out. 'Never mind that yer wife's ill and needin' some carin' for. All you can think aboot is yersel an hoo it's goin' tae upset *your*

147

applecairt. Ye're a' the same, you men, selfish buggers. If there wis anither sex, women would never be bothered wi ye!'

She began to clear up the crumbs-and-butter mess on the counter with angry, jerking movements.

Johnnie took stock of the situation and realised that he was handling it badly. He recalled some of the principles of people management he had been learning. How could he have made such a mess of such an important negotiation? He had allowed his panic – and his hunger – to get in the way. He had alienated a potential ally, a classic error of judgment. He rose thoughtfully and schooled his features into a mask of hurt concern.

'Aggie, how can you think that of me? Of course, I'm worried about my dear Kate and I blame myself for not seeing that she has been getting over-tired. I want to give her all the care and attention she needs to get better. I just don't know how I am going to cope with looking after her *and* my mother *and* get to my work… I've come to you, my dear, because I know you are a woman of great resourcefulness and I know you would never see your only sister stuck.'

'That should do it,' he thought: a nice mix of loving concern, humility, neediness, flattery and appeal to family loyalties. He felt better than he had done since his orderly life had been reduced to a shambles last night. He felt in control again, doing what he did best – managing and manipulating people.

Aggie absorbed the various strands of his statement thoughtfully. It *was* a problem, she could see that. Part of her wanted to tell him to sod off, that it was not her concern: plenty of families had had much worse to cope with and without such comfortable circumstances to start from. But part of her could not but acknowledge that what he said was true: Kate *was* her only sister and she, Aggie, *was* a woman of great resourcefulness.

It was just *soft soap* from him, of course, trying to get on her good side, but, still, it sounded good and it made her feel good.

'Let me think aboot it, Johnnie.' She played for time. 'Ah cannae dae onythin' this mornin'. The shop'll be openin' in a meenit. Ah'll come ower later on, at denner-time, an we'll see whit we can work oot. No…' as he made to protest, '…that's ma best offer. Ye'll hae tae tak a morning aff an dae the bizness yersel at hame. Surely a high heid-yin like you can dae that easily enough? Jist tell them ye're awa at anither daft meetin'!'

Aggie was not Eck's wife for nothing and she had absorbed at least a little of her husband's scorn for Johnnie's working day. She pushed past him now and went to open the shop door as the first of her early birds arrived.

Johnnie admitted defeat and remembered another management principle: *Know when to retreat as long as the door is left open for further negotiation.* He trudged wearily over the crossroads, not responding to the surprised greetings from some of the men on their way to the pit.

Aggie, busy buttering rolls and exchanging banter with the men, spared a thought, half-amused, half- sympathetic, for her brother-in-law. *He'll ken a' aboot it noo. He'll be richt glad tae get back tae his work fur a rest!*

The mid-morning lull came at last as the early surge for bread and rolls died away. Later in the morning would come the pre-dinnertime rush for pies and bridies; the afternoon belonged mainly to cakes and teabread, although there were a few rotund devotees of such fare who hit on them for a mid-morning snack. Annie, of course, with her love of sugary doughnuts and cream cookies, was one such.

Aggie brewed a fresh pot of tea and selected the largest, juiciest apple turnover from the tray under the counter: breakfast at last. Johnnie's problems had been shelved to the back of her mind as she dealt with the steady stream of customers, moving from cheery banter with the early-shift men into nodding acknowledgement and sympathy for the women's groans and gossip, with her own brand of sharp wit and wry comment salting it all. Now, with the shop becalmed and a comforting mouthful of turnover on board, she focused on his situation.

Johnnie might have demonstrated remarkably little problem-solving skill – which, for a man with ambitions to rise in middle management was regrettable – but he *had* shown an unerring instinct for passing his problem on to the right person for which, at least, he deserved some points. Aggie, for all her shortcomings as a housewife, was a good organiser. Housework, cooking, childcare and entertaining had never appealed to her and, as long as these had been the only arenas open to her, she had presented as slovenly and disorganised. But, with the opportunity to become a business woman and earn her own money, a new woman had emerged and with her a self-belief and drive that had surprised everyone and terrified Eck, who felt the shaky rock of his power-base crumbling still more.

Aggie considered the situation from all sides, analysing the needs, setting possible solutions against them, listing the pros and cons of each solution, refining and fashioning the best, most achievable one, then moving on to develop an action plan. She did all this efficiently before she had finished her tea-and-turnover break. She could have taught those working lunches in St Andrews a thing or two.

She tidied away teapot, cup and plate, leaving the back-shop neat and clean, an orderly habit which had never been transferred from shop to home. Then she put two doughnuts and a cream cookie in a bag, hung the *back in a few minutes* sign on the door and went up the street to begin the implementation of her favoured solution.

She thought at first that the draper's shop was closed; the door refused to open at her first attempt. Peering through the smeary glass, however, she spied Annie's bulk crouched on the floor, struggling with a large cardboard box. It was this which was wedging the door shut and there were several others of various sizes littered around the front shop, some open and spilling out their contents.

Aggie rapped on the glass, attracting Annie's attention. With much puffing and panting, a red-faced, sweating Annie manoeuvred the door open far enough to let Aggie in.

'Wid ye look at a' this stuff,' Annie wailed. 'Ah'll never get it a' sorted oot – *or* sold. There'll be nae bloody room fur customers onyway, there's that much o' it.'

'But, whit is it? Where did it a' come frae?' Aggie was temporarily diverted from her pressing mission. She looked more closely at some of the contents: garments of all kinds, both outer and under, large and small, all with one thing in common – a dreary, washed-out colourlessness.

'It's ma order frae ma clothes supplier, ma stock for the New Year. But the cheeky buggers have sent me a hale load o' auld stock they want rid o', as weel. Bargain prices, they're sayin'. Bloody rip-aff, mair like. They're clearin' oot a' the auld wartime stuff they couldnae get rid o' when the rationin' wis on. Jist look at it, Annie. Dis onyone want tae be reminded that we had tae wear this sort o' stuff?'

She held up a selection of deeply depressing garments: skimpy, badly-cut blouses, already fraying at the seams; lank, greasy-looking underskirts; brassieres made out of what looked like old sacks; jackets with one padded shoulder noticeably bigger than the other; skirts cut so economically that sitting down would be a hazard and bending down unthinkable. And all of them miserably devoid of anything approaching a definite colour.

The *piece de resistance* which she held up was a tweed costume intended for a woman of very generous proportions. It was the colour of tea that has been stewed from leaves used over and over again then left to go cold in the pot over night and now beginning to film over – perhaps a fitting reflection of wartime life. The jacket lapels hung at odds so that the button-holes did not quite meet the buttons and the shoulder-pads were lumpy and uneven. Worse still was the skirt which, while *wide* enough to qualify as outsize, was so skimpily cut that it was literally broader than it was long.

'An look at these.' Annie was on a roll now. She displayed an enormous pair of sagging bloomers in air-force grey: 'Parachute silk, nae less!'

Aggie whistled. 'Classy! Ye'll be a bonnie sicht, Annie, wi them hingin doon below that wee skirt.'

The cold glass in the door misted over as the two women burst into helpless peals of laughter at the picture thus conjured up. Annie had an ability to laugh openly at her size and shape and a comfortable self-acceptance that sometimes made slimmer but less confident women feel quite jealous.

'How-some-ever,' Annie made a supreme effort to compose herself, hiccupping a little, 'one good thing is that they've sent some nice navy skirts and bonnie white blouses, like ye asked me aboot a few weeks ago – there's even twa or three wi frilled collars. An that stuff is brand new, just made fur this year, no like this mouldy auld rubbish.'

She kicked over one of the smaller offending boxes and a heap of scratchy, shapeless khaki gloves fell out. 'Ye'll need tae be quick, though, there's no many. Why no shut up early at denner-time and nip in fur a quick look afore ye gang hame tae get Eck his denner?'

Aggie was recalled to her purpose in coming to the draper shop.

'Ah've brought ye a wee treat, Annie – on the hoose this mornin'. Looks like ye're needin' a wee break after a' this excitement wi Lili Marlene.' She indicated the tea-leaves costume and the two women almost slipped back into a state of helpless mirth.

'Ye're richt there, Aggie.' Annie wiped her eyes then narrowed on the bakery bag greedily. 'Ah'm fair in need o' some sustenance after a' that work.'

Aggie forbore to remark that she knew of no-one less in need of sustenance, especially of the doughnut and cream-cookie variety. She held out the bag but did not let it go when Annie's fat hand clamped greedily on to it. The two women's eyes met over it.

'Ah've something tae discuss wi ye, Annie. Ah need yer help. Well, no me, exactly. It's someone else that needs help.'

Annie nodded. She had been expecting the call all morning though she had thought it might come from Johnnie himself. She had been gearing up for scene two of her performance as an important, trustworthy person, a central figure in an unfolding drama. She felt a little put out that Aggie had also come on stage and obviously in a leading role. Better establish her superior position immediately:

'Ye'll be talking aboot Kate,' she said airily. 'Ah wis jist wonderin' hoo she is this mornin' and whit Johnnie's goin' tae dae. He's got a wee bit o' a problem on his hands.'

'An no ane he can solve sittin' at a desk,' smirked Aggie. 'It's time tae call in the folk that really mak the warld gang roon!'

She winked at Annie and, for the second time that morning, the little shop echoed to the laughter of the two women.

A queue was forming outside the closed bakery shop. The women huddled into their coats, tied scarves tighter round shivery necks and stamped frozen feet on the icy ground. There was some half-hearted blethering - about the weather, the forthcoming Christmas party for the children at the Welfare Club, Hogmanay plans and so forth – but the damp, bitter cold, seeping into their bones was winning.

'This is a damn lang few meenits,' observed Nellie in some irritation. She had left the baby and the two-year-old asleep at home and run all the way to the shop, expecting to be in and out and haring back home within 'a few meenits'. Now she had been standing here for at least ten and was getting not only freezing cold in her thin, inadequate jacket but also anxious and fearful.

Jeannie, who was standing a little behind her in the queue heard her and guessed at once why she was so worried. Jeannie had watched Nellie slipping out her door and setting off at a run. Her neighbour's

152

anxious backward glance at the house, as she made to turn the corner out of the cul-de-sac, had given her away.

'Leavin' they wee bairnies a' on their own again. It's a scandal,' Jeannie had thought, quite forgetting the occasional times she had done likewise when her twins had been babies, though she had always called out to a neighbour to keep an eye and ear open for them. *Why does Nellie no ask me?* In her heart, she knew fine the answer to that. No woman in her right mind would give Jeannie Gilhooley a free-rein invitation into her empty home. It would be tantamount to taking out an advertisement in the Methil and Buckhaven Courier, declaring the state of one's marriage, finances and cupboards, fleshed out by tidbits from personal letters, receipts and unpaid bills.

It could be different. It will be different, she had resolved as she set off herself to do her own morning's messages.

But now, stamping her small feet on the frozen ground, she turned to Senga behind her and opened her mouth to expose and vilify Nellie's childcare practices. The cold was numbing her brain and making her forget her changed heart.

She was saved this fall from grace so early in her career as a reformed character by the good Senga choosing that very moment to say: 'Are ye looking forward tae the Get-thegither this year, Jeannie? Ah'm that excited, it's no been in ma hoose fur mony's a year. Ah think the last time wis . . . '

Senga launched into a rambling memory, freely peppered with anecdotes about her children, other people's children, the black-market food she had managed to provide despite the stranglehold of rationing, who had been expecting and who had just given birth to whom, how those long-ago babies were now faring as ten-year-olds...

By the time she paused for breath, prior to launching into a detailed description of the tablecloth she was embroidering for the forthcoming occasion, Jeannie had almost lost the will to live, let alone to initiate slanderous gossip. In any event, and to the vociferous relief of the queue, Aggie appeared and wafted up the side of it to a tide of complaints and taunts.

'Do ye think we've got a' day tae wait fur you?'

'Ma feet's frozen tae the grund.'

'Been awa at the beauty salon again, Aggie – it disnae show!'

'Been havin' a wee quickie wi yer fancy man?'

Aggie flapped her hands in dismissive rebuttal of their sallies. She affected a mock posh voice: 'Now, now, then, ladies, control yourselves. There will be plenty for all of you, sumptuous fare, all the best of stuff and well worth waiting for!' She was picking up phrases, intonations and accents from her new friends in the choir.

The women growled as mobs will do when mocked. Aggie, seeing that valour in this instance was demanding discretion rather than stagey foolhardiness, hastily unlocked the door and darted behind her counter.

Business boomed; Aggie's stock whittled nicely. She was coming through from the back-shop with a fresh tray of pies and bridies when she stopped, her ears pricked up. Senga was still ear-bashing Jeannie but, having finally exhausted the minute details of the tablecloth, had moved on to another topic.

'Ah'm a wee bittie worried aboot Kate, ma next-door-neibour. Ah saw her oot the windae yesterday afternoon crossin' the road. She wis staggerin' like she wis blotto – near caused an awfy accident wi twa fellas on bikes an Jimmy-frae-the-brewery's horse. Ah ken she's been goin' oot on Wednesday afternoons but Ah niver thocht she'd be *drinkin'*! An her curtains were no open till ten o'clock this mornin' though it wis licht by half-eight. Ah'll cry in later an see whit's goin' on. Ah've a cherry an almond cake baked for her onyway. It's a new recipe. Ye start wi putting the butter in a pan and meltin' it...'

Jeannie, who had been conserving her sanity by paying only the most minimal attention to Senga's ramblings, now turned full attention on her. She raised her voice to cut across Senga's talking recipe: 'Ah think we should a' leave Kate alane. The puir lassie's got enough on her plate withoot onyone else stickin' their oar in. Ah, fur ane, am going tae mind ma ain bizness!'

It sometimes happens in a buzzing throng of people that there is a momentary lull into which someone's last remark seems to fall as into an echoing chasm. This was one such moment so that Jeannie's astonishing pronouncement assumed the nature of a public declaration of intent.

There was a stunned silence as, for the second time in two days, Jeannie heard the words *mind my own business* fall from her own lips. Yesterday, there had been only a fraught and fevered Kate to respond with disbelief; today there was a whole shop-full of women. Incredulous mutters began to eddy slowly around the group in the shop and wash out to the shivering overflow on the pavement. And, for the second time in two days, Jeannie saw herself as others saw her.

After the first surge of satisfaction - *That's better. Ah got it richt that time* - in the initial silence, she felt acute embarrassment but, as the incredulous, derisory muttering began, she moved into defensiveness. She looked defiantly around, staring the bold ones down, sweeping a scornful glance over the more cowardly. Then she moved towards the counter.

'Ah ken it's no ma turn yet, Aggie, but ye micht as well tak me since naebody else seems tae be batherin' aboot gettin' served the noo. Ah'll hae fower bridies, a wee broon loaf an…'

As she watched Aggie's large, bony hands roughly bagging up her purchases, she was reminded of her interest in Aggie's clandestine connection with the Methodist Church. Aggie's fingers were broad-tipped, the nails bitten, the skin rough, her hand-movements brisk and strong. They did not look like embroiderer's hands; not at all like Senga's, which were dainty and dexterous, noticeably well-cared for, smooth and supple, the nails always neatly filed and buffed.

Embroidery classes, ma foot. Ah'm sure she's up tae somethin' else a' thegither. Ah wonder… She was on the point of chewing greedily on some fresh speculative fodder when she remembered her new mantra: *mind your own business.* It was not proving easy to slough off the habit of a lifetime. She made an effort to divert her attention from temptation:

'Senga's fair cairried-awa wi hersel the noo. The Get-thegither's at her hoose this year. Ye'd think it wis the royal gairden pairty at Holyrood Palace the wiy she's goin' on. Mind, Ah aye say it *is* the best bit oot a' the Hogmanany and New Year shenanigans. Are ye lookin' forward tae it yersel, Aggie?'

Aggie almost swallowed the pencil stub she was licking, prior to jotting down the prices of Jeannie's purchases.

'Whit's it got tae dae wi you whether Ah'm goin' or no?' she demanded aggressively. 'Ah thocht ye jist said ye were goin' tae mind yer ain bizness?'

'*Bloody hell!*' thought Jeannie. '*Ah cannae dae onythin' richt.*' Frustrated and confused, she snarled: 'Oh aye? An who was it wanted me tae dae her dirty work an stick ma nose intae her ain sister's bizness fur her? An no very lang ago, either. Well, Ah'll no be tellin' *you* whit Ah've fund oot aboot Kate. Ye can damn well find oot fur yersel!'

She turned to flounce out the shop but Aggie laid a quick, repentant hand on her arm.

Jeannie's mention of Kate had recalled her to that day's present and pressing needs – January the second's problems would have to wait. It had also reminded her of their shared, prurient interest in Kate's excursions, about which, she now realised, she had heard nothing for several weeks. Wrapped up in her singing practices and plans, and with her own interest in gossip always likely to be fleeting and fragile anyway, she had forgotten all about it. Now, it occurred to her quick brain that Jeannie was already involved in the unfolding Kate drama and might be useful – especially if she really meant to do a bit of serious own-business-minding for once.

'Ach, Ah'm sorry, Jeannie, dinnae rush awa. Ah wis hopin' tae speak tae ye. Will ye be in later on in the afternoon? Can Ah come roon? Ye micht be able tae help a wee situation that's arisen. It's aboot Kate hersel actually.' She lowered her voice confidentially: 'She's no weel, ye see, no weel at a'...'

She broke off in some astonishment. Jeannie was nodding sagely with no sign of this being news to her.

'Tak yer time, you twa. Dinnae mind us. We've only been hingin aboot this damned shop fur hoors. Ah've a guid mind tae go an get the bus tae The Store in Leven – at this rate Ah could hae been there an back twice!'

'Aye, an had time fur a wee paddle on the beach! It's a damned disgrace!'

The remaining women had recovered from the shell-shock of Jeannie's declaration and had re-grouped, though the idea of dipping toes in the winter sea on Leven beach sent a collective frisson through them.

The mob was turning ugly, Aggie saw. Finding out how Jeannie knew about Kate's illness – for know about it she did, Aggie was certain - would have to wait. 'Can Ah come roon tae see ye at the back o' five, then?' she asked quickly.

Jeannie's knowing nod confirmed the hunch.

As the last of the pies went off to grace hungry dinner tables, the talk was all of Jeannie Gilhooley. Was she having them all on? Was it a ploy to lull them into a false sense of security so as to worm more information out of them? Could she possibly have meant it? And why was she talking like this?

One of the more imaginative women suggested she might have been taken over by the 'Men from Mars'. There was talk of such things and her man had read a fanciful book about rockets going into space.

One thing was certain: it was a day that would go down in the annals of the little shop, indeed of the little community. Years later women would tell their grandchildren: *Ah mind the day in Aggie Fairweather's wee shop...*

Icy sleet was scourging the dark streets as Aggie trudged wearily up the road from the Methodist Church. She had had to run to the kirk to be in time to tell one of the ladies on their way in to the choir practice why she would not be there tonight and reassure them it was only a temporary problem.

Now she thought regretfully of the familiar comfort of her peaceful tea-and-woodbine hour, the promise of refuge from the cold making it especially alluring tonight. But, demanding and exhausting as the day had been, it was not yet over.

Johnnie owes me ane fur a' this, dis he no? An Kate an a', though she's fair senseless the noo an disnae ken wha's doin' whit, puir lassie...

Though not naturally given to a sympathetic response to weakness or sickness – as her daughters had known only too well when they were growing up, often being sent to school when other children would have been tucked up in bed with a thermometer in their mouths – Aggie had nevertheless been shocked by the sight and sound of Kate.

Her sister had appeared scarcely to know her as she lay in sheets soaked in sweat, barely able to sip water through cracked lips or swallow it over a swollen, infected throat. Aggie's natural tendency to bracing dismissiveness of others' problems and ailments had shrivelled in the face of such obvious infirmity.

She had gone over to the house at noon, shutting up the shop early as Annie had suggested but not for purposes of mere frivolous clothes shopping: that would have to wait.

An heaven help that fat slob if she sells a' the skirts and blouses Ah asked her tae get, that'll be the last doughnut she gets aff me.

She found a harassed Johnnie in the kitchen, attempting to peel potatoes, hang dripping sheets on the pulley and deal with an overflowing bucket all at the same time. He had started peeling the potatoes with some notion of making chips for their dinner. Then the washing machine had stopped its cycle and, quite forgetting about using the spin drier or thinking about any other means of rinsing and wringing the water out of the sheets, he had let down the pulley and begun dragging a soapy, dripping sheet out of the machine drum and over the four poles of the pulley. The end of the sheet had slapped against the already full, kitchen-scraps bucket into which he was dropping the potato peelings; the bucket had spilled over the floor and he was in the process of trying to gather the slimy, smelly contents back into the bucket with his bare hands. The sheet continued to relentlessly drip soap suds on the whole sorry pantomime.

Aggie had let herself in; she had borrowed the key from Annie earlier – first point of the action plan. She rarely visited Kate's house these days and had not been in it since the old mother had come to stay. She knew, however, which bedroom was Kate and Johnnie's and she pushed open the door expecting to see her sister in bed. She was taken aback to meet the belligerent glare of Old Maggie and a pungent smell that was a complex mixture of lavender water, bleach, bad breath and dirty underwear.

'Aye, about time,' cried the old woman. 'It doesnae look like that lazy bitch is goin' to get up out o' her bed this side o' Christmas an my poor laddie cannae be expected to do a' this. It's no man's work. If *she*'s no goin' to do it, we'll need another woman. I'm wantin' egg-an-chips for my dinner, wi the yolk runny so I can dip the chips in, an I like a wee bit tomato sauce on the side – on the *side*, mind, no slathered a' over the chips.'

Aggie closed the door with a sound that was half-giggle, half-shudder. Obviously Kate had ceded the master bedroom to the old woman and she and Johnnie must now be in one of the other smaller ones across the lobby. Her recollection of the geography of the house was hazy and the first door she pushed open, immediately opposite Maggie's room, turned out to be the bathroom and here a disaster scene met her eyes and assaulted her nostrils: the bucket from the commode had been approximately emptied into the toilet pan but without lifting the wooden seat first so that the foul contents of the bucket had splashed all over it. The toilet had not yet been flushed. The still-dirty bucket lay on its side, possibly thrown down in haste when another urgent demand overtook the task or possibly kicked over as Johnnie stumbled over the towel that lay on the floor. *This* had obviously been used as a hasty, makeshift receptacle for vomit, though fortunately not a large amount – Kate had coughed herself sick but had had very little in her stomach. The commode bucket was dribbling out the last of its miserable load in a greenish-brown trickle that met Aggie at the door.

Mother o' God! Whit's happenin' here?

She thought of the house-on-the-corner she remembered: always spotlessly clean, smelling of polish and home-baking, with matching soaps and towels in the pretty bathroom and not a speck of dust on the multiplicity of ornaments, trinkets and photographs. Her daughters had loved visiting their Aunty Kate when they were wee lassies, being allowed to play with all the fascinating trivia, listening to their aunt's stories about each souvenir and photo frame, helping her to bake fairy cakes, curling up on her welcoming lap to eat them and listen to more stories.

Kate's home had been all that their own was not, exuding order, security and routine, magically combined with loving indulgence and interesting activity. Aggie had been only too aware of how its comforting stability threw her own haphazard approach to motherhood and home-making into sharp relief. How its emotional security highlighted the tightrope of fear and dread that her daughters often walked in their own abusive, violent home. Maureen and Robbie had known a happy, easy childhood with parents who loved each other and laughed often together. Agnes and Maisie had known constant tension, stabbing sarcasm they did not understand but felt the pain of, unpredictable, terrifying flare-ups with shouts, screams, blows, kicks, doors slamming and angry boots stamping off down the road, echoing with the threat of a too-soon return.

The next room she looked in had once been Robbie's tiny bedroom but was now a tangle of the accoutrements of old age and disability: a walking frame; a wheelchair; a pile of elasticated long-socks; a metal foot-rest; pillows and quilts; and an enormous pile of brown paper parcels, all unopened, all labeled 'female incontinence pads'.

'Ah wonder if they mate wi the male anes and hae wee bairnie pads. Looks like they're no goin' tae get much else tae dae.' A note of hysteria began to creep into her thoughts.

'It's no the bonnie hoose it was, that's fur sure.' Any sense of long-deferred satisfaction faded, however, when she opened the last door in the lobby.

This had been Maureen's bedroom, full in those days of girlish fripperies and girlish dreams. Now it was crowded with the occupancy of two middle-aged adults and was cluttered and uninviting. The bed was technically a double but was considerably smaller than the one

Old Maggie was lolling in. Aggie briefly wondered how Johnnie managed to accommodate his stringy length in it with any degree of comfort.

Kate was lying on her back with her mouth open. She appeared to be just below the surface of sleep, her fingers occasionally plucking fitfully at the knotted, sweaty sheet. In her restlessness, her head had slipped down off the bolster then pushed back up against it, so that the long, marriage-bed pillow was now curling against the bed-head and flapping over her face, further impeding her laboured breathing. The curtains were still closed and the grey half-light of the dreich December day barely showed at their edges. The only real light in the room was from a small, one-bar electric fire which was creating an airless miasma in the claustrophobic space.

Aggie swore under her breath and moved instinctively to open the curtains and the window, gulping in the cold, damp breeze like a diver coming up for air from the depths of a murky pool. She moved over to the bedside and stared down at her sister, a mix of emotions and memories coursing through her: nausea and disgust, a spontaneous physical reaction to the last few minutes; an unworthy thread of downright glee; a whisper of rising panic; a surge of compassion; but, supreme over all these, remorse and growing anger.

If the things could get into this state in one short evening and morning, how had Kate been managing to cope with it all on her own? How could they all have turned their eyes and their backs away from her situation? She thought with burning shame of the day she had callously rejected Kate's request for help with Old Maggie before the Wednesday outings began. She closed her eyes and groaned when she thought of how she had set pernicious wee Jeannie Gilhooley on Kate, not even because she particularly cared what Kate was doing, but just because she had needed a diversion from her own miseries that day. And she had squirmed as she realised that, having thus released the dogs of war on Kate, she had immediately lost interest when her own life took a new and absorbing turn.

Ah jist dropped her in the shit and then forgot aboot her. An Jeannie's been hard at it, that's definite. She's squeezed some juice oot o' it, Ah could tell by her face this mornin'. God knows whit trouble she's goin' tae cause noo fur Kate. An it's a' ma fault...

Tenderly, almost mournfully, she lifted her sister's head and pulled the bolster back under it. Kate's hair was sticky and wet; the back of her neck on Aggie's hands was burning hot. As Aggie looked down at the tears oozing out from swollen eyelids, the cracked lips and Kate's harried, careworn expression, she felt the anger explode within her.

Enough! Annie was a woman of action and the time had come.

She became aware suddenly that the low, steady thrumming noise, that had been filling the house since she had come in, had stopped. She heard the squeak of the kitchen pulley being let down then, a moment later, a crash followed by a loud and colourful oath from Johnnie. She followed the sounds to arrive at the kitchen door and at the final disaster scene.

Johnnie, seeing her, rose from his knees with an exclamation of relief and advanced hastily and unwisely towards her. He slipped on a dollop of old porridge from the bucket and grabbed out in panic to stop from falling. His hand closed around a trailing end of the dripping sheet. He fell anyway, pulling the steaming, soapy sheet down on top of himself and rolled along the floor in it, fetching up with a painful bang to his back against the unused spin drier.

In that moment, Aggie realised that the strategy she had devised with her apple turnover that morning, and the subsequent action plan she and Annie had drawn up, would need to be redrafted. Their plan had been to tell Johnnie to manage the rest of this first day himself and thereafter Aggie and Annie would be taking turns to come over and spend a few hours each day seeing to both invalids and helping out with washing, cleaning, shopping and cooking.

Annie planned to come in the morning and Aggie in the afternoon. They had discussed asking several local women to provide cover in their shops to enable them to do this without losing business. Aggie had women in mind to whom, she was sure, the lure of unlimited free bakeries would prove irresistible and Annie's best bet, they thought, would be Senga with her love of clothes, soft furnishings and haberdashery.

'Ah'll hae nae embroidery thread left,' Annie had prophesied. 'Never mind. She's aboot the only ane that buys much o' it onyway.'

Aggie had planned to begin asking her chosen henchwomen this afternoon and Annie was, at this very moment, engaged in persuading Senga.

But, fresh from her unguided tour of the house and confronted with the mayhem in the kitchen, Aggie acknowledged that Johnnie could not be left alone a minute longer. The man was *completely oot amangst it – no safe tae be left in charge.*

She took off her coat, rolled up her sleeves, and spent the next hour sorting out the kitchen as best she could, though both washing machine and spin drier were a mystery to her. Once he had changed his clothes, however, Johnnie proved to be good for something and managed to remember enough of his tutorial from Dr Jim the night before to spin-dry the sheets, empty the washing machine and fill it up with rinsing water, run the sheets through it again and then spin-dry them once again.

It seems like an awfy palaver tae me. Aggie favoured an overnight 'steepie' in the bath then a half-an-hour with the wringer over the bath next day. Rinsing was not something she ever gave much thought to.

With the kitchen floor cleaned up and the full pulley hoisted on high, Aggie turned her attention to the tattie-peeling.

'Dae something aboot that hell-hole o' a toilet,' she said bluntly to Johnnie. 'The deil himsel wouldnae pee in there even if he wis burstin'! Ah'll mak the chips.'

Johnnie looked vaguely mystified as he went off to do her bidding. He had no memory of the state he had left the bathroom in. Truth to tell, his morning had passed in a blur of frantic responses to one emergency after another with no time to complete any one task. His mother had soaked her bed twice and splashed sloppy, milky porridge all over it for good measure. She had complained constantly about lack of attention, about lumpy porridge, about being kept waiting, about being ignored, about being pushed and pulled around. She had ended each tirade, however, by exonerating her son: 'It's no you should be even tryin' to do a' this. Get that lazy wife o' yours up! What's a young lassie like that doin' lyin' in bed?'

In vain, he had explained how ill Kate was. Maggie had no ears for such feeble excuses. Kate herself had demanded nothing but she had fallen out of the bed twice as she thrashed about deliriously. He had managed to get two of Dr Jim's pills down her throat but then she had been immediately seized with a violent coughing fit which had ejected them, and the sparse remaining contents of her stomach, in a projectile vomit. He had been about to bathe her face so the towel he had laid on the bed had served as a receptacle.

He yelped in horror when he opened the bathroom door and saw the mess he had left. He stumbled back into the kitchen with some vague notion of asking Aggie to swap jobs. This might have resulted in more edible chips – Aggie was making her usual poor job of these – but she gave him short shrift.

'It's your mess, your hoose, your mother and your wife,' she declared, her intransigence rooted in a fierce determination to avoid the unenviable task herself, and he had to hold his breath and do his best to restore the bathroom to as near normal as possible. It would have gladdened the heart of some of the men at the pit – and given Eck one of the happiest days of his life – to have seen their up-and-coming deputy manager scraping shit off the floor and washing the filthy lavatory pan and seat.

Old Maggie began shouting again and he almost seized upon this excuse to abandon the task half-done, but Aggie stopped him in the lobby.

'Ah'll see tae her,' she said, inexorably. 'You finish whit ye're doin'.'

She was brisk and brief with the old woman.

'Ye'll get yer denner when it's good and ready, Maggie. If ye mak me run back and forrad tae ye, it'll tak twice as lang. Now jist wait yer patience, for ony's sake!'

And the old moaner, taken aback by such bluntness, subsided, muttering 'Bloody cheek! I aye kent those Kelly sisters were just scum. One lyin' about her bed like Lady Muck an the other settin' me up cheek…' But she had ceased shouting and waited – though perhaps without the patience Aggie had suggested – till her plate of egg and chips had eventually appeared.

It said much for the effect of Aggie's earlier stern treatment that she forbore to bewail the burnt chips, the rock-hard egg and total lack of tomato sauce.

Aggie caught sight of Annie coming out of Senga's gate at twenty-to-one and, leaning out the window, accosted her.

'Is Senga goin' tae oblige?' Then, as Annie gave the GI-Joe thumbs-up sign, 'Get back an ask her if she'll start this afternoon. Ye should see the state o' things in this hoose. It's a bloody war zone. We cannae leave it till the morn. He's no copin' at a'. Ye'll need tae come ower an help this afternoon.'

As Annie obediently turned back, she added, on an afterthought: 'An run roon tae ma hoose an tell Eck whit's happenin'. Tell him Ah dinnae ken when Ah'll be hame the nicht either.'

Annie baulked at this last command. 'He's no goin' tae be best pleased, Aggie. He'll be fair scunnered, nae denner afore his shift. Ah dinnae fancy bein' the ane tae tell him. An Ah've no had ma ain denner yet masel, Ah'm starvin'.'

163

Aggie fished in her pocket and threw the shop key down to the woebegone woman on the pavement.

'Gang through the back and tak the last fower bridies. Ye can eat twa yersel as ye're walkin' roon and gie the ither twa tae Eck. Oh, an mind ye tell him Kate's at death's door. Lay it on wi a trowel. He's aye had a soft spot fur her. It'll no rattle him sae much if it's *bonnie wee Katy* that's causin' a' the trouble.'

Annie, instantly mollified by the promise of food, especially two of Aggie's large, savoury bridies, still warm on the back-shop's hot-plate, accepted the commission without further demur.

Aggie reflected, as she closed the sitting-room window, that Eck would likely be a great deal more moved by Kate's plight than he had ever been by his own wife's or daughters' illnesses. She could remember being doubled up with the searing pain of mastitis after Agnes was born and getting no sympathy or exemption from wifely duties, neither kitchen nor bedroom. For a moment, the old jealous resentment was sour in her mouth. Then she spat it out and turned back to the exigencies of the moment. *It's a' water under the bridge noo.*

And so, the afternoon and early evening had somehow been got through, with Aggie and Annie running back and forward between their shops and Kate's house. Johnnie had been positively ordered off to his office in the middle of the afternoon as it became increasingly clear that he was more of a liability than a support and he had gone humbly, shamefacedly, quite without his accustomed confident swagger.

Dr Jim had been impressed when he called mid-afternoon and found his patient tucked up in fresh sheets, propped up on clean pillows to help her breathing, and the room warm but well-aired. He sensed some commotion in the rest of the house and he could hear raised voices in the old woman's room but he pursued his lifelong policy of non-intervention, confining himself to instructions about Kate's nursing care and medication.

'…and a tepid sponge-down two or three times a day will help keep her temperature down. I'm sure she'll soon turn the corner with such good care. Well done!'

Annie, deferentially seeing him along the lobby to the inside door, preened and thought that she must remember to share this praise with Aggie. He turned in the doorway:

'I can see why Johnnie is being groomed for management. He can obviously handle an emergency.'

Going down the carpeted stair, he wondered at the slam of the inside door and… *Was that a bellow of laughter or rage?* He had hurried on to his next house-call.

Now it was nearly seven o'clock, a measure of order and calm prevailed in the house-on-the-corner and plans were in place for a system that should meet the demands of the next two weeks.

Johnnie was profuse in his gratitude and admiration but, unlike in the morning when it had been mere flattery to get his own way, now it was genuine. Now he had a full appreciation of the magnitude of the task and a healthy horror of ever again being left to face it alone.

Aggie turned into Jeannie's cul-de-sac some two hours later than the time they had agreed that morning but she was still confident of her welcome. She knew that Jeannie would be desperate to be in on the drama. She was less sure of how the meeting would go and her tired brain struggled to recall her impressions of the morning.

What did Jeannie know? How had she found it out? And what was she going to do with it. Perhaps had already done with it?

God help me, Ah'll no furgive masel if Kate's name is blackened a' ower the place an her lyin' in that awfy hoose in sich a state.

She straightened her aching back and rang Jeannie's doorbell determinedly.

CHAPTER NINE

JEANNIE

Jeannie had been on hecklepins all afternoon, unable to settle to anything, even her beloved scribbling, an escape route which normally never let her down. She had tried to slip into her world of fiction but reality had refused to let go of its hold on her. Over and over she had replayed the events of yesterday afternoon, marveling at all she had learned and taken part in.

Occasionally, her truant mind would go down the road of *Wait till Ah tell... Imagine her... Folk are no goin' tae credit it!* But each time she would catch herself and try again to school her mindset and realign it with the new person she was hoping to become. It was proving a minute-by-minute task.

In the anonymity of the noisy, steamy tearoom, in the oasis of their little corner table, Kate had talked and talked, sometimes rambling towards incoherence. Exhaustion and impending illness had loosened her tongue and she had spilled out the whole story: her desperate longing to go and be with her children and grandchildren; the five year wait rendered meaningless by the arrival of her mother-in-law to take up residence; the hideous grind of caring for an incontinent, demanding old woman who would do nothing to make it easier and who, far from expressing any gratitude, treated Kate with disdain and carping dissatisfaction; the housebound, miserable days and broken nights that stretched into the foreseeable future; the way her lovely home, which had always been her pride and joy as well as her sanctuary, was being destroyed.

Then had come a shaft of light through, of all people, Angus Smillie, the butcher. Jeannie had heard the whole story of the day he had been taken ill in his own shop, Kate's cavalier treatment of him that day and subsequent remorse, her apologetic visit to him in hospital

166

and the friendship that had grown out of it, leading to her Wednesday visits to his house.

And now, they had plans, great plans - and she, Jeannie, was in on them, had even been given a part to play and was sworn to secrecy. She hugged herself when she thought of it.

Ah mustna blow it. Ah'm goin' tae haud ma tongue if it kills me. But as she waited impatiently for Aggie, she thought it just might. She had cleaned the house several times, hunting restlessly through the small domain for occupation. Nellie, spying her polishing her brass door-bell for the third time, had muttered; 'That wumman's got bugger all tae dae wi hersel. She should cam' ower here and Ah'd gie her a proper job.'

When Aggie at last appeared, Jeannie almost dragged her into the cottage.

'Whaur hae ye been? Whit's goin' on? How is Kate the day? Is Johnnie managin'? Wha's lookin' after the auld mither? Has the doctor been? Whit did he say? Is it…?'

Aggie was too tired and too cold to feign politeness or to find Jeannie's usual barrage of questions amusing.

'Fur peety's sake, shut up, wumman, an let me in the door. Mak me a cup o' tea and let me tak this wet coat aff. Then we'll sit doon an Ah'll tell ye whit Ah've come fur. An it's no jist tae answer a' yer questions so ye can go flappin' yer nasty, wee mooth a' ower the place. Ye'll be telt whit Ah choose tae tell ye an no a morsel mair.'

She took off her dripping coat and handed it to an open-mouthed Jeannie. 'Careless talk costs lives,' she concluded with a dramatic flourish, borrowing a phrase from wartime posters. She marched uninvited into Jeannie's sitting-room and held her chapped hands out to the welcome blaze of the fire.

Stung by such treatment, Jeannie lashed out: 'So, wha needs ye? Ah'll bet Ah ken a lot mair than ye do!'

Aggie turned and warmed her backside, John-Bull-style. She eyed Jeannie speculatively. 'Ah could see this mornin' in the shop that ye kent aboot Kate bein' ill…' She kept her voice neutral, encouraging. It almost worked.

'Ye can bet on it, hen. Wha else wis wi her yesterday? Wha else cam' hame wi her? Wha else went tae…' - Jeannie heard the warning bell tolling in her head - '…tae mak sure she got hame a' richt,' she concluded lamely.

'Hame frae where?' Aggie was bland, smiling now as the fire warmed her cold buttocks and thighs.

Jeannie recovered her wits: 'Och, she wis jist goin' tae see her pal in St Monans like she telt ye and Ah happened tae be on the bus as weel. Lucky thing Ah wis there. She wis took richt bad an Ah made sure she got hersel awa hame tae her bed.'

'An whit were *you* doin' on the bus tae St Monans? Do you have pals there as weel?' Aggie was all sweet reason.

'Bob has an auntie in Anstruther. Auld Lizzie,' Jeannie fabricated, now enjoying this fencing match as much as Aggie. 'We heard she'd fell and broke a leg. Ah wis goin' tae see if it wis true.'

'An is it?'

'Is whit it?'

'Is it true she's broke her leg?'

'Wha?'

'Puir auld Auntie Lizzie.'

'Oh…her… Ah never went tae see her after a'. Ah turned roon wi Kate afore Anstruther when Ah saw she wis ta'en sae bad and Ah cam' hame wi her.'

'But,' Aggie prepared to deliver the winning thrust, 'Ah heard Senga telling ye she saw Kate gettin' aff the bus. She'd no have been telling *you* that like it wis news if ye were there wi Kate yersel.'

Jeannie parried swiftly. 'Ah got aff at the top o' the avenue. Kate said she could mak it hame frae there on her ain.' She breezed off through to the kitchen and Aggie heard her humming a Glenn Miller song as she made the tea.

'Ah'm missin' somethin',' thought Aggie. *'There's mair to this than she's lettin' on. What is it she's no tellin' me?'*

She sank wearily down into Bob's armchair by the fire. What did it matter, after all, as long as Jeannie could be made to keep her trap shut – whatever it was she had found out and was so smugly hugging to herself – and persuaded to pitch in with the execution of the rescue plan?

Jeannie appeared with not only a welcome tray of tea and toast but a half bottle of sherry and a packet of woodbine as well and the two women buried the hatchet, exchanging grins which tacitly acknowledged that the match was a draw for the moment.

Several sherries later, the tea-and-toast eaten and the room wreathed in woodbine smoke, Jeannie laid her cards on the table.

'It's jist like this, Aggie – Ah've turned ower a new leaf. Ye can sneer if ye like and Ah dinnae expect ye tae believe me a' at aince but it's the God's honest truth. Ah'm fed up wi gossipin' and havin' a'body either runnin' awa frae me in case Ah tell a'body their business or else runnin' taewards me askin' whit the latest dirt is so they can spread it aroon a bit mair.' She puffed vigorously on her cigarette, a determined glint in her eye.

Aggie regarded her doubtfully. This beggared belief. 'Are ye sure ye werena goin' tae Damascus yesterday an no Anstruther?' Then, seeing Jeannie's look of incomprehension, 'Ach, never mind me! A' they nichts at the methody kirk must be gettin' tae me.'

Jeannie leant forward eagerly. 'Whit nichts would that be, Aggie?'

Aggie regarded her severely. 'Ye'll no be needin' tae ken that, will ye? No noo that ye've turned into St Jeannie, patron saint o' *reformed* gossips.'

Jeannie groaned but, to Aggie's surprise, she subsided meekly enough. A short silence ensued, the only sounds being the cheery crackle of the fire and the distant rattle of a loose gate-catch in the snell wind. It was a silence pregnant with assumptions and questions.

Aggie knew in her bones that Jeannie was keeping a secret about Kate. It bothered her less what this was than the perplexing fact that it *was* being kept. Jeannie's remarkable promise of a 'new leaf' remained to be seen and tested – Aggie would not have put any money on it. And she was also sure now that Jeannie knew something about her own nights at the choir – there had been exactly the same look on Jeannie's face when Aggie had let the fatal words 'methody kirk' slip out as there had been in the bakery that morning when she had told her about Kate being ill: unsurprised, smug, ahead-of-the-game.

Aggie found herself at a loss. Talking to Gossip Jeannie, who had always been avid for information about anyone and generous with its exaggerated and ornamented redistribution, had been one thing. Everyone had had years of practice and most people had developed some skill in using her as an information point, a reliable conduit and publicity machine, even as a kind of free private investigator, at the same time being as careful as possible not to give away their own secrets to her. Talking to New Leaf Jeannie, who was proclaiming her reformation so openly, was quite another thing.

Aggie no longer felt on solid ground. The belligerent approach she had resolved on in order to slap Gossip Jeannie down no longer seemed appropriate; but fashioning a brand new way of relating to her was too difficult for Aggie who had been up since half-past-four that morning, had not had a square meal or a moment's rest all day and had solved more problems than ten management meetings.

The clock struck into the silence: eight o'clock. Aggie roused herself. Abandoning all subterfuge, she addressed Jeannie woman-to-woman.

'Kate's got a bad case o' the influenza and the doctor says it's somethin' ca'd 'pleurisy' as weel. She's tae stay in her bed an keep awa frae a'body – especially the auld mither – fur a fortnicht. Johnnie can nae mair manage things there than flee in the air. Ah'll no pit ye through the mess he got himsel intae this mornin'. It wis doonricht pathetic! Annie and me've worked oot a system tae tak turns tae gang ower and look after things durin' the day. Ah've got Bessie, Nellie and Mina comin' in tae look after the shop fur an hoor each in the afternoons and Annie's got Senga doin' the mornin' fur her. But Ah cannae dae breakfast time, there's ower much tae be doin' in the shop then, and Annie cannae get oot o' her bed afore half-eight - so she says.'

Aggie personally thought this a ridiculous foible and had been on the point of saying so to Annie when she had remembered how much she needed her for the rescue plan. Wisdom and expedience had triumphed over free expression.

'So, Jeannie, will *you* dae the early shift? Gang up there aboot seven o' clock and see tae Johnnie's breakfast, get the auld wuman sorted oot an look after Kate? Annie'll be ower by half-nine or ten, once she's got Senga organised in the shop...'

Jeannie rose and began gathering up the evidence of their little feast.

'It will be ma pleasure, Aggie,' she stated grandly. 'Ye can coont on me.'

'An ye'll no be spreadin' ony dirt aboot Kate?' Aggie was determined to do the job thoroughly. The time for playing games was over. 'Ah cannae think o' her lyin' helpless in bed while the rest of the warld is pickin' ower her bones and judgin' her. An her no even kennin' or bein' able tae stick up fur hersel.'

'Whit dirt wid that be? Ah dinnae ken whit ye're talkin' aboot. Besides,' Jeannie was magnificent now, as she swept through to the scullery, 'Kate's ma guid freend an Ah widnae *dream* o' doin' sich a'thing, even if Ah kent onythin', *which...*' - she placed especial emphasis on this last phrase - '...*which*, of coorse, Ah dinnae!'

'Weel…' Aggie heard the ring of protest-too-much in this last phrase and battled with her suspicion and scepticism. Then, hearing the clatter of Bob's boots outside the back-door, she accepted that she could do no more tonight. She would have to risk it.

'So, ye'll start the morn?'

'Ah'll be there,' said Jeannie happily, as she turned on the cooker to heat up the large pot of stew she had made earlier. She had a sudden generous impulse.

'Wid ye like me tae gie ye some o' this stew fur you and Eck the nicht? It sounds like ye've had a damn busy day an Ah cannae think ye feel like goin' hame an startin' tae cook.'

Aggie, who had given no thought at all to supper, realised suddenly that there was no food in her house beyond a few sprouting tatties and some stale cakes.

'That wid be grand, Jeannie. Thanks, hen. Ye're a pal,' she said warmly and was surprised to feel that it might actually be the truth.

Jeannie decanted a generous helping of the stew, which was thick with root vegetables – a complete and delicious meal in itself – into a smaller pot. Aggie's stomach suddenly rumbled so loudly that Bob, appearing in the doorway of the kitchen, exclaimed: 'Oh, pardon me, ladies. Ah'm that hungry ma belly thinks ma throat's cut!'

The two women burst out laughing but did nothing to disabuse him of his assumption of guilt.

'Ah'll cry ower tae the shop and get the pot back the morn's mornin' when Ah'm finished at Kate's place. Mind ye dinnae slip wi it. Ye'd get yersel in a fine mess an it wid be an awfy waste o' good food.'

The warning was well given as the streets were now covered with fast-freezing slush. Aggie walked the short distance home bearing the precious pot aloft as if it was the Holy Grail itself. Eck had been reconciling himself to spending the little that remained of his week's pocket money on a bag of chips and had not been looking forward to going out into the bitter weather again. He greeted Aggie and her holy grail with the nearest thing to a cry of joy she had ever heard from him.

Bob closed his eyes in ecstasy. A large plate of beef, carrot, parsnip, onion and potato in a rich gravy steamed gently in front of him on the table. He caught Jeannie round the waist as she passed him on her way to sit down for her own meal and turned her round towards him.

'Ah dinnae ken whit Ah'm wantin' tae eat first – yoursel or this braw denner,' he murmured as he buried his face, moist from the steam of the stew, in her belly, nuzzling her like an importunate lamb.

Jeannie giggled as she wriggled out of his grasp and took her seat opposite him.

'The stew'll get cauld - better eat it first. *Ah'll* still be hot later.'

Bob beamed at her. He had come home in a bad mood or as near as his equable temperament would allow. It had been a grueling shift: they were still shorthanded at the pit, due now to the outbreak of influenza, and the strain of working with a reduced team for weeks had reached a new peak today. The easy banter and sense of comrades-in-arms' solidarity that made the pit bearable was, if not dead, then certainly ailing. It was being replaced by irritable selfishness and personal attacks, mainly verbal up to now but likely to turn physical any time. Cutting insults and crafty points-scoring went over Bob's hapless head - and he certainly never returned any of it, with or without interest – so the men largely left him alone. But he had sensed the atmosphere of grim, smouldering endurance and had shrunk still further into his isolation. It had been a long seven hours, broken up only briefly by the shortened piece-break, which now seemed a long time ago.

To make matters worse, Eck had been binding on about Aggie on both journeys to and from the pit. Bob had only been half-listening, especially on the way home – something about her not being there to give him any dinner before the shift and maybe not going to be there after it either. Bob had briefly wondered why Eck was so bothered about this since most of the time Aggie served up inedible food anyway, according to her dissatisfied husband. He had been glad to leave Eck at his front door, drearily complaining that the house was in darkness which meant Aggie was indeed not yet home.

But, as always, his Jeannie, with her lovely food and her lovely wee body ready and waiting for him, had revitalised him just by their sight and smell before he even tasted either of them. He attacked the stew obediently, feeling the residue of strain and weariness being replaced by contentment and expectation.

As the fiercest hunger pangs ceased their growling, he looked across at his wife. *Man, wis that no a sicht fur sore een. Jeannie's*

172

lookin' awfy bonnie the nicht…an richt perky…this might be a good nicht tae try…'

'Ah've somethin' tae tell ye, Bob.' She cut into his optimistic fantasy. 'Ah'm gettin' up early the morn, aboot half-six. Ah'm goin' roon tae Kate Cruikshank's hoose.'

Eck had been speaking about Kate at one point, he recalled now. Something about Aggie not coming home at dinner-time because she was at Kate's.

'She's no weel and it's serious.' Jeannie spoke with all the gravity of an elder stateman pronouncing on the state of the economy. 'We've a' tae put oor shoulders tae the wheel and dae oor bit.' Now she sounded like Churchill exhorting the nation to endurance. Bob half-expected a burst of stirring rhetoric which might make reference to beaches, hedges and finest hours but she contented herself with a portentous nod which culminated in a lady-like burp.

'That's richt guid o' ye, darlin',' he approved.

She simpered. The small hand she had put up politely to the burp remained at her mouth, trailing lightly over the lips. Her tongue came out and licked a fingertip whilst her gaze never left Bob. Entranced and excited, he sought to think of something that would keep her attention.

'Eck wis talkin' aboot Kate – Aggie's been roon there a' day, Ah think. Oh, an…' he suddenly remembered something that was bound to get her really excited: 'That lad Graham's back in the pub. Ah saw him pittin' oot the empties at the back o' The Toll when we were passin' on the way tae the pit. Will Ah gang in the morn's mornin' an ask him whit he fund oot when he followed Kate that time?'

He was delighted that he had remembered this, confident it would be his passport to new levels of ecstasy that night.

'Naw, dinnae worry aboot him, Bob. Ah'm no needin' him ony mair.'

'But Ah thocht ye were desperate tae ken whit Kate wis daein on Tuesdays?'

'Wednesdays, Bob. But never mind aboot it noo.'

'But, why no?' he burst out in frustration, shoveling a large forkful into his mouth for comfort. He could see his exciting, innovatory plans becoming less and less likely to be realised.

'Ah already *ken* a' Ah need tae. But, it disnae matter because Ah'm no really interested in ither folk's bizness ony mair. Ah'm a new wumman!'

173

Jeannie was now sitting very upright and eating with exaggerated daintiness, as prim and proper as a Victorian governess. Bob threw his fork and knife on to his empty plate and leapt up unable to contain himself a moment longer.

'Ye saucy wee minx,' he yelled, excitedly. 'Ah'll gie ye playin' at being a' buttoned up and prissy as a prune. Ah'll gie ye new wumman!'

The twins, arriving home an hour later, finished off Jeannie's half-eaten meal and scraped the cold stewpot to fill their sandwiches. 'Would you listen to those two?' whistled Dave, as Jeannie's shrieks and Bob's roars of laughter came from upstairs. 'They're goin' their mile the nicht! It's no natural at their age.'

'Ah meant it, Bob.' Jeannie's head appeared from out the long, white nightdress she had thrown over her head. She slipped into bed beside him.

'Surely no?' he murmured sleepily as he turned to her, one of his big hands beginning to move up her leg, pushing up the nightdress. She smelled of roses from the special soap which she kept hidden in the kitchen, away from the marauding twins, and always used when having a wash after their love-making.

His smell was still more animal than botanical. She pushed him off: 'Go an hae a wash an pit yer pyjamas on, fur ony's sake.'

Bob groaned. Jeannie could be amazing - inventive, permissive, uninhibited - during lengthy love sessions, but she had the ability to revert immediately afterwards to the fussy, bossy woman who ruled her home and husband with a rod of iron.

It was part of her charm for him, in a way, that her two personae were so different and he lived for the moment when he broke through from the public face of the prim housewife into the secret 'saucy minx' only he knew. For her, too, it was equally exciting, when placid, hen-pecked Bob turned into her demanding, dominating sexual partner. The interplay of these four characters kept their marriage vibrant and a constant source of wonder to their sons.

As he settled back into bed five minutes later, she said again: 'Ah meant whit Ah said.'

'Surely no,' he replied again. 'Ye're no really goin' tae ...' he was thinking of some of the outrageous suggestions, promises and mock-threats that Jeannie always used to spur him to greater heights and greater delights. It was a game which had been part of their foreplay from an early stage of their sex-life and, though never as inventive as she was, he happily joined in and occasionally came up with fantasies that surprised them both.

Jeannie ignored the allusion. She never acknowledged or referred to anything they had said or done whilst in their secret personae - though quite a lot of it found its way into her racier stories.

'Ah've made up my mind,' she pursued. 'Nae mair gossipin' an diggin' up dirt. Ah'm goin' tae become someone folk can trust.'

She dwelt fondly on the memory of Kate's vulnerability and dewy gratitude when she had finally brought herself to believe that she could actually leave her fate in Jeannie's hands and rest easy. It was sustaining Jeannie now in the struggle to live out her decision to change.

'Ye see, Bob, whit happened in Anstruther wi Kate...'

She shifted to accommodate him as his large, meaty hand pushed up between her thighs. It was not that Bob had any hopes of, or indeed energy for, further action: he simply liked to fall asleep intimately attached in some way to her. The hand settled comfortably, rather like a hot water bottle, between the tops of her thighs and he slipped happily into sleep.

Jeannie talked on. She was well aware that he was asleep but this did not bother her; she often discussed things with him when he was asleep and, in truth, frequently got as much useful response out of him as she did when he was awake.

When she had told him all about Aggie's visit and her own role not only in the rescue plan for Kate's illness but in a much bigger, more exciting and completely secret plan also involving Kate, she explained that in her newly reformed character she must, albeit regretfully, lay down her plans to snoop on Aggie.

'It's just no ma bizness, Bob,' she said, stroking his head, which lay heavily on her shoulder. 'Now there, did ye ever think ye'd here yer Jeannie say that?'

Bob gave an answering snore and grunted as she gently pulled his hand out of her crotch, smoothed down her nightdress and wriggled demurely down into her own place in the bed beside him.

It was after half-past ten next morning when Annie finally disengaged herself from Senga's clutches. That good lady had risen to the occasion the day before and 'minded the shop' for most of the afternoon. Annie had had little time to explain things to her and had had to hope she would use her common sense and cope somehow.

Annie made a big effort and turfed her bulk out of bed at ten past eight so as to be at the shop before nine and ready to give Senga her belated induction but Senga had already opened up with the spare key Annie had given her and was hard at work. Annie goggled when she saw what Senga had spent her first shift doing, the day before.

With not many customers out and about in the miserable weather, she had tackled the despised boxes of old wartime clothes. Annie had briefly referred to them, giving one of them a disgusted kick, indicating that they were going to be sent back with a note that pulled no punches and made sure the 'cheeky chancers dinnae try it on again'.

But Senga, casting around for something to while away the darkening afternoon hours, had had a brainwave and had proceeded to act upon it. She had created dozens of 'lucky dip' bags, each one containing a selection of the horrible clothes, making sure each bag had large items whose material could be dyed and used for dress-making, smaller items with buttons that could be cut off and saved, socks that could be used as furniture polishing mitts...

Annie might not have much imagination about the use of such stock but Senga knew how resourceful and creative many women had learned to be during the long years of rationing and shortage. She also knew that the serendipity of buying a mystery bundle would appeal to them. She had even made attractive labels for the bags out of old stock cards, decorating these with witty drawings.

'Ah thocht we could tie some bonnie ribbon round the top of each bag and maybe mak a pile of them in the windae wi a big notice – something like: *Mystery Bags for All: Why Not Try Your Luck?*' she suggested. 'Of course, we need tae dae a deal wi the supplier first and beat them doon tae a knock-doon price fur the lot. Then we can work oot how much we need tae charge tae mak a profit oot of selling the lucky bags. Ah've coonted them an there's twenty-eight. So if we charge five bob for each and we offer the suppliers a fiver fur the lot, we'll mak twa pounds profit.'

She beamed at Annie. 'Of course, we dinnae gie them the ribbon awa wi them, that wid reduce oor profit. That's jist fur show in the windae. We can iron it and roll it up again fur sale afterwards.'

Before Annie could express her opinion of this masterly business and marketing strategy, Senga had launched into a whole stream of other business ideas. She had fallen asleep last night, for once not thinking about embroidery, but with her brain spinning through dozens of ideas for transforming Annie's dreary little shop.

The window, for example, should have a good Christmas display once the lucky dip bags were all sold, something bright and lively. Annie's window had not changed for years, the liveliest thing about it likely to be a trapped bluebottle in summer whose carcass would eventually go to augment the sad pile of corpses in the dusty corner.

Annie listened with a growing feeling that she might have unleashed a tiger which was about to tear up her comfortable little shop and her comfortable little life. Senga was energised in a way neither of them had ever experienced before, her excitement unquenchable and even a little contagious.

Annie found herself agreeing and approving, Senga's enthusiasm stirring her own sluggish imagination and almost shaking her comatose ambition awake.

'She'll be givin' that Marks and Spencer a run fur their money,' she chuckled to herself as she crossed the road to Kate's, having at last managed to escape from Senga's list of improvement and development proposals. Not that Annie had ever been in such a shop but Graham, the new man at The Toll pub, had told her about the one in London when he had called in to buy a pair of gloves.

'Everything you need, choice and variety, lots of it, all under one roof – it's the way forward,' he had declared. 'The day of the small draper's shop is over.' Then, catching her black look: 'But, of course, there will always be a place for the small trader in a small community like this one.'

She was wheezing with guilty apologies as she hurried up the short stair and into Kate's house. *Ah hope it's no been too much fur Jeannie and pit her richt aff comin' the morn. She's no used tae lookin' after auld folk.*

The first thing she noticed was the noise: a wireless was turned up to full volume. The second thing was that the door to the smallest bedroom was lying open. Annie knew from her weekly searches that this only ever contained uninteresting and unused equipment for the old woman. Today, however, it appeared to be very much in use.

The wheelchair was gone and one of the packets of *female incontinence pads* had been opened and it looked like one or two of them had actually been taken out. *She's never got that stubborn auld goat tae actually pit one on! Ah never even dared suggest it.*

She found Maggie's bed empty and stripped and the old woman herself sitting in the wheelchair by the bedroom window, looking out and cackling at something coming from a very loud wireless which sat on the sill. The door to the sitting-room was closed and, above the racket from the wireless, she could make out no noise behind it. She peeped into Kate's room and found all neat and tidy, the invalid propped up and appearing clean and comfortable, even managing a wan smile as Annie waved cheerily from the door.

Going through finally into the sitting-room, she saw that Jeannie was in the kitchen cooking. Already a good smell of frying onions filled the air, mingling with another delicious smell – could that possibly be *scones baking*?

Jeannie turned and greeted Annie calmly, dismissing her apologies for the late hour with: 'Is it that the time a'ready? Time flies when ye're enjoyin' yersel, richt enough!'

The kitchen was in apple-pie order: there was no sign of the bedding stripped off Maggie's presumably soiled bed, nor of any other nursing tasks; and dinner was obviously underway. Jeannie calmly completed her culinary task and turned the gas down under the mince-and-tatties.

'Ye'll hae a cup o' tea, Annie? An a wee scone wi butter an jam? They're fresh oot o' the oven.' She indicated a laden cooling-tray with a clean tea-towel covering the scones to keep them warm.

'Geez,' thought Annie, *'there'll be nae keepin' up wi her. She's jist showin' aff. Thank God Aggie's no goin' tae be any trouble tae shine ower. Trust Jeannie tae mak it intae a competition! She aye has tae be the wee Smart Alec.'*

She watched in some despair as Jeannie laid two neat little trays, covering them with prettily embroidered tray-cloths (no doubt presents to Kate from Senga at some time) and put a thick mug on one and a fine china cup and saucer on the other. She buttered and jammed a scone and put it on the tray with the mug then handed the lot to Annie.

'That's fur the auld yin. Ah'll tak Kate's cup intae her masel. She'd no manage a scone with sich a sair throat but Ah'll try her wi a wee rich tea biscuit dunked in the hot tea tae soften it.' Jeannie bustled briskly out of the room.

'*Yes, sir, no, sir, three bloody bags full, sir,*' muttered Annie as she did what she was told.

Old Maggie had to be tapped on the shoulder to get her attention, so immersed was she in *Housewives Choice* bellowing out from the wireless. Annie turned it down and addressed her.

'Are ye a' richt, Maggie? It's me, Annie. Has Jeannie been lookin' after ye weel enough?'

Commonsense was telling her that it was in all their interests for Old Maggie to be content and compliant but she could not repress a sneaking hope that the old troublemaker would prove too much for Jeannie. Annie had been enjoying the sense of superiority the Wednesday afternoons had given her when Maggie had continued to compare her favourably to Kate. She was not liking at all the idea that Jeannie was overtaking her in this race.

'Yon's a braw wee woman,' enthused Maggie. 'Right sympathetic and kindly. An smart as paint, kens what I want before I ask for it.' She chuckled and reached out for her tray. 'Is that a home-made scone, fresh out o' the oven? I thought I smelt somethin' bakin'. Can ye turn up the wireless again, Annie. I'm fair enjoying this programme: Jeannie suggested it.'

Annie tried to tell herself this was what she wanted to hear. It would make all their lives easier during the temporary rescue regime and maybe even make Kate's life easier when she was recovered and back on the job, but... *Ach, whit's the point*? she conceded drearily to herself. *We'd be wastin' oor time tryin' tae upstage Jeannie Gilhooley. She's aye been sharper than a tack and bossier than the Gestapo. One puir auld wifie has nae chance against her.*

It was perhaps the first time anyone had ever thought of Maggie Cruikshanks as someone to be pitied rather than feared.

She could hear a low conversational mumble coming from Kate's room. The door was closed and she moved towards it intending to go in and join them. She had her hand on the door handle and could almost make out Jeannie saying something like: 'Dinnae you fret, dearie, Ah'll see tae it a' masel.'

As Annie began to open the door, the next sentence came more clearly to her and stopped her in her tracks: 'Your Angus has it a' in hand.'

Jeannie had her back to the door but Kate, sitting up in bed, was facing it. Her flushed face registered a flicker of horrified panic when she saw Annie coming in and Jeannie, catching it, whirled round.

'Hoo are ye doin' the day, Kate?' Annie sailed into the bedroom as only one of her girth *can* sail. 'So, ye've the flu an somethin' else bad Ah hear? Never mind, we're a' here tae help. Jist you tak yer rest an dae whit Dr Jim tells ye. We'll hae ye weel again afore the New Year.'

She had some vague notion of the need to establish the corporate nature of the rescue package and to cut Jeannie - who was obviously suffering from delusions of grandeur and in danger of assuming all the credit and responsibility - down to size. She was taken aback at the effect her words had on them both.

Kate gave a hoarse scream and covered her face with shaking hands. Jeannie straightened her back so far she almost reared up between the advancing Annie and the bed, moving forward and blocking her way.

'*Like a bloody lioness in front o' her cubs,*' thought Annie.

'Whit's the *New Year* got tae dae wi it?' hissed Jeannie.

Annie boggled, completely baffled. She needed time to ruminate at her usual ponderous pace on the mention of 'Angus' but had been already looking forward to doing so with Jeannie as an informed ally. Another delicious hippos-in-the-mud session seemed to be beckoning. Now both Jeannie's words and attitude threw her. Why was she being so belligerent? What did she know? What was going on between her and Kate? And why had the innocent mention of the *New Year* called forth such an immediate, hostile reaction?

There was a moment's silence in the small bedroom. Jeannie saw at once from the owlish expression on Annie's moon face that her swift over-reaction had made matters worse and had only served to intensify Annie's suspicion. She knew Annie well enough to know that it would take her a few laborious thinking sessions to come to any conclusions, however, so she moved swiftly to damage limitation. Whether Annie had heard the mention of 'Angus' or not was one thing – she would have to deal with that later. The first priority was to divert her off the *New Year* track.

'Kate's no tae feel under any pressure tae hurry up an get weel. Worryin' aboot gettin' weel can jist set a body back,' she pronounced with a gravitas that would not have discredited Consultant Simpson

180

himself. 'The New Year's jist roon the corner so we'll hae tae wait an see hoo she is by then.'

She backed Annie purposefully out of the room, calling over her shoulder to Kate: 'We'll go an hae oor ain cuppie. Ah'll pop ma heid roon yer door afore Ah leave and say 'cheerio' if ye're no sleepin'. Dinnae you worry aboot a thing.'

Once they were back in the kitchen, Jeannie invited Annie to sit down at the little kitchen table with their own tea and scones.

*'As if it wis **her** hoose an Ah wis a visitor – does she no tak the biscuit?'* thought Annie.

The next ten minutes left her feeling even more baffled. The mud-wallowing session she had confidently expected did not materialise: Jeannie fended off all of Annie's enquiries with a patchwork of half-truths, complete lies, flights of fancy and occasional facts, making Annie's head spin as she tried to guess which was which. By the time Jeannie rose to take her leave, Annie was wallowing, not in the happy-hippo mud of spicy gossip but in a quagmire of perplexed uncertainty.

What was worse, Jeannie had somehow managed to convey that Annie's interest in Kate was rather unsavoury and that she, Jeannie, found it quite reprehensible. She did not actually give another airing to yesterday's over-used phrase concerning the minding of one's own business but she conveyed exactly that same message.

It was completely uncharted territory for Annie and she had to make a conscious effort several times to close her gaping mouth. In the curiosity engendered by the tantalising snippet she had heard, she had quite forgotten her own resolution of the day before to live up to Johnnie's description of her as *'someone so trustworthy'* but it seemed that, if she could not manage to achieve trustworthiness, she was to have it thrust upon her.

On her way out, as she put on her hat and coat in the lobby, Jeannie gave Annie her handover briefing.

'Johnnie had forgotten tae pit a pad on his mither at bedtime last nicht and the pair auld soul wis fair soakin' when Ah got here. The pads are in the wee room if ye need tae change her again – but Ah'm sure ye ken that since ye've looked after her afore. Ah dinnae ken hoo tae work they machines in the kitchen but Johnnie does, he says. So Ah said Ah'd jist leave the dirty sheets in the big ane an he'll see tae them the nicht. There's mince an tatties cookin' fur the denner – Ah brocht some mince roon masel an there wis onions and tatties here a'ready.'

For the second time in half-an-hour, Annie boggled. 'Ye actually got the auld yin tae pit on ane o' they continental pads?'

Jeannie frowned. '*Incontinence*, no 'continental',' she reproved. 'Of coorse. Wha else wid they be fur?'

'But…but… Kate said… Ah didnae dare even mention them. Hoo on earth did ye persuade her?'

Jeannie shrugged uncomprehendingly. It had never occurred to her that there *would* be a problem. She vaguely recalled some of Kate's ramblings of yesterday covering Maggie's toileting problems but she had been much more interested in what was going on between Kate and Angus Smillie in Windygates and their forthcoming secret plans. The adventure of her own visit to the anxious butcher had further superseded in her mind such trivial details as soiled beds and endless washing.

When she had arrived that morning to find Maggie's bed a disgusting mess, she had simply blamed it on Johnnie.

'Ye puir auld thing,' she had cried. 'He's forgot tae pit on yer pad last nicht. Noo, whaur are they?'

She had quickly located them and noticed the wheelchair at the same time. 'It's a damn shame,' she had sympathised as she cleaned up the old lady, put an incontinence pad on her and bustled her into a clean nightdress and into the wheelchair. Still talking volubly, she had stripped the bed: 'Ah expect ye didnae want tae mention it tae him, him bein' a man an a' – an yer son. But it's no fair. Ye need tae keep yer dignity, Maggie, ye've aye had dignity, Ah've aye admired that aboot ye. Jist you mak sure he sees tae ye properly the nicht at bedtime. It's the least he can do when the rest o' us are doin' a'thing else.'

And Maggie, perhaps because she had known Jeannie for years as a neighbour and seen her in bruising action with her own household or perhaps because she was seduced by the magic word 'dignity', had simply succumbed. In any case, she had no hope of getting a word in edgewise. Jeannie talked as fast as she worked and had tamed the daunting list of early-morning demands by nine o'clock, sending Johnnie off to work mightily relieved, both to know that his home, his wife and his mother were all in extremely competent hands *and* to escape the sound of Jeannie's voice.

How he had ended up agreeing to see to all the household washing as his part in the package he was not quite sure. He would have to consult his management theory book. He was not sure if it covered the management of an individual quite like Jeannie Gilhooley. In fact, he strongly suspected he was the one being managed here and that she could teach him a thing or two.

The regime which Jeannie established the first day proved very workable. She arrived prompt at ten-to-seven each morning and had both invalids sitting up enjoying fresh tea and toast by quarter-past.

Johnnie had been told to be up and getting washed in the bathroom before she arrived and the bedding he used on the couch in the sitting-room to be already rolled up and hidden behind it. He obeyed her to the letter and was rewarded with an excellent cooked breakfast on the table prompt at half-past-seven.

By nine o'clock, Kate and Maggie would both have been given smaller versions of Johnnie's feast then had their beds either straightened up or changed. She made sure both her charges were washed and into clean nighties by half-past-nine ready for Annie's shift – just in case Annie was ever on time.

This became increasingly unlikely as the days rolled by, partly because Annie relaxed more and more, knowing Jeannie had everything so well in hand and partly because getting away from Senga with her string of enthusiastic suggestions and progress reports became harder every day. In fact, there was really no need for Annie to go into the shop in the mornings at all after the first day: Senga was very much at home and in command of the situation. It was more a fear on Annie's part that there was a kind of gradual takeover being effected. Showing her face each morning was her way of hanging on to the fact that she *was* still the proprietor and Senga the mere helper. Not that Senga acknowledged this fine distinction: increasingly, she treated Annie as a mere sounding board for her ideas, many of which were already well on the way to being implemented.

Whilst she waited for Annie to arrive, Jeannie cooked, baked, ironed and cleaned. She shopped in the afternoons and kept the house provisioned, including the makings of the midday dinner. Aggie was told to bring pies and other bakeries in with her in the afternoon for the high tea at six o'clock.

Johnnie manfully did his duty with steamie and screamie in the evenings. Old Maggie continued to accept the 'continental pads',

183

indeed she even asked for them and roundly condemned Kate for not giving her them in the past.

'*She* doesn't care about ma dignity, that one,' she declared. 'No like Jeannie.'

Annie and Aggie at first muttered resentfully to themselves and each other at Jeannie's cool, unstoppable assumption of authority but, in their hearts, they were glad to let her get on with it. They had their shops to run and their temporary helpers to supervise. Their lives had already been full enough, their time and talents stretched.

Jeannie, with her boundless energy and restless imagination, lacking the outlet which their businesses gave them, had poured herself into the management of the rescue package and achieved fast and remarkable results. Observing how quickly she had overcome not only the immediate problems but even some longstanding ones – and with his own humiliating efforts fresh in his memory - Johnnie reflected that the mining industry could do with someone like her in a senior position.

'*Damn pity she's a woman. What a waste! She's a hundred times better than most of those high-falutin' fellas at the working lunches in St Andrews,*' he thought.

Kate, groggily but thankfully aware that the household seemed to be running on oiled wheels, was able to take the total rest prescribed as her illness ran its course.

Dr Kenny congratulated Johnnie on the excellent measures he had put in place to care for his wife and ensure her recovery. He also congratulated himself that, once again, a little straight talking to a self-centred husband had improved matters for a sick wife.

And so, unbelievably, out of what had seemed a disaster, came a situation where everyone was happy.

Johnnie basked in Dr Jim's approval and admiration and Aggie basked in Johnnie's when she handed over to him at tea-time, since he seemed to think the speedy and spectacular success of the rescue plan all due to her.

Bessie, Nellie and Mina were delighted with their free bakeries, as were their hungry children, and Senga was entranced with her new position and excited by her awakening business skills.

Once she had recovered from the shock, Annie began to be excited herself by Senga's ideas for the long-stagnant business and was already wondering if Senga would be interested in continuing after the crisis was over.

Even Eck seemed as content as he was ever likely to be, encouraging Aggie to take her time and make sure Kate got all the attention she needed – and to be sure to give his best wishes to her for a speedy recovery.

Old Maggie's behaviour and temperament seemed to improve daily under Jeannie's clever management – most of which was down to Jeannie simply assuming Maggie wanted to behave well and giving her no scope to pursue the other option.

Kate relaxed, reassured that all was well in her home and happy to put her trust in Jeannie for the other great matter on her mind.

There was only one person who was not happy. But he was an outsider, not part of – not even aware of – *Operation Rescue Kate*. Cut off, even, from any news of her though, for the moment, he held the key to her happiness.

At last the week was over.

Angus rose at the crack of dawn and spent a fussy morning, fiddling his way through unnecessary household chores, which had already been done several times over during the past restless week. His energy was returning now at a rapid pace and he was finding these last few weeks of convalescence extremely dull.

He made his now daily pilgrimage down the hill to the local shops and walked slowly back up with his few purchases. He no longer needed the services of the kindly neighbour who had kept him provisioned in the earlier housebound weeks.

He spent longer than usual choosing a few delicacies and carried them like precious cargo up the hill; then he spun out the task of setting them out and putting together a particularly inviting tea-table. He had a bath and attended meticulously to his own toilette, cleaning the bathroom again before leaving it, replacing the clean towel which he had barely used with a fresh one.

'Ah'm like somethin' oot o' that 'Good Housekeeping' magazine! A' Ah need is a frilly apron an a wee feather duster. Ma granny wid hae been prood o' me. God, Ah'll be glad tae get back tae work.'
Though he was making more and more of an effort to 'speak proper' after his moment of identification with Mr Swanky Simpson in hospital, he still tended to revert to broad dialect in thought.

It was almost time: quarter-past-one. She usually came just after half-past. Unable to think of one more petty, pointless task, and reduced to pacing round and round the beautifully-set low tea-table in the middle of the warm sitting-room, he decided to break with their established routine and walk down the hill to meet her.

What did it matter if people saw them together now? There would be very few more Wednesdays like this now – it was all going to change and soon everyone would know everything anyway.

He banked up the already enormous fire, put the guard securely on it, struggled into his long, thick winter coat, donned his hat and set off, whistling cheerfully. He felt a welcome return of his old jaunty, jack-the-lad instincts and it showed in his gait.

'Mr. Smillie's gettin' a lot better, Ah see. It's wunnerfu whit they can do noo-adays,' said the kindly neighbour, who happened to be looking out her window.

The bus was late and he made it all the way down the hill, round the corner and along the main street to the bus stop. It was a cold, bright day and the sparkling winter sunlight reflected his mood of devil-may-care optimism as he waited in the little bus shelter.

At last it hove into sight and he went forward confidently to meet it. He could see six or seven standing passengers waiting to alight. He craned his neck to see which one was her. The bus ground to a shuddering halt. The standing passengers lurched and grabbed at the nearest pole or person then thankfully righted themselves and began to jump or lower themselves down off the platform, depending on age and agility. A lad of about fifteen leapt off first before the bus had completely stopped; a young mother with a heavy shopping bag helped her small child off; two old men descended with careful dignity and went off chatting together; a surly-looking man of indeterminate age jumped off and immediately began lighting up his next cigarette; and, last of all... He stared in horrified disappointment.

There was no mistaking Mrs Jeannie Gilhooley *this* week: gone were the bedraggled, old-fashioned clothes which had seemed so incongruous with the mane of streaming-wet, abundant black hair; gone were the strange, clomping, shoes and the funny old-lady's handbag. She wore a smart winter costume and well-fitting court shoes with a modern matching bag. Her hair was tightly tamed into a gleaming, perfectly formed bun which lay submissively on her neck, just below a tip-tilted felt hat. Jeannie in her Sunday Best and a pleasure to behold.

What's she come again fur? Whaur is Kate?

Jeannie alighted nimbly, last off because she had been berating the driver for his poor braking skills. Not expecting to see Angus at the bus stop, she sailed past him without looking up, her indignation with the driver's answering gesture lending her even more impetus than usual. She set off at a spanking pace towards the foot of the hill.

Angus looked blankly after her. It had never occurred to him that it would be Jeannie who would come again this week. When she had brought the news to him a week ago of Kate being taken ill and having to go home without coming to see him, he had been disappointed, resigned but not unduly concerned. He had imagined a bad cold, maybe a wee bit fever, nothing a couple of days in bed with plenty of hot drinks and a few Beecham's powders wouldn't cure.

He hesitated, running the possibility through his mind that Jeannie was in Windygates on an errand of her own and Kate might be on the next bus. Maybe something had held her up and she had not been able to escape as early as usual.

The bus revved up enthusiastically and, with a belch of stinking black smoke, charged off on its merry way. Obviously the driver's take-off skills matched his braking ones.

Angus choked on the fumes as they hit him full in the face. By the time he cleared his lungs and wiped his eyes, he saw that Jeannie was rounding the corner and heading up the hill towards his house. *She's definitely comin' to see me. She'll get a locked door.*

Suddenly, Jeannie seemed like a very important person to him. Bearing, surely, news of Kate who must be seriously ill. *Maybe, Ah'll have to go and visit **her** in hospital. That would be a turn-up for the book!*

Galvanized, he set off at a run after Jeannie. It was the first time for many a year that he had tried to run: previous portliness and recent illness had seen to that. At first it felt good, an enjoyable flexing of his strengthening muscles, an exhibition of his new, slimmer self. By the time he reached the corner to turn up the hill, however, his heart was hammering uncomfortably and each breath was more painfully drawn than the last.

He stopped at the foot of the hill and looked up at Jeannie who, unencumbered by either excess weight or ill-health and fit as a fiddle – her nightly exercise routine in the marriage bed saw to that – was setting a cracking pace. She seemed to be scaling the hill with all the ease of a mountain goat.

Defeated, he sat down heavily on the low wall that wound round the corner. Waves of nausea washed over him, recalling him to the miserably weak, early days after his operation. He tried to regain the rhythm of his breathing and to think of clear, icy water running over a sunlit burn – an image which one of the nurses had suggested to combat nausea and which he had found helpful in hospital.

After a time, he became aware of a sharp pain in his left buttock. Exploring cautiously with a shaking hand, he found the sawn-off stump of a railing which had been one of thousands taken away some twelve years ago for the making of wartime munitions. There was actually a whole row of them along this wall, he now realised. With a considerable squeeze, he managed to wriggle both buttocks between two railing-stumps and ease the pain.

He was breathing more easily now and his heart was slowing but he knew that the sickening dizziness was still lurking, ready to pounce if he tried to move. He groaned.

She'll be there by now. What will she be thinkin'? What if she goes awa and I never find oot aboot Kate? Common sense told him that she would have to come back down the hill again for the bus home eventually but common sense was cold comfort at that moment.

Jeannie peered through the bay window. A roaring fire, welcome sight on this frosty day; a low table in the middle of the floor, covered in a rose pink damask cloth and beautifully set for two with dainty china, silver milk jug and matching sugar bowl; and, standing at the side of the table, an impressive three-tier cake-stand. She hauled a large empty flower-pot over to the window, turned it upside down and stood on it for a better view.

The room was spotlessly tidy, cushions plumped, rugs straight, furniture shining, fireplace swept, tiles gleaming, polished brass companion set with poker, tongs, brush and small shovel winking in the firelight.

The cake stand sported tiny crustless sandwiches, cut into triangles, on its first tier, scones and pancakes on the second and two large strawberry tarts on the top one.

He's expectin' company, a' richt. But, whit a spread and the place like a palace.

188

Jeannie had had a lot of experience of men in her life, having grown up with noisy, messy, feckless twin brothers, earlier versions of Jeannie's own twins. They had sadly paid the ultimate price for their fecklessness, which had been charitably described in dispatches as bravery in the soldierly execution of duty. She was used to Bob's obedient, bumbling attempts at household tasks or her sons' uninspired, forced-labour approach to them. *This* level of achievement she would have judged to be way beyond male competence.

He's either a nancy boy or he's fair besotted wi Kate. She doubted the former, remembering the butcher's ready line in cheeky innuendo and his roving eye with younger, prettier customers - or even with more mature ladies if they still had their looks, it would seem.

Dusting down her skirt, she replaced the flower-pot and tried the door-bell again. Where on earth could he be when he was clearly expecting Kate any minute?

She recalled Kate's tale of the day in his shop when he had disappeared into the back and she had gone in search of him, laughed openly at the noises and smells he was making in the toilet and then later discovered he had been seriously ill. Could he have been taken bad again and be inside, unable to get to the door? Maybe he was lying on the floor in the bathroom or bedroom in terrible agony.

Jeannie's fertile imagination painted a ream of possible scenarios, each one more alarming that the last. *Maybe Ah should try an get in. Ah cannae break doon the door, Ah'm no strong enough. Is there a windae open somewhere?*

Fired with the dramatic possibility of coming to the rescue of a dying man, of saving his life and becoming a heroine, she marched resolutely round to the back of the house.

Time passed. He wasn't sure how much as he focused fiercely on the image of the clear, babbling burn, terrified that he might throw up in the street.

Then, suddenly, he could *taste* the water in his mouth, feel its iciness attacking the nerves in his gums. He choked a little as he swallowed the first cold draught. He opened startled eyes and saw the wrinkled, rosy-apple face of his kindly neighbour, very close to his own as she held the cup to his lips. Behind her loomed a tall man, the owner of the wall he had been sitting on for the past ten minutes.

'Tak yer time. Dinnae choke yersel.' She spoke soothingly, as to a child.

The water was a very good idea. He felt better almost at once and within a few minutes was struggling to free his backside from the straitjacket of the railing stumps.

'Tak yer time,' she reiterated. 'Here, lean on me.'

This seemed an impractical proposition, since he was six feet tall and probably weighed twice as much as her, even with his new, slim physique. The tall man, new to the area and not really known to Angus, moved quickly round to his other side and, putting his arm under Angus's elbow, briskly manhandled him to his feet. He kept a strong, firm hand under the elbow as Angus swayed a little, then steadied and nodded thanks and reassurance that he was not going to collapse again.

The man, military in bearing, seeing that his task was done, nodded politely, turned on his heel and went back into his house.

'Keeps himsel tae himsel,' explained little Mrs Clancy, who did not and whose kindness had given her access to considerable knowledge of her neighbours' lives and personalities. 'Widower, was in the RAF, spends his time makin' wee models o' planes an writin' books aboot them.'

She linked her arm into Angus determinedly. 'Are we goin' tae try it? Jist real slow, now...'

He was feeling much stronger now and would much have preferred to go it alone, partly for reasons of pride and dignity, partly because she was so much smaller than him that she felt more like a weight dragging on his arm than any kind of support. But there was no shaking her off and the incongruous duo began its laborious ascent.

When they paused halfway up at her insistence for a rest, she said: 'Och, Ah near furgot tae tell ye! Ye've a visitor, a lady, she wis ringing yer bell and lookin' in yer windae. That's whit caught ma attention an made me look oot. Then Ah looked doon the hill an saw ye sittin' on the wa an Ah kent somethin' wis wrang wi ye. Ah saw ye settin' aff and Ah wis jist thinkin' hoo much better ye were lookin' tae. But ye've jist pushed the boat oot ower far. These things tak time. Ah mind ma cousin in Pittenweem took near a year tae get back tae his auld sel...'

'Is she still there?' Angus cut into these reminiscences abruptly. He craned his neck anxiously to see the front of his house. 'Is she...'

'It's no yer usual lady visitor,' said Mrs Clancy, knowledgeably, 'This ane's a lot wee'er, but awfy weel-dressed – no that yer ither lady isnae aye smart tae. Ye're lucky tae hae sich bonnie visitors.' Her eyes gleamed a little though she kept her voice neutral.

Angus groaned. Since his parents had died and he had settled into his bachelor existence, he had largely been able to keep his distance from his neighbours, even ones he had known for years. And that was how he wanted to keep it. He hated being caught up in or, worse still, being the subject of gossip. He observed enough of it going on, often right under his nose, in his shop.

With an effort, he restrained himself from asking anything else about his visitor and he made no response to her observations about his circle of female friends. Once again, with expressions of gratitude and reassurances that he no longer needed help, he attempted politely to remove her arm from his, but she hung on, limpet-like.

They reached the top of the hill and he could see his front garden and door clearly. No sign of Jeannie. *Whit can hae happened tae her? Has she gone intae someone else's hoose?*

He cast a searching glance at the other four houses in the cu-de-sac besides his own and Mrs Clancy's. Their net-curtained windows were impenetrable, their gardens deserted, their doors closed. All was silent and lifeless.

There came a crash, the sound of glass breaking, a scraping, sliding noise and a high-pitched yell. It came, unmistakably, from behind Angus's house.

With one alarmed look at each other, he and his self-appointed nurse rushed over to his gate and hurried round the side of the house. The scene that met their eyes, and its accompanying soundtrack, brought them up short. Jeannie, swearing loudly and colourfully, was picking herself up from behind the metal coal bunker.

She had climbed up its sloping top to reach the kitchen window which had looked to be off its catch. When she had got near enough to see it properly, she had seen that it was not actually undone enough to pull open and she had begun fiddling with it. At first, she had wisely used only one hand for the fiddling and the other to hold on to the sill for balance and safety; but, becoming frustrated with her ineffectual one-handed attempts to free the catch, she had rashly employed the other hand as well. This had certainly resulted in success but, as is often the way with awkward devices that we fiddle with impatiently and at length, success came so suddenly that she was caught off-

191

balance, and began to slip backwards down the bunker lid. Its thin layer of ice and her high-heeled shoes hastened her progress and in terror she had grabbed at the swinging window. She could not sustain her grasp but she did swing it open far and fast enough to crash it resoundingly on to the wall of the house, smashing the glass.

Jeannie had fallen off the bunker on to an old coal sack, full of fire-ash and cinders, which had mercifully broken her fall and saved her from injury but had wrought havoc with her appearance. Her stockings were torn, one of her shoe-heels was broken, her face and clothes were covered in ashy dust and, once again, her hair was tumbling down her back in the most abandoned fashion.

'Michty me!' exclaimed Mrs Clancy blankly. 'Wha on earth is that?'

CHAPTER TEN

KATE

Maggie snorted awake from her mid-morning doze. The shrieks of laughter which had awoken her were coming from Kate's bedroom. *Aye, she's well enough to be laughin' her silly head off, but no well enough to get up an look after her family... Ach, serves her bloody well right!* One of the shrieks had ended in a hacking bout of coughing.

Jeannie was sitting on the end of Kate's bed regaling her with a blow-by-blow account of her escapade in Windygates the day before. With her storyteller's flair for description and detail, she had painted a graphic picture of the scene that had met Angus and Mrs Clancy at the back of his house.

Kate's spontaneous shout of laughter, even if it had brought on a bout of coughing, probably did her as much - if not more - good than Dr Jim's wee white pills. When she had recovered enough to sip from the cup of tea Jeannie held to her lips, she gasped: 'Whit on earth did ye dae? Tell me mair, Jeannie, but, fur the love o' God, dinnae mak it sae funny. Ye're killin' me!'

Jeannie took a fortifying gulp from her own cup. 'Weel...'she launched again into her tale.

It had been a bad moment, standing there looking like a refugee from the blitz, meeting their astonished stares. Many women would have been overwhelmed by embarrassment. Fortunately, Jeannie was made of sterner stuff. She simply straightened her shoulders and, making no reference to the dilapidated state of either the window or her own appearance, marched - as far as a broken shoe-heel allows for marching – past them and round to the front of the house. They hastily trailed round after her. At the front door, she indicated with a directive nod to Angus that he was required to produce the key and he hastily complied. As soon as he pushed open the front door, she sailed into the house without a backward glance.

Angus gestured helplessly at Jeannie's retreating back, the gesture intended to indicate that he didn't know what to make of it all but interpreted by Mrs C as his need to go in and see to his guest and, therefore, her own dismissal. She prided herself on being able to take a hint: 'Ah'll be aff, then,' she said briskly, 'you tak care o' yersel, Mr Smillie.'

He called his thanks to her which she waved away as she closed his gate. *His mither wad turn in her grave. That's the third wumman in as many weeks!* She had not recognised the earlier smart, well-groomed woman in the Cinderella who had risen, phoenix-like from the ashes, at the foot of the coal bunker.

Jeannie had already found his bathroom and was closeted in it, attempting to repair some of the damage. Her ash-covered jacket, battered hat and broken shoe were left lying on the floor outside the door. It took her the best part of half-an-hour not only to clean herself up, but to try and bring the bathroom back to its spotless state – no easy task given the amount of grit and ash in her hair and on her hands and face. She had to concede defeat over the originally pristine white towel. Not even all *her* determination and housewifely skills could restore it. She considered trying to hang it up in a way that hid as much of the dirt on it as possible but was not able to bring herself to leave it in place.

She brought it out with her and into the sitting room saying, 'Ah'm sorry, Mr Smillie, ye're goin' tae need a clean ane in there...'

She tailed off in surprise when she saw what he was doing. He had unearthed his father's old shoe-mending box and was delicately tapping tiny nails through the sole of her shoe into the heel to hold it in place again. Her surprised gaze also took in her jacket and hat lying on the couch: both had been brushed clean and looked, if not quite good as new, certainly a great deal better. A large sewing basket sat on the couch beside them.

'You might find something to mend your stockings in that,' he said diffidently, not looking up, continuing to tap the tiny nails. 'It was my mother's.'

She had felt a rush of gratitude to him and had begun to see what attracted Kate.

'He jist accepted whit had happened and got on wi it – nae mountains oot o' molehills. Never even asked me whit Ah wis doin' fallin' aff his bunker.'

'But ye surely telt him?' pressed Kate.

'Oh aye, an, ye ken, when Ah telt him Ah'd been worried he'd been took ill again and wis lyin' at death's door needin' help, he wis richt touched. *'You risked getting badly hurt trying to come to my aid, that was very kind and brave of you'* - that's what he said.' Jeannie preened remembering it.

'An whit aboot the broken windae?'

'He never even mentioned it an Ah furgot a' aboot it till Ah wis on the bus hame!'

'Aye, he's a real gent,' Kate smiled, thinking it was just like the man she had come to know. 'He does awfy kind things an never taks ony credit, disnae even let ye thank him hauf the time.'

There was a sound on the stair and Jeannie rose, collecting the cups. 'That'll be Annie.'

Kate laid a restraining hand on her arm. 'But whit aboot a' the arrangements? Has Angus seen tae... does he ken Ah want tae...?'

Jeannie patted the anxious hand. 'It'll a' be jist the way ye want it. Ah telt him everythin' ye said and he's got it a' weel in hand...' She broke off as Annie came into the bedroom.

'They're at it again,' thought Annie. *'Ah wish tae hell Ah kent whit it is they're aye whisperin' aboot. If Jeannie'd cam' aff her high horse and stop pretendin' she's God's gift tae folk wi secrets. That'll never last!'*

Jim Kenny removed his stethoscope from his ears, rolled it up and put it into its pouch. 'Much better!' he approved. 'Your chest is almost clear and your lungs are sounding more like lungs again.' He grinned at her.

'Instead o' like a coo wi the colic, ye mean?' laughed Kate. 'Aye, Ah'm feelin' a lot better. Can Ah get up oot o' this damned bed, then?'

Another week of confinement had gone by and the bedroom which had seemed like a blessed haven of rest at the beginning of her illness had recently begun to feel like a prison. The impotence of illness was breeding a detachment that she was beginning to feel a little afraid of. She sensed that her home – her precious little kingdom

195

– was being turned into something different by those running it and she knew that she ought to care deeply. But somehow she couldn't and the sense of languorous indifference frightened her more than anxiety would have. She really must make an effort to care...

'Certainly, by all means, begin getting up for short periods and perhaps doing a few light tasks you feel up to, but nothing too strenuous and not for any length of time. You *are* much better but your pulse is still a little erratic and your blood pressure low. We do not want to undo all the good we have done. A *phased return to normality* is what we're after, if you get my meaning.'

Kate did not. She might have been able to work out what 'phased return' meant if she had thought about it, but the concept of 'normality' was beyond her. Nothing had felt 'normal' to her for years and for the last six months she had felt like a foreigner wandering without a map. ''*Normality' sailed awa years ago on a big ship,*' she thought wistfully.

Mystified by the sad, faraway look in her dark eyes, Dr Kenny attempted to close the discussion. He had a great many other house calls on his list that morning.

'Begin by getting up for one hour the first day, two the second and so on. If you feel you are getting tired and breathless, go back to bed. Don't rush it. I'll call in again in three days' time and see how that regime is working for you.'

Kate came back from her faraway place and forced herself to ask: 'But whit aboot the hoose, an Johnnie, an the auld yin? Ah cannae expect Jeannie an Aggie an Annie tae go on pamperin' me furever. It'll soon be Christmas and New Year. They'll hae their ain bizness tae attend tae. It's aye a busy time.'

The doctor laughed. 'Oh, I think you'll find they're rather enjoying themselves. Especially Mrs Gilhooley,' he added drily.

Despite his policy of non-involvement in his patients' lives, he was a keen observer of human nature. 'I'll have a little word with them on my way out and explain what I want done.' He left her then and found Jeannie and Annie in the kitchen: Annie was being given her instructions for the day.

As soon as he had closed the bedroom door, Kate threw back the covers and rashly jumped out of bed. *Praise be tae God, Ah'm better!*

The resulting wave of dizzying weakness and painful breathlessness restored her to reality and she wiped the tears of frustration and impatience away shakily. *Ca' canny. Ye're no goin' tae be climbin' ony mountains jist yet.*

Gingerly she rose and donned her dressing-gown. She contented herself with spending some time at her dressing table, tidying the contents of the drawers and re-arranging the bottles and brushes on it. Then she looked out the window on to the row of back gardens and thoughtfully watched the birds squabbling over some left-over food Senga had put out.

She realised that, although she was longing to be fully recovered, she knew she was not simply indifferent to her home: she was actually dreading what she was coming back to. The very thought of seeing Old Maggie again and resuming her duty of care for the old woman made her quite sick. *Ah could run a mile frae it a'. No jist frae the mess and a' the work but frae her snake's tongue. Ah wish the auld bitch wid hurry up and dee!*

Appalled, she made a hasty sign of the cross. *May God furgive me.* More tears, this time of pent-up, deep unhappiness, released in the emotional vulnerability of early convalescence.

But there was a beacon of light on the horizon and she focused on that. If Angus did not let her down, if all went according to plan, this would be the best New Year ever, with or without Maggie Cruikshanks.

Johnnie bent down and kissed his wife's forehead, gently brushing back the strands of dark hair. Annie had helped Kate wash her hair that morning for the first time in two-and-a-half weeks and it felt silky-soft again, restored to its customary clean, shining glory. As she slept, her breathing was still more audible than normal but it was regular and untroubled; the forehead he kissed was dry and cool. *Thank God she's over the worst.*

Seeing her like this, sleeping peacefully, this beautiful woman he was married to, and contrasting it with the exhausted, delirious, sick creature of a couple of weeks ago, he realised how much he loved her. His panic at the start of her illness had been initially self-centred – Aggie had been right to condemn him roundly that first morning in her shop – but, once the rescue regime was in place and he could think straight again, he had become aware of a very real concern for his wife.

Over the past two weeks, as she had been nursed back to health and his home had been efficiently run, including the care of his mother, by *The Holy Trinity* (as he had privately dubbed Aggie, Jeannie and Annie), he had experienced several emotions new to him: initial relief which gave way to admiration and gratitude to *The Trinity*; humility after his own pathetic attempts to cope; growing understanding of what he had done to Kate in simply moving his mother in and leaving her to get on with it; remorse that he had so taken her for granted.

Wrapped up in his developing career opportunities, he had not even noticed how tired and unhappy she was. *I'm supposed to protect her.* He remembered his marriage vows: *to love and to cherish… An I never even noticed what was goin' on under ma own nose.*

Kate stirred. 'Is that you, bonnie lad?' she murmured – an old endearment from their early days. He took her hand and raised it to his lips and her eyes flew open at the courtly gesture. She giggled softly. 'Wha do ye think ye are? Prince Charmin'?'

'Tis no more than a bonnie princess like you deserves,' he replied, twinkling at her.

'Weel,' she came fully awake and wriggled up on her pillows. 'Ah'm a lot bonnier than Ah wis this mornin'. Whit a relief tae get ma hair washed. It wis stickin' tae ma heid. It's sich a palaver washin' it, though, it's that thick an lang. Ah never usually notice but Ah wis near exhausted wi the effort the day. Maybe Ah should get it cut short.'

'You've got to take it easy,' he reminded her. 'Today was only your second day up out of bed. Easy stages, that's what Dr Kenny says.'

He stroked her hair with his other hand and whispered, 'And please don't talk o' cutting your hair. I've aye loved it.'

'Ah ken,' she sighed, barely noticing the compliment. 'But it'll be Christmas next week an no a card bought tae send tae onyone. An then there's the New Year…' Her eyes slid away from him as she said the last two words and a little flush crept up her neck and chin.

He did not notice. 'Don't you be thinkin' o' any o' that stuff,' he said sternly. 'No-one will be expectin' you to do anythin' about any o' it.'

'But…' she hesitated, weighing up what she must say and what she must *not* say. 'Ah'll no be fit tae gang first-footin' this year so Ah wis thinkin'… Whit if we have a wee party *here* on Hogmanay evenin'? Start early an get a'body here lang afore the bells. That wiy

Ah'll see a'body without goin' oot in the cauld an then folk can leave an dae their first-footin' frae here. Whit dae ye think?'

She had the fingers of her other hand, hidden under the bedclothes, tightly crossed.

'Well,' he considered, 'it's no a bad idea, ma darlin'. If you think it won't be too much for...'

'No, no,' she broke in eagerly. 'Ah'll get Aggie tae bring in stuff frae her shop, Jeannie'll bake and mak up the sandwiches, Annie and Senga'll help wi settin' oot a' the chairs and laying oot the booze.'

'I see you've got it all planned,' he laughed. 'Well, it'll be a good way to celebrate your return to health and...' he coughed modestly, ' . . . my promotion!'

'Yer whit? Ye never telt me!'

'Oh, it seemed less important that gettin' you well again, sweetheart. But, yes, young Mark has decided he doesnae want to come home from his honeymoon at a'. Seems he met an old school pal in Paris who offered him a job – more fool him, that laddie's useless - an his fancy wife likes it better there. I've been asked to carry on as the deputy manager permanently.'

'God, Johnnie, there'll be nae haudin ye noo! Will Ah still be guid enough tae be yer wife?'

For answer, he leaned down and this time the kiss was not on her forehead and it lasted much longer.

It was Saturday afternoon. In less than a week's time, it would be Christmas Day. Kate sat in one corner of the bay window with a tray-on-top-of-a-cushion on her knee, writing the dozen Christmas cards she always sent to family and friends. In the other corner, Old Maggie dozed in her wheelchair. The fire crackled from time to time and an occasional car drove cautiously along the frosty road but otherwise all was quiet, both indoors and out. The men were all at the match as usual, cheering for the local football team. They would come pouring down the road in an hour or so, either - depending on the results - slapping each other on the back and crowing delightedly or arguing vociferously and consigning the referee to eternal perdition.

In the doorway between the sitting-room and the kitchen, Aggie had the ironing board up and was working her sweaty way through a pile of Johnnie's white shirts. One of the hard things about being a nurse, she had discovered, was that the sick and the elderly need to be in a consistent, warm temperature whereas the work that they generate makes those nursing them hot and frequently bothered, longing for a cool draught.

She had discarded as many of her own clothes as was decent but was seriously considering stripping down to her underslip – at least until Maggie woke up. Only the thought of that sad garment's stained and frayed condition was stopping her. She had done enough of the ironing in Kate's house over the past three weeks to know that no garment as old or as dilapidated would ever be found here.

Niver *mind, Ah've got ma smashin' new skirt an blouse fur the concert.* Annie's supplier had come up trumps. *Maybe Ah should go the hale hog an get a new petticoat as weel.* It was an exciting, radical idea.

'Are Uncle Matt and Auntie Cath still at the same address, d'ye think?' Kate broke into her musings. 'Ah thocht Ah heard they were maybe movin'.'

Aggie frowned. Keeping up with relations, especially ones who lived as far away as Glasgow, had never been an exercise she saw any purpose or value in. Wasting good money on tinselly cards and postage stamps for people you never saw seemed tantamount to throwing your purse on the fire. However, she had settled Kate in the window with her cards, envelopes and little address book indulgently, like a mother putting a child in a playpen with its toys.

'Nae idea!' she replied cheerfully. 'They could be deid fur a' Ah ken! Nae loss, either, from whit Ah remember o' them. She wis aye a soor-faced besom an he stank tae high heaven, aye fartin' but silent-like so ye never got any warnin'.'

Kate giggled. 'D'ye mind that time when we were sent tae stay wi them fur a week when Oor Ma wis no weel? We had tae sleep in that cabinet bed that kept jumpin' aff the flair and trying tae fold back up wi us in it. You had the bricht idea of getting twa bricks oot o' the back green an putting them on the end o' the bed tae weigh it doon...'

'An then you kicked ane o' the bricks aff the bed during the nicht an the bloody bed shot up in the air like a seesaw...'

'An the ither brick went fleein through the air an hit the mirror ower the fireplace! The pair o' them cam' runnin' ben, thinkin' the hoose wis bein' burgled...'

'An then Auntie Cath never stopped goin' on fur the rest o' the week aboot seven years bad luck fur breakin' a mirror. Superstitious shite!'

'Ach, weel,' Kate wiped her tears of laughter, 'they had a lot o' funny auld sayin's in they days. They didnae ken ony better. Now whit aboot this address? At this rate, it'll be next Christmas afore Ah get ma cards written, never mind posted!'

'Jist send it tae the address ye've got. Pit yer ain address on the back, though, under 'sender'. That wiy, it'll cam' back tae ye if they're no there an it'll save ye wastin' anither ane next year.'

Kate nodded and bent to her task. Silence fell again as she laboriously penned one of her customary little news-update notes on the card: 'We are all well here and hope finds you same. Johnny now has bossis job at mine. His mother is fine'...*mair's the peety*... 'and lives here with us now. I have had the floo but getting better thanks to Aggie looking after me and two good frenns as well.' She wrinkled her brow and held the card out at arm's length.

'Hoo d'ye spell 'freends', Aggie?'

'F-R-I-E-N-D-S'

Kate scored out and wrote above her own attempt at the word. She squinted at it doubtfully. 'Are ye sure? It looks funny.'

'Ah'm sure,' said Aggie briefly, wiping her hand over her hot brow and looking dispiritedly at the four remaining shirts lying in a heap on the chair.

'Weel...if ye're sure. Ye were aye streets ahead o' me wi the reading an writin'. But it still looks funny tae me.'

Aggie slapped another shirt on the ironing board. 'Tak it or leave it,' she said curtly. Weariness and the uncomfortable heat made her snap: 'Ye can ask Jeannie if ye dinnae believe me. Ye seem tae think she kens a'thing an can dae nae wrang!'

Her shoulders hunched resentfully as she banged the iron up and down Johnnie's long shirt. '*God,*' said an astonished voice in her head, '*Ah'm surely no jealous o' Jeannie an Katy bein' pals? Whit dis that matter tae me? They're welcome tae each ither!*'

Only yesterday, at early afternoon handover time, Annie had been lamenting to Aggie about the two conspirators: 'They're thick as thieves, aye whisperin' an then stoppin' when Ah cam' intae the room. But, if Ah ask Jeannie whit's goin' on, she jist simpers like a damn lassie wi her first monthlies an says she cannae speak aboot it. Do *you* ken anythin', Aggie?'

201

Aggie had declined to engage in speculation. 'Och, haud yer tongue or stick yer nose intae someone else's affairs.'

Aggie too knew that Jeannie and Kate were *up tae some cairry-on* but, as long as Jeannie kept her promise to refrain from gossiping about it, Aggie was content to let them get on with it. In her opinion, they all had more than enough to do keeping the rescue regime running at this busy time of year. Right now, Nellie was probably messing up the Christmas Club savings calculations again and Bessie, who would be relieving Nellie in ten minutes, would no doubt compound the shambles, leaving Aggie to sort it out on Monday morning and face telling some customers that they had been given too many vouchers and must hand some back – not exactly guaranteed to put a smile on their faces.

Kate glanced sharply at Aggie then laid down her pen and looked thoughtfully out the window. She saw Annie chatting with an exiting customer in her shop-doorway. Annie glanced up at the window before going back in, saw Kate and waved cheerily. Kate returned the greeting briefly, absent-mindedly, then turned to look again at her sister.

Over the years, Kate's home and children had been the envy of many in the community. Other people's children squabbled and scrapped noisily, irritating and setting up cheek to their tired parents, often ending up being brutally leathered by angry fathers, whilst mothers looked helplessly and fearfully on. Kate's family life had always seemed a model of peace and harmony.

Maureen and Robbie could have been as quarrelsome and aggravating as any other siblings, and Johnnie might well have been as short-tempered and ready with his hands and his belt as the next man, but she had always been able to sense trouble brewing long before things got to that stage. She had been able to pick up on potential quarrel-fodder and head it off with a quiet, loving *wee word in yer ear,* with some extra attention at bedtime or a complicit wink at the table while she slipped the malcontent an extra-big helping of a favourite pudding.

Her children and her husband had each been supremely confident of their own special place in her heart and her attentions so that any competitiveness had always been still-born.

She had even been able to extend this skill to other, visiting children so that Agnes and Maisie had often arrived spitting at each other like wildcats and left giggling happily, hand-in-hand.

Aggie's marriage and parenting style had been confrontational and crisis-ridden, Jeannie's benevolent despotism. Kate's had been sure-footed, peace-making diplomacy and the results spoke for themselves. Agnes and Maisie had grown up restless, insecure and still quarrelsome; Jeannie's twins had turned into foolish, feckless lads, always up to some rebellious prank; Maureen and Robbie showed well-mannered maturity, remarkable self-assurance and mutual love and respect.

Kate had thought her parenting skills no longer needed, rusty and redundant. But now she saw that they must be dusted down and once again pressed into action.

'Och, Jeannie's a smart wee wumman...in some ways,' she agreed tranquilly, 'but *she's* no the ane that's built up a smashin' wee bizness in a few short years an single-handed at that.' She paused, re-arranging the envelopes on her tray, not looking at Aggie. 'An we a' ken that man o' hers is an awfy nice mannie but he's a big, saft shite – he jist dis whitever she tells him and thinks the sun shines oot o' her wee bum. Ah'm thinkin' that's no quite the road *you've* had tae travel wi that man o' yours a' these years but ye're still here tae tell the tale an wi twa fine, grown-up lassies tae yer credit.'

She sneaked a glance at Aggie. Her sister was silent, her face unreadable, but the resentful shoulders had relaxed and she was now *ironing* the shirt rather than administering corporal punishment to it.

Kate decided that a hat trick was called for. 'An there's ae thing fur sure, she cannae sing like you – naebody can! Are you practising somethin' new fur oor party on Hogmanay?'

The effect of this question, meant only to confirm Kate's good opinion of her sister, was quite unexpected. Aggie froze and only the smell of singeing cotton under the iron recalled her to the moment. Fortunately the iron was only on the cover of the board and not on the shirt so the brown, iron-shaped burn-mark only joined a whole family of other similar accidents from over the years. She hastily stood the iron up on its end.

Kate's innocent words had brought the problem of the *Messiah* concert right out into the spotlight of immediacy. Caught up in the daily whirl of the usual heavy demands in the shop at this time of year, of managing her rota of willing but inexperienced afternoon helpers and of doing her daily stint in the rescue regime, she had simply shelved the problem. Apart from that first chaotic Thursday when the Kate crisis had first broken, she had managed to attend all the practices, though recently having to run all the way from Kate's house once she had served up the evening meal and handed over to Johnnie.

The members of the choir were reaching fever pitch and she shared avidly in the mounting excitement as the big day approached. But just how she was going to escape for the best part of the entire day on the second of January, missing the Women's Get-together, she still had no idea. Each time her uneasy mind flicked over the problem – usually while she was walking home from choir practice, her mind full of the expectant buzz – she simply let the unease peter out in a panacea of *Ah'll think o' somethin' near the time.*

Now she suddenly realised it *was* near the time, horribly near, less than a couple of weeks away. She began to belabour the unfortunate shirt once more. The problem of her escape to the concert, which she had been treating as no more than a little hillock on the smooth plains of her happiness and anticipation, suddenly reared up before her, an impossible cliff-face to scale.

Whit if Ah cannae get awa? Whit if they're a' on stage waitin' fur me an Ah'm stuck here? Whit if Ah jist go an then a'body here finds oot? Whit if Eck finds oot whit Ah've been doin' behind his back a' these weeks?

She felt a rush of panic and lashed out: 'Whit the hell's that got tae dae wi' you? Ah'll sing whit Ah like.'

Kate rose carefully and, turning, laid the cushion and tray on her seat. Old Maggie groaned and shifted in her chair. Kate froze and waited immobile until the old woman slowly subsided back into a drooling doze. Then she turned to look across the room at her sister.

Aggie was now folding the poor shirt, making as bad a job of that as she had done of its ironing. Every few seconds she let her clumsy, jerky hands drop on to the mangled garment while she stared sightless into the fire. Her brow was creased and she was biting her lip.

'There's somethin' mair here than a wee bittie jealousy o' Jeannie,' thought Kate. *'Aggie's in some kind o' trouble.'*

It was not a big room and Kate crossed it in a few steps but, to the two sisters whose eyes met over the ironing board, it felt as if a long bridge had been crossed.

'Whit's wrang, Ag? Ye can tell *me* surely? Ah micht even be able tae help. God knows, *you've* done enough fur *me* these past few weeks, ye've been a treasure.'

It had been years since anyone who really knew her had spoken to her so sweetly. The compliments she received from strangers at the choir were one thing; these gentle expressions of admiration and appreciation from her sister were quite another. Aggie felt her eyes fill with tears and was unable to stop them running down her flushed cheeks.

Kate lifted the work-worn hands off the sadly mistreated shirt and gently pulled Aggie out from behind the ironing board. With a quick glance at the softly snoring Maggie, she led her sister out of the sitting-room, down the lobby and into her own bedroom.

Aggie plumped herself heavily on the side of the bed. Kate hastily closed the door as her sister gave vent to a stormy bout of noisy tears. Aggie had not cried like this for many years, perhaps not ever: not about her loveless marriage and Eck's brutality; not about her dreary, unsatisfying life before she had started running her shop; not about her daughters emigrating; not about either of her parents dying. She had allowed herself a *wee greet* over the Novello rejection but nothing like this full-blown howling match. This had its own momentum, becoming increasingly abandoned. It was as if she had decided to cry for all the ills in her life, past and present.

Kate let her cry, handing her one of Johnnie's large white handkerchiefs out of a drawer in the room. In the past she had often experienced this kind of cataclysmic end to one of her diplomatic interventions with the children, when the subject of her attentions finally admitted what was troubling him or her. Then the floodgates would open.

Characteristically, Aggie's bout of self-pity was brief and, within a few minutes, the racking sobs diminished to sniffles and hiccups. Finally, a trumpeting nose-blow brought the show to an end.

'Ah dinnae ken whit's wrang wi me. Bloody ridiculous, greetin' like that. Ah must jist be gettin' ower tired. It's aye sich a busy time. There's been that much tae think aboot. Maybe Ah've caught the flu aff ye.'

'*An* there's something on yer mind,' Kate was gentle but inexorable. This too was familiar territory: the denial and attempt to dodge away from the issue once the cathartic bout of weeping was over; as if somehow the problem had been solved because it had been allowed its moment of glory. 'Ah can see ye're worried aboot something.'

They heard a faint cry from the sitting-room: Maggie waking up and, like a baby bird in the nest, moving immediately into *feed-me* mode.

'Come on, Ag, nae mair messin' aboot. Whitever it is, ye can tell me. Ye can trust me. Ye ken it'll be safe wi me, Ah'm no ane fur gossipin', ye ken that. Ye're *needin'* tae tell somebody, that's half the trouble. Ye aye tak it a' on yer ain broad shoulders and try tae dae it a' by yersel. Sometimes ye have tae let someone else help ye.'

Those broad shoulders now slumped as Aggie recognised the truth in what her little sister said: she *was* tired of trying to do it all herself. Not so much juggling the normal demands of her business at this busy time of year with the extra ones imposed by the rescue regime: rather it was the strain of preserving her *secret* life and trying to meet *its* demands.

Despite – or maybe because of – how much she loved the choir and shared in its excited anticipation, it had, because of its secrecy, become a very demanding part of her life, occupying only a few actual hours a week but dominating her daytime thoughts and night-time dreams. And she was lonely, she suddenly acknowledged, tired of going round and round in her own head with no-one to talk to about it, no-one to share not only in the stresses its clandestine nature brought but also in the pleasure and excitement.

Maggie's cries were becoming stronger and Aggie gestured despairingly at the closed bedroom door.

'Never mind her, she gets plenty attention.' Kate was not about to give up now: she could see how close she was to a break-through. 'The worst she can do is pee on her "continental pad".' Annie's solecism had become a nickname they all, even Maggie herself, now used. It seemed to invest a necessary embarrassment with a touch of glamour.

So, in the few minutes available before Maggie's cries brought the house down, Aggie told her.

'God, Aggie, that's smashin'! Ah've aye said ye should be on a big stage. Ye deserve a better audience than the drunken rabble in this place on a Hogmanay. Mind when ye were young ye used tae sing at charity concerts at the club? It used tae bring the hoose doon. That wee half-wit o' a singin' director in Leven, him that said ye were too auld tae sing yer Novello stuff, he disnae ken whit he's missin'. Ah'm tellin' ye, his loss is the proddy kirk's gain!'

Oh, it was good to have such hearty, unreserved loyalty, such generous praise and encouragement! Aggie glowed. Then, she remembered the nub of it all.

'But whit am Ah goin' tae dae aboot gettin' awa tae the concert? Hoo can Ah get oot o' goin' tae Senga's fur the Get-thegither?'

'Weel, it's nothin' tae be ashamed o'. Ye could jist tell Senga the truth.'

'But a' the wummen wid be . . . They wouldnae understand. They'd think Ah've turned intae a religious maniac. The Catholics wid a' be runnin' tae the priest tae tell him. An if Eck finds oot Ah've been goin' tae it every week behind his back an plannin' tae go up on the stage at The Alhambra without tellin' him, he'd be furious. He aye gets flamin' mad if anyone maks a fool o' him.' Aggie shivered a little at the thought of Eck's anger.

Kate understood only too well the drive to protect a plan so precious that you feared to expose it to the cold wind of public scrutiny or the over-bearing opinion of a husband.

Her Johnnie could be self-centred and sometimes self-important but he was always good-natured and often kind, with a quirky sense of humour that Kate had come to appreciate and enjoy over the years. Even so, she had not felt able to share her own secret with her husband and she could well understand Aggie's reluctance to share hers with Eck.

He had never been anything but gruffly amicable to Kate over the years, indeed she thought she had even caught him looking at her occasionally with an indulgent gleam in his narrowed eyes, but she knew the life he had given his wife and children. She had seen the bruises and belt-marks, heard the sobbing tales from Agnes and Maisie, admired but often feared for her indomitable sister. It was no surprise that Aggie recoiled at the thought of his finding out. At the very least he would be scathing and derogatory; if her discovered deception really angered him, he would be implacable and even violent.

The old woman was yelling her head off now and, when she paused for breath, there came the sounds of men singing as they made their happy way down the road from the football match. Their team had scored in the dying minutes of the game and the men were ecstatic and vocal.

Kate rose and, taking Aggie's hands, pulled her to her feet too. 'Leave it wi me, hen,' she said. 'Ah'll think o' something. Ye'll be on that stage, the star o' the show, ye'll see!'

Senga chattered happily on and Kate leant back on her pillows and let the tide of ambitious plans wash over her head.

It was mid-afternoon the following Monday and Kate had been mulling Aggie's problem over for two days now without much progress. She was beginning to regret her rash promise to her sister. Kate's strengths lay in gentle, skilful people management but manipulating events, devising and executing clever strategies, had never been her forte.

She had been drifting helplessly in her own unhappiness a few months ago until Angus Smillie had taken her in hand and helped her work out and set in motion an ambitious plan. She thought of him now, as Senga prattled on about the potential of Annie's wee shop to turn into a modern emporium, a trail-blazer of cutting-edge fashion and business practice.

Ah wish Ah could speak tae Angus aboot it. He'd ken whit tae dae. He's that guid at findin' wiys roon things. Nothin's ever ony bather tae him.

She missed him, she thought now, and sighed. Still, luckily, Jeannie had swung into action as the *Mata Hari* of Methil. Kate smiled to herself remembering Jeannie's attempts at spying and her daft disguise. Kate had been too frightened, too unwell and too self-absorbed that day in Anstruther to appreciate the humour of the situation but, now that she was on the mend, confused memories of it made her smile. Indeed, the two women had chuckled often together over it, their shared laughter working like a tonic on Kate.

And Jeannie had been amazing: her cheerful willingness to act as go-between to Windygates in order to finalise The Plan; her staunch maintenance of complete confidentiality, fulfilling a promise that Kate had privately thought her incapable of; her management of the rescue regime and handling of Old Maggie, even to the 'continental pads' victory. Kate had had to swallow her pride and irritation as Maggie had told her, only yesterday, how only Jeannie had understood that the old woman's *dignity* was being compromised by all the wet and shitty beds, how Kate hadn't cared enough to give her the pads.

Kate had damped down an angry, defensive retort. She was enough of a people management strategist to know that this unfair condemnation and Maggie's self-righteousness was small price to pay for the excellent outcome: a lot less work for steamie and screamie and no more nauseating beds to change. She knew that Maggie would never wittingly do anything to make her daughter-in-law's life easier and she realised now that she had been less than clever presenting the pads under this banner. Jeannie had cleverly sold them to the old woman as no more than her right and an important part of preserving her dignity and public image – two things Maggie Cruikshanks had always prized highly.

The more Kate thought about Aggie's problem, the more she conceded that they needed help. Kate considered the voluble Senga who was just embarking on an account of her plans for the January sale in the shop – Annie had not so much asked Senga to stay on as accepted that she was doing so. In truth, Senga had instituted so many new systems in the shop and raised so many expectations among the customers in the past three weeks that even Annie realised she could not go back to the former inferior service and poor selection.

Certainly, enlisting Senga's help for Aggie would have merit since the Get-together was in her house. And Senga was not really a gossip: her interest in tittle-tattle was always cursory and her ability to remember it rarely enough for her consciously to pass it on. On the other hand, she talked a great deal, often without fully realising what she was saying, and she had been known to let slip, in all innocence, information that constituted juicy gossip-fodder for others. The more excited she was, the more she talked and the less discreet she was liable to become. This was in evidence right now as she prattled on about her plans for the shop and recounted tales of recent sales she had made, unthinkingly revealing some quite intimate details about her customers' sizes, shapes, underwear and finances. No, the excitement of being the hostess of the Get-together would make her an unreliable conspirator in any plan to ensure Aggie's escape that day.

Senga finally ran down and rose regretfully. 'Ah could yammer a' day aboot the shop, Kate, Ah'm enjoyin' it that much. Ah should have got masel a wee shop job years ago. Ye should think aboot it yersel aince ye're better. Weel, maybe no this meenit, richt enough...' Old Maggie could be heard arguing with Aggie in the sitting-room.

Kate had earlier retreated to her bedroom to escape their altercations and Senga had found her lying on top of her quilt, reading from an old jotter. 'Ah brocht ye some mair magazines – here they are – looks like ye're needin' them if this is a' ye've got tae read.' She picked up the dog-eared jotter and glanced doubtfully at it. 'Whit is it onyway? Ane o' Robbie's or Maureen's auld school things?'

Kate hastily removed it from her hands and slipped it under the bolster. She did not answer Senga's question but only accepted the pile of magazines gratefully, immediately engaging Senga in discussion about a free knitting pattern that was offered with one of them and diverting her from further investigation.

At last her kind-hearted, loquacious neighbour took her leave and wandered through to the sitting-room to say cheerio to Aggie and Maggie.

Kate breathed a sigh of relief. She had promised Jeannie she would be careful with the jotter and it had almost fallen into the wrong hands. She had been complaining to Jeannie yesterday of being bored with the endless magazines and wishing she had something more interesting to read. This had led to an enjoyable blether about books they had both read and ones which only Jeannie had read and would recommend, this latter category being at least ten times bigger.

'Jings, Jeannie, ye must spend an awfy lot o' time readin'. Do ye dae onythin' else in yer spare time?' Kate had reasonably asked.

'Weel,' Jeannie had suddenly become mysteriously coy, 'Ah dae a wee bittie *writin'* as weel.'

Kate had been astounded. People who read books were rare enough in her world; someone who *wrote* them would be as alien as Men from Mars – or so Kate had thought. But here was Jeannie Gilhooley, just an ordinary miner's wife, whom they had all known for years, sitting on the end of her bed, revealing that she was an…an *authoress*!

'Have ye written a hale book yet?' Kate's voice had conveyed awe and wonder.

'Weel,' Jeannie had hesitated, seeming…Kate might have said *shy and uncertain*, if those two words would not have seemed so incongruous when attributed to her assertive, supremely competent friend. 'There's a few wee books but maistly they're short stories, though…'she had paused thoughtfully as a new idea struck her, '… a lot of the stories follow on frae each ither aboot the same folk so Ah suppose, if they wis pit thegither, ye micht ca' them books.'

'God, Jeannie, ye're a dark horse, an nae mistake! Go an let me read some of them. Ah'd love tae see them.'

Jeannie had been diffident, requiring coaxing, and again Kate had been struck by such out-of-character behaviour. In the end, she had somewhat reluctantly agreed to let Kate have 'ane o' ma jotters wi a few wee stories in it. An dinnae worry aboot readin' through it a' if ye get fed up.'

This morning, she had handed Kate the jotter casually. 'If ye're still fancyin' somethin' a wee bit different tae read. It'll pass the time fur ye.'

Nothing in Jeannie's demeanour had betrayed the hours she had spent sifting through the dusty piles under her bed, appraising, discarding, short-listing and finally settling on this well-thumbed one. Nothing in her face betrayed her feelings as she handed it over though a mother, who had thought herself barren and now presented her long-awaited first child for inspection, would have identified with her expression. 'Dinnae tell onyone else, though. Ah'm no wantin' it talked aboot a' ower the place.'

Kate had smiled to hear Jeannie, erstwhile arch-gossip, reveal her own vulnerability. *Seems like we've a' got oor wee secrets. A' Ah need noo is tae ken whit Annie and Senga have got hidden at the back **their** cupboards!*

Kate had begun reading through it with more curiosity than expectation. It was one of Jeannie's collections of interlinked stories. Soon she was immersed in it, regretfully stopping for dinner and glad to find an excuse, when Aggie and Maggie had begun one of their frequent, protracted arguments-about-nothing, to escape back to her bedroom to consume more of the fascinating, racy tale. Senga's interruption with more of the dreaded magazines, though kindly meant, had not been at all welcome, though Kate would never have betrayed this by so much as a fleeting expression.

Now, she thankfully extracted the jotter from under the bolster and settled down to the last three stories in it.

She finished reading an hour later and thoughtfully hid the jotter at the bottom of her corset drawer. She wandered through to the sitting-room to find Maggie in the bay-window with a box of tangled, tinselly paper-chains on her knee, painstakingly attempting to sort them into useable condition. Jeannie firmly believed in keeping the old woman either entertained or gainfully occupied and always had wireless programmes lined up for her in the morning, which Annie was to make sure she listened to, and *wee jobs* laid out for her afternoon sojourn in the sitting-room, which were Aggie's responsibility to supervise.

Kate marveled at how docilely both women implemented Jeannie's wishes, perhaps because they quickly saw that both the entertainment and the gainful occupation worked wonders for Maggie's mood once she was settled into them. Sometimes, as had happened earlier this afternoon, it took some persuading to get her started, resistance and an unwillingness to accept that anything was for her own good being in the nature of the beast.

Aggie was in the kitchen laying two tea-trays. It said much for Jeannie's authority that even Aggie now automatically laid a clean, embroidered cloth on each tray first, then made sure that one had the easy-to-drink-from mug for Maggie and the other had dainty china to tempt Kate's convalescent appetite. Kate smiled behind Aggie's broad back to see her sister engaged in a task she would have scorned as *a lot o' bloody nonsense* a few weeks ago.

Aggie was humming, the tune swelling towards a climax and, unable to contain herself, she burst into song just as the kettle began to boil. Kate did not recognise the music but she did recognise its beauty – and the beauty of the voice singing it. She stood in the doorway smiling and spontaneously clapped her hands in appreciation when the song ended.

Aggie whirled round, her expression immediately defensive but, seeing Kate's genuine delight, relaxed into a slightly embarrassed grin. 'Ach, Ah didnae mean tae be givin' a gran performance. Ah jist got cairried awa wi masel. Furgot whaur Ah wis fur a meenit!'

'Ah'm no surprised.' Kate shook her head in wonder. 'That's aboot the loveliest thing Ah've ever heard. Is it whit ye'll be singin'…'she lowered her voice with a quick glance over her shoulder at the wheelchair in the bay window, '…at The Alhambra?'

Aggie turned to catch the kettle as it began to whistle. Her back was once more to Kate as she poured the boiling water into the big brown teapot and Kate saw her shoulders – always a giveaway to her feelings – tense and then droop. '*If* Ah ever get tae the damned place,' she growled.

Kate came to a decision. 'Cheer up! Ah think Ah micht ken whit tae dae aboot that. Gie Maggie her tray an then bring mine an yer ain cup through tae ma bedroom. Ah've somethin' tae talk tae ye aboot.'

CHAPTER ELEVEN

AGGIE

Aggie disgustedly swept the small Christmas puddings off the glass shelf under the counter where they had reposed for the past fortnight. Now it was five o'clock on Christmas Eve and the last chance of their being sold had gone. It had been a new line from one of her suppliers this year but had met with little success. The women had been suspicious of such anglicised fare, strongly resisting the attempt to sell the idea of 'Christmas Dinner' to them. Their focus was on next week's Hogmanay and New Year celebrations and their money and their club vouchers were being kept for the steak pies, black bun, shortbread and, of course, the alcohol that would need to be bought.

Christmas was just a 'day for the bairns'. Children hung up one of their mother's old woollen stockings at the side of the fireplace before going to bed on Christmas Eve and joyfully found them filled with treats in the morning. There was always an apple and an orange in the foot with maybe a coin or a halfpenny chew in the toe and, hopefully, a couple of wee presents filling out the leg – a knitted soft toy or rag doll for the girls, a wooden train or dinky car for the boys. In wealthier families there might be books laid out on the chairs as well: a *Dandy* or *Beano* Annual and the ever-popular *Oor Wullie* or *The Broons* book which the adults loved as much as the children.

A few of the women were beginning to make more of a fuss of Christmas, encouraged by the mail order catalogues which were beginning to appear as post-war austerity gradually lessened. Senga was one such and Aggie had had to listen just this week to a detailed account of all the presents she had bought, thought of buying and decided against, ordered but not received, might save up for next year. However, not even Senga had yet transferred any interest from presents for the bairns to food for the table so the wee puddings would just have to form staple fare for Aggie and Eck for the next few weeks.

213

Maybe Kate'll try ane oot. She's startin' tae dae mair but she's no up tae much cookin' yet. Ah'll tak a couple ower afore Ah gang hame. An Ah suppose Ah can aye coont on Annie tae eat onythin', especially if it's free.

She had decided to close the shop on Christmas Day and had had a warning sign in the window for the past week, remaining resolute and unmoved by the women's complaints about having to eat two-day-old bakeries, though she had made a concession and stayed open today until five o'clock instead of taking her usual Wednesday half-day. Her two day closure on first and second of January was always accepted without demur as it was simply part of the general upheaval in the community at this time but closing for Christmas Day was a new departure.

Aggie did not even have children in her life anymore and Eck would be off down the pit as usual so her decision to close baffled and irritated them. But she had a lot on her mind and desperately needed a day to herself when Eck would be safely out of the way for seven or eight hours and she would be uninterrupted by customers and commercial demands.

Kate had declared herself well enough to manage without help now but had promised to let one of *The Trinity* know at once if she did feel things were getting too much for her. In any case, the likelihood of Jeannie staying away for any length of time was slim. She and Kate were indeed *thick as thieves* and their friendship seemed to have been very much a part of Kate's restoration to health.

Aggie had damped down her jealousy now that she understood the basis for the burgeoning friendship: Kate had not specified what it was that Jeannie was helping her with - *If ye dinnae mind, Ag, Ah jist want it tae be a gran surprise fur a'body and Ah dinnae want tae tempt fate by sayin' whit's goin' tae happen* – but she had extolled Jeannie's virtues so thoroughly as a resourceful, reliable and discreet conspirator that Aggie had begun to readjust her view of the former gossip queen.

The last choir practice was tomorrow night as well and it was to be a dress rehearsal. She wanted plenty time to get herself ready, have a long bubble-bath and try out her new clothes. But most of all, she wanted to be able to enter into all the excited chatter with an untroubled mind. As the big day drew nearer and excitement mounted, she found it increasingly hard to ignore the spectre of her escape problem.

The last straw had been the week before when the group of sopranos, whom she had got to know particularly well, had announced that they were all planning to go for 'an early light lunch' at the newly-opened cafe in Kirkcaldy before the afternoon rehearsal at The Alhambra. They were going to make their own way to Kirkcaldy and ask the choirmaster if they could join the choir's private bus as it passed through on its way to Burntisland.

'We thought we'd have some fun together before the serious business of the day begins. Do come, Aggie, it won't be the same without our wonderful soloist,' said Margot, who seemed to have a real soft spot for Aggie. She had mumbled something about *'having to see'* and her *'sister still being ill and maybe needing her'* but it had thrown the problem of the whole day into sharp relief, let alone an extra hour at the start of the afternoon for the 'light lunch', whatever that was.

She could put it off no longer, she had decided. Contrary to her airy, sanguine hopes that *something would work out nearer the time*, she knew that she was facing a brick wall into which her hopes and dreams were about to smash if she did not do something fast. A couple of days ago, Kate had made a suggestion at which Aggie had at first baulked then grudgingly agreed to consider. But it was quite alien to her natural instincts and went against the practice of years.

'Ask Jeannie tae help? Tell her a' ma bizness? Trust her tae keep her mooth shut? Ah'd be as weel get a'body thegither for a public announcement an sell tickets fur it intae the bargain.'

But Kate, who only a few short weeks ago would have held exactly the same opinion, had not accepted this damning prediction.

'She's changed, Aggie, honest. Ah had ma doots at the beginning, Ah'll no kid ye. But, as it happened, Ah didnae really hae ony choice, the wiy things worked oot. Ah'll tell ye a' aboot it after…weel, later on. But Jeannie's been a real diamond, Ah dinnae ken whit Ah'd hae done withoot her. An she's never breathed a word o' it tae a soul. No even tae Bob, her man, an she says she used tae tell him a'thing. But he's no the sharpest nail in the toolbox an Jeannie's feart he'd let slip somethin' without meanin' tae.'

Aggie had spared a moment's wonder for this secret that Kate was guarding so carefully. It seemed to be something that was going to make not only her but everyone else happy. What it had to do with the Wednesday trips to Windygates, St. Monans, Anstruther, or anywhere

215

else in the Kingdom of Fife, was unclear. But Aggie had to admit one thing *was* certain: Jeannie, who obviously knew all about it and had somehow become involved, had *not* used it as gossip-fodder, not even to her crony, Fat Annie, who had been complaining bitterly to Aggie for weeks about feeling left out.

'But, even if Ah did risk tellin' her, whit guid wid it dae? Whit can *she* dae? Ah dinnae see hoo that's goin' tae help me.'

Kate had been reading more of Jeannie's stories these past few days and, the more she read, the more she came to appreciate the mind at work in them. Jeannie was not only good at creating delightful, believable characters and scripting sharp, entertaining dialogue; she also constructed amazing plots with inventive, devious twists and turns.

Kate had a simple, straightforward approach to life and was quite unable to come up with any clever solution to Aggie's dilemma herself. But she felt sure that doing so would put no strain on Jeannie's fertile imagination.

'Tak it frae me, Ag,' she had said earnestly. 'Jeannie'll hae an answer. An she'll no jist think ane up fur ye, she'll help ye an mak sure it works. She's amazin'! She's like a bloody dynamo! An she'll keep it a secret, if ye ask her tae. She's proved she can dae that as weel, noo.'

Aggie made her way determinedly up Burns Avenue with her bag of little Christmas puddings slapping against her leg. It was a clear, frosty night with a thousand stars twinkling and something of the sweet expectant hush of Christmas Eve spoke to her anxious spirit as she rounded the corner into Jeannie's cul-de-sac. A kind of peace came over her, an unexpected sense of optimism and safety. She recalled a verse from poetry classes at school: *God's in his heaven; all's right with the world.*

Jeannie opened her door to Aggie without surprise. She had paid a visit to Kate that afternoon and they had spent a happy hour chatting about the forthcoming Hogmanay party at Kate's house and sharing plans and secrets. As she had risen to take her leave, Kate had suddenly given her an affectionate hug, close to grateful tears, and Jeannie had felt that all her strenuous efforts to create and maintain her new role as trustworthy confidante and resourceful friend had been richly rewarded.

Then Kate had said: 'Ye're jist the best freend a wumman could want, Jeannie. An there's someone else micht be askin' fur yer help.

216

Ah hope ye dinnae mind but Ah said tae Aggie that ye micht be able tae help her. Ye ken whit she's like - she'll no find it easy tae ask ye - but Ah telt her she'll no find onyone better.'

Jeannie had been intrigued and curious. With difficulty, and mindful of her reformed character, she had restrained herself from plunging into a string of questions, contenting herself with a determinedly casual: 'Weel, if she wants tae ask fur ma help, she kens whaur Ah live.'

But she had been pondering for several hours now on the possibility of Aggie turning up on her doorstep, feeling sure that, whatever her problem was, it must in some way relate to her clandestine connection with the Methodist Kirk.

'Come awa in, Aggie.' Jeannie was welcoming and - Aggie did not fail to note - unsurprised. *Kate's maybe telt her a'ready. Damn it! Am Ah pittin' ma heid in the lion's mooth here?*

Her sense of optimistic calm began to drain away. Uneasily, she let Jeannie take her coat and sat down in front of the roaring fire. She noted with amusement that two of Jeannie's old woollen stockings lay on the hearth rug ready for the twenty-year-old twins to hang up that night when they finally came home from the pub. Jeannie acknowledged them rather shamefacedly.

'Och, the laddies still like tae hang up their stockin's. Ah pit wee bits an pieces in them - razors, fags, sweeties, a new tie…that sort o' thing. They really jist like openin' the parcels.'

Aggie thought of her daughters, barely older than the twins, who were bravely making their way in the New World. She had sent a small parcel to them several weeks ago, just some ribbons and buttons with an old postcard of Anstruther harbour to remind them of childhood holidays. She knew from their letters that anything she could send would be vastly inferior to what was available in the shops out there and it had seemed pointless to waste money on postage. She had not thought to turn these modest gifts into separately wrapped parcels. Give them real Christmas presents. Briefly she hoped someone else out there would do this for them.

Jeannie appeared suspiciously quickly with a loaded tray – a pot of tea, buttered pancakes, jam, iced biscuits, a bottle of sherry and the inevitable packet of woodbine. Obviously she had been expecting company. Aggie resigned herself to her task, never being one to waste time or energy in beating about the bush.

'Did Kate tell ye Ah wis goin' tae ask ye if ye could help me wi a wee problem?'

Jeannie concentrated on pouring the tea and adding sugar and milk to the two cups. She handed Aggie her cup with a grave nod, took her own cup and settled back in her chair, assuming the air of inscrutable guru.

'Ah'm at yer service, Aggie,' she intoned. Nothing in her grave, attentive attitude betrayed her inner glee. *This is jist the best wiy in the warld tae learn a'thing aboot a'body! Ah should hae thocht o' it years ago!*

Unlike Kate, who had taken the best part of an hour that day in the steamy Anstruther tearoom to reveal her secrets and throw herself on Jeannie's mercy, Aggie explained her problem succinctly and outlined her need for help in less than five minutes. Jeannie had not even consumed one jammy pancake before she finished her account and ended with a challenging: 'So, whit's the answer? Kate said ye would ken and ye would help me. An keep yer mooth shut aboot it. If ye start gossipin' this a' ower the place, Ah'll hae yer guts fur garters. Ah widnae be here askin' *you* if Ah wisnae desperate.' Aggie slapped jam on to her own pancake beligerently.

'Ca' canny!' protested Jeannie. 'There's nae need tae be nasty. Ah'm sure Kate's telt ye that Ah can be trusted these days tae keep a secret or ye widnae be here at a'.'

Aggie flushed and shifted uncomfortably. The heat from the fire was making her sweat now and she moved her chair away from it, catching the leg on one of the woollen stockings on the hearth-rug. The few moments that it took to untangle and re-arrange the hopeful stocking gave both women time to reconsider their attitudes.

Jeannie poured two generous sherries and offered the woodbines. As the smoke from the two cigarettes curled up into the warm room, she considered her response to Aggie's situation. *Softlee, softlee, catchee monkee.*

First she congratulated Aggie on being chosen as soloist and echoed Kate's opinion that such recognition of Aggie's wonderful musical talent was well-deserved and long overdue. Then, like Kate too, she consigned the Novello show director to a place fit only for small-minded, unimaginative people who spent their small-minded, unimaginative lives missing the boat.

218

Aggie relaxed visibly and lit a second woodbine while Jeannie topped up their sherry glasses.

'But, it seems tae me, Aggie,' Jeannie sipped her sherry thoughtfully, 'that ye're makin' this a lot harder than it needs tae be. Why no jist tell a'body aboot it? Ye're daein nothin' wrang. Some folk micht be picky and likely jealous but whit dae they matter? Some o' us would be richt proud o' ye – Ah ken Ah am, an Ah'm damn sure Kate is. We'll both stan by ye an Ah'll tell onyone that says different that they can jist go an bile their heid!'

Aggie grinned. She had no doubt that Jeannie would do just that and, although those thus abjured might draw the line at actually boiling their heads, they would certainly shut their mouths and think twice about expressing contrary opinions again.

'But there's the priest, though, if it gets oot that Ah've been in the proddy kirk every week an me hardly ever at mass these days…'

Jeannie snorted. Father Brian might be one of the old school of diehard bigots who thought that crossing the door of a Protestant church was tantamount to selling your soul to the devil but he was also quite elderly and rarely sober these days. He had only a tenuous grasp on who was who in his parish or who attended mass regularly. In Jeannie's recent experience, he could be easily confused and dissuaded from condemnation by a little judicious massaging of the facts and assertive presentation of edited truth.

'We'll work roon him, dinnae worry. A wee bottle o' Haig's Dimple should do it.'

'But a' the ither Catholics would be sayin'Ah shouldnae be gettin' mixed up wi proddies an singin' kirky sangs.'

Again Jeannie snorted. 'D'ye no think they'd a' jump at the chance tae be up on a gran stage wi a big orcherstra, gettin' clapped? Geez, maist o' them would stan on their hands wi nae knickers on if they thocht they had a chance!'

Aggie burst into peals of laughter. 'Bloody guid job they dinnae hae a chance then! *That* would be a sicht that no even a blind man would be glad o'.'

The two women indulged themselves in a few moments delicious contemplation of some of the sights that such unseemly antics would provide. Then Aggie sighed.

'But if a' the wummen get tae ken, they'll tell their menfolk an it'll get back tae Eck. Ah've no telt him onythin' aboot it. He'd be blazin' mad if he fund oot that Ah've been goin' tae the practices a'

these weeks without him kennin'. An as fur singin' on the stage...'
She stared into the fire, her laughing face falling abruptly into a
harried, miserable frown.

This was new territory for Jeannie and she struggled to identify
with Aggie's feelings and fears. Like everyone else in the community,
she knew Eck was a heavy-handed, sharp-tongued bully but she had
always thought, as did everyone else, that Aggie was more than a
match for him. When any of them had sought in the past to express
sympathy for her black eyes and painful limps or to offer support after
the frightening sounds of a particularly vicious row had emanated from
No 22, Aggie had always brushed it off, declaring that she had given
as good, if not better, than she had got and that *the bad-tempered
bugger'll think twice afore he starts his cairry-on again.*

Of course, he always *had* started it again and usually quite soon
after but Aggie's determined defensiveness had made it impossible for
anyone to point this out or offer help.

When the two girls had been young, people had muttered about
'telling *The Cruelty*' but no-one had ever quite had the courage,
fearing Eck's temper and Aggie's tongue. As the years had passed and
the girls had grown up and left home for the New World, the
Fairweather household had ceased to be a talking point: Eck now
seemed more of a smouldering presence in the background than the
fiery threat he had once been. Since Aggie had started her bakery
business, her confidence had visibly grown and, conversely, his
seemed to have shrunk. There had not been a decent row at No 22 for
several years – at least not one that the neighbours could hear. Aggie's
obvious fearfulness came as a surprise to Jeannie.

'But he disnae hit ye any mair surely? An he lets ye get on wi yer
shop. He'd likely no bather aboot ye singin' in a choir, even if it is a
proddy ane. It's no like he's sich a staunch Catholic. I havenae seen
him at mass fur...' Jeannie could not actually ever remember seeing
Eck kneeling in St. Agatha's pews though he had presumably been
there when his daughters were baptised. Jeannie would have been
more interested in looking at boys of her own age at that time than old
married men in their twenties.

'Ach, he kens better than tae lift his hand tae me these days and he
jist took instruction frae the priest tae please ma faither afore we got
wed. He never bathered wi it after that. If a priest cam' roon tae the
hoose, he used tae send him awa wi a flea in his ear. Ah mind there
wis ane awfy earnest young Irish lad started goin' on tae him about us

no havin' mair than twa bairns. Richt there on the doorstep – Eck never let them in – he wis tellin' Eck that we must be goin' against the will o' God, "unnatural practices", an a' that. He telt Eck that he wis "wastin' seed".'

Jeannie goggled. 'Did the lad hae a' his marbles or wis he on a dare or somethin'? It must hae been afore Ah cam' tae live here.'

Aggie smiled ruefully remembering the scene which had been the talk of the village for weeks. 'Ah wonder ye've never heard the tale. Eck picked him up by his dog collar, dragged him doon the gairden path and threw him oot the gate. An he bawled after him so as the hale street could hear: "You're the ane that's bloody wastin' seed. Bugger aff hame tae yer Irish bog!" Then he ca'd him a few choice names and telt him no tae darken oor door again. We've no seen much o' any o' the priests since then. Ah sometimes used tae gang tae mass if Ah got up in time on Sunday mornin' but since Ah started wi the bakery Ah'm up sae early a' the ither mornin's that Ah'm fair desperate fur a lang lie on a Sunday. An Eck never goes at a'.'

'So, whit does it matter if he gets tae ken aboot the proddy choir then?' pressed Jeannie.

As Kate had rightly assessed, it would have been no trouble to Jeannie to devise an escape strategy for Aggie on the second of January and undoubtedly, as Kate had also predicted, she would happily have taken an active part in ensuring its successful execution. But, for the life of her, she couldn't fathom why Aggie was making such a palaver out of it all. Married herself to a man whom she had been able to twist round her little finger with increasing dexterity over the years and who would have been *prood as punch* to see his adored wife starring on a big stage, Jeannie was finding it hard to grasp the need for subterfuge. If Eck didn't give a damn about the Catholic-Protestant issue and if Aggie was no longer afraid of his physical violence, what else was there?

Aggie rose abruptly and began to pace fretfully about the small living-room. Jeannie forbore to remark on the irreparable damage she was doing to the twins' Christmas stockings as the heels of the heavy winter boots ground them into the fireside rug. *Lucky Ah've got plenty mair auld stockin's up the stair.*

Jeannie watched Aggie and waited in silence, every instinct telling her that she was about to learn something that lay very deep in Aggie's soul and which had rarely, perhaps never, been put into words before.

Eck looked in pleased surprise at the plate in front of him. Supper-time fare had been particularly poor for the past few weeks with not even badly cooked chips appearing on the menu some nights, just some blackened toast to complement a few slices of corned beef or boiled ham. He had been on the verge of revolt several times but had always damped down his anger when Aggie had reminded him of the extra commitments in her day's schedule, looking after Kate and her household in the afternoon then going back, before coming home, into the bakery shop to sort out any messes her afternoon helpers had made.

His expression always softened whenever Kate's name was mentioned. Aggie swallowed her resentment and wisely used this weakness to her own advantage. If he had noticed that Kate had been particularly needy on the three *Thursdays* involved and kept Aggie exceptionally late, necessitating fish-and-chips in newspaper wrappings rather than home-cooked food on a plate on each of those evenings, he had made no comment. In truth, the chippie's offering was vastly preferable to anything his wife ever served up and he had simply wolfed down the slimy fish, greasy batter and salty, vinegary chips with relish.

But now he was looking at thin slices of succulent lambs' liver with tiny purple shallots in a rich gravy, cheerful little orange rounds of carrot and a mound of fluffy mashed potato. It looked and smelled wonderful. He looked doubtfully across the table at his wife. She looked the same as ever: unkempt hair; pasty skin with the inevitable 'plook' on a chin that was beginning to sprout hairs; crumpled clothes only infrequently washed; mind obviously miles away from this dreary kitchen.

She was already attacking the food on her own plate hungrily. Jeannie had come up trumps again, offering Aggie a generous share of the dinner she had cooked earlier for herself and Bob.

'But whit aboot yer laddies?' Aggie had protested.

'Och, they'll have gone straight tae the pub frae their work an they'll likely go fur a black puddin' supper on the wiy hame. They never coont on me keepin' onythin' fur them an they jist tak whit they find when they get hame or gang withoot if there's nothin' they fancy.' Jeannie had been already ladling the liver and onion stew into a casserole dish and topping it with mashed potato. 'There! Jist heat that up. It'll be a guid start tae oor plan tae get yer Eck in a guid mood.'

Aggie had accepted the casserole gratefully though she had no expectations of it working such a miracle, however tasty it was. She and Jeannie had talked for two hours and she had had even less time to devote to cooking Eck's supper. Her only contributions to the meal were a small farmhouse loaf from the shop, one of the wee Christmas puddings which was simmering on the stove and some lumpy custard to go with it.

Jeannie had been right. Eck cleaned his plate with a chunk of bread torn off the loaf and sat back with a satisfied belch. As usual he poked unattractively at his yellow teeth with a long, bony finger and gave the lurking remains of his meal to the waiting dog. But he looked more relaxed and approachable than Aggie had seen him for a long time. When she put a bowl of the hot, fragrant, spicy pudding in front of him and offered him the jug of custard, he almost smiled.

'Whit dae ye ca' this?' he mumbled through a large mouthful.

'It's Christmas pudding. They hae it in England, so Ah'm telt, on Christmas Day. The place Ah get ma black bun frae sent me some tae try in the shop but nane o' ma customers wanted it.'

'Mair fool them,' he grunted. 'It's grand! Ye can gie me that onytime ye like. But dinnae worry aboot the custard.' He poked disparagingly at the yellow lumps. 'Ah'll jist hae some milk on it.'

'Weel, Ah'm richt glad ye like it. There's a hale bag o' them tae get eaten.' Aggie toyed with her spoon, nervously scraping minute smears of the pudding off her empty plate. 'It *is* Christmas the morn, ye ken.'

'Is it? Aye, ye're richt. It'll be Hogmanay next Wednesday. Ah'll need tae hae a few practice drinkin' sessions at the club this week. Ye'll be makin' plenty money in the shop next week so Ah'll no gie ye as much housekeepin' as usual.'

Aggie opened her mouth to protest at this high-handed, unilateral realignment of their financial arrangements: *That's him a' ower, selfish pig. Jist tellin' me, never askin' me.* It was exactly the kind of spark that had ignited some vicious and often violent flare-ups in the past. Then wily wisdom whispered to her and she swallowed her resentment.

'Ah'm thinkin' o' goin' tae midnight mass the nicht. Maybe it's the puddings that've pit me in the mood...'

'Dinnae expect me tae go wi ye, then. Ah cannae be bathered wi bible-thumpin'. Ye ken that.' To her relief, he made no other comment on her proposed religious outing and, once he had departed for the club to make a start on his training schedule for Hogmanay, she was free to turn her mind to the plan which she and Jeannie had concocted. Tonight, in the over-crowded, candle-lit, incense-laden church it would roll into action.

Father Brian O'Malley glanced with satisfaction at the packed pews as he processed regally up the centre aisle of his church, a gaggle of altar boys following him like so many ill-assorted bridesmaids. Midnight mass was always a sure-fire winner for raking in the crowd, even if some of the men had to be ejected later for drunk and disorderly behaviour as the service progressed. There would be a few fainters, of course: the sticklers, who observed the church's ruling that no food could be consumed before taking Holy Communion at quarter-to-midnight, would have been fasting all day and the heat from dozens of candles, the choking fumes of liberally wafted incense and the smell of two hundred bodies, some only infrequently washed, would see them off. But, still, it was a gratifying moment in the liturgical calendar.

'*Et introibo ad altare deo,*' he intoned mellifluously as he stopped before the altar.

'*Ad deum, qui laetificat juventutem meum,*' responded the altar-boys dutifully.

Aggie glanced at Jeannie's missal which lay open between them on the shallow pew-shelf. The Latin which the priest and the boys were chanting was written in red on one side with a translation in black on the other. *I will go unto the altar of God; to God who giveth joy to my youth.*

Joy to my youth: she pondered the words. Growing into womanhood, she had not been aware of much joy. Her exhausted, painfully thin mother had been obsessed by the need to get her two daughters married off, knowing what they did not guess, that she was dying before their eyes of a slow-moving but irrevocable cancer. She had been dead a few months before Aggie's wedding to Eck but had been irresistibly forceful in promoting it.

With Kate having already secured a good match and Aggie having had no other offers, there had seemed no option. Aggie had been only too aware of her own awkward, scrawny body, having been forced to compare it daily for years with her younger sister's blossoming curves and graceful charm. Her mother had been brutally frank, as only those running out of time can be: 'Ye'll no get anither offer, Aggie. He's nae oil paintin', but nether are you. Ye dinnae want tae be left on the shelf.'

So she had resigned herself to a loveless marriage, thinking it could not be any worse than the life she had already. She had been wrong.

Once he had her trapped, he had shown his true colours. The first ten years had been characterised by escalating brutality. Naturally spirited by nature, she had constantly exacerbated his vile temper, resenting and resisting his attempts to crush and dominate her. She thought back to nights when he had literally kicked her out of the house and she had prowled round the windows, shivering, often only in her nightdress, terrified to leave him alone with the two young children who would be cowering under the bed they shared. Neighbours had shaken their heads and closed their curtains more tightly, unwilling to witness or be drawn into this 'man-and-wife' altercation.

The second decade had been slightly easier once the little girls were old enough to recognise the warning signs and escape before the violence began. They had run to their Aunty Kate's house, knowing she always had a reassuring cuddle for them. Sometimes they had poured out their fears to her but, if Uncle Johnnie was there, they had not. Once he had threatened to go round and *sort the bugger oot* and only their hysterical pleading had dissuaded him. The thought of their father's anger turned on them because they had prompted such unwelcome intervention had reduced them to terrified, trembling wails and Johnnie, against his better judgment, had given in.

Then had come the night that she always thought of as the turning point. Eck had been in a particularly black mood that night – she could not now remember why – and Agnes and Maisie had fled as soon as he came home from work. Within half-an-hour, she and Eck had been screaming at each other and he had already struck her several times. Although she was strong for a woman and wiry, Aggie knew she was no match physically for her brutal husband. However, she also knew that, mentally and verbally, she could leave him standing and, over the years, she had developed a fine line in taunting sneers that he experienced like poisoned needles in his flesh.

The impotence that had plagued him for years, ever since a bad bout of fever, was fertile ground for insults and Aggie used it unmercifully. After each unsuccessful attempt at reaching a sexual climax, he would starkly command her not to tell anyone about it - or *Ah'll bloody kill ye* - and she would scathingly reply: 'Dinnae fash yersel, Casanova. Ah've got better things tae talk aboot than you an yer wee ha'penny biscuit.' And she would finger-flick his flaccid penis scornfully, jump out of bed and race to safety behind a locked bathroom door. But sometimes she did not make it: he would catch hold of her hair or the tail of her nightgown and drag her back to be punished for her cheek.

That night, she had hurled such a hellish insult at him, despite her throbbing face and rising panic, that he had simply put down his head and charged at her, roaring like a maddened, wounded bull. Quick as a flash, with all the skill of a matador, she had sidestepped at the last moment. He had gone headfirst into the doorjamb with a sickening crunch and dropped like a stone to the floor.

For one joyous, appalled moment, she had thought he was dead. But after a few moments, he had thrown up on the kitchen floor, grabbed the hem of her skirt to wipe the blood and vomit off his face, then staggered upstairs to the bathroom. She had stayed downstairs in the kitchen, barricading the door with the table, peeing in the sink and sleeping on the old rocking chair by the range.

The next day there had been two of them sporting bruised faces and split lips and Aggie's reputation for giving as good as she got had been established. The men down the pit had made sly jokes.

'Ah met a wumman the day wi twa black eyes an a puddin' lip. Ah asked her whit happened tae her.'

'Oh, aye, whit did she say?'

'She said: 'Ye should see the ither fellow'!'

Eck could growl and grind his teeth but there was nothing he could do to retrieve his reputation. He had got his comeuppance, and *hell mend him* was the general opinion.

After that, there was a slow but marked change in the dynamics of the Fairweather household. It would be several years before Eck finally stopped lashing out but the violence slowly tapered off and, by the time his daughters emigrated, it had ceased completely. They would never love him but they did at least come to a place of resigned acceptance and felt they could safely leave their mother to fend for herself against him.

With the gradual loss of his powerbase as a physical bully, however, had come an ever-present, simmering fury that expressed itself in mean, slit-eyed glares and terse, bitter remarks. Learning from Aggie, who was past mistress of the barbed comment, he developed his own repertoire of poisonous commentary. Listening to them sometimes, Agnes and Maisie had often wondered if the days of honest blows and kicks had not been better. Their parents had developed a fine expertise in openly despising and degrading each other's opinions, ideas or achievements. After so many years of dedicated practice, they knew no other way to relate to each other.

Aggie was recalled from her musings by the congregation rising for the readings from the bible: the Epistle and the Gospel – *piss an gas*, her father had called them, though never, of course, in the priest's hearing.

Then it was time to sit down for the sermon, for thumb-sucking bairns to snuffle off to sleep and the drunks at the back to begin snoring. Father Brian had a rich Irish brogue, quite unalloyed by forty years in his Scottish parish. His parishioners did not expect to understand what he was saying and even the most pious of them did not try.

The mass was in Latin and the sermon was in Irish brogue, neither of them comprehensible, that was how it was and the good folk in the pews had no quarrel with this system. As long as they could slip into the confessional box as often or as seldom as their consciences dictated and *get their slates cleaned* to be ready to receive Holy Communion, that was all the theology they wanted. Many of them had been married or baptised by this priest, some both, and he was the first person they turned to when there was a death, or someone looking like death, in their families. He was an institution in the community and they neither queried his authority nor questioned his judgment.

Aggie looked intently at the priest as he spoke and anyone watching her might have been impressed by her studious concentration on the sermon. She was not, however, weighing theological premises. Even supposing there were any in the sermon: who could tell? She was considering the man himself and wondering if she and Jeannie could really pull off their plan for tonight.

Jeannie had been relentless in her systematic probing until Aggie's problem had been reduced to twin pillars that must be demolished: the Catholics in the community must be silenced and Eck must be softened.

'So that's a',' Jeannie had concluded. 'It jist comes doon tae twa men that need sortit oot. And that,' she had declared with all the confidence of a woman who has been told she is beautiful every night of her life for the past twenty-two years, 'should be nae trouble tae twa fine lassies like us!'

Aggie, who had never been told she was beautiful, had been less confident. 'Aye, but ane o' them is a priest an the ither is Eck Fairweather.'

The sermon ended and the mass moved on through its centuries-old process, arriving at last at communion. 'Mind,' whispered Jeannie, 'we're no goin' oot wi the rest o' oor row. We're waitin' tae the end an bein' the last twa he serves – that wiy he'll maybe remember us.'

'We shouldnae be goin' oot at a',' whispered Aggie back. 'We baith had big helpin's o' liver and onion a couple o' hoors ago, an Eck an me had Christmas pudding an custard as well.'

'God understands.' This was pronounced very quietly but with such certainty that Aggie stilled her qualms obediently and did not query Jeannie's intimate knowledge of the mind of the Almighty. *Ah widnae be surprised if **He** dis whit He's telt as weel. Kate wis richt. The wumman's a dynamo!*

It caused no little stir, their refusal to go out for communion with the other people in their pew. Askance looks were cast at them implying that they must be in mortal sin, unshriven, in need of confession and absolution for some dastardly crime. When they rose and, heads bowed piously, joined the end of the last line of communicants in the centre aisle, their fellow pew-members were mystified: 'Whit are they twa up tae? Are they jist chancin' it after a' an hopin' God'll no ken they're in a state o' sin? They'll burn in hell fur that!'

Aggie was acutely uncomfortable, aware of the stares, nudges and whispers, but Jeannie simply ignored them and sailed regally back down the side aisle to regain her seat. Aggie resolutely kept her eyes on her clasped hands. Jeannie calmly met the accusing stares of the curious faithful. She even smiled and nodded to those she had some acquaintance with and they hastily dropped their gaze and resumed their eyes-tight-shut prayers.

'*Ita missa est. Deo gratias.*' Aggie smiled, remembering how their schoolteacher had had to explain to them that the response, *deo gratias*

228

– thank God – after the priest's *ita missa est* – the mass is over – was *not* intended as an expression of relief, despite the ring of impatient thankfulness in the altar-boys' cheerful reply and the immediate scuffle to escape that broke out in the congregation.

Tonight she and Jeannie did not join in the surge of tightly packed bodies thronging the aisles and heading for the front porch. Father Brian always made his own way round the outside of the church, once he had gone out by the door at the side of the altar, and would then stand at the front door of the church for the purpose of greeting his parishioners. Those who made good their escape before he managed to reach the front door were spared this face-to-face meeting and anyone with reason for avoiding the priest's eye was wise to take this chance. The elderly priest was not the keen-eyed, shrewd man he had once been but his legend lived on and those who had grown up under his watchful, unrelenting eye were too conditioned to notice the lessening of his control over their lives. They still reckoned he could see right through them to the murky depths of their miserable souls and would not hesitate to tell them so if he thought they needed to hear it.

Aggie and Jeannie waited in their pew. Jeannie was all bland smiles and nods to neighbours and acquaintances but Aggie could not bear to meet their *we-havnae-see-you-here-fur-a-while* looks and comments. She knelt down and buried her face in her hands in an attitude of deep prayer. She remembered enough from her church-going days to know that this was always a good way to choke off unwelcome conversationalists.

Her mind was racing and her heart was beating uncomfortably. *What am Ah doin' even thinkin' o' tellin' the priest aboot the choir?*

It had been one thing to spill it all out to Kate in response to her irresistible kindness. Then, with some trepidation and considerable risk assessment, but desperate for help, she had opened her heart to Jeannie. But to tell Father Brian was to expose it to the ruthless spotlight of the sectarian divide that ran through their community as strongly and surely as the seam of coal ran through the mine which had created the community.

Aggie had hoped that Jeannie would, as Kate had confidently implied, simply come up with some brilliant scheme that would enable her to escape for the whole day on the second of January, would satisfy the wagging tongues at the Get-Together and would ensure continued and complete secrecy. But Jeannie had seen it differently.

'But whit aboot *after* the concert? It soonds tae me like this choir is enjoyin' itsel far too much tae stop after jist ane performance. Ye micht get asked tae perform somewhere else. An it'll likely keep meetin' an start learnin' somethin' else an get asked tae dae mair concerts. Are ye jist goin' tae gie it up after this concert? Disnae soond like they'll let ye go, no if ye're their solo singer an they think sae much o' ye. Ye cannae keep it a secret furever.'

She was right, of course, Aggie realised at once. Already members of the choir were talking about new music and other venues. In her single-minded desperation to work out how to get to The Alhambra for this first concert, she had not looked ahead. Now the thought of the choir going on meeting, learning new pieces, performing at other concerts, all without her, filled her with despair. If it was only a one-off event and the choir disbanded after it, she would be sad but resigned and at least she would have the memory of her moment of glory to cherish. But if the choir was going on, possibly from strength to strength, and she could not be part of it… They would get another leading soprano to take her place…

Jeannie had seen at once that her point was well taken and had pressed home her advantage. 'So we need tae sort it a' oot aince an fur a'. An then ye can dae as much singin' as ye like, whaur ye like, an naebody'll stan in yer wiy.'

It *was* a joyous prospect and Aggie had been sufficiently seduced by it to agree to this midnight mass ploy with a view to tackling Father Brian afterwards. But now, as she contemplated actually doing so, her heart failed her and she found herself *really* praying rather than just play-acting.

God help me. It's your son, Jesus, Ah want tae go an sing aboot. I know that my redeemer liveth… ' The words and music drifted through her mind. It had been a long time since she had prayed, really prayed with this kind of earnestness. Probably the last time, she thought, had been when her mother was dying. *An a fat lot o' guid that did…*

Jeannie poked her sharply in the ribs. 'Come on, it's time tae go.'

'Ah'm no sure Ah think this is sich a guid idea…'

But Jeannie was already out of the pew and marching down the centre aisle towards the front porch of the church to join the last few lingerers.

Father O'Malley was pleased with the way the mass had gone. Neither of the older altar-boys had dropped their incense-wafters; the three younger ones had not pushed and shoved each other, giggled hysterically or – he remembered one occasion with horror – pee-ed themselves; there had been only one drunken brawl, hastily stifled and ejected by the burly, stalwart believers he always chose for this duty; only four people had fainted and they had all luckily been sitting at the end of their pews; and his sermon had been met with the usual rapt concentration from his parishioners. It was an old, re-cycled one but it had been five years since its last airing and he had been confident that no-one would notice.

Now he was looking forward to settling down by the fire in his study with the remaining third of a bottle of Johnnie Walker. Yes, everything had gone well and, of course, he hastily reminded himself, just as they had just sung in the closing carol, *Christ **was** born - in Bethlehem.*

He turned to give his last two handshakes of the night to the two women bearing down on him.

'Mrs Gilhooley,' he shook her hand and smiled with professional warmth. 'How is Mr Gilhooley and your fine sons?' Jeannie was a regular attender, which meant Bob was as well, although it had been quite a while since the twins had been able to get out of their beds on a Sunday morning after as much Saturday night debauchery as they could find or afford.

He turned to Aggie. She looked vaguely familiar but he could not recall her name: *not* a regular attender. 'It's...it's... I don't think I've seen you here for a while, have I?'

As always when nervous and defensive, Aggie became belligerent.

'Ah'm Aggie Fairweather. Ye married me tae Eck Fairweather – mair's the peety – an ye baptised baith ma bairns. Ah'm runnin' a shop these days an Ah cannae aye find time . . . '

As the priest recoiled a little from this attack, Jeannie moved swiftly.

'A Merry Christmas tae ye, Father,' she said smoothly. 'That was a beeyootiful mass the nicht and yer sermon was jist lovely.' She slipped her small foot on top of Aggie's large one and bore down mercilessly. 'We were jist sayin' that tae each ither, were we no, Aggie?'

Aggie took the hint and cast around in her mind for a way to augment Jeannie's strategic flattery.

'Really?' He was amazed. No-one *ever* talked to him – or, as far as he knew, to each other - about his sermons. 'What was it that you particularly liked about it?'

Jeannie was stumped and cursed herself for digging her own grave. Then to her amazement, Aggie said solemnly: 'It's aye guid tae be reminded that *The Lord God Omnipotent Reigneth.*'

'Indeed,' said Father Brian, visibly gratified. He did not think these words were actually *in* his sermon, though they sounded vaguely familiar, but he could not fault the sentiment. 'I'm glad you took that from my message.'

Jeannie recovered from her astonishment at Aggie's scholarly and effective intervention. She hastened to press their advantage. 'We were wonderin' if we could hae a wee word wi ye, Father. We've a wee problem.'

'What, now? Can't it wait till tomorrow?' He saw his happy hour with JW fading.

'We need...' Jeannie sifted through her extensive vocabulary. 'We're in need o' some o' yer *pastoral care*, jist like they wee sheep that we were singin' aboot, that the shepherds were watchin'.'

She saw his look of depressed resignation and guessed its cause. She played her master card. Opening her large bag, she showed him its contents.

'We thocht, since it's Christmas Eve an we've a' been starvin' oorsels a' day fur communion afore midnight, we would bring ye some nice wee bits an pieces tae eat an drink. We can hae a nice wee feast, the three o' us, while we tell ye oor story an get the benefit o' yer wise coonsel.'

There was a slab of black bun and a tin of Petticoat Tails shortbread in the bag – Aggie had paid a quick visit to her shop on the way to the church and broken into the large order that had been delivered for selling next week – but these were not the focus of his interested gaze. It was the sight of a uniquely shaped bottle, full of amber liquid, that held his attention: Haig's Dimple, one of the best whiskies on the market, from the local distillery a few miles away in Markinch.

'Well,' he said jovially, 'far be it from me to turn two lost lambs away at Christmas. Let's go over to the house. There's a good fire on in my study. We'll hear all about your problem there.'

CHAPTER TWELVE

JEANNIE

She awoke to the sounds of her sons laughing over their Christmas stockings. For a dreamy moment she was back in the days of their childhood, imagining two little boys on the hearth rug, agog with the wonder of what Santa had brought them. She remembered running downstairs in the pre-dawn dark at the first sound, anxious not to miss one second of their wide-eyed, whooping excitement, trying to throw old blankets over their pyjamas to keep them warm but losing out to their impatient leaping and lunging. They had not noticed the cold, even though it was sometimes, technically, still the middle of the night when their anticipation roused them and they could wait no longer. It had been the one morning of the year when she had been permissive and they had always made the most of it.

She snuggled up to Bob's broad back and tried to drift back to sleep. She could see the alarm clock over his shoulder on his bedside table: five-past-eight. Much later than her normal rising hour though Bob, when on back-shift, never rose much before nine. Usually she would have their breakfast all ready when the boys came down at quarter-past-eight but it had been almost two o'clock in the morning when she had crept into bed, hugging a hot water bottle, depriving herself of the usual close body contact with Bob which was far more effective than any such artificial bed-warming device. He had been fast asleep, emitting his usual unique combination of a snore, a cat's purr and a satisfied smirk. She had made sure he was a happy lad before she had set off for midnight mass with Aggie. He had offered happily to come with her – they had often gone to it together over the years, especially when he was back-shift and did not have to get up

233

early next morning. But she had been adamant and, from his point of view, rather mysterious.

'Ah hae ma reasons, Bob. Ye'll hae tae trust me on this ane. Ah'm keepin' a secret fur somebody the noo but Ah'll be able tae tell ye a' aboot it in a week's time.'

A few weeks ago, she could not have imagined being able to restrain herself from sharing it with him – and several others – but she was finding it easier in this, her second, outing as Jeannie, trustworthy confidante and saviour. 'So ye cannae come tae mass wi me.'

'But hoo can goin' tae midnight mass be a secret? The church'll be fair packed. Hunners o' folk'll see ye.'

'Dinnae try tae fathom things like that oot, Bob. Ye'll never manage it. Ye'll be telt a' aboot it soon enough. Noo…' With all the skill of an experienced courtesan, she had enticed him away from thinking about matters too weighty for his simple mind and had lured him upstairs for a quick hour, leaving him smiling broadly and able to accept her absence for a few hours.

'Though it'll no be the same goin' aff tae sleep withoot ma bonnie wee wife beside me,' he had grumbled.

She had promised to make it up to him in the morning, hinting at one of his favourite fantasies; then had hurried through to the twins' bedroom to unearth the bottle of Haig's Dimple whisky which she knew was hidden at the back of a drawer. Rab had been given it as a thank-you present from one of his fellow dodgy-dealers, in whose way he had put a bit of business. He was hoarding it for Hogmanay and had, so far, managed to keep it out of the hands of his brother and his father.

But it was a small house and Jeannie was a meticulous cleaner: nothing in her domain ever remained a secret from her. She had had a slight pang of guilt as she stowed it at the bottom of her bag but she had reminded herself of all the times the twins had helped themselves to things *she* had tried to keep for special occasions: memories of cakes half-eaten before she had time to ice them, bowls of trifle half-demolished before guests arrived and once a whole box of expensive bath crystals – one of her mother-in-law's pretentious presents – emptied lock, stock and barrel into the hip-bath, causing a high tide of scented foam to surge all over the tiny bathroom and into the living-room.

Ah'll see if there's enough money in ma post office savings tae buy him anither ane – or at least get him somethin' like it, even if it's no Dimple. Everyone, even non-whisky drinkers like Jeannie, knew that Dimple was a *posh* brand.

The lads finished opening their parcels and, realising that there was no attentive mother on hand, threw together a slap-dash breakfast of burnt toast and messy marmalade. They consoled themselves that at least having no Jeannie there meant they were let off the bothersome task of clearing up the shambles of wrapping paper, orange peel and tinsel in the living-room.

Once they had roistered their way out and roared off in the latest borrowed car, Bob turned over and extracted last night's promise from Jeannie so that it was late morning before she had time to herself to remember the events of the night before. Once Bob had gone off to the pub for his usual pre-dinner dram, she treated herself to hot milk and honey – always a comfort for mild hangovers - and half-an-hour in her fireside chair whilst she reviewed progress so far in The Aggie Project.

It had been half-past-one when Jeannie had finally left Aggie at her door and walked down to her own house. The two women had been 'as high as kites' on their way home, Jeannie glowing with a sense of her powers of manipulation and Aggie almost hysterical with incredulous relief. Every time they looked like calming down, one of them would say the magic words, *Omnipotent Reigneth,* and off they would go again, hooting with laughter and clutching each other.

There was certainly no doubt that Aggie's astonishing proclamation in the church porch had been the beginning of their victorious progress. It had set the tone for the discussion which had lasted for the next hour in Father Brian's cosy little study.

In all his years in the priesthood, he had never had a parishioner comment on one of his sermons, let alone express a truth they felt they had gained from it. He had been thrilled. *'I've waited fifty years for this,'* he thought. *'It's come at last. God is good!'* As they followed him round the church and across the path to the priest's house, Jeannie dug Aggie in the ribs.

'Have ye only mair whaur that cam' frae? He's like a cat that's swallied the cream. He'll be putty in oor hauns.'

Aggie had grinned and replied. 'Ah've got twa hoors worth, but Ah'll jist try an choose the best bits.'

'Well, jist watch me an tak yer cue frae me.'

They played the old man like a fish on a hook, encouraging him to have two generous drams of liquid gold and to continue to talk about his sermon. Aggie continued, courtesy of Handel, to trot out remarkable responses which caused him to gasp, beam and nod vigorously.

When, warming to her task, she clasped her hands and declared piously, 'Ye see, Father, after yer sermon, I *know* that my redeemer liveth' – and Jeannie nodded sententiously, endorsing this with a ringing 'AMEN!' - he even wiped away a tear.

A contemplative hush fell in the hot little room; then he started up saying: 'But you ladies are not drinking. Of course, ladies like *sherry*. I'm sorry.'

As he busied himself finding a bottle of Harvey's Walnut Brown, Aggie mouthed at Jeannie; 'When are we goin' tae tell him aboot...?'

Jeannie's raised finger silenced and reassured her. It was a question of judging things very finely. Jeannie wanted Brian O'Malley inebriated enough to be ready to resonate emotionally with the story she was about to tell and to respond generously to it but not so drunk he could not remember his promises in the morning. She watched him as he poured out two very large sherries and settled down for what he fondly imagined was going to be more theological discussion and more praise for his preaching. She allowed him one sip of his third dram before striking.

'Ye're maybe wonderin', Father, hoo Aggie here kens sae much aboot God and Jesus and has sich a grasp o' a' this stuff when she disnae cam' tae mass much these days?' she began.

The priest frowned a little irritably. Just at that moment, he was much more interested in hearing how his wonderful preaching had taught Aggie so many deep truths than in dwelling on this bothersome detail. Obviously, she would have to get herself down to confession as soon as possible and get forgiven for all these weeks or months – or years? – of missed Sunday masses. Then she must start attending regularly, of course.

But these were mere procedural details. Plenty of his parishioners were never out of his confessional box (barely giving themselves time to sin between each visit, really) and were forever at mass, weekdays and Sundays, but did not evince a fraction of this woman's understanding of the Christian faith.

He opened his mouth to stimulate anew the paean of praise for his sermon but Jeannie beat him to it. She launched into a description of 'ma freen here'.

Aggie, listening incredulously, barely recognised herself or her life. With all her storyteller's skill, Jeannie painted a picture of an innocent young girl, with the voice of an angel and a deep religious faith, finding herself hastily married off to a non-Catholic in order to assuage her dying mother's anxiety and allow her to go to her eternal rest knowing neither of her daughters would suffer the terrible fate of becoming elderly spinsters.

'Ah hope her pal, Annie, disnae hear her sayin' that,' Aggie thought, suppressing a grin.

This beautiful young girl (Aggie privately thought Jeannie was stretching the truth a bit too far there and Father Brian glanced a little doubtfully at Aggie at this point) had virtually been sold into a life in which she was not allowed to express her faith or her musicality. Her domineering husband had simply gone through the motions of converting and making promises to the Roman Catholic faith. He had had no intention of sustaining it or of allowing his wife to do so. But, amazingly, because she was such a special person with such a saintly faith and unquenchable spirit, she had never lost her longing to express both her burning faith or her singing ability. After years in the wilderness, she had recently been given the chance to do both by joining a church choir.

Sadly, this was not a *Catholic* choir *as such* (here, Jeannie paused to pour a fourth dram for the priest and to pat Aggie's hand consolingly). Of course she would so much have preferred if it was, but she had been too ashamed of her years of absence to come back to her old church, too unsure of her welcome from the Catholic God (another consoling pat on Aggie's hand and a complicit sniff from Aggie). She had been very nervous of going to the choir, not knowing if she would be received into *any* fold of the Christian faith. Imagine her joy when she had not only been made welcome but had been chosen as soloist. As she had sung their songs, she had rediscovered her *Delight in the Lord* (Jeannie had borrowed one of Aggie's phrases here) and had come back to her own church tonight.

'But didn't I see you taking communion tonight?' he interposed. 'If you have been estranged so long from the church, you know the rules, you should not have...'

'That's jist it,' Jeannie broke in hastily, cursing herself for this inconsistency in her strategy. 'Aggie's been that long in the wilderness that she'd forgotten a' they rules an she wis jist desperate tae come back. An then yer wunnerfu sermon and the wiy ye've made us that welcome the nicht...'

Father Brian had thrown his scruples to the wind. 'It's The Prodigal Son!' he cried, leaping up and refilling their glasses generously. 'This, my son, was lost and is found!'

He topped up his own glass and offered them more black bun. 'His father celebrated when he came home, had a party for him. This is just what we are doing for Mrs Fairweather tonight. Drink up, ladies!'

And he had proceeded to set them a splendid example.

After that, it had been child's play to get him onside about the concert. 'Of course, you must sing, my dear. I may even come and hear you. Handel's *Messiah* is quite famous though I have never heard it myself. Of course, he wasn't a Catholic, but still...'

Aggie was about to elaborate on the need for him to direct his flock to take a similarly encouraging and tolerant position but Jeannie caught her eye and shook her head.

'Time we were takin' oor leave, Aggie. Father Brian's had a hard day and a long nicht an he'll be up tae say nine o'clock mass the morn. We'll jist leave the whisky, Father, an a Merry Christmas tae ye.'

As he courteously ushered them out of the house, he laid a hand on Aggie's arm. 'God has blessed you with a voice to sing his praises, my dear. Who are we to question where He sends us to use our gifts? Perhaps he is calling you to shine the light of the true faith among these well-meaning but sadly misguided Protestants.'

Aggie was unable to stop herself asking anxiously: 'But will a' the ither folk in *oor* church see it like that, Father? Ah'm worried that...'

'I shall preach a sermon on it, my dear.' He winked at her. 'I hope you'll be in church to hear it. And I shall look forward to discussing it with you afterwards.'

'Ye can bet on it!' Aggie positively skipped down the path to join Jeannie.

'Why did *you* no ask him that? That's mair important that onythin' if Ah'm tae get awa frae the Get-thegither.'

Jeannie smiled. 'Ah wanted him tae think it wis his ain idea. Ye nearly spoiled it, there at the door, but then he had his wee brainwave aboot doin' a sermon on it. He'll be awa gettin' his wee books an bibles oot richt noo, Ah widnae be surprised, burnin' the midnight oil. Ye've gied him the impression that his sermons are better than whit that lad Moses brocht doon frae that big hill on tablets o' stane.'

'Ye mean the ten commandments?'

'Aye, there'll be nae haudin him noo. Ah jist hope he disnae think his sermons need tae be ony langer. Ye can never mak oot a word he says onyway. He'd be as weel readin' oot the Miscellaneous Sales page in the paper.'

'Puir auld mannie.' Aggie was feeling magnanimous in victory. 'Wis that no a laugh when he asked me… An Ah said…'

And so began a blow-by-blow replay of the encounter with much mimicry and mirth, so that, by the time they reached No. 22, they were hiccupping and staggering like two old sots.

'Ah hope tae God naeone saw us oot their windaes,' Jeannie thought now as she drained her cup and rose to begin making Bob's dinner. *'Ye'd hae thocht it wis laughin' gas we'd been on an no jist sherry. Whit a result, though!'*

As she rubbed flour into knobs of margarine to make pastry, she began to turn her attention to phase two of The Aggie Project: the softening of Eck. She needed a very different approach here, she reflected. *And* she needed an ally, someone with a path to one of the most unapproachable men she knew.

She frowned as she rolled out the pastry. Then her expression lightened. *Whit am Ah worryin' aboot? Am Ah no married tae the very man that walks tae work wi him every day an listens tae a' his moans an groans sae patiently? Bob, ma bonnie lad, ye're aboot tae earn yer keep. Ye maybe thocht that wee thrill Ah gied ye this mornin' wis free gratis but ye're aboot tae find oot different!*

Bob chased the last few crumbs of the feather-light pastry round the edges of his plate then, in exasperation, laid down his knife and fork and lifted the plate up to lick it. He caught a look of severe reproof from his wife and hastily lowered it. Jeannie daintily finished her own smaller helping of the pork sausage pie. She eyed Bob speculatively, then rose to clear their plates. 'Ah've a wee puddin'.'

Bob smirked. 'Aye, Ah ken. Ah had a guid haud of it this mornin'!'

Beyond a dismissive *tut* as she went through to the kitchen, Jeannie gave no sign of hearing this indiscreet reference to their early morning activities. She set one of Aggie's Christmas puddings, a gift from yesterday's late afternoon visit, down on the table between them and poured perfect, silky-smooth custard over it.

Bob leaned forward and inhaled spicy fruitiness overlaid with warm, milky vanilla. 'Whit in the name o' God is that? It smells braw!'

'Christmas pudding, Bob. This *is* Christmas Day.' Jeannie sounded as if they had been eating the stuff for years on this day of the year and he tried to look as if he had known this all along. 'Och aye, of course.'

As he tucked into the lion's share of it, she tackled him. 'Hoo are ye gettin' on wi Big Eck these days?'

'Weel,' Bob slurped at the custard moat around his dollop of pudding. 'Weel…'

People did not really think in terms of *getting on* with Eck. You ignored him, you avoided him, you suffered him and occasionally, if you felt the need for a bit of excitement in your life, you played the rile-him-and-run game. When Eck really lost his temper, you could sell tickets for the show but most of the time he was more like a caged wild animal, pacing angrily but abortively, snarling whenever his cage-bars were rattled.

Jeannie pressed on. 'Whit dae ye talk aboot when ye're walkin' tae and from the pit?'

'Weel… Ah dinnae really talk at a'. Maistly Ah jist listen.'

'So, whit dis *he* talk aboot then?'

'Ach, this 'n that, Jeannie. Ah dinnae aye listen tae a' he says. It's the same stuff a' the time.'

'Like whit?'

'The union, the pit, the fitba…'

'Whit aboot Aggie? Hoo much dis he ken aboot Aggie?'

Bob blinked. 'She's his wife, Jeannie. He kens a'thing aboot her. Like Ah dae aboot you, ma wee darlin''

Jeannie sniffed. *Ah widnae bet on it, Bob.* She smiled at the thought of Bob knowing or understanding what she and Aggie had been up to last night, for example.

'Has he said onythin' aboot whit she's singin' these days?'

'Singin'? Oh aye, that's richt, she's a gran singer. Mind that Hogmanay when she…'

Jeannie cut in. 'Ah wis askin' ye if *Eck*'s mentioned onythin' aboot her singin'.' She fixed him with an intent stare and he obediently puckered his forehead in concentration.

'Weel…let me see… He's aye goin' on aboot whit a hellish cook she is an whit a state the hoose is in. But singin'… Wait a meenit, he did mention that he'd heard her singin' some churchy stuff, like a hymn or somethin'. That wis weeks ago…he wis goin' his mile aboot whit he'd dae if she wis turnin' intae some kind o' religious…religious… Och, ah cannae mind exactly the word he used but he went on an on aboot it that day. Ah telt him no tae be worryin' aboot it. Ah mean, it's no very likely, is it? But he jist telt me tae belt up an no stick ma nose in. He's no mentioned it again since then.'

Jeannie sighed. It was not looking like a fruitful seam after all. The chances of Eck paying any attention to Bob were obviously minimal. He saw her disappointment and attempted to regain her favour. 'Ah could ask him if she's still goin' tae the embroidery classes, if ye like.'

Jeannie swept him a contemptuous glance. 'Can it, Bob,' she spat angrily. 'We baith ken that wis a load o' muck ye cam' oot wi that day.'

She rose and moved into the kitchen to begin clattering the pots and crockery. Bob sighed, glanced at the clock and moved reluctantly through to begin putting on his boots. Then he had a brainwave.

'Ah'll tell ye ane thing, Jeannie,' he called through to her, raising his voice to be heard above the din of her washing-up. 'Eck's been awfy guid aboot the time that Aggie's been spendin' at her sister's these past weeks. He's had tae pit up wi even worse meals, sometimes nae meals at a', when she's been seeing tae her sister and the auld mither-in-law. But he's no said a bad word aboot it. Ah thocht he'd be flamin' mad an moanin his damn heid aff. He's got a real soft spot fur the sister, it seems tae me. He even talked aboot buyin' some flooers an takin' them roon one day. Imagine Eck wi a bunch o' flooers in his haun! Ah dinnae think he's done it, like, but even him thinkin' aboot it is a miracle.'

He was struggling into his working coat as he spoke but he was stopped short by his wife trying to encircle his ample waist with her arms. He turned and delightedly held out the sides of the coat so she could snuggle into his chest. He happily nibbled the hair on the top of her head as Eck's rap came on the front door and his shout of 'Are ye ready there, Bob?' echoed though the cottage.

Jeannie tilted her head back. 'Will ye dae somethin' fur me, Bob?' she murmured. 'Will ye ask Eck a wee bit mair aboot hoo he feels aboot Kate?'

There was no time to expound as Eck was rapping ever more impatiently. She had to content herself with giving him a soft kiss full of promise and a meaningful nod as he let himself out the back door and trudged off round the house to meet Eck.

She finished the washing up and prepared a bag with a small piece of the sausage pie and some potato salad to take round to her father-in-law. She added one of the four Christmas puddings Aggie had given her and a cup of custard. As she walked round to the old man's house, she pondered this new twist in The Aggie Project.

Eck sweet on Kate? 'A soft spot', Bob had said. Not a phrase she, or anyone else, would associate with Eck. But Jeannie, as all writers must be, was a keen observer of human nature, and she knew that there were always surprises and unplumbed depths in everyone. It might just be the key.

It had taken all of her extensive ability to imagine herself into situations beyond her experience in order to understand Aggie's extreme reluctance to tell Eck about the concert. Once Aggie had begun to talk about it yesterday, it had been as if a floodgate opened. A huge dam of bottled up anger and misery had finally broken and the torrent that flowed out had left Jeannie appalled into silence and Aggie exhausted and shaking.

A story emerged of two decades of growing hatred. Aggie's description of her marriage was terse and stark: a vicious spiral of growing mutual denigration, the physical violence gradually being replaced by even more damaging mental cruelty. They had reached a place now where they communicated only through sneers and insults. She described how Eck poured scorn on everything she did, predicting failure for her every plan, sullying everything she did by wounding, derogatory comment.

From small things like a new haircut which was laughed at derisively – *ye cannae mak a silk purse oot o' a sow's ear* – to big things like her business enterprise in the bakery - *ye'll mak a pig's ear o' that like ye dae o' a'thing, ye'll hae us in the bankruptcy court* – he never failed to stick the knife in.

'But ye've made a gran success o' yer shop. Even *he* must see that,' Jeannie ventured.

'Och aye, but Ah've tae hide half the profits Ah mak. If he kent Ah mak a lot mair than he dis doon the pit, he'd hae a fit.'

242

She talked about the way he looked at her, flicking disgust from her face down over her body but still manhandling that body remorselessly in attempts to achieve sexual satisfaction, never considering any needs that she might have. Jeannie blushed to hear such things talked about in her living-room and thanked God secretly for the rich, loving relationship she enjoyed with her own dear Bob.

Aggie talked about Eck's constant, carping dissatisfaction with her home-making and culinary efforts and his unstinting prediction of failure for her business. Even when it had become apparent that she was succeeding beyond anyone's expectations, he still disparaged it at every turn. Indeed, if it had not been for the encouragement of her daughters, she would never have started it. They had seen the problems their cousins were having with their Aunty Kate and had thought to head off at the pass any similar barriers to their emigration plans by getting their mother immersed in the new venture.

'But he cannae deny ye're a lovely singer. A'body kens that,' Jeannie attempted to salvage some glimmer of light. So Aggie told her about the times when, after enthusiastic applause and calls for several encores at community gatherings, his only comments had been: 'Mair o' yer sentimental shite. We're a' fed up listenin' tae that crap' or 'Ye looked a bonnie sicht standin' up there in front o' a'body. Ye're like a bag tied in the middle an yer hair's like straw hingin oot o' a midden.'

The very thought of Eck being allowed to exercise his venomous tongue on her forthcoming debut at The Alhambra filled her with dread and Jeannie, her heart wrung for this skinny, unattractive but immensely talented and enormously brave woman, at last understood why.

'Dinnae greet, Aggie,' she had consoled. 'We'll manage it. Leave it wi me.'

Now, as she turned in the path to her father-in-law's cottage, she wondered just what she had promised. Father Brian and his bigoted flock had been one hurdle, in the end remarkably easily and enjoyably overcome. But this one was not so much of a hurdle as a ten-foot-high fence with barbed wire on the top.

Maybe Ah'd better be sayin' ma rosary fur this ane.

'Weel?'

Bob had barely emerged from the little bathroom still towelling his thick, springy hair, when she pounced on him. 'Weel whit?' he growled, looking meaningfully at the two places set on the table.

Jeannie took the hint. Even Bob had his sticking point and, after a seven-hour shift at the coalface, it was always best to feed him before expecting any sense out of him. She hastily dished up a huge platter of 'stovies' – onions and potatoes cooked in the dinner-time sausage dripping and laced with corned beef - and he attacked it without ceremony.

With difficulty she possessed her soul in patience until he had wiped his plate clean with a chunk of bread. 'Did ye find oot any mair aboot hoo Eck feels aboot Kate?'

Bob leaned back in his chair and grinned. He saw a distinct possibility opening up in front of him.

'Ah micht have…' He toyed with the knife which he had not used, having simply shovelled the stovies into his mouth with the fork. 'Ah micht have. But ye micht hae tae find a wiy tae get it oot o' me.'

Jeannie saw at once how the land lay. This was territory in which she was a confident, seasoned traveller. She brushed past him as she made her way through to the kitchen with their dirty plates, making sure her breasts touched his shoulder. She served up the pudding: tapioca and bramble jelly. He consumed it in three spoonfuls before she had even resumed her place opposite him. She resigned herself – she did not like tapioca anyway. She pushed her plate away, leaned over the table and took his hand in hers. She turned the big, calloused hand over and considered it thoughtfully.

'Now, now, Bobby.' She had her schoolmistress's voice on. 'Ye ken Ah dinnae like secrets. Are ye goin' tae be a guid lad an tell me or do Ah have tae gie ye the strap again?'

An hour later, she came downstairs to clear the table and tidy up the kitchen. She left a dish of stovies for the boys – it was a big favourite with them. She hummed as she worked: it was all coming together nicely.

Bob, once they had played out the delicious fantasy which Jeannie had concocted, had been happy to tell her that Eck, in response to Bob's simple enquiry as to how Kate was progressing, had waxed positively lyrical (*not* Bob's words but Jeannie's construction) about what a wonderful woman Kate was, what a lovely wife and mother she was and a lot more than that *cock-a-doodle-dandy Johnnie Cruikshanks* deserved.

'*Ah think Ah'll jist run roon fur a wee visit tae Kate the morn,*' she thought as she switched the lights out on a spotlessly tidy kitchen and living-room – though with no expectation of finding it in similar condition tomorrow morning, the twins not yet being home. '*She got me intae this. She can get me oot o' it!*'

CHAPTER THIRTEEN

KATE

Kate smiled blandly at her mother-in-law as she removed the sodden pad and replaced it with a new one. 'There we are, Maggie,' she said cheerfully. 'A' clean and comfy again.'

She pointedly ignored the old woman's mutterings. She was armed with Jeannie's reassurances that the auld yin was happier with the new regime: *Dinnae tak ony o' her lip. She's used tae it noo.*

'Ah'll bring yer tea an biscuit through in a wee while. Jist ye listen tae yer programme on the wireless the noo.'

She closed the door decisively and breezed out of the bedroom back to the kitchen '*Nae sheets tae wash. Whit a relief! Thank God!*' She had so much to thank Jeannie for, she reflected. Returning to her unwelcome duties had not been as hideous as she had feared, thanks to the changes that her friend had wrought.

She moved slowly round her kitchen not with the sprightly bustle of former years nor even with the dogged, increasingly dreary, determination of the last many months. She still felt dreamily detached, more like a visitor than the mistress of the house. But the dread of it had gone and even the indifference was waning as she reclaimed her territory and slowly reacquainted herself with dear, familiar things.

There came the *ping* of the doorbell and the muffled sound of feet on the carpeted inner stair. Senga's husband Jim, being handy with his toolbox, had fitted a device to the outside door which stopped it short of closing totally and snapping the Yale lock on. During the time when *The Trinity* had been coming and going so much, it had become a burden having to run up and down stairs to open it for each other. Most people in this community never locked their doors anyway but

246

the council had had the locks and door-closers fitted when the houses were being built. Now she was glad to be able to leave the house open to callers – it was what she had grown up with.

'Are ye there, Kate?' came Jeannie's voice as she pushed open the inside door.

Kate brightened. She had not seen Jeannie for a few days and she was missing not only her cheerful, bracing presence but also their secret, conspiratorial discussions of what lay ahead in the near future.

Jeannie moved across the sitting-room to the fireplace. She brought a breath of cold, snowy air and the scent of winter-out-of-doors. Kate inhaled it longingly. Dr Kenny had decreed that she must wait another week before going out into the bitter weather and breathing in the chimney-smoke-laden air.

Jeannie brushed flakes of snow off her shoulders and stood on tiptoe to remove her hat, lean into the mirror, check her appearance, smooth the hair on top of her head and tuck a few stragglers into her bun at the back. Kate smiled to watch her. Aggie would have had a ragged scarf over her head and she would have whipped it off without regard to the state of the hair underneath or so much as a glance in the mirror. Jeannie was never less than primly well-groomed, no matter what the task in hand. *Except fur that day in Ain'ster. She wis a bonnie sicht that day. We baith were.*

'It's gran tae see ye, Jeannie. Tak yer coat aff. Ah wis jist goin' tae mak the tea fur me an Maggie.'

Jeannie moved towards the kitchen door. She waved a round tin which purported to contain ginger snaps but was actually full of home-made scones. 'Ah'll soon see tae that,' she said briskly. 'Ah've brocht some bakin'.'

Kate moved more quickly than she had done for about a month. She intercepted Jeannie and gently wrested the tin from her grasp. 'That's guid o' ye, Jeannie,' she said firmly. 'Tak a seat by the fire an get yersel warmed up. Ah'll manage the tea fine by masel.'

Jeannie opened her mouth to protest as a sense of loss, almost of outrage at ingratitude, swept through her. Then common sense prevailed. *Let the lassie hae her ain hame back. It shows ye've done a guid job an she's getting weel again.* But there was no denying a surge of nostalgia for the days when she had been the one in control in this house.

'Ye can tak the auld yin's through tae her, if ye like.' Kate reappeared a few minutes later with a tray bearing a mug of tea and a large, golden scone, thickly spread with butter and raspberry jam. 'That'll pit a smile on her face. Since it was you made the scones, ye micht as well be the ane that gets the smile.'

Vera Lynn was yearning loudly for *The White Cliffs of Dover* when Jeannie opened Maggie's door. She waited till the song ended then moved forward to turn down the wireless. The old woman was sitting in her wheelchair by the window, wireless on sill. The bed was neatly made up but obviously the bed linen had not had to be changed. Jeannie nodded approvingly to see that the routine she had established was being adhered to.

At the sight of the inviting scone, Maggie allowed something approaching a smile to cross her girny old face. 'Are ye back, then, Jeannie?' she said hopefully. 'Things are no the same with that silly bitch up out o' her bed again.'

Jeannie gave this conversational lead no rope. 'Ah've popped into see ma good freen, Kate, and enjoy a blether wi her,' she said firmly. 'An Ah'm glad tae see ye lookin' sae weel yersel. Noo, a' we need is tae get Kate lookin' half as weel. That's whit we a' want, is it no?' And she turned up the wireless again, leaving Old Maggie to enjoy a *White Christmas* with Bing Crosby.

Kate and Jeannie enjoyed a happy twenty minutes over their tea and scones rehearsing for the umpteenth time the details of the plan which was soon to be executed. It was all well in hand with no hitches and there was really nothing more to do now than wait. But these regular repetitions gave Kate, who had been forced to take a back seat the past few weeks and learn only at second hand how it was all going, an injection of faith and hope that it *would* really happen.

Jeannie understood this and she wanted Kate feeling as buoyant and optimistic as possible before she changed the subject. When Kate finally leaned back in her chair with a contented sigh and a little wriggle of happy anticipation, Jeannie grasped her opportunity.

'Aggie came tae see me last week. She said *you*'d telt her Ah could help her wi a wee problem.'

Kate had almost forgotten about Aggie's needs once she had referred her on to Jeannie. This was partly because she had such confidence in Jeannie's problem-solving ability and partly because, as her own big day approached, she really had no room in her head to think or care about anything else.

'That's guid. Ah'm glad she took ma advice an asked ye whit tae dae.' With an effort she drummed up enough interest to ask: 'So whit's yer plan tae get Aggie awa tae her concert wi naebody ony the wiser?'

Jeannie shook her head. Short-sightedness obviously ran in the Kelly family. 'Whit wid be the point o' that? It's no jist *this* concert – she's an important member o' an important choir noo. She'll be carryin' on goin' tae practices every week and gettin' dressed up tae gang on stage regular-like. She cannae spend the rest o' her life sneakin' aboot an hopin' naebody notices. Sooner or later somebody wid see her or find oot. Naw, whit we've got tae dae is mak it a' richt fur her tae dae it, richt oot in the open, an naebody sayin' nothin' aboot it!'

Kate nodded slowly. 'Ah telt her it wis nothin' tae be ashamed o' an she should jist tell Senga the truth aboot whaur she's goin'. But she's worried aboot the priest an a' the ither Catholics.'

Jeannie chortled. 'No ony mair, she's no!' She proceeded to regale Kate with a full account of the midnight mass triumph, mimicking Aggie's solemnity as she had delivered her quotes from the *Messiah* and Father Brian's gratified Irish-brogue purr as he had responded.

'It wis a match made in heaven tae listen tae the pair o' them.' She described how he had gone off happily to prepare a new sermon that would explain to his flock just why they should all endorse and support Aggie's involvement in the choir.

'But whit guid will that dae?' wondered Kate. 'Naebody listens tae his sermons. Ye can hardly mak oot a word he says at the best o' times, but when he gets up on that pulpit and his voice jist kinda rumbles roon an roon the church…'

'It disnae matter. The main thing is *he* thinks it's makin' a difference an so we can tell a' the Catholics that Father B is quite happy aboot Aggie's choir an if they dinnae believe it they can go an ask him themsels.'

'That's a wee miracle ye've worked there, you and Aggie.'

'Aye, weel… Ah suppose Christmas Eve *should* be a guid nicht fur miracles.'

A short lull fell in the room. Both women were now thinking of the other half of Aggie's problem; each was wondering how much the other knew and hesitating to reveal her own knowledge. What Aggie had shared about her marriage was so deeply personal and so painfully sad that talking about it openly seemed almost indecent.

But eventually, Kate ventured tentatively: 'An whit aboot Eck? Wha's goin' tae tell *him*?'

'Weel, Kate, that's jist the thing, ye see.'

Family Favourites was blaring out of Maggie's room: *The British Forces Broadcasting Network in Germany* was performing its weekly task of enabling relatives at home to send musical messages to their boys doing National Service in regiments still stationed there ten years after war had ended. It was late Sunday morning, almost dinner-time.

Kate had everything ready for Maggie's runny-egg-with-chips-to-dip-in-it and a grand big fry up of bacon, sausage, black pudding, eggs, beans and fried bread for Johnnie. She might just manage an egg and some toast herself, her appetite not being yet up to strength. Indeed she had lost weight and she rather liked it. Senga had brought over a selection of new frocks in smaller sizes for her to try on and she had chosen a beautiful, tailored one in soft, clinging peach-coloured wool for Hogmanay. It accentuated her new slimmer waist and thighs, which in turn enhanced her full bosom and the swelling curves of her hips.

Johnnie had gone off to church, looking every inch the Kirk elder in his Sunday suit, stiff white collar, sober tie and shining shoes. Like Eck, he had gone through the motions of converting to Catholicism in order to marry Kate – that had been another thorn in Maggie's flesh, another axe she had to grind with the Kelly family – but, also like Eck, he had not maintained either interest or adherence. When he had begun to rise through the ranks in the mine some seven or eight years ago, he had judged it politic to return to the Church of Scotland and rub shoulders of a Sunday morning with the bosses.

Two years ago he had been invited to join the Kirk Session and become an elder, a position which he took seriously, always dressing the part at Sunday services, arriving early to hand out hymn books and offer formal greetings as people arrived, taking up the collection every week, handing out communion three times a year and attending terminally dull Kirk Session meetings once a month. This conscientious and conspicuous behaviour had not gone unnoticed by his bosses and had certainly done his career no harm.

To give him his due, he was equally assiduous about the unseen duties of an elder, visiting elderly, sick and housebound church members, delivering the church magazine and being the *kent face* in the church for the large list of members allocated to him.

Kate watched out the bay window as his tall, striding figure appeared at the crossroads. It was beginning to snow again, the sky an impenetrable steel-grey. He hurried across, turning up his coat-collar against the wind which was threatening to turn into a blizzard. She moved through to the kitchen.

Johnnie came to the end of a lengthy and – he thought – witty description of an incident at the kirk that morning, involving two old ladies, both very deaf. One was obviously not very good at dressing herself and the other was determinedly 'pass-remarkable', with a very loud voice. The whole congregation, while the organ was playing soft music during the taking up of the collection, had heard the latter tell the former three times, with escalating clarity, that her skirt hem was tucked into her knickers. The former had then told the latter, even more loudly to *Mind yer ain bloody bizness. At least ye ken Ah've got knickers on, no like some folk!*

Johnnie chuckled. 'The minister could hardly say his wee prayer when they brought the collection plates up the front, he was tryin' that hard no to laugh.'

Kate was barely listening. Now that the tasks of the morning were done, her mind was returning to the preoccupations that had kept her awake for a large part of the night. When Jeannie had first explained Kate's starring role in the Taming of Eck Fairweather, Kate had simply been incredulous.

'Ye're barkin' up the wrang tree there, Jeannie. Ah've hardly ever really spoken tae him. After seein' whit he did tae Aggie an her bairns ower the years, Ah've nae time fur him but Ah jist keep oot o' his wiy. Ah widnae ken whit tae say tae him aboot onythin', let alone mention Aggie tae him. He'd no tak kindly tae *ma* interference.'

She had been frankly appalled at the very thought of broaching any topic likely to ignite Eck's well-known smouldering fire. 'An he an Johnnie have been at daggers drawn fur the past twenty years. That wid mak it even mair difficult.'

But Jeannie had been inexorable. 'It's doon tae *you*, Kate, an *quick*. We've nae time tae think o' anythin' else. Bob has telt me a' the things Eck says aboot ye, *has* been sayin' fur years.'

251

At Jeannie's insistent probing, Bob had dredged up memories of Eck's remarks about Kate, some going back many years: even the fact that she had produced a son, which his own unsatisfactory wife had not. Eck would dearly have loved a strong, manly son to take down the mine with him rather than his uninteresting daughters with their trivial, girlish pursuits, a man to stand drinking and swearing beside him in the Miners' Welfare rather than silly lassies skirling off to *The Dancin'* in Kirkcaldy. All this and more, he had revealed to Bob over the years and, when Jeannie had pieced it together, she had arrived at a picture of a man who was in love with one sister and bitterly disappointed in the other whom he had married. It went some way to explaining the hell of a marriage that he and Aggie had created for each other.

Kate passed an anxious hand across her brow. It was a task she would have given much to avoid and felt quite unequal to. But Jeannie had summed it up as she had turned on the stair and looked back up at Kate's woebegone face.

'Aggie's been a guid sister tae ye these past weeks an noo she needs yer help. Dinnae let her doon. She deserves a wee bittie happiness.'

Kate heaved a tired sigh and tried for the umpteenth time to imagine herself – or indeed anyone - persuading Eck of anything. Even if she could compose some kind of script for this unimaginable dialogue, how on earth was she, in her convalescent captivity, going to get the chance to speak to him alone? She began agitatedly to gather the dirty crockery together, her hands shaking so that it rattled slightly.

Johnnie stopped talking and looked in concern across the table at his wife.

'Right!' He rose briskly and, with one step, was at her side. He firmly removed the plates from her hands. 'I'll do the dishes and see to mother. *You* are goin' to have a wee lie-down. We're no havin' you exhaustin' yourself before Hogmanay. I still think this party is over-ambitious, too much for you. Maybe we should cancel it.'

'NO!' Her instant, fierce retort put a stop to any such ideas.

Unwilling to tire or excite her further by arguing, he held his peace and simply led her gently through to the bedroom. 'Nae worries, sweetheart, nae worries,' he murmured as he kissed her brow, closed the curtains and left her to sleep on top of the bed under its quilt.

'Nae worries,' she echoed wistfully. 'Aye, that'll be the day…'
But her senses were already dizzying and she fell almost at once into
an exhausted doze.

The dog was in her dream again, yawning widely and panting its
hot breath in her face. She recoiled in terror at first but gradually she
saw that it was actually *laughing*, its eyes lit up with pleasure, inviting
her to join in. The fangs she had feared so much in previous dreams no
longer seemed frightening and destructive. They were so beautifully
white (all that cleaning?) and the big, waggling, bright pink tongue
was like a jolly flag. The tongue was stretching out to lick her nose
and she *was* laughing too. A large paw came up and rested heavily on
her shoulder, not scratching or pushing, just a warm, comforting
weight.

'Katy, Katy! What are ye laughin' about? Are ye dreamin'?'
Johnnie's long hand was on her shoulder, not moving, just resting
weightily as he tried to wake her. She came to with the sound of her
own laughter in her ears.

'By, that must have been some dream,' he laughed himself now.
'I thought someone had slipped into the bedroom and started tellin' ye
jokes when I heard you laughin' so loudly.'

He handed her a cup of tea. 'Mother's snoozin' in her chair in the
sitting-room and she'll be fine for a wee while. The weather's got a lot
better.'

He moved over to open the curtains and sharp winter sunshine
flooded in. 'It looks that lovely out there now – a winter wonderland
after the snow. Ye dinnae mind if I go out and have a walk in the park
for a wee while before it gets dark, do ye?'

'Of course not,' she responded sleepily, still a little in thrall to
her dream.

'I'll likely meet Eck walking that old dog of his. He aye does that
on Sunday afternoons. I can wish him a Merry Christmas. That'll be a
fine waste o' time!'

Kate snapped out of her trance. The dog! It was surely a sign! 'If
ye see Eck, tell him Ah want tae see the dog again – auld Gypsy – Ah
havnae seen her for years. And Ah used to be richt fond o' her. Tell
him tae cam' hame wi ye an bring the dog tae see his Aunty Kate.'

Johnnie regarded her doubtfully. 'That smelly, old bitch? She'll stink out the house.'

'*A bit like yer auld mither*,' thought Kate briefly, then returned to the attack. 'Ah want tae see her,' she declared. 'Jist tell Eck and bring them hame wi ye. Please, Johnnie. Ah jist have an awfy fancy tae see the auld thing. Please.'

Johnnie shook his head in wonder. He was committed to giving Kate whatever she wanted at the moment until he could again feel sure of her health and strength. Up to now, this had been easy, Kate being the most reasonable and undemanding of women. But this request was quite without precedence or parallel. *I hope she's no goin' funny on me. Ye hear o' folk that are never the same after some illness or other.*

'I'll try,' he said uneasily. 'But ye ken whit Eck's like. He might no come, especially if it's *me* askin'.'

'Tell him it's nothin' tae dae wi *you*. Tell him it's *me* wants tae see him. An dear auld Gyp, of coorse.'

Mystified, but obedient, Johnnie went off to get 'happed up' against the cold and venture forth.

Maggie had been safely restored to her room and Kate was peering fretfully out the bay window, straining her eyes in the failing light of the short winter afternoon. At last – her heart flipped – she saw two figures emerge at the far end of the street and begin to come down towards the crossroads. Their pace was necessarily slow to match that of the old dog dawdling behind them.

She took a deep breath, feeling it plumb the depths of her healing chest, and went through to the kitchen. She began by taking out the box containing the remains of Jeannie's scones from yesterday. On a sudden inspiration, she opened the cupboard where the Hogmanay party goodies were being collected. Already, excitingly, it was almost full and she allowed herself a moment's respite from the exigencies of this frightening moment to dwell upon the forthcoming party. Then she selected a delicious-looking sultana cake.

It had been lightly iced and was decorated with a frilly scrap of gold-shiny paper which, on closer inspection, was seen to bear the motif: *A Happy New Year from Aggie's Bakery*. It seemed like a kind of talisman and, if nothing else, might at least provide a conversational starting-point.

She put the cake on the larger tray with three cups and one of Jeannie's scones on the smaller tray for Maggie; then, on reflection, put the scone back in the box and cut a generous slice off the end of the sultana cake. It might look less like an obvious ploy if they had already started on the cake.

The two men tramped up the stairs and into the lobby in silence, the old dog trailing after them. It had been a silent, uneasy walk from the park and Johnnie was mighty glad to get home.

As he had foretold, he had seen Eck and old Gypsy quite soon on entering the park: indeed they had been the only figures in its frozen wasteland that afternoon. The snow had been too late in stopping to allow for the hordes of sledging children its slopes always attracted: they would come tomorrow. He allowed himself quarter-of-an-hour's peaceful tramping in the deep, crunchy snow, then, mindful of his promise to Kate, made his way over to the little spinney of trees in one of the corners. He thought how almost unbearably lovely it looked: thick snow on the branches roseate in the setting-sun rays; the stark shape of the old trees in the unflinching winter-light. The man and his dog seemed to belong in the picture, black figures against white background, tiny figures against huge trees.

'How are ye, brother-in-law?' he accosted the hunched figure, trying for a note of camaraderie. Eck did not even turn round although, of course, he had heard Johnnie's crunching progress across the virgin snow and had been waiting for him.

Johnnie tried again. 'It's been quite a snowfall, hasn't it? I hope we don't get any more before Hogmanay or it'll make the first-footin' hard for folks.' Still no response. *'Third time lucky?'* he thought, *'Well, here goes an then I'm givin' up. Kate cannae expect me to make a complete silly bugger o' myself.'*

'We're lookin' forward to seein' you an Aggie at our party on Hogmanay. Folks have been right good about sayin' they'll come out for it though I ken they usually like to be in their own hooses when the bells ring out at midnight. But then,' - he was getting into his stride - 'everyone's been wonderful about Kate's illness, so many people helpin'. And no-one more than your wife. She's been such a star! Kate is right grateful to her.'

At the mention of Kate's name, Eck turned at last. 'Hoo is she?'

His rough voice was a sharp contrast to Johnnie's nervous, lightweight chatter, like an Alsatian's gruff bark cutting across the

255

yapping of a wee Yorkie terrier. Johnnie seized on the three words like a drowning man on a rope.

'She's been awfy ill but she's turned the corner an, praise be, she's comin' on well now, thanks to all the care and help she's had from Aggie and all the other folk she drafted into help. I don't know what we'd have done without them.'

He remembered the real reason he had sought out this conversation and put himself through this ordeal. Looking at old Gyp who was dejectedly and unsuccessfully trying to ghost up a decent smell from the frozen ground, it seemed to him that, as a reason for luring Eck back home with him, it was unconvincing.

It dawned on him that Kate wanted to see Eck himself, for some reason - the dog was merely some kind of cover story. Why she should desire such an unpleasant encounter, Johnnie could not imagine. But he had set himself on a path of expiating his previous negligence and this meant doing her bidding however inexplicable. He called upon all his man-management skills.

'And don't think, Eck, that either of us is unaware of how much *you* have had to sacrifice as well these past weeks. We know Aggie has been at full stretch with her business to run at this busy time of year as well as organisin' all the help for us and showin' such wonderful care for her sister. I'm sure you've had to put up with meals not ready on time - or even missed - and less being done in your home than usual.'

It had been years since Johnnie had been in No. 22 and he had forgotten that it had never been a home that looked like much was 'done' in it and that meals were so awful that missing them – and resorting to the chippie - was something of a relief.

Eck was about to point this out angrily when Johnnie, unwittingly, struck exactly the right note. He remembered what his wife had said: *Tell him it's **me** wants tae see him.*

'Kate wants to thank you herself for all yer patience and kindness. She told me to ask ye back to the hoose just now. She wants to see you…and old Gyp,' he added as an afterthought and passing nod to Kate's cover story.

Eck had harrumphed and hesitated but in the end, the thought of being personally invited by Kate had won – *and* the thought of their clean, cosy house with its roaring fire rather than his own dirty, dreary abode, the fire probably out by now, Aggie having gone down to the shop to do some much-needed tidying and stock-taking in the guaranteed peace of a Sunday afternoon. With no more than a cursory nod to Johnnie and a whistle to Gypsy, he had followed his brother-in-law out of the park.

Now he hesitated on the threshold of the sitting-room, taking in its welcoming warmth and orderly comfort. Kate appeared in the doorway through to the kitchen.

'Eck! It's gran tae see ye!'

He was taken aback at the enthusiasm in her voice. 'An Gyp, of coorse.' She hastily remembered her cover story. 'Ah wis jist fair longin' tae see auld Gyp.'

The dog slipped past him and headed for the fireside rug where she sat shivering and salivating with relief at the sight and touch of the blaze. Kate moved to fondle the dog's ears and Gyp turned pleading, mournful eyes on her.

'Och, a' richt,' Kate was laughing. 'Ye havnae forgotten then, ye still ken whit yer Aunty Kate has fur ye.'

She went back into the kitchen and returned with a bowl of milk into which she had crumbled some digestive biscuits. Gyp consumed this treat-from-long-ago in five seconds and then collapsed, spread-eagled, taking up most of the rug and exposing as much of her body as possible to the flickering warmth. She heaved a sigh of pure bliss and slipped into happy oblivion.

'That'll be that, then.' Laughing, Kate turned to the two men. 'Come and get a seat at the fire, Eck. And, Johnnie, will ye come an carry the tray through fur me. It's heavy an Ah dinnae want tae drop it. Ah'm still no quite as strong as Ah was.'

Johnnie, instantly solicitous at this reminder of her recent illness, followed her through to the kitchen. Kate drew him away from the door over to the other side of the room. She indicated the two trays.

'Tak a cup aff the big tray and pit it on the wee ane. Ah want ye tae tak yer ain cup o' tea through and hae it wi yer mither. An stay there talkin' tae her fur a while.'

'Talkin' to her? What about? Why?'

'Ah've somethin' Ah need tae talk tae Eck aboot an it'll no work if *you're* there. Ye ken whit he's like aboot ye. Jist get yer mither tellin' ye aboot whit she's been listenin' tae on the wireless. Jeannie can get her talkin' fur hoors. She wis listenin' tae *Family Favourites* this mornin'. Ask her whit sangs folk asked fur and whit messages they were sendin' oot tae the sodgers. Get her bletherin' aboot her memories o' the war. Ach, use yer brain!'

257

She ended on a note of impatience and, anxious to keep her happy, he obediently moved a cup and saucer to the small tray and nodded, mystified but compliant. '*I was right,*' he thought. '*It **was** Eck she wanted to see. Daft nonsense about the old dog. But what on earth is she up to?*'

But there was no time to ask her for she was already moving back through to the sitting-room to join Eck at the fireside, pulling the pouffee over to the side of the sleeping dog.

When Johnnie had laid the big tray on this and taken himself off with the smaller one, silence fell in the firelit room. Kate busied herself with all the palaver of serving tea, milk, sugar and cake. Eck had time to enjoy his first cup of tea and slice of cake in peace whilst she cast around desperately in her mind for an opening gambit. As she was cutting him a second slice, she had to lift the gold-paper decoration off to do so and she remembered why she had chosen this cake out of her store-cupboard. She braced herself: *It's noo or never! Here goes. God help me.*

'A Happy New Year from Aggie's Bakery,' she read out. 'Is it no amazin' whit an institution that wee shop's become in jist five short years? Ye must be richt prood o' her.'

Eck curled his lip and shrugged, which was not encouraging, but Kate ploughed on. 'Ah ken Johnnie wid be awfy prood o' me if Ah'd done onythin' like that.'

Eck looked hard at her. '*You* dinnae need tae dae onythin' like that, Kate. Any man wid be prood tae have ye as his wife, jist the wiy ye are.'

The compliment barely registered with Kate, partly because she was simply not a vain woman and partly because men had been saying things like that to her all her life so that she barely noticed or paid them any credence. It was the reason she had unwittingly kept Angus the butcher dangling for years and ready – to her surprise - to become her willing slave at a moment's notice.

'Ah've aye thocht, if ye dinnae mind me sayin' so, Eck, that you an Aggie wid get on a lot better if ye took some pride in each ither. If you each took an interest in whit the ither's doin' an whit ye care aboot.'

He said nothing, staring morosely into his teacup. She gulped. *Mak it aboot him.* She struggled on: 'Ah mean, Ah ken *you've* aye been richt keen on yer union stuff, on gettin' a fair deal fur the men, better pay an workin' conditions an a' that…'

She had touched a well-spring and she had to allow him several precious minutes of airtime while he thumped his tub, railing against unfair working practices, slating the mine-bosses, despising the scabs who were too lily-livered to stick to their principles and fight for their rights, extolling the virtues of workers' solidarity.

She recalled him to the basis of their conversation. 'An it hurts ye that Aggie is no interested in any o' that? Because it's sae important tae ye? Because ye're sae...sae *passionate* aboot it?'

He made a sound that encapsulated all his disappointment and disgust. Then he shrugged. 'Wha cares aboot that silly bitch? Ah dinnae need *her*. She thinks it's jist a' *ma stupid union shite* an it's whit's kept me frae gettin' ony promotion. No like *your* man through there.' He jerked his head in the direction of the old woman's bedroom and the muffled sounds of a mother-and-son conversation.

Kate ignored this red herring. 'But dae *you* care aboot onythin' that *she* dis? Onythin' that she's, like, passionate aboot?' Again that word *passionate*: it had surprised them when she had said it a moment ago and here it was again.

He frowned at her. 'Whit dae ye mean? Whit is there tae get excited aboot? Plesterin' aboot wi rolls an wee fancy cakes? Oh, aye! Awfy excitin'. That wid get onyone feelin'...' He could not bring himself to say the word but it hung in the room on the breath of his sneer. 'Ah've telt her she'd be better at hame gettin' the place cleaned fur aince an learnin' tae cook me a decent meal.'

Kate felt a surge of anger. What a pig the man was! No wonder Aggie didn't want to tell him about... She heard Johnnie's voice raised or had he perhaps opened the door of Maggie's room and was getting ready to come back through? She had so little time.

'Ah wisnae talkin' aboot her shop – though Ah think she's done awfy weel in it. No, Ah wis talkin' aboot somethin' else.' She took a deep breath and winged a quick, desperate prayer, before plunging into the deep end. 'Aboot her singin'!'

Eck frowned. What had Aggie's singing got to do with anything? She had always sung, often, in his opinion, at singularly inappropriate and irritating moments, when she should have been concentrating on other, more important, things – like housework, childcare and cooking.

Kate pressed him: 'She's a wonderfu singer, is she no?'

He conceded, grudgingly, that she was.

'Do ye *tell* her that? Do ye show that ye're prood o' her an interested in whit she sings?' Kate knew very well he did not, that, in fact, the opposite was true, that he ruthlessly and regularly derided and denigrated her – as she did him, of course.

'Ye see, Eck…' She could hardly believe the stuff that was coming out of her mouth. Her earlier panic had gone, she felt sure-footed and skilful, just as she used to feel when arbitrating in childhood disputes between Robbie and Maureen. 'If you dinnae encourage her in something that *she* loves doin', it's nae surprise she disnae tak ony interest or think much o' yer union stuff, an a' yer politics and principles, that are sae important tae *you*. It's got tae gang baith wiys.'

It was a new idea to him and one he would certainly have dismissed out of hand if it had come from anyone else. Indeed, in his bumbling, inarticulate way, Bob Gilhooley had attempted, over the years of listening to Eck binding on about his miserable marriage, to say something of the same. Eck had not even heard him and would not have paid any attention to such a sentiment if he had. But this was Kate, looking at him earnestly out of her beautiful dark eyes, her face soft in the darkening room still lit only by the flickering fire. He hesitated, unsure of what she wanted him to say but anxious to please her.

'Weel… Ah dinnae stop her singin'. She'll be singin' at yer party on Hogmanay, Ah'm sure.'

'Ah'm no jist talkin' aboot that kind o' singin', Eck.' She took a deep breath that challenged her still tender airways. *This is it! God in Heaven, please let me get it richt.* 'Ah'm talkin' aboot proper singin', like wi an audience, on a stage.'

'On a *stage*?' He stared at her, suddenly catapulted back in memory to the first time he had ever seen Aggie. The tall, willowy girl in the green dress and black sash, delivering a performance that had rocked the Welfare Club that night. And he had wanted her: not for her face or figure, he could see they were not of any interest; but for the feisty look in her snapping eyes and her supreme confidence up on that stage. He had wanted to possess her: not sexually particularly; rather he had wanted to be the man who reined in her spirit and subjugated it. So he had married her but he had never tamed her, despite sustained physical and mental cruelty.

He thought back to other times in the early days of their courtship and marriage when she had sung on a stage – at the club or occasionally in a hall at a wedding. He remembered the feeling of possessive smugness as he had watched the audience reaction while she sang, the hush that always followed her performance. No instant, facile applause, but a stunned silence, then slowly the clapping would start and swell and swell till everyone was on their feet, demanding an encore. He had shrugged off the other men's comments of 'That's a richt cracker ye've got there, Eck, ye're a lucky man,' but, deep down, he had been delighted and, yes…proud.

But, no, he had never told her so and, as their marriage deteriorated into the battleground it soon became, he had begun to sneer and mock, turning his fire on her weak spot, her appearance, and assaulting her confidence mercilessly. It was no wonder she had stopped singing in public these past ten years.

'But she disnae sing on stages these days,' he said now, bewildered.

So Kate, hearing Maggie's voice drifting through the now open door of her bedroom and rushing her fences perforce, told him in three short sentences: how Aggie had joined a big choir in the Methodist Kirk and had been instantly made their solo soprano; how the choir was to perform at The Alhambra in five days' time; and how Aggie had told *him* nothing of all this, afraid he would try to stop her. But now he had to know.

'Ye see, Eck,' Kate had a sudden, brilliant inspiration, 'Aggie wid dearly love *you* tae be in the audience. Get a day aff yer work an go tae the concert. In spite o' a' the bad blood there's been between ye ower the years, ye're still her man an it wid mean a lot tae her if ye were in the audience. An think hoo prood ye'd feel, sittin' there among a'body clappin' and kennin' that wis *your* wife up there!' Unconsciously, she was echoing his memories of a moment ago.

*Aggie'll kill me fur this. The last thing she's wantin' is **his** soor face there.* But, she was going with her instinct now, the years of experience in manipulating growing children coming to her aid, informing her every move. She felt as if she was being guided. 'An Ah'm tellin' ye, Eck, Ah can promise ye, if *you* dae this fur her, she'll tak an interest and support ye wi they gran union things ye were tellin' me aboot, ye'll see. Ah jist ken it! An naebody will be mair happy than me tae see the twa o' ye gettin' on better. It micht be a new beginnin' fur ye.'

'Ah'll need tae get on tae Aggie quick an tell her tae dae it,' she thought frantically, as she delivered this last homily.

She waited, every instinct telling her she had said enough. She heard Johnnie closing his mother's door as he came out of her room. *Please, God... have Ah managed it or no?*

Eck looked piercingly at her and she met his gaze. He spoke: 'But hoo am Ah goin' tae get a day aff ma work, jist like that?'

She drew a long, slow breath, registering the triumph that was beginning to ring in her head. 'Ach, that's an easy ane. Do we no hae Mr Deputy Manager himsel richt here under this roof? It's time we got some guid oot o' a' this promotion he's aye talkin' aboot.'

He stiffened. 'Ah'm no askin' Johnnie fur ony favours, no me!'

She grinned at him and winked. 'No,' she agreed. 'Ye're no. But *Ah* am!'

And Johnnie, tentatively sticking his long nose round the door a few moments later, was utterly astonished to find them chuckling together and looking up with guilty, complicit giggles as he came towards them.

CHAPTER FOURTEEN

AGGIE

Eck trudged slowly, almost dreamily, home through the empty, snow-covered streets. Despite the intense cold, for the temperature had dropped again and the soft snow was beginning to freeze, he was in no hurry.

He wanted to play and replay the past hour over and over in his mind. For that all-too-short time, alone with Kate by the fireside, old Gyp snoring between them, it had almost felt like *his* home, *his* wife. Stifled, ill-formed fantasies from the past twenty years had finally been indulged, albeit briefly. Their chuckling, conspiratorial moment as Johnnie came back into the room was like a delicious spicy glow inside his mouth, sliding down his throat and warming his cold body. It felt a bit like the Christmas puddings he had been eating for the past five days but even richer and juicier.

Maybe, he thought, as he stopped to let Gyp create a yellow hole in the snow, if he had had a wife like Kate – indeed a wife who *was* Kate – he might have been able to overcome the black dog of depression that had plagued him since adolescence, to master his terrible temper and control his violent urges.

Certainly, he could not imagine himself ever striking or shouting at Kate. He recoiled in horror at the mere idea. But then, *she* would never defy and argue with him, shout insults at him. She would - he smiled grimly to himself as he acknowledged what had happened to him – sweet-talk him and get her own way but leave him feeling good about it, just as she had done tonight.

Nae wonder Johnnie aye looks sae pleased wi himsel. He disnae ken whit's happenin' tae him half the time! Eck chuckled out loud, greatly to the surprise of Gyp who had never heard her master make such a noise before.

But even at the pace of Gyp's arthritic crawl, he did at last, reluctantly, reach his own gate and trail slowly round to his back door. As soon as he opened it, he could hear Aggie singing.

At once he was recalled to the burden of his conversation with Kate. He had been so immersed in the feelings it had generated in him, the delight of simply being the focus of her attention, of being physically close to her and alone together - and then the thrill of conspiring with her to score a point off Johnnie - that he had not thought at all of *what* they had talked about.

Now, as he heard Aggie's golden voice soaring through the house, he was forcibly reminded. As he took off his snow-encrusted boots and damp socks, he listened intently. He remembered now hearing something of the same a few weeks ago. It had been one of the nights when her offering for supper had been so disgusting and inadequate that he had resorted to the chippie. She had been singing as he left the house, her complete lack of contrition or care evident in the full-throated aria, which, as always, had angered him even more. '*Churchy stuff,*' he had thought then, momentarily puzzled, and now, as he recalled Kate's revelation of the kirky choir and the forthcoming performance, he understood why.

Insolent bitch. Keepin' it frae me a' these months, no tellin' me onything aboot choirs or concerts, sneakin' aff behind ma back. And then, jist singin' the stuff, richt oot loud, as bold as brass, under ma nose. She thocht Ah widnae notice…

He paused on the way through the kitchen to the sitting-room where she was engaged in re-lighting the fire. He had *not* noticed, he realised now, apart from that one wondering moment in November and a few passing expressions of anxiety to Bob, quickly forgotten.

He remembered Kate's suggestion that he and Aggie needed to take more interest in each other's lives, that Aggie might actually come to care about and encourage his passion for his union work if he were to do likewise about her business and her singing.

That must be how other couples did it, he thought. Bob and Jeannie were always like youngsters - *bloody sappy billin' an cooin'*, he had always dismissed it as – and Kate and Johnnie always laughing together: that was how he thought of them over the years. How he had hated Johnnie for being able to bring the light of laughter so readily to those beautiful eyes!

He had always felt completely outside the charmed circle of couples with obviously good relationships, baffled by them. He had scorned them and refused to consider that he could learn anything from them. And now, Kate had asked him to try and find a few strands in the ugly, washed-out, felted fabric of this loveless, destructive marriage that could be untangled and re-woven into something fine and fresh.

Dae it fur me, Eck, please. Ye baith deserve a bittie happiness after a' these years.

They had been briefly alone together again in the lobby as she saw him out, Johnnie being busy banking up the fire. She had laid a beseeching hand on his arm and reached up to plant a soft kiss on his stubbly cheek. He could still feel the warmth of her breath and smell her perfume. There had been pecks-on-the-cheek from her before, of course, on Hogmanay when it was time to wish each other Happy New Year, but those were public and perfunctory. This kiss had been unsolicited, unwitnessed and completely unexpected. He would take the memory of it with him to the grave. How could he refuse her anything?

He stood in the doorway of the sitting-room and looked at his wife. She was kneeling over the fireplace, sweeping up dusty cinders and tipping them on to a roughly arranged pyramid of paper, sticks and coal in the grate. Her singing dropped to a breathy whisper as she finished the task, hung up the brush and shovel and groped above her head for the matches on the mantelpiece. Once she had put a light to the pyramid, she sat back on her haunches and watched it intently as it emitted more and more smoke. He was about to step forward when the fire suddenly burst into bright flames and Aggie simultaneously burst into song.

Hallelujah! she sang over and over again. Then: *For the Lord God Omnipotent Reigneth. Hallelujah! Hallelujah!* Then, for no apparent reason, she began to laugh uproariously.

'*The wumman's daft,*' he thought. Again he was about to step forward when she changed completely and began to sing a soft plaintive song: *Where'er you walk... cool gales shall fan the shade; trees where you sit... shall crowd into a shade...*

The firelight flickered brightly on her face which was full of intent pleasure as she caressed the words, investing them with a poignant sweetness that made him catch his breath. Her face and figure were as plain and unattractive as ever at this moment but there was, in the

265

totally absorbed look on her face and the rapt posture of her body, a strange kind of beauty that fascinated the watching listener. As if a beautiful, alluring spirit inhabited the ordinary, uninviting person of his familiar, despised wife.

She finished the song and its last notes drifted round the room on a few spirals of escaped smoke. She sighed deeply then turned with a startled cry as Eck laid a hand on her shoulder. She made as if to rise but he pressed his heavy hand down and looked at her with narrowed, accusing eyes.

There was no need to ask if he knew. It was written in his measured, thoughtful gaze and in the pressure of his hand. She flushed and prepared to stand and fight. She had always known in her heart that it would come to this: that he would find out and there would be a show-down. Her lovely secret world was about to be invaded by a snorting, fire-breathing beast, whose foul breath would contaminate it forever. Her dream was over but she would not let it die without a fight. She owed it that much at least.

Abruptly he loosened his hand and turned away. She waited for the first broadside of his assault.

'Ah've been roon at Kate and Johnnie's hoose,' he said. 'That's why Ah've been sae lang.' His voice was - she sought for the word – *calm, neutral,* even *offhand.*

She floundered, wrong-footed, not quite knowing what to do with the battle armour she had been hastily donning. 'Oh… aye?'

'Ah met Johnnie in the park an he said Kate wanted tae talk tae me.'

'Did he? Did she?'

'Aye, he said she wanted tae thank me fur pittin' up wi you aye bein' sae busy these past few weeks when ye've been helpin' tae look after her and the auld mither.'

It occurred to him now that Kate had never mentioned this at all. *'That wis jist a ploy tae get Johnnie tae bring me roon. Is she no the sly wee minx? She can fair tak Mr Deputy Manager fur a ride!'* The thought brought a smile to his face and Aggie stared at him, further baffled by his behaviour.

'She telt me aboot yer concert in Burntisland.' He considered telling her that Kate wanted him to go to it and might even at this very minute be engaged in persuading Johnnie to arrange a day off for him for the purpose. He thought better of it. He did not want to commit himself yet. He was not sure that this might not be a bridge too far –

even to please Kate – and Johnnie might not be able to get him a day off at all. He was still only a *deputy* manager, after all.

Aggie was astonished. She had been trustingly waiting for Jeannie to work a miracle with regard to the Eck problem, just as she had with Father O'Malley. That Kate would be the one to tackle Eck had never occurred to her. Had Kate done it off her own bat? Or had Jeannie asked her to? And why? Of course, he had always been sweet on Kate - she had known and resented that for years - but she had not thought it was obvious to other people. She felt a flick of humiliation. *Wha else kens that he wishes he'd married the ither sister?*

Eck was talking again: 'Ye'd nae damn bizness goin' tae choirs ahent ma back and agreein' tae stan up an sing on stages – an a' by yersel - withoot tellin' me. But…when a' said an done…if that's whit ye want tae dae…well… Ah ken ye've aye liked singin' an naebody can deny ye're guid at it. Ah suppose there's nae harm in it.'

He petered out, his stock of goodwill exhausted. He could hear Kate's voice in his ear, abjuring him to *tell her ye're prood o' her*, but this was asking too much and the words stuck in his throat.

She stared at him, struck dumb by this completely unexpected attitude. If the victory over Father O'Malley's bigotry had been a minor miracle, this seemed like one of Rubicon proportions.

'Ye dinnae mind, then? Ye'll no try an stop me?' She was dazed at her good fortune. 'Ye'll no be aye makin' yer sly, nasty comments aboot it an sayin'… sayin'… makin' me feel…'she ran out of steam suddenly and subsided on to the armchair by the fire. How to express to him, of all people, what his sneers and mockery did to her? *Ah dae the same tae him, of coorse. We dae it tae each ither, God help us.*

But he had stomped off back through to the kitchen growling, 'Is there onything worth eatin' in this damned hoose fur a change?'

Aggie grimaced. *Back tae normal, then.* But she was smiling as she moved to the kitchen sink to wash her coal-blackened hands. 'There's twa onion bridies,' she said tranquilly. 'Are ye wantin' beans or peas wi them?'

She wiped her sweating brow with a floury hand, adding a white wing to the front of her pepper-and-salt hair. *Thank God it's five o'clock at last. Ane doon and twa tae go.*

She had expected these last three days of the old year to be busy, of course. She had thought of asking one of her recent afternoon helpers to come in for a few hours each day but had quickly become aware that choosing one of them would cause strife among them. And she could not face having all three, one after the other, as she had done during the rescue package time. There had been constant confusion over three different ways of working and three different understandings of how the shop was run.

Aggie had had enough of sorting out their muddles, especially over the club vouchers. She had ended up out of pocket, having to mollify irate customers who insisted that either Mina, Nellie or Bessie had short-changed them. Even worse had been when they had given some customers too many vouchers and Aggie had tried unsuccessfully to re-coup these.

So, she had simply squared up to the relentless workload herself and let *the three stooges* go back to spending their afternoons gossiping in each other's houses. She thought enviously of Annie who still had Senga coming in every morning and whose business was positively booming as a result so that the wage she was paying her was easily offset by the new profits.

As if on cue, she heard the shop-door open and cursed that she had not yet put up the *closed* sign. Coming through from the back-shop, she saw Annie's bulk filling the doorway.

'Ah'm closed,' she said discouragingly. 'Ah jist havnae turned ma sign roon yet.'

'It's nice tae see you too, Aggie,' replied Annie dryly. 'But Ah'm no wantin' tae buy ony mair, dinnae worry.' As usual, she had already consumed an impressive quantity of the bakery's goods that day. 'Ah jist cried in tae see hoo ye're survivin' the rush.'

Aggie shrugged. 'Got tae. Naething else fur it.' She was wondering what the real reason was for the visit. She did not have to wonder long.

'Are ye goin' tae Kate's Hogmanay party on Wednesday night? It's a funny idea, is it no? Ah dinnae ken if Ah'll hae the energy. Ah usually hae a guid sleep frae aboot eight 'till half-eleven an then get ready tae go first-footin' That wiy ye can last through the nicht. But if we've tae be at her hoose fur nine – or even earlier tae help wi a' the preparations – that'll no work sae weel.'

She paused for breath but got no reply beyond an impatient shrug from Aggie who knew fine that this was not what was really bothering

Annie who could just go home and skip first-footing if she wished. It was not like there were folk waiting with bated breath for her visit or like there were not dozens of other people thronging the streets and her presence would actually be missed.

Annie got to the heart of the matter at last. 'Ah think there's mair tae this party than meets the eye. Ah widnae be surprised if it's no somethin' tae dae wi whit Kate and Jeannie have been whisperin' aboot fur weeks. Ever since that Wednesday Kate cam' hame no weel an took tae her bed. Whit dae *you* think, Aggie? Ye're her sister, after a'. She shouldnae hae secrets frae *you*.'

Aggie snorted but forbore to comment on this shaky premise. 'Ah ken nothin' aboot it.'

This blunt answer had the ring of truth and Annie's frustration and sense of exclusion boiled over. 'It's no fair,' she burst out. 'Jeannie aye used tae tell me a'thing an many's a time she's been glad o' ma help tae find things oot fur her or tae pass on the word aboot things that are goin' on aroon here.'

'Aye,' thought Aggie. *'We a' kent hoo it worked between the pair o' ye. But noo Jeannie's bailed oot o' the partnership an left ye high an dry.'* She turned back unsympathetically to continue her preparations for shutting up shop for the night.

'Can ye turn the sign roon as ye go oot, Annie?' she called dismissively over her shoulder. Then she was arrested by the sound of a sniff that ended in a sob.

Och, that's a' Ah need. Annie greetin' a' ower me because Jeannie's gien her the boot! Aggie weighed up the possibility of pretending she hadn't heard and hoping Annie would take herself and her grief away. Then she remembered how much she owed Jeannie - and Kate too, it would seem now. The last thing they needed was Annie poking discontentedly into whatever it was they were nursing so close to their bosoms.

With a sigh, she came back into the front shop and surveyed the fat woman. *She looks as tired as Ah feel.* Aggie thought of Annie's lonely existence without husband or children, forever tagging along with any couples that would have her, as she would do for the first-footing. *She's a bloody auld gossip an a greedy pig intae the bargain. But, still, it's a damn shame fur her. She thinks she's lost the only pal she had.*

She looked out the shop-window and squinted down to The Auld Toll pub on the corner. The street lamps had recently been electrified and folk said the light was not as good – *awfy bare, no as cosy as the gas* – but then folk never liked change.

The thrusting young manager of the pub had recently launched an audacious new venture: a *Ladies' Bar*. He had erected a partition to screen off a large corner of the main saloon and furnished it tastefully with velvet seats and pretty table lamps. It had its own door from outside so that the ladies did not have to pass through the main pub and it sported a discreet sign on this door. Graham Currie was a forward-looking business man and he had been impressed by such arrangements in several pubs he had heard about when at a brewery event in England.

So far, it was slow to take off in Methil where women did not go unescorted into pubs and men were not slow to express horror at such an idea. But, little by little, a few women, especially the younger ones, were starting to patronise it and there had even been a hen-night there before a wedding a few weeks ago. Aggie came to a daring decision.

'Hoo dae ye fancy a wee drink the-gither afore we gang hame? We're baith workin' oor bums aff the noo an we deserve a wee treat. Hoo aboot tryin' the new Ladies' Bar?'

She did not need to explain what she was referring to - it had been the talk of the community ever since it had opened, creating a spectrum of opinion from downright scandalised through secretly delighted to openly determined to try it. Most women were somewhere in the middle, covertly longing to go to it but having to pretend shocked disapproval to their husbands. This had already invested the Bar with considerable risqué allure.

Annie perked up at the very mention of its name. She had been yearning to cross its threshold ever since it opened but felt that a woman going *alone* into a bar – even one just for ladies - was going just a bit too far.

'Whit a braw thocht, Aggie,' she beamed. 'Get yer coat.'

The Bar was warm, softly-lit and welcoming. Aggie and Annie looked round appreciatively as the manager himself came through to serve them.

He made a point of this, trusting to a combination of gallant good manners and boyish charm to win over hesitant first-timers. It worked well: the older women responded either like mothers proud of a good-looking, well-brought-up son or with girlish coquetry; the younger women simply fancied him and simpered, jostling for his attention.

There were six low tables with comfortable chairs and benches around them but only one other table was occupied, with two women laughing together at it. Aggie's heart sank when she recognised one of them and she turned her head quickly away. But she was too late.

'It's Aggie! How nice to see you! Of course, you live near here, don't you?' It was Margot from the choir, crossing the room towards them.

Aggie gulped and Annie goggled.

'Isn't this a delightful place? I feel so wicked! Howard will get such a shock when I tell him. But he won't be able to say anything. That's *his* sister over there, she's up from London for a wee holiday over Christmas and New Year. She says they have lots of *Ladies' Bars* down there now and she positively *forced* me to come. Not that I put up much resistance...' Her musical laugh tinkled out. 'Do you come here often?' She looked enquiringly from Aggie to Annie.

Aggie mumbled something unintelligible. Her thoughts were reeling. What if Margot mentioned the choir? But, of course, it didn't really matter now; not now that Eck and the priest both knew and were all right about it. But she hadn't told Senga yet that she wouldn't be at the Get-Together. And was this really how she wanted the news to break? Through Annie?

Margot was talking again. 'Of course, Aggie, you have a shop near here, your bakery, I remember you told us about it the night you brought us those lovely wee cakes. In fact that was the night we first heard about...'

'This is ma freend, Annie,' interposed Aggie hastily. 'She runs the draper's shop on the corner.'

'I see! Two businesswomen having a drink after work together. How frightfully *modern*!' The tinkling, mirthful laugh again.

It was an imaginative feat on her part as no-one looking at Aggie and Annie would have dubbed them remotely – let alone *frightfully* – modern.

Margot was moving to return to her racy, bar-frequenting sister-in-law and Aggie was letting her breath out on a slow, thankful sigh, when Margot turned.

'How is your poor sister, Aggie? Are you going to be able to get away for our light lunch in Kirkcaldy before the concert on Friday?'

Annie negotiated the humps and bumps of frozen slush with the elaborate care of the inebriated. The slight thaw of the early afternoon had lasted only long enough to turn the lovely white snow into grey slush; then a fresh freeze had descended and now the pavements were more treacherous than ever. She hummed a happy little tune and, if it had not been for the conditions underfoot, might well have accompanied it with a jig.

She was *in the know* again, on the inside of a big secret and this time she definitely had a starring role.

The promise of being an important part of the Kate story had never been fulfilled. She was still not quite sure how that had happened, considering *she* had been first on the scene with the Wednesday outings, actually in Kate's home looking after Auld Maggie and there to receive Kate home and put her to bed when she fell ill. She had been poised to become Johnnie's trusted henchman and even to have a go at being discreet and *trustworthy*, as he had called her that first evening. But somehow, it had all slipped through her grasp once Jeannie came on the scene and took over in her inimitable fashion.

The fact that Jeannie had assumed the managerial role in the rescue package would not have bothered Annie who was too lazy and too unimaginative to have sustained it anyway. It would have been all right if it had been the old Jeannie: Annie would happily have slipped into her accustomed role of listening, speculating and doing what Jeannie told her to further the gossip cause. But Jeannie had metamorphosed into a clam and her smug, secretive demeanour had infuriated Annie whilst at the same time leaving her bereft and isolated. She had lost a friend and been shut outside a charmed circle. To make matters worse, whenever she had attempted to penetrate the circle and ghost up some gossip-fodder, Jeannie had reproved her prissily, as if such deplorable behaviour was unknown.

Annie felt as if she had been sent like the scapegoat into the wilderness, bearing the sins of many, whilst the many were basking in smug self-righteousness back home. And she was sick to death of it.

But now her exile was over and she was to be at the epicenter of breaking news. '*Stick that in yer pipe an smoke it, Jeannie Gilhooley,*' she thought happily as she let herself into her cold, dark house. The fire which she had smothered in slow-burning, packed dross as usual before leaving home that morning had not survived the extra two hours. Only the faintest glow came from its depths when she poked it hopefully.

Too tired and tipsy to contemplate cleaning out and resetting it, she settled for putting on the gas oven at full belt and leaving the oven door open. Too hungry to wait for food to cook or heat up, she opened a giant tin of peaches, emptied them into a bowl and poured a whole tin of evaporated milk over them. This, along with the remaining half of a slab of angel cake, constituted her supper. Sitting on the kitchen floor beside the oven, she savoured each detail of the evening along with the sweet, cakey, creaminess.

She had known as soon as the posh woman with the funny laugh had accosted them that she had stumbled on hidden treasure. Aggie's face, wreathed in all the guilty horror of one caught in the act, said it all. Annie had been all ready to try and worm it out of Aggie when the necessity for such efforts was obviated by the posh woman herself.

Her throwaway question as she turned to leave them – 'Are you going to be able to get away for our light lunch in Kirkcaldy before the concert on Friday?'- completely blew the gaff. The question, called across the room as Margot was half-way back to her own table, reverberated round the intimate little bar and even the wee table lamps seemed to be holding their breath.

Aggie turned beetroot under Annie's interested gaze and a fast series of emotions flickered over her red face, culminating in a final defiant lift of her head and
characteristic squaring of her shoulders.

'Aye, Ah am, Margot,' she said loudly. 'Ah'm fair lookin' forrad tae it. Whit time are we meetin'?'

Margot returned to their table. 'Twelve noon at the church. Howard and a couple of the other husbands who have cars as well are going to drive us to Kirkcaldy to the café and then the choir bus is coming to pick us up at two o'clock. So we'll have plenty of time for a leisurely lunch and a good chat. It'll help settle our nerves before the rehearsal. At least, I hope so! I am *so* excited. It's going to be a bit of a rush getting back from the hairdresser's and getting all dressed before twelve but I expect we'll all manage. Some of us are trying out that new hairdresser in Leven. I just hope they do us proud. Which one are you going to, Aggie?'

Margot looked thoughtfully at Aggie's straggly, greying frizz, with its strange white streak at the front, as if measuring the extent of expertise that was going to be needed.

Annie was further entertained. The idea of Aggie singing in a choir, of her going for 'lunch' in a 'café' with this high-falutin' woman, of her getting driven in a car by someone called Howard: all this paled before the prospect of Aggie going to a hairdresser. Annie had only ever known any woman to do such a thing on her wedding-day and, even then, most local brides settled for the ministrations of their sisters or cousins.

Aggie's hair had been cut by her mother until she had left home to get married, then occasionally hacked by her own hands for several years but mostly simply bundled up in a hairnet or scarf and washed infrequently. Young Maisie had had a flurry of interest in hairdressing in her teenage years and had practised perms and dyeing treatments on her mother's hair, leaving it in the poor condition from which it had never recovered. Now it scarcely grew enough to need cut and she rarely thought about it at all, its only ablution being a cursory weekly dip in scummy, cooling bathwater.

Aggie was caught on the back foot by Margot's question, feeling totally out of her depth. She even momentarily forgot about Annie sitting agog beside her. She had tried on her new clothes several times, even dug out some old make-up and perfume that had belonged to her daughters and tried some rouge and eye-shadow, bursting into laughter at the sight of her clown-like face in the mirror and deciding to settle for a slick of vanishing cream, a dusting of face powder and a smear of lipstick.

But it had never occurred to her that anything could or should be done with her hair. Of course, she knew it was hardly her best feature: even in her youth the best that had been said about it was that it was long and dark. Even then it had been flyaway and inclined to be dry and dull, unlike Kate's thick, glossy mane. But she had always just accepted that that was what her hair was like – she could no more change it than buy herself a new pair of legs, an idea she sometimes fancifully and wistfully envisaged after twelve hours on her feet in the shop.

'Well… Ah havnae really thocht aboot it,' she murmured uncomfortably. Then, seeing Margot's anxious glance at the grey frizz, 'Ah expect Ah'll get ma sister, Kate, or ane o' ma freends…'

Annie found her voice. 'Ye could aye ask Mina,' she put in conversationally, as if discussing Aggie's beautification needs leading up to a grand public appearance - alongside people who were married to men-with-cars called Howard and who went for light lunches in cafes - was an everyday occurrence. 'Mina's a dab haun at the shampoo an set. She's even got a fancy big hairdryer-thing that ye sit under. She got it frae her cousin twa year back when her wee hairdresser shop in Elie went bust. Ah heard ane o' the hairdressers had his haun in the till. Some folk said he wis a bit o' a Jessie but they never thocht he had licht fingers an a'.'

'Aye, that's it,' Aggie interrupted hastily, seeing a baffled look beginning to cross Margot's face. 'Of coorse. Ah'll ask Mina. Ah've been meaning tae. Ah've jist been awfy busy. This time of year in the shop...'

'Oh, you important businesswomen,' Margot trilled happily, relieved of her worries about Aggie's hair. 'How you get time to do it all... And you've been so good about attending all the practices. She's hardly missed one, you know,' - she turned to address Annie - 'thank goodness. With her being our soloist - and what a voice! It would have been very worrying if we had not felt we could rely on her. But she's always there.'

'Och aye, ye can coont on Aggie. She's a legend in these parts,' Annie agreed tranquilly and Margot beamed at her.

Then the racy sister-in-law appeared at her elbow, swept a city slicker's disdainful glance at the two old-fashioned, hopelessly provincial women to whom Margot had inexplicably been talking for the past ten minutes and pointed out that their bus home was due in a few minutes.

Margot chattered off, giving a final cheery wave and call of 'See you on Friday, Aggie. And you too, maybe, Annie. Why don't you come and hear us?'

The little bar seemed unnaturally silent once her effervescence finally died away. Annie settled back comfortably on the padded, velvet-covered bench and waited.

They both knew there was no going back. Margot had innocently and thoroughly laid the whole scenario bare and very kindly included Annie in it. To the delight of Graham, who saw an encouraging portent of his *Ladies' Bar* venture at last beginning to take off as he hoped, they recklessly ordered round after round of port-and-lemons, a satisfyingly more expensive drink, from his point of view, than the sherries and shandies that had so far constituted the trade from the *Bar*. A considerable assault on the seasonal profits of the bakery and drapery was underway.

By the second round, Annie had heard all about the *wee shite* at the Novello audition; the Methodist choirmaster had been caricatured and chuckled over but his excellent taste and discernment in the choice of solo soprano had been admired; the other choir members had been enthusiastically described and their kindness applauded.

By the third round, Aggie's worries about the disapproval of the priest and the whole Catholic flock had been aired. Annie had been brought up by devout Presbyterians and had been a mainstay of the Sunday School in her rotund youth. However, since taking over the draper's shop twelve years ago, after the death of her demanding parents, she almost never rolled out of bed before midday on Sundays, confining her church-going to a sentimental bout of carol-singing at watch-night services on Christmas Eve. But she understood, as they all did, the solid sectarian boundaries that were upheld in their community and did not wonder that Aggie had been worried.

By the fourth round of drinks, Aggie was well into her stride as raconteur: her description of Father O'Malley's unexpected experience after midnight mass was masterly and Annie was laughing so hard she had to plead with Aggie to *ca' a halt fur a meenit* while she availed herself of the *Ladies' Powder Room*, as Graham had rechristened the women's toilets.

With regard to her husband and her agonies over his finding out, Aggie did not, in spite of her alcohol-loosened tongue and the bonhomie now flowing between them, paint for Annie anything like as graphic a picture as she had done for Kate or for Jeannie. She had, for the time being at any rate, exhausted her need for intimate revelations: her soul had been bared twice and amazing grace had followed but her soul was now safely back in its protective clothing.

As they regretfully agreed that the fifth round must be their last, she encapsulated months of anxiety into: 'Ah thocht Eck micht pit a spoke in ma wheel - he can be funny aboot things sometimes,' and her still half-incredulous understanding of what had passed between Eck and Kate into: 'Kate telt him it wis a guid thing an he aye minds whit *she* says.'

Then she had pre-empted any comment from Annie on this interesting phenomenon by moving smoothly into arrangements for the circulation of the news. Would Annie explain it all to Senga tomorrow in the shop and then perhaps the two of them could mention it to anyone else they came into contact with?

The little draper's shop would see almost the entire female complement of the community over the next two days. Senga had managed to procure a consignment of the sheerest nylon stockings seen in Fife since the departure of the Yanks at the end of the war. She was not simply selling these, however: they were a 'free gift' to anyone who spent a certain amount in the shop on particular goods (these being the ones that had been hanging heavy on Annie's hands for the past two or three years).

By the time the shop closed on Hogmanay, Annie would have finally sold the damn stuff, made a tidy profit, generated valuable goodwill through the 'free' nylons, passed on a fascinating new titbit of news about Aggie-from-the-bakery and reinforced the shop's status as information centre. It really was all very satisfying. Annie was humming tunelessly but happily as she added the large bowl to the heap of dirty dishes in the sink, turned off the oven and made her ponderous way to bed.

CHAPTER FIFTEEN

JEANNIE

The draper's shop was crowded next morning when Jeannie slipped in to buy her usual set of new underwear for Hogmanay (not only her house but her person and clothes, from the skin out, must be spotlessly clean when the bells rang out at twelve – otherwise, the ensuing year would be full of murky trouble).

Pressed up against the back wall, she could hear Annie and Senga chatting busily as they served their customers and she could also see that the women exiting with their bags full were looking extremely pleased with themselves. A quick bit of eavesdropping soon told her that they were delighted with their 'free' nylons. Jeannie was not herself gullible enough to spend three times the value of the stockings on a lot of old clothes and haberdashery that she would never wear or use. She was just glad she still had some decent stockings left over from last Hogmanay that were not yet out of their packet.

From force of habit, she found herself tuning into scraps of conversation in the shop.

'Fancy! Big Ag frae the baker's goin' tae be singin' at The Alhambra!'

'Geez, Ah hope she washes her hair first – it's aye sich a mess.'

'She's an awfy bonnie singer, though, Ah've heard her often.'

'Can ye believe the nerve o' her, joinin' a proddy choir, goin' tae practices in the Methodist Kirk?'

'Father O'Malley'll kill her.'

'Aye, an that bad-tempered bugger she's married tae will help him!'

Jeannie was transfixed. The news was out already! How could this have happened? She and Aggie had agreed that, once they were both

278

satisfied that the two men – priest and husband – had been dealt with, then the happy task of going public would be Jeannie's responsibility.

She was just on her way now to visit Kate to find out how it had gone with Eck and thereafter had intended to call in at the bakery to hear Aggie's side of things. With only three days to go till the concert, there was no time to lose and Jeannie had been up early, cutting a swathe through her housework and cooking chores so as to have the morning free to devote to the job. If everything had gone according to plan and the Eck equation was solved, she had intended to spend the rest of the morning moving around the little cluster of shops at the crossroads talking to as many women as possible. As back-up, just in case there was any household not yet apprised of the facts by the end of the day, she intended to explain it all to Bob tonight and ask him to spread the word around the men at the pit and in the pub tomorrow.

But she had clearly been pre-empted. Sharp disappointment, mixed with a sense of foreboding, gave her extra strength and she thrust her way through the throng, tramping on toes and elbowing ribs. As she reached the counter, she was just in time to hear Annie responding to one customer who was wondering aloud what Big Eck would say and do about it and beginning to speculate – not without some lip-smacking anticipation – that Aggie had better be ready to run, and fast.

'Naw, ye're wrang there,' Annie was reassuring her. 'Eck's a' richt aboot it. Says she can dae it if she wants.'

'But, she's been keepin' it awfy quiet a' these months – Ah bet she never telt him eether - an he'll no like that. An when Eck's no happy, weel…We a' ken whit he's like. Ah mind hoo the twa lassies used tae cam' howlin' an greetin' oot o' the hoose, screamin' that he wis goin' tae murder their ma.'

'It's fine, Ah telt ye.' Annie handed her the change and turned to the next customer.

'But, hoo did she manage tae persuade him? We a' ken they hardly even speak tae each ither,' persisted the woman.

'*She* didnae.' Annie was becoming exasperated. 'It wis no her that did the persuadin'. It wis…'

Jeannie broke in loudly, elbowing the persistent woman aside. 'Annie! Can ye spare a meenit? There's somethin' awfy important Ah need tae talk tae ye aboot. Senga!' She called through to the back-shop where Senga had gone to fetch another box of the sought-after nylons. 'Senga, can ye haud the fort here fur a wee while?'

Senga appeared in the curtained doorway and was surprised to find little Jeannie virtually manhandling large Annie towards it. Indeed, she barely had time to step through it and out of their way.

Jeannie pushed Annie against a table in the corner of the back-shop and reached behind her to pull the curtain down over the doorway, creating at least an illusion of privacy. She fixed Annie with a gimlet glare.

'So ye ken a' aboot Aggie's concert, do ye? Ah dinnae ken hoo ye fund oot but Ah hope ye're sure she wants ye tae be tellin' the warld!'

Annie smirked: revenge was sweet. She knew at once why Jeannie was so incensed. Aggie *had* mentioned that Jeannie expected to be the chosen one for the news-spreading task but, such had been the warm fellow-feeling engendered by the intimate Ladies' Bar and its excellent port-and-lemons, that she had magnanimously designated the honour to Annie.

'Jeannie'll no mind,' she had declared optimistically. 'She's got a big enough starring role at the moment onyway between a' the stuff she's done fur me an the ither thing she's doin' wi…'

Aggie had stopped herself in time. Even in her cups, she still had a fine disdain for gossip and she did not want any dirt dug up about Kate now – not when she had taken such pains to repress it some weeks ago when Kate first fell ill.

So *Annie* had been charged with the job of telling the community about the concert, making sure they all understood that both priest and husband had no objections and that Aggie would not be at the Get-together this year having been called to higher things at The Alhambra. It was a delightful task, made all the more delightful by the knowledge that she had usurped Jeannie in it.

She grinned at her erstwhile gossiping buddy and pointedly assured her that Aggie herself had told her all about it and specifically asked her to be the means of circulating the news. 'Ah'm that well placed here wi a'body comin' in the day fur their free nylons and wi havin' Senga here as weel. The Get-thegither's at her hoose of coorse, so it maks sense that she should ken first an help tae tell a'body else, wid ye no agree?'

Jeannie would not, logic and common sense playing second fiddle to disappointment and frustration, but she recognised a *fait accompli* when she saw one and was never one to expend time and energy futilely.

She moved to salvage her pride and re-establish her authority: 'Aye, Aggie *an me* thocht ye widnae mind helpin' oot wi tellin' folks once we had cleared up a couple o' wee problems,' she stated grandly and Annie caught her breath at the sheer audacity of the woman whilst dimly admiring a level of quick-thinking to which she knew she herself could never aspire.

'Jist let me mak ae thing clear,' continued Jeannie, getting into her stride. 'Kate's name is no tae be mentioned in the same breath as that bugger, Eck Fairweather. Ye ken whit they're like aroon here. They'll pit twa and twa thegither an mak twenty-six!'

Annie bristled. Aggie had said something of the same in a rather blurred afterthought just before they had parted but Annie had not been able to resist doing a bit of dodgy arithmetic herself and coming up with a few interesting sums. She and Senga had mulled it over when she had been briefing Senga before the shop opened that morning. They had come to the conclusion that, whilst it beggared belief that *anyone* would want to be having a relationship with Eck, illicit or otherwise, the situation might nevertheless bear watching.

'Ye jist never ken,' Senga had declared. 'An Kate *wis* behavin' a mite strange afore she got ill. Ah mind seein' her comin' stottin across the road an near causin' an accident wi the brewer's cart that afternoon. We ken noo she wis no weel, of coorse, but we niver got tae ken whaur she had been.'

Sensing Annie's defiance, Jeannie reiterated her warning that there was to be no whispering campaign against Kate, no linking of her name with any clandestine relationship, however unlikely. Having taken such pains over the past month to guard Kate's real secret and preserve her good name, she was horrified to think that this spurious tale might now threaten it.

And it would be all her fault since she had been the instigator of the contact between Kate and Eck. She realised now, on quick reflection, that this had always been a threat. The fine nuances of Eck's feelings for Kate, stretching back over the years and culminating in his rapid, recent capitulation to her request, would be delicious gossip-fodder if they ever became known. They would be picked over, misunderstood and embroidered handsomely: much more interesting, really, than a mere kirky concert and a bit of religious boundary-blurring. She blamed herself for not foreseeing this problem - it was a casualty of the regrettable but necessary speed of operations – but she exerted herself now to contain and limit the damage.

'We baith ken that Kate only spoke tae the bugger tae help Aggie oot.'

'Aye. But why? There's nae love lost between the twa sisters. We a' ken that.'

'Och, they're better pals these days - ye ken that yersel - an Aggie's been richt guid tae Kate helpin' her oot these past weeks an Kate is richt gratefu tae her.'

'*May*-beee…but that disnae explain tae me hoo Kate had tae be the ane tae talk tae Eck. An hoo he's cam' roon sae easy an is eatin' oot o' her haun like a wee lapdog, it wid seem.'

Jeannie snorted. 'Ah widnae like tae be in *your* shoes when *he* hears ye callin' him that.'

She had struck home at last. Appeals to Annie's reasonableness and compassion were always likely to fail when she had the scent of gossip in her nostrils but she was not a brave woman and men were by and large a mystery to her. Men like Eck filled her with baffled fear and she avoided them instinctively. Jeannie pressed home her advantage.

'If Ah wis you, Annie, Ah'd stick tae tellin' folk aboot the concert and settlin' their hash if they start on aboot Aggie goin' tae a proddy kirk an aboot whit the priest's goin' tae say. That'll be enough fur them a' tae be goin' on wi. Ye dinnae want tae hae Eck Fairweather breathin' doon yer neck, Ah presume.'

Annie most certainly did not and her crestfallen look told Jeannie that the job was done. 'If folk ask aboot Eck, jist tell them that he's no batherin' whit she dis as long as the priest's happy. Richt?' She fixed Annie with a final meaningful look. 'An, fur the love o' God, tell Senga tae say the same.'

However, they both had less concern about Senga whom they knew would probably have forgotten this aspect by now, being simply concerned with the reason that Aggie would not be at the Get-together in her house. There were times when Senga's self-absorption and resulting lack of gossiping acumen could be a blessing.

Coming out of the draper's some ten minutes later, new knickers and under-slip having been duly purchased, Jeannie had to run the gauntlet of several knots of gossiping women on the pavement. Each group hailed her with the news: had she heard about Aggie from the bakery who was going to be the star of a big show at The Alhambra, who had been going *to the Methodist Kirk,* no less, for weeks and singing in their choir? And it would seem the priest was going to let her carry on, might even go to the concert himself. And even her man, that well known firebrand, Eck Fairweather, wasn't going to stop her. Who would have thought, to look at her, that she was capable of getting up to such a thing? *And* hiding it so well all these weeks, just carrying on as if butter wouldn't melt in her mouth. It just went to show… You never knew with folk . . . Who knew what else might be going on? Where would it all end?

Jeannie met each barrage of comment and speculation head-on. 'Och, Ah've kent aboot it fur ages,' she declared blithely, feeling that she could be forgiven for a little exaggeration to soothe her disappointment. 'Aggie telt me hersel but she didnae want it broadcast a' ower the place until near the time. Hoo'ever, we thocht that it wis time tae tell Senga this mornin'. Wi the Get-thegither at her hoose this year, it's only *polite.*'

She considered this a master-stroke as it removed all the kudos from Annie, implying that Senga was the key figure and Annie and her shop were involved only because Senga worked there of a morning.

The chattering women absorbed Jeannie's reaction with some amazement, even incredulity. That Jeannie had known about it 'for ages' *and kept it secret* was bigger news than the news itself.

Then some of them remembered being in the bakery about a month ago and hearing Jeannie declare that she was going to *mind her own business.* It had caused quite a shock and been the main topic of conversation for several days. On reflection now, they all realised with some surprise…*richt enough*…there had been no new gossip from her since then. Indeed, she had not even been seen around much or, when seen, had been bustling with brisk importance, giving the air of someone with no time to stop and engage in idle gossip.

It was all very strange. Folk seemed to be changing. Nothing was the way it used to be. All very unsettling… The women chattered on in the pale winter sunshine while Jeannie worked her way up the street towards the bakery. She felt better and better as she dealt with each little knot of chatterers, leaving them in no doubt as to her status in the affair.

By the time she reached Aggie's domain, her good spirits were quite restored. So long as no-one was in any doubt about her own superior importance, she felt she could afford to be magnanimous towards Annie's attempts to grab a little of the limelight. *Puir auld, Annie. Her nose has been awfy oot o' joint lately wi her no gettin' tae ken whit's goin' on wi Kate an me. Ah suppose Aggie took peety on her.*

The queue in the bakery was moving even more slowly than that in the draper's and for the same reason. Those women who had already heard the news from Annie or Senga were agog to hear more from Aggie; those who had gone to the bakery first and were still innocent of it provided a wonderful audience for those who already knew.

Aggie was looking, Jeannie thought, like a child who has been at a wonderful but extremely tiring party: exhilarated, over-excited and absolutely exhausted.

In truth, the cocktail of relief, happiness and anticipation was almost proving too much for her in her weakened physical state. Two hangovers in the bakery's busiest week of the year were taking their toll. She was doing very little business, however, at the moment as she attempted to answer questions, correct misapprehensions, acknowledge compliments and explain mysteries. Such was the excited buzz in the shop that she was beginning to doubt if she would ever manage to finish a sentence again. Jeannie took all this in at once and moved swiftly to the rescue.

'Dearie me!' She swept a disapproving look around the shop and its dozen or so customers. 'At this rate, the New Year is goin' tae be comin' in tae some awfy dirty hooses wi nae food or drink in them fur their first-footers.'

To a woman, they started guiltily, recalled forcibly to a housewife's pressing duties on the day before Hogmanay.

Jeannie moved to the counter. 'Ye're run aff yer feet,' she pronounced. She moved to join Aggie behind it. 'You dae the money an the club vouchers: Ah'll bag up the stuff.'

She raised her voice and favoured the assembled throng with a wide, serene smile. 'We dinnae want ye gettin' too tired tae sing at yer concert, dae we? No when we've *baith* been lookin' forrad tae it fur sae lang. Now then, wha's first?'

It was one of Jeannie's finest hours. By physically aligning herself alongside Aggie behind the counter and talking easily and familiarly about the forthcoming concert, she established not only that she had known about it long before Annie or Senga but that she had been

284

Aggie's trusted and trustworthy confidante, actually guarding this exciting secret, actually *not* gossiping it all over the community.

As the women left the shop, they were undecided whether the most amazing news of the day was Aggie's concert or Jeannie's conversion.

'Can ye credit it, Mina?' Bessie was loth to end their discussions as the two lingered at the crossroads, before going their separate ways. 'A' that time we were goin' in tae help in the shop in the afternoons an she never said a word. Ah mean, *we* should hae been telt somethin', d'ye no think?' She was aggrieved that they had had no advantage and had just had to learn about it along with everyone else. 'Ah mean, it's no every day we get the chance tae...'

Mina smirked. Aggie had just asked her to exercise her hairdressing skills early in the morning of the concert. Mina had been dying to get her hands on Aggie's disastrous hair for a long time but that was not the only reason she was so pleased to be asked. As Bessie was saying, it was not everyday they got the chance to help someone famous!

'So...' Jeannie said almost an hour later - there was a lull and Aggie was putting the kettle on - '...ye decided tae ask *Annie* tae spill the beans. Guid idea! Annie's aye a lot easier tae handle if she thinks she has an important job tae dae an this'll stop her goin' aff at half cock an bletherin' a load o' muck.'

Aggie was in general too straightforward to practice deviousness to this degree and in particular too tired and too preoccupied at this moment to take any interest in such manipulative measures. 'Och, her an me jist happened tae be havin' a drink thegither in the new Ladies' Bar.'

Jeannie snapped her head up from the bucket under the tiny sink where she was pouring out yesterday's tea-leaves. 'Ye never went in tae that place! Ye brazen hussies!'

'No we're no! We're jist' - she recalled Margot's description - 'jist twa businesswomen havin' a drink after work. Awfy modern, ye ken.'

Jeannie stared. Fat Annie and Scraggy Aggie: *businesswomen? modern?* She burst into helpless giggles, holding on to the sink for support and, after a moment of pretending affront, Aggie joined in.

'Ah tak it Kate did the bizness wi Eck, then? He's a' richt aboot it?'

'She worked some kind o' a miracle! He's been nice as ninepence aboot it. Ah'll hae tae try an leave somethin' half-decent fur his denner that day. Keep him sweet. Well, as sweet as *he's* ever likely tae be.'

'Tell him he can cam' roon an hae a bite tae eat wi me an Bob afore they gang aff tae the pit, if he wants.'

'Thanks, Jeannie. Ye're a pal.'

A short silence fell in the little back shop as they drank their tea and ate the apple tarts Aggie had selected for their snack. Jeannie wandered through to the front shop and looked across the road at the off-license. 'The queue's no sae bad at the booze-shop fur the moment. Ah think Ah'll nip ower the noo.'

'Buying yer New Year bottle? Ye'll no get much choice noo – the shelves'll be gettin' fair empty.'

In fact, Jeannie, being a meticulous planner of her household budget, always saved up and bought three or four bottles of spirits at well-spaced-out intervals in the six-months between June and December. At this very moment two bottles of whisky, one of sherry and one of Advocaat were awaiting their unveiling tomorrow night. They had spent the last few months in the cupboard under the sink, modestly hidden behind a box of washing soda and a large packet of Lux Flakes, safe from the marauding hands of the twins who would never have any reason to touch either of these cleaning products.

'Naw. It's a wee matter o' replacing a bottle o' Haig's Dimple.'

Aggie moved to the money drawer under the counter and pulled it out to its full extent. She reached past the piles of copper pennies and silver shillings for the roll of banknotes at the back.

'Here.' She handed a pound note to Jeannie. 'That bottle went on *ma* guid cause. Ye've done enough tae help me withoot bein' oot o' pocket as weel.' As Jeannie nodded and accepted, she added: 'Ah jist hope that priest minds whit we talked aboot. Noo that a' body kens, there'll be some o' them beatin' a track tae his door the day wantin' tae hear whit he has tae say aboot it.'

'He's mindin' a' richt,' Jeannie was confident and complacent. 'Ah nipped his heid again on ma wiy oot o' mass on Sunday mornin'. He said he wis goin' tae be preachin' aboot it this Sunday comin'. Och, an he wis lookin' fur ye, wonderin' whaur ye were. Ah had tae tell a wee white lie an say ye were no weel. Ye'd better come tae mass this Sunday an tell him his sermon's wonderfu. Tickle his fancy wi some mair o' that stuff ye're singin' at the concert.'

Aggie groaned. 'But Ah'll be *banjaxed* after Hogmanay, New Year's Day an then The Concert. An then, on Saturday, Ah'll hae tae tidy up here an re-stock an then a'body'll be needin' stuff after Ah've been closed fur twa days. The last thing Ah need is havin' tae get up an gang tae mass on Sunday!'

'Geez, Ag, ye're makin' me tired listenin' tae ye! Whit ye're needin' is an *assistant.*'

'Dinnae think Ah havnae thocht aboot it. But if Ah ask ane o' them, the ither twa'll be flamin' mad. An Ah'm no havin a' three o' them again, ane after the ither, like when Kate wis no weel. Ye should see the mess they made o' the vouchers an the stock orders. The richt haun didnae ken whit the left wis doin'. It wis a bloody shambles!'

'Maybe ye should think o' gettin' someone else a'thegither?' Jeannie was toying with an alluring new idea. She had rather enjoyed the past hour helping in the bakery and already her sharp eyes had observed areas ripe for improvement and her busy brain was sifting through ideas.

'Aye. Maybe. But wha?'

'Weel…' Jeannie was coy but her meaning was unmistakable.

Aggie ran the idea quickly round her cluttered, over-tired brain. She was under no illusions, having seen how it had worked with Annie and Senga, that being the proprietrix of the business would necessarily save her from the danger of a bossy takeover bid. However, forewarned was forearmed and she counted herself a lot smarter than Annie. And there would certainly be no doubt about Jeannie's competence and reliability. Aggie was still reeling from the efficient way this wee woman had dealt with the problem of her getting to the concert and had even, quite beyond her wildest dreams, paved the way for her ongoing involvement in the choir. Jeannie would be an asset, albeit one that would need careful managing.

'Can ye start the morn? Hogmanay is aye bedlam. Ah've that mony orders tae prepare afore Ah even open in the mornin' an then…'

Jeannie shook her head decisively. 'No the morn, sorry, Ag. Ah'll be awa maist o' the day so Ah cannae even cam' in fur a few hoors. But after that, Ah'm yer wumman. Ah'll start on Saturday. Hoo much dae Ah get paid?'

Aggie named a salary which sounded like a fortune to Jeannie who had never had any money of her own, having gone straight from living at home and handing all of her small wage from the factory over to her mother to being given her weekly housekeeping from Bob.

The shop began to fill up again and Jeannie took her leave to go and stand in the off-license queue. It wasn't until she was hurrying home with the dinner-time pies that Aggie thought to wonder where on earth Jeannie could be going on Hogmanay that was going to take her away for most of the day.

Returning home towards midday dinner-time, Jeannie saw at once that the twins were at home. She could see their latest borrowed car outside the house and was pleased to see that it was a comfortable family saloon and not one of the daft, low-slung sporty models they sometimes indulged in, which had difficulty accommodating the driver let alone any passengers.

She quickened her step and prepared to strike while the iron was hot. The boys were 'between jobs' at the moment (the word 'unemployed' never crossed their lips) and were hence simply cruising from one dodgy bit of business in the car world to the next – 'free-lancing' was Rab's airy description of their doubtful activities. Jeannie did not like this unpredictable state of affairs normally but was glad of it for her own purposes right now. It meant they would be free to dance to *her* tune tomorrow.

She breezed cheerfully in and expressed her pleasure that they would be joining her and Bob for dinner – a rare treat for them all. The twins exchanged uneasy glances: *She's wantin' us to do somethin', fur sure!* Their uneasiness was somewhat mollified by a delicious dinner of home-made broth with dumplings followed by one of their favourite puddings: rice 'n raisins. Once Bob had clumped off to the pit, she cleared the table and served them cups of Camp coffee with plenty of sugar and hot, foamy milk – another of their favourite treats. Their suspicions returned.

'Now, you twa . . . ' She sat down at the table with her own abstemious cup of tea.

Their hearts sank. Jeannie considered them and weighed up two possible approaches: she could dominate them and demand obedience, something they were well used to though nowadays less and less likely to respond to satisfactorily; or she could seduce them into compliance, a tactic she was also well-versed in though hadn't used for some time.

She rarely saw enough of them to spend the time it took to implement. Today, however, they seemed in no hurry to rush off and she had made their coffees scalding hot. She smiled conspiratorially at them and leaned across the table to create a sensation of tripartite intimacy.

'Ah'm goin' tae let you twa intae a big secret,' she began. The voice was one they instinctively recognised and responded to as they had done from infancy. It conveyed all the promise of a wonderful story, made up specially and shared only with them. If they had not been great, lumbering, grown-up lads, they might well have crept, thumbs in mouths, on to her lap and gazed up at her in rapt attention. Years of such bedtime stories, some developing into whole sagas that lasted for months, were imprinted on their memories and still exerted a powerful influence over them. They leaned forward and the three heads formed a close, exclusive circle.

'An aince Ah've telt ye it, Ah want ye baith tae dae me a big favour. Will ye promise me that?' They nodded solemnly, almost banging their heads together.

When she finished talking, their eyes were as bright with excitement as her own and they were full of glee at the important role they were to play in the wonderful secret.

'Ye've tae promise me ye'll no tell a livin' soul aboot it. Mind! No even yer faither: he's nae guid at keepin' secrets, he'd jist furget whit he wis sayin' doon the pub an blow the gaff. Promise me. Ah'll tear ye up fur lavvie paper if Ah hear that ye've...'

She checked herself and slipped back into seduction mode: 'It's oor secret an when it a' comes oot the morn's nicht, there'll only be us an Kate that kens it's goin' tae happen. Is that no braw?'

It was not strictly true: there were several other people involved; but the twins were unlikely to work this out and the important thing was to make them feel that it was in their own interests to keep silent. She put her finger to her lips and winked. It was another reminder of childhood, a game they had sometimes played with her to prepare surprises for their father or their grandfather. As of yore, they imitated the two gestures and the pact was sealed.

It was not until later that afternoon that it dawned on them that they had willingly agreed to give up their entire Hogmanay. It had been their plan to meet up with pals and begin drinking mid-afternoon, reaching insensibility by early evening. This would then give them time to sleep it off and wake up in time to greet the New Year at midnight and begin all over again. They had attempted this feat last year but had failed to wake up until two in the morning, thus missing 'The Bells' altogether and losing out to those in their circle who had managed it. They had been in training for some months now and were feeling quietly confident of a better performance this year. But now, they had surrendered their chance and would have to wait till next year to try again.

'It had better bloody well be worth it,' groaned Rab. 'Is that ma o' oors no *some* wee wumman?'

Jasper Gilhooley patiently turned down the wireless for the fifth time and sighed. At this rate he would never find out if the filly he had backed in the two-thirty at Goodwood had won or not – it was a photo finish and they were waiting on the evidence being developed.

His daughter-in-law seemed unusually excited and in need of an audience. Usually, Jasper just let her get on with the baffling number of small tasks she always seemed to find to do during her brief afternoon visit and usually she would chatter her way through them but not demand his attention or a response. It was a formula that had served them both well for several years. Today, however, she kept coming back into the room and demanding a sensible answer to questions he had not been listening to.

Did he mind having broth and dumplings for his tea? It was really dinner-time fare but it was all she had to give him today.

He did not mind, he assured her.

Did he mind that the raisins were all through the rice? She had forgotten to keep part of the dish raisin-free for him and she knew he didn't like them mixed in.

He would put up with it for once, he agreed.

Was he remembering that tomorrow was Hogmanay but that she and Bob were going to Kate's evening party *before* the bells? So they'd have to come in earlier than usual to wish him *Happy New Year* if he wanted to get away to bed before twelve. If he wanted to wait up, they'd come and first-foot him.

He would be going to bed at ten o'clock as usual, he said, he was too old for staying up all night and had never been much of drinker anyway, usually passing out in a corner after the third whisky.

Would he like her and Bob to come and help him along the road to Kate's party? He didn't have to feel left out, though the streets were hazardous with frozen slush at the moment and walking was difficult for someone as feeble on the legs as him. But he would be quite welcome. Kate had made it clear it was open house for all.

He shuddered at the thought of going out late at night into the bitter weather and re-iterated his intention to be in bed by ten – and perfectly happy to be so.

The fifth interruption was obviously more important and he realised she had been working up to it through the preceding series. She sat down beside him on a small stool, her head no higher than his shoulder. '*Here it comes,*' he thought, and momentarily forgot the two-thirty.

'Wid ye mind if Ah start bringin' yer tea roon a lot earlier? Like aboot one o'clock? An Ah'll no be able tae stay an blether ony mair. Ye see, Ah've got masel a job!'

There was no mistaking the triumph in her voice and Jasper could not help smiling back at her excited, beaming face. He was very fond of Jeannie and much appreciated her unstinting attention, not to mention her excellent cooking. He was genuinely delighted to see her so happy and he was also thinking with pleasure of how much easier it would be to listen uninterrupted to the wireless in the afternoons.

He had to forego finding out the Goodwood result today, however, whilst he listened indulgently to her prattle. Aggie had asked her to work in the bakery in the afternoons, initially alongside her but, as soon as Jeannie felt confident (which they both knew would be no more than a matter of a day or two), taking over the job of opening up after dinner-time and running the place single-handed until four o'clock when Aggie would return to help with the cleaning and closing-up jobs in the last hour. Aggie was already happily contemplating the after-dinner snoozes which her body often craved – not surprising when she arose at an hour most people would consider the middle of the night.

Jeannie had to be reassured on several counts: that Jasper would be quite happy to go along with whatever suited her new schedule; that he was delighted for her and hoped she would enjoy her new job; that she had no need to upbraid herself for having less time to spend with him each day from now on. It was proving hard for her to relinquish the routines of years and to accept that they were not, after all, indispensable. But he loved her enough to give her the time she needed to talk it out and reach a place of acceptance.

'Thanks, Faither,' she said as she rose to take her leave. 'Ye've aye a wise word tae sae.'

He forbore to remark that *he* had said almost nothing, certainly nothing *wise* – only listened, nodding and shaking his head at the right times, patting her hand occasionally. It was a role he excelled in, having had years of practice when his wife was alive.

The telephone box at the crossroads was occupied when Jeannie descended upon it half-an-hour later. A woman and two small children were crammed into it, the woman gesticulating vehemently as she talked on the phone, the children busy drawing weird and wonderful designs in the condensation of its large glass panels. When they saw Jeannie take up her stance as a one-woman queue, they turned their attention to making weird and wonderful faces at her, pressing snotty noses stickily against the panels and dangling impudent tongues to lick the snot as it ran down the glass. Jeannie glared disgustedly at them. *Ah ken whit they'd get if they were mine.*

Across the road, Kate was watching anxiously out the window. She had just settled the auld yin back in bed after her afternoon sojourn in the sitting-room and had been on the point of drawing the curtains against the falling darkness. She had spotted Jeannie hurrying up to the crossroads and over to the phone box. There could be only one reason for Jeannie making a telephone call and Kate was desperately impatient to know its outcome.

The mother of the two budding little mime-artists was in no hurry. Twice she put more pennies into the slot and carried on waving her hands about and nodding vigorously. Getting colder and colder, Jeannie at last lost patience and rapped on the door, making some unmistakable gestures herself.

The woman spun round and became flustered. Her demeanour became even more frantic as she added the pressure of haste into whatever mix of emotions was fuelling her excited conversation. Another three or four minutes passed; Jeannie rapped again. This time, she got a result: the woman yelled something unrepeatable, which Jeannie could not hear but could easily guess at, and slammed the receiver down. She pushed the giggling bairns out of the box and emerged exclaiming enigmatically:

'Well, dinnae say Ah didnae warn them!' She grabbed her bairns' hands and stomped off, their little wellies sliding in the slush to keep up with her.

The phone box was at least warm from their presence, the glass panels opaque with steam and the heavy black receiver slippery in her grasp. She fished the slip of paper from her purse along with the four big pennies. Smoothing out the paper to read the number she dialed slowly and deliberately, keeping her finger in each hole as it returned each time to the zero position. Her heart was beating a little faster than normal: It was only the third or fourth time she had ever used a phone box and the machinery felt threatening, each action seeming to initiate a serious and irrevocable consequence.

At last the dialing was done and she heard the ringing tone. She visualised the comfortable room, the fire blazing, the little table by the bay window with the phone on it.

Hello? With a sigh of relief, she pressed button A and heard the satisfying clatter as the pennies dropped and she was connected.

Angus had had a very busy day. It was really a good job that he was now feeling so much stronger and able to cope with the pace. Up and down the hill twice: laying in provisions the first time; collecting laundry the second time - it had not been ready in the morning.

Then there was the house to clean for the umpteenth time, especially the bathroom – he was worried about sharing such an intimate space with her – and the lady's bedroom to prepare, making up the spare bed with the freshly laundered sheets and lavender sachets under the pillows, laying out fresh towels on the chair, polishing the furniture and bed-head till they shone, putting coat-hangers in the empty wardrobe and finally arranging a small vase of Christmas roses from the garden, all just as Jeannie had instructed on the neat note she had left him.

Then there had been crockery and cutlery to bring out from long captivity in the big sideboard, plates to wash and silver to clean. He had taken great pains setting the table in the dining-room starting with a freshly laundered white damask tablecloth with matching napkins. It was the first time the room had been used for five years and he and Jeannie had had a long discussion about it the last time she had called in her role as Kate's emissary.

There had been several such visits over the past few weeks and Mrs Clancy next door had watched these with interest. Obviously the first pretty, plump lady had been passed over for this smart wee one who had been peering in his windows the day he had been taken poorly at the foot of the hill. Of the strange disheveled one who had been trying to break into the back of his house there had never been another sighting. It was all very intriguing.

He had just sat down to enjoy a well-earned rest and read of the paper when the telephone shrilled. With a tired sigh, he rose to answer it. He held the receiver well away from his ear since Jeannie did not quite trust the technology and made a creditable attempt at simply shouting loud enough to be heard across the intervening five miles. When the brief exchange was over, he sat down again and pondered the small detail she had left him to smooth out.

Accustomed to dealing with slow-witted Bob and with her self-absorbed, inattentive sons, Jeannie had found Angus a revelation. She had even slightly revised her opinion that men as a whole were mentally inferior to women and, as such, had to be humoured, manipulated, treated as devoid of sense and considered as generally unreliable. Angus had proved intelligent and totally dependable, executing every detail of their plan perfectly and even thinking ahead, spotting potential problems and heading them off at the pass. Jeannie had been amazed and impressed.

'Ye'd mak some wumman a gran man and lucky she'd be tae get ye,' she had declared at their last meeting, a considerable accolade from her, at which he had grinned and given back a cheeky, slightly risqué reply more suited to his old butcher-shop persona. She had, to his surprise, replied in kind, almost making him blush and certainly making him revise his opinion of prissy wee Mrs Gilhooley. Then she had instantly reverted to her accustomed prunes-and-prisms manner and he had been left wondering if he had imagined the exchange.

Now he pondered this final wee detail she had left him with, frowning as he drank his cooling cup of tea. Then his brow cleared. *Of course, the lad Terry's coming roon tonight fur a wee game o' dominoes. I'll ask him. He disnae drink at a', bein' one o' they Baptists, an he cannae do enough for me. He's got an eye to the main chance, of course, but who can blame him?*

Jeannie glanced at the clock outside the post office as she hurried across the road: ten-to-five already. Where had the day gone? Lucky she had been up some twelve hours ago and had finally polished off her housewifely Hogmanay responsibilities before Bob and the twins were out of bed.

She ticked these off in her head as she let herself in through Kate's gate. Her little house was spotless, every cupboard cleaned out, every cobweb banished, all washing and ironing up to date. All the food and drink had been bought and stored away ready for first-footers and for the family New Year's Day dinner – it was her turn this year and both Bob's sister and her own cousin would be coming with their attendant spouses and children to crowd into her living-room round the annually enlarged trestle table. She had two large steak pies and two bowls of trifle keeping cold in the metal box on the wall outside the house. She would have a bath and wash her hair later tonight, once Bob's demands had been met, but she would keep the nice new knickers to change into before the party tomorrow night. She could pop into Father O'Malley's confession box tomorrow night before the party to make sure her soul was as spotless as her house and person in time for the bells at midnight.

Kate greeted her with gratifying enthusiasm. Jeannie spared a thought for the way most people used to greet her and wondered at the change that had been wrought in so short a time. Certainly, Aggie would never have thought of asking her to work in the bakery a few short months ago – that would have been tantamount to letting the whole world know both her private as well as her commercial business – and Kate had only ever treated Jeannie in the past with distrust and dislike, not even making use of her as a publicity machine, as some people had risked doing.

Life was undoubtedly a lot more interesting this way. '*And a helluva lot busier!*' she thought ruefully as she toiled up the stairs to meet Kate who was standing impatiently on the top step.

There was much to catch up on and very little time as Johnnie would be home in less than an hour and old Maggie would soon be looking for food. The two women did not even waste time on cups of tea for once.

Jeannie had to hear all about how the magic had been worked on Eck; Kate had to be congratulated on a spectacular success and apprised of the latest developments regarding Annie and Senga publishing the news. A few minutes were spent admiring the effrontery of Aggie and Annie going into the Ladies' Bar and laughing over them calling themselves 'modern businesswomen' for doing so.

'Though, mind you, Kate, Ah micht have tae start behavin' like that masel noo. Ag's asked me tae become her assistant in the shop. Ah start on Saturday afternoon.'

Kate was pleased for her. As she had got to know this woman over the past weeks, she had come to realise how much of her past addiction to pernicious gossip had stemmed from simply not having enough outlet for her sharp brain and boundless energy. Managing her home, husband and grown-up sons, she could do with one hand tied behind her back and her mind scarcely getting out of first gear.

Aggie'd better watch oot, though. It'll be 'Jeannie's Bakery' afore lang – and likely hauf a dozen ither shops opening up as weel!

Relief was expressed that Mina was going to take Aggie's hair in hand. This had been worrying Kate. Indeed, she had been toying with the idea of offering to do it herself but had feared to offend her sister. And so, at last, for the moment, the subject of Aggie's concert was laid to rest and, for the remaining quarter-of-an-hour before they heard Johnnie's footfall on the path, they dwelt lovingly on the last details of their own immense and imminent secret.

Once Johnnie joined them, conversation turned to acknowledgement of how much better Kate was looking, how grateful they both were for Jeannie's care and friendship and how much they were all looking forward to the party tomorrow night. It was going to be quite a novelty having everyone together in the house *before* the bells.

'We'll have to send someone outside before twelve – a tall, dark, handsome man – and make sure he has a lump o' coal in one hand and a packet of tea in the other. The window will be opened before midnight, of course, so if we turn the wireless up, he'll hear Big Ben strikin' twelve and ken when to chap the door an be our first-foot.' Johnnie was exercising his forward-planning skills.

He had sat down to take his boots off and put on the slippers warming on the fender so did not see Kate and Jeannie exchange looks, their eyes dancing with excitement.

Bob thought that he had never seen his Jeannie looking better. Her dark eyes were snapping with excitement, her cheeks were flushed

296

from running home as fast as the slippery pavements would allow, then dashing about the warm little house hastily throwing together a supper of herring-in-oatmeal with plenty of mashed potato to cushion the fish bones and some pickled beetroot from one of the big preserving jars which she filled every summer.

She had eaten her own meal very fast, talking all the time, and now she was leaning across the table, still talking, her bosom heaving in a most entrancing way.

'Are you listenin' tae me, Bob?'

'Ah certainly am, darlin'.' His eyes were on her pert little breasts which were now resting invitingly on the table, still heaving.

'So what did Ah jist say?'

'Ye were sayin'…emm… Och, aye! That ye're goin tae be takin' ma faither's tea roon tae him earlier in the afternoons frae noo on an he disnae mind at a'.' Bob beamed triumphantly at this impressive demonstration of his powers of recall.

'An *why* am Ah goin' tae be doin' that?' Then, as he frowned hard but did not answer, 'Did ye no hear me tellin' ye aboot ma new JOB?' She almost shouted the word, partly in excitement, partly in frustration.

'Job? Oh, aye. Richt enough. Ye did say aboot maybe goin' tae help Aggie in the bakery sometimes, wis that it?' He caught sight of her face, realised he had totally missed his cue and sought to make amends. 'If it's important tae you, darlin', it's important tae me as weel, of coorse.'

She flounced angrily through to the kitchen with their dirty plates and returned to dump a lemon meringue pie on the table, her face as sour as the fruit used to make it. He tried harder. 'Now, that looks real interessin'! Whit d'ye ca' that? An it smells lovely.'

'It's the kind o' thing ye'll be seein' a lot mair o', that's whit it is. It's a new line in the bakery. Aggie gave me ane tae try. Ye see, Bob…'

Unable to sustain her chilly manner as her excitement re-surfaced, she began to talk again about the job. 'An Ah've decided Ah'm no goin' tae spend the money Ah mak. Ah'm goin' tae save it in a separate post office account until we've enough tae get oorsels a nice wee holiday next summer. Whit dae ye think?'

Bob blinked. No-one he knew had had a holiday since the end of the war. They had all got out of the habit during it and, with the lack of fuel for transport and people's absorption in simple survival through the years of post-war austerity, the concept had ceased to be a part of their lives. Then he suddenly threw back his head and roared with laughter.

'D'ye mind that holiday we had at Carnoustie afore the war? The lads were only babbies. Ye had knitted yersel that bathin' costume an it looked smashin' on ye until ye went intae the water an it a' stretched and sagged. Ye never realised whit wis happenin' an ye cam' walkin' oot of the water wi it a' runkled roon yer waist an yer bonnie titties on show fur a' tae see!'

'Bob!' She had no wish to be reminded of that embarrassing moment. The knitted costume had gone straight into the bin that day and she had never worn one – knitted or otherwise – again.

But his laughter was infectious and she softened, remembering too that she needed to have him in a happy and compliant mood before he went off to sleep that night. She served out the lemon pie and they ate it appreciatively. Then she went and stood at his side and placed a firm hand on his shoulder.

'It is most un-gentlemanly o' you to remind a lady o' sich a moment, sir. You must make amends.'

She held out the back of her hand daintily inviting him to kiss it, as a lady would to her devoted troubadour. Bob gurgled delightedly: this was one of his favourite fantasies and it had been some time since they had given it an airing. She nudged him with the elbow of her other arm, prompting him, and this time he did not miss his cue. He dropped to his knees, kissed her hand and breathed: 'Whit wid ma lady hae me dae fur her?'

She bent down and whispered her wishes in his ear and he squirmed excitedly. Then he leapt to his feet, scooped her up, threw her over his shoulder and charged upstairs, bellowing; 'Yer wish is ma command! Hey nonny nonny and a haw chaw chaw!'

She had no trouble some time later in persuading him to accept that she would be gone most of the day tomorrow, that he would just have to help himself to the remains of today's broth and dumplings for dinner with the last of the meringue pie for afters. There was going to be so much food at Kate's party in the evening, she assured him, that he would only need a wee snack when he got in from work in the early evening – the pit always closed early on Hogmanay – and she would be home by then.

When he protested sleepily that he didn't understand where she was going, she simply stroked his head as it lay on her sweaty bare stomach and said firmly: 'Such things are no fur you tae ken. Ah'm your lady an you're ma chiel – that's like a slave, ye ken. Ye jist dae whit Ah tell ye.'

He grunted happily and slipped into a deep, sonorous sleep, giving her the chance, at last, after a very long day, to relax and wallow in the deep, rose-scented hip-bath she had promised herself.

CHAPTER SIXTEEN

HOGMANAY

Jeannie was up with the lark despite not having finally fallen asleep till nearly two o'clock. Fortunately, she was one of those rare people who need very little sleep. In fact, the busier and more exciting her life was, the less sleep she needed. It was only on dreary, uninteresting days that she felt the need for an early night. And there had not been many of those lately.

When the twins had returned home at nearly midnight, they had been surprised to find her still up, sitting on the hearth rug, drying her long dark hair by a still lively fire. She was flushed, rose-scented, wrapped in her old candlewick dressing-gown and scribbling busily in a jotter, which she hastily closed and thrust under the rug when she heard them coming in.

After a long leisurely bath, she had taken her time for once, clearing away and washing up the supper things. Then, still at a slow, thoughtful pace, she had prepared everything for the morning, ready for their early start. Finally, she had laid out the makings of two substantial sandwiches for the lads and, still not sleepy, had slipped upstairs to get her latest jotter. Bob had not even stirred as she had quietly closed the bedroom door and come back down to the fire. Her mind was still processing all that had happened and all that was about to happen whilst at the back of it lay the other delicious, new prospect of her job at the bakery.

She thought back to that moment of truth in the rain on that bleak November afternoon in Anstruther. Thank God she had listened to the inner prompting of that moment. Her life had taken such a turn for the better that she hardly recognised it. Now she was attempting in her latest story to portray a similar life-change in one of her characters and it was proving a self-analytical, cathartic process.

The boys were almost over-whelmed by her indulgent good-humour as she made them hearty sandwiches and a big pot of tea, chatting affectionately with them over it and wishing them a loving good-night as they yawned off to bed. They were not surprised, therefore, when she had called them back in a whisper when they were half-way upstairs.

'Mind we'll be leavin' at eight sharp. Ah'll have yer breakfast ready at hauf-past-seven an Ah'll chap ye up at seven. Nae messin' noo – Ah want ye up richt awa.'

They groaned at the thought but, always creatures of the moment, refused to let it spoil the pleasure of happily subsiding on to their beds and falling instantly asleep.

Jeannie spent another half-hour with her jotter but at last felt the pull of sleep and, resorting once again to the second-rate charms of the hot water bottle, slipped into bed beside Bob without disturbing him. Her eyes were smarting after the hours of concentration and she thought, *'Ah'll hae tae gie in soon an get specks. But they National Health frames are that ugly.'*

Then a smile had spread over her sleepy face. *But Ah'll be able tae afford the private frames noo - wi ma ain pay!*

Now it was seven o'clock in the morning and she was preparing two large, thickly- sugared mugs of tea for the boys. She had already breakfasted and was fully dressed with a voluminous apron covering her new outfit. She had made herself a smart grey skirt with material culled from one of Senga's mystery parcels and she had knitted a fine, lacy-pattern jumper in soft butter-yellow from her favourite wool-shop in Leven.

It was really her Hogmanay outfit for tonight but she would just have to be careful today and get no stains on it. What she was doing today was more important, more deserving of a new outfit, than a drunken rabble at midnight in this place, she told herself. She would keep her new knickers for tonight and that would have to do for the bells.

It took a skilful mix of cajoling and threatening to get the twins up and ready to leave by eight. The promise of a spectacular cooked breakfast helped.

As he used the last piece of fried bread to wipe egg yolk off his plate, Rab suddenly said, 'Here, Ma! Funny thing: I've a bottle o'

Haig's Dimple hidden in ma bedroom for the nicht. It was in a box. An noo…it's no! Do *you* ken what happened to the box?'

Jeannie, heading for the stairs with a mug of tea for Bob, was stopped in her tracks. *Damn-it!* She had quite forgotten about the box, having thrown out the original one when she 'borrowed' the whisky on Christmas Eve. As Aggie had predicted yesterday, there had not been a great deal left in the off-license and she had been lucky to get the last bottle of Dimple. It was the one that had been out on show in the shop and Tam, the 'Offie-man', had not been able to find the box. He had given her a wee bit off the price and she had been too thankful to get one at all to quibble.

She briefly toyed with the idea of telling them the truth but it was a story too long for the time available and with too many subtleties and complexities for them to understand. In any case, she did not think it a good idea for them to know how *fond of the whisky* their priest was. They most certainly did not need that kind of example.

'Ah think Ah cam' across it when Ah wis cleanin',' she said vaguely. 'Then Nellie-ower-the-road asked me if Ah had a box she could use fur sendin' some things tae her auld granny in Tayport fur the New Year, an Ah thocht ye widnae mind. It wis only a box…'

She disappeared hastily upstairs to terminate the discussion and Rab shrugged, accepting the fabrication at face value.

Bob had difficulty making sense of Jeannie appearing fully dressed and immaculately groomed at the side of the bed and thought at first he was still dreaming. As he propped himself up to take the mug from her, he blinked owlishly. 'Is that you, hen?'

'Ah'm jist aff.' She planted a kiss on his furrowed forehead. 'Noo, mind Ah telt ye: Ah'll no be hame till aboot six. Ah'll see ye when ye get in frae work. If ye're hame afore me, get yersel washed an ready fur the party. We've tae gang tae confession afore it – we'll gang on the wiy tae Kate's hoose. But we've tae cry in an say Happy-New-Year-when-it-comes tae yer faither first. There's yesterday's broth an dumplings on the cooker tae heat up fur yer denner and the last bit o' the Lemon Meringue Pie is in the cold-box ootside.'

Bob blinked harder and tried to make sense of it all. Some of it was ringing bells from last night…

'But, whaur are ye goin'? Whit fur? Whit are ye daein? When..?'

'Too many questions, ma lad.' Jeannie made a snap decision and broke the habit of a lifetime. Leaning over, she whispered in his ear: 'A chiel disnae question his lady. A chiel only has to obey.'

302

A huge smile spread over his sleep-blurred face. It was the first time she had ever so much as acknowledged a night-time fantasy in the morning.

'Yer wish is ma command,' he mumbled and reached out a hopeful hand but she slipped easily out of his grasp, pausing only to give him a queenly wave from the door that made him groan in frustration.

Dave play-acted the chauffeur, standing to attention, even essaying a salute and a Teutonic click of his heels like in the old newsreels at the pictures, as he held open the back door of the car for Jeannie. Rab cranked the car into action, threw the starting handle into the boot then leapt into the driver's seat. 'Whaur is it we're goin' again, ma?'

'Windygates,' she said serenely. 'An dinnae spare the horses!'

Looking out the window, she saw Nellie and her oldest daughter, open-mouthed, at their window. For the second time in five minutes, she raised her hand in a regal wave.

Standing at her kitchen window, Kate looked out at the long shadows lying across the back gardens. It was a fine winter day. The weather had at last taken a turn for the better and an overnight thaw had cleared the dirty slush from the pavements. Now a weak sun was gradually drying up the puddles. She opened the window and leaned out. No wind, the air soft with even a hint of spring. A false promise, of course, with all the misery of January and February to come, but still alluring and, to the long-imprisoned Kate, irresistible.

'Wid ye mind if Ah went oot fur a wee while, mither? It's sich a lovely mornin' an Ah've an awfy hankerin' tae get oot o' the hoose...'

She paused, realising the insensitivity of this remark to someone who never got out and had no prospect of doing so. *We'll hae tae try an get the auld soul oot fur a wee hurl in her chair aince the winter's ower.*

If she saw the ironic relevance to her own plight, however, Old Maggie gave no sign, being absorbed in the Hogmanay edition of *Housewives Choice,* which had fittingly dedicated today's programme to playing requests from Scottish listeners. She merely nodded and turned up the wireless again.

Since Kate had resumed full care of the old woman, their relationship had undergone a change. Under Jeannie's watchful eye, neither had slipped back into the old groove. Maggie continued to accept the routines so smoothly established by Jeannie, including the blessed 'continental pads', and Kate swiftly grew into a new role that was at once more calm and confident and yet also more compassionate. They would never like each other or be friends but they had reached a place of scratchy mutual tolerance that might just get them through to the end of this period of enforced closeness.

Kate stood on the doorstep outside and breathed in deeply, looking around and drinking in the scene greedily, like a man released from a long prison sentence. The familiar scene seemed suddenly inexpressibly dear to her, as to a returning exile, and she choked on the comparison, thinking of her children and where they both were at this moment.

She thought of the last time she had been on this path, coming through this gate. She had been so feverish, so focused on staggering across the road and getting to the sanctuary of home, that she could now barely remember it. Senga had told her that she had nearly killed herself – and a few others into the bargain - causing an accident with the brewer's dray and a couple of cyclists but she had no memory of this and put it down to Senga's propensity for exaggeration.

But she did retain a strong memory of the Anstruther tearoom, although quite how she had got off the bus there and into the shop was only a blur. So much had flowed from that day: a metamorphosis in Jeannie which, astonishingly, had proved permanent and a friendship with her that Kate would never have previously contemplated or considered possible; a remarkable thaw in her relationship with her sister, Aggie, after years of constraint and resentment; a very welcome change in Old Maggie's behaviour and her acceptance of the new order; a new – no, *reclaimed* – relationship with Johnnie who was again the caring, companionable husband she had grown to love in the early years of their marriage; and, perhaps, best of all, a sense of being once again mistress in her own home, of being able to make things happen for good in it, of no longer being simply swept along on a tide of others' needs, demands and assumptions.

She felt strong again in a way that was not simply physical, as if not only her body but her spirit too had been healed.

'*We've a' changed,*' she thought. Even Eck - she still shivered when she thought of screwing up her courage to talk to him last

Sunday - whose acceptance of Aggie's new interest was nothing short of miraculous. Even Annie whose shop was so improved it was barely recognizable. And of course, Senga, who had wrought this sea-change and was fast turning into quite the entrepreneur, displaying all the vision and daring that such a role required, trailing a bewildered but delighted Annie behind her.

Thinking of her, Kate looked over the crossroads to the draper's shop. In fact, she could see Senga now, crouching in the small window, busy changing the display. *Again! That's the third time in a month. An it hadnae changed fur five years afore that!* Kate chuckled and decided to do a little shopping.

Senga was still in the window when Kate went into the shop. Not having been in it since the advent of Senga, she marveled at the changes. Gone was the uninviting, heaped-up clothes rail jumbled with garments and coat-hangers; gone were the messy piles of buttons, ribbons, pins, reels of thread, knitting patterns and other stock that had always littered the counter; gone was the faintly fusty smell that had always seemed to hang in the air. The clothes rail was almost empty, the counter was quite clear and there was only a fresh, floral scent emanating from a large vase of chrysanthemums on it. Everything looked brighter, probably due to energetic cleaning of the window and long-overdue washing of the light-shade.

This would be a quiet day for the draper's, most of the women having bought their new clothes or any haberdashery needed earlier in the week and today belonging to the purchase and preparation of food and drink. A good day to change the window display, therefore, Senga had decided. She was too engrossed in her work to notice Kate crossing the road but, hearing the shop-door bell, she hastily jumped down out of the window into the front shop. She was still holding in her hand a large white card with the word *SALE* on it in bright red letters

'My, Senga,' Kate's glance took in the sparsely stocked rail and empty counter, 'whit are ye goin' tae pit in yer sale? It seems tae me like ye've sold a'thing a'ready!'

Senga's twin-pronged assault on all the old and unwanted stock, through first the mystery parcels then the free nylons, had in truth left very little. And all the desirable new stock – like Aggie's skirt and blouse for the concert – had been snapped up by women desperate for something fresh and fashionable at last after years of privation.

'Ah, weel, Kate,' Senga twinkled at her. 'that's anither story.'

Kate grinned and settled herself on the edge of the window shelf, happy to hear some more of Senga's amazing exploits. It seemed that the budding businesswoman had an auntie in Cupar – *weel, no really an aunt, she wis jist oor neibour when we were growin' up an we were aye in an oot her hoose* – who had two daughters, now grown-up and working in England *in the rag-trade.*

'Whit kind o' trade?' interposed Kate. 'Ye're surely no goin' tae be tryin' tae sell us *rags* next? A' that auld wartime stuff an a' Annie's auld mouldy stock wis bad enough!'

Senga explained that in Manchester, where her old neighbour's daughters worked and where there were dozens of clothing manufacturers, this was the new phrase used for the industry. She had made the bus journey to Cupar one afternoon and the result had been that the daughters had been written to and had proved most helpful, giving Senga names of rag-trade companies springing up in Scotland.

'So the upshot is,' Senga was in full flood now, her plump face flushed and her chins wobbling with excitement, 'there'll be a wee van on *The Fifie* next week fu o' smashin' new clothes fur oor shop. Ah've got a new supplier in Dundee. Ah took a wee sail on the ferry-boat ower the River Tay last week tae meet him an see his stuff. It's smashin', far better than the stuff Annie's been gettin' fur years frae that ither place she's aye used. Ah've ordered a hale lot o' it. But…'she smirked, suddenly looking wily, 'Ah drove a hard bargain an said the first lot had tae be at a knock-down price tae see if ma customers wid like the stuff. That means Ah can afford tae sell them cheaper an *that* means we can still hae oor January Sale – see?'

Kate did see. She saw a woman who had found her métier at last and was blossoming. She saw that things would never go back to how they had been before her illness. She saw that the change in Senga was a mirror of what was happening to them all: Aggie with her choir and concert; Jeannie with her new approach to life and her new job; and Kate herself… Well, her life was going to be different too, after tonight.

'Now,' Senga was brisk, 'is this jist a wee social visit or are ye wantin' tae buy onythin'? 'Cause, if no, Ah'll need tae get on wi this windae.'

'Far be it frae me tae keep ye frae sich important work,' laughed Kate and prepared to take herself off. 'Whaur's Annie the day?'

'She's havin' a lang lie. She wis fair worried aboot no gettin' a wee sleep the nicht afore the bells, wi havin' tae come tae yer pairty.

Kept on an on aboot hoo she wis goin' tae be fair buggered and wid likely no see twelve o'clock. So Ah telt her tae tak the mornin' aff an stay in her scratcher.'

Fired up with all her new ventures in the shop and full of excitement about the forthcoming Get-together in her house, Senga had enough energy for two people, which was proving very lucky for Annie, who rarely had enough for one.

Kate made her way up the street towards the bakery. She spared a glance across the road at the Auld Toll pub. Jeannie had long since confessed the use of 'the new lad' as Kate's original stalker. *Maybe the lad'll come the nicht an see whit it wis a' aboot. Ah hope so.*

It was a morning of queues: at the off-license, as unlucky women whose men had already drunk their New Year bottle had to spend their house-keeping on another one; at the butcher's van along the main road where numerous orders of steak pies were being collected; at the grocery van, up from The Store in Leven, with all the bowls of trifle; and, of course at the bakery where Aggie's stock of shortbread and black bun was diminishing fast. As she approached the bakery queue, Kate was greeted by cries of: 'It's yersel, Kate! Hoo are ye? It's grand tae see ye up an aboot again.'

She moved up the queue slowly, chatting to them all, assuring them of her improving health, asking after their own health and that of their families, feeling like a returning hero and realising with some surprise how much she had missed being part of this community. Assuring them all that she was not going to be buying anything and was therefore not queue-jumping, she moved up to the counter to greet her sister.

Aggie was very busy with customers and Kate had the chance to observe her unnoticed. Aggie was working briskly, with a speed and competence that almost took Kate's breath away. There was about her an air of happy energy and confidence that triumphed over the unkempt hair, the crumpled clothes and the uncared-for skin. As she frisked from task to task and dealt with each customer, she hummed a happy, tuneful air.

As Eck had done on Sunday when he had returned from his snowy tramp home with the dog, Kate saw that a beautiful spirit inhabited this plain woman. *She's happy. She's gettin' tae dae whit she was born tae dae. An it shows.*

Suddenly the frightening effort of talking to Eck paled into insignificance. If this was the result, all her terror had been worth it.

Between them, she and Jeannie had achieved a resounding victory and the result was before her very eyes, which suddenly filled with tears as she remembered the miserable, fraught woman whom she had led away from the ironing board in her sitting-room only ten days ago.

She did not linger, contenting herself with a cheery wave to her sister as she left, calling out: 'See ye the nicht, Ag.' She was tiring now and her last coherent thought as she made her way home was for the shuttered butcher's shop, still sporting the now fading sign, *closed due to illness*.

But it would not be closed much longer and she thought with a sudden surge of pleasure of it being open again, of Angus back in his place behind the counter, of popping in daily as before, but now it would be so different.

The pub was very quiet today. Graham busied himself with the chores that are always waiting to be done in any busy shop and his only customer, big Bob Gilhooley, contentedly sipped his usual pre-dinner dram and browsed through the customers' copy of *The Sporting Herald*. It was another of Graham's innovations: to have a selection of newspapers and magazines that appealed to his male customers. It helped them to linger and sometimes to decide they needed another drink. He was planning to introduce some into the Ladies' Bar as well but needed to consult an expert first. Women's magazines were a mystery to a bachelor like him.

It felt strange to have time to potter like this. The last two weeks had been hectic as the men got into training for Hogmanay and the cold winter weather had made the thought of a warming nip of whisky all the more tempting. Even the Ladies' Bar trade had picked up nicely. First there had been that smart, posh-voiced woman and her friend on Monday evening; then those women from two of the local shops had ensconced themselves and consumed an encouraging number of expensive drinks. They had also been happy to try one of his new lines – tattie crisps – and give him their verdict. It had been favourable enough to lead to the purchase of several packets after their free sample and he had felt quite confident to offer them on the Tuesday night to a rowdy gang of factory girls spending their end-of-year bonuses. Yes, things were going well, despite his enforced three-week absence when his grandmother died.

He sighed, thinking of her now. Keeping busy was a good antidote, or perhaps just a camouflage, for grief but in the quiet moments it sneaked up on him. And this time of year, when families got together and hatchets were buried in a swell of goodwill, he was especially conscious of his solitary state.

There had been time in the two days before Granny died, in her brief periods of lucidity, for a few last, precious chats. Her thoughts had been all of him: of her pride in his successful career; of her memories of his childhood; and of her hopes for his future. He had realised, as never before, how much he owed her.

As a child he had simply accepted that, with his mother and father gone, his granny would take care of him. As an adult, he now saw how much sacrifice and commitment that entailed and he had attempted to thank her, to let her know how much he appreciated all she had done for him.

She had waved his expressions of gratitude away. 'You were a blessin' to me, son. I was just that glad to have you... all I had left. I could have laid down and died maself after your mother was taken and then yer father so soon after. You lit up ma life, God bless you, kept me goin'...'

But then, in their last conversation, she had grown fretful. 'You need to find yourself a nice wife...settle down...have some bairns of yer own. I want to look down from heaven and see ma great-grand-children. Promise me you'll find a nice lassie soon. Dinnae leave it too late.' And he had promised, of course, racked with sorrow and desperate to soothe her.

He thought of the noisy, brash factory girls in the Ladies' Bar last night: no, definitely not his type. But what was? He had been so busy building up his career with the brewery, moving around from pub to pub, 'married to his work' people said of him. But he was thirty now and all his old school pals were husbands and fathers. Soon there would be no eligible lassies left. He'd had a few short-term girlfriends and lots of one-off dates but he had never seriously considered any of them as wife material. But then, he had not considered himself as husband material. If he was to fulfill his promise to Granny on her deathbed, he was going to have to start thinking of himself and the women he dated differently.

It'll have to be my New Year resolution: to go courting. But who? Where? How? He felt no joy at the prospect.

'*You* look like ye've lost a shillin' an fund a sixpence, lad. Cheer up! It's Hogmanay!' Bob had come up to the bar for a pint to chase down his whisky.

'Ach, Bob,' Graham put a pint glass under the beer tap, tilting it expertly to ensure just enough, not too much, head of foam, 'I'm not really in the mood for celebrations this year.'

Feeling the need to confide in someone and trusting this gentle, placid man whom he had got to know over the past few months, he added sadly: 'I always spent it with my Granny. We used to sit up and hear the bells on the wireless and then have a nice wee drink together. She loved Jimmy Shand on the accordion and we would put one of his records on her old turntable and have a wee dance together.' To his horror, he felt his eyes filling with tears.

Bob might not be much good at the quick thinking and quick talking that was his wife's forte, but he was a kind man with deeply compassionate instincts. He cursed himself for his insensitivity in trying to jolly up the young man at such a vulnerable time. He laid a large, solid, understanding hand on Graham's arm and left it there in silence until the young man regained his composure. Then:

'So, whit *are* ye doin' the nicht?'

Graham shrugged and essayed indifference. 'Nothing, really. Early night. Been a busy week.'

'Naw, naw.' Bob was definite. 'That's no the game at a'. Hogmanay's Hogmanay – especially in Methil! Ye cannae spend yer first Hogmanay here goin' awa tae yer bed. It's agin the law!' He ended with a rare joke and guffawed appreciatively at his own wit.

Graham shrugged again. 'I know you all go first-footin'. I've heard you all talking about it. But I don't really know anyone well enough. I mean, I've never been in anyone's house before.'

'Nae problem!' declared Bob. 'Ye're in luck. *This* year it's a' different. There's a big party ower at Johnnie Cruikshanks's hoose, startin' at nine o'clock.' He gestured out the window, 'A'body's invited, a'body's welcome! We're a' bringin' in the New Year there 'cause Kate, his wife, she's been awfy no weel.'

'Is that the lady your wife wanted me to follow to Windygates a couple of months ago? An then you said your wife wasn't interested any more. That was just before I had to rush through to see Granny…'

'Aye, that's her. She's no fit tae gang oot first-footin', so we're a' goin' tae bring in the bells wi them an then gang aff an dae oor first-footin' after. Ye've got tae come! It's goin' tae be gran!'

Bemused, Graham found himself assenting to this plan. It had to be better than mooning over old records and dancing with his shadow.

Johnnie looked out his office window at the gang of men assembling at the pit-head for the back-shift. They all seemed in high good form, laughing and jostling each other good-naturedly. Of course, it helped that the shift on Hogmanay had been reduced to five hours, with the early one not starting till eight in the morning and this one ending at six in the evening.

This had been one of Johnnie's small victories since moving into the corridors of power five years ago. He had argued the case determinedly, wanting the men to see that he had not forgotten their needs and priorities, just because he was now wearing a smart suit to work. The older managers in the industry had dug in their heels, muttering direly about thin ends of wedges, giving the men ideas, and so on.

But Johnnie had persisted, arguing the case from the point of view of safety. The men did not have their minds fully on the job on Hogmanay. It might be regrettable and reprehensible but it was also an incontrovertible truth. By the last two hours of the shift, the men were tiring, longing to get away home and get a few hours rest before the night's jollifications commenced. Concentration was at a severe low and accidents were more likely.

Accidents were damned expensive things – quite apart from any tragic consequences to life and limb – and the mine-owners hated them. It had eventually been this argument that had won the day. It had been his first campaign and he had learned a lot about persuasion and manipulation within mining management structures. Of course, the union had insisted that the early shift be reduced as well which meant a mercifully late start for those men.

Sadly, the men did not know that the boon of the shortened Hogmanay shifts (without any loss of pay) was Johnnie's doing and he had not found a way to make it known without appearing to be bragging.

The line at the pit-head grew and he saw Eck join it, talking to Bob Gilhooley. Johnnie watched him intently. It was true, he thought, Eck did look more relaxed, more at ease with himself and the world. The look he cast round the yard was really quite cheerful and he

311

actually laughed – a rusty sound like an old dog remembering how to bark – when two of the younger men in front broke into a ragged rendition of the *Sailor's Hornpipe*, attempting the steps and gestures of the nautical jig, tripping over their own feet and landing in a tangle on the ground.

What Katy said last night... It's true. He's changed. She's changed him.

They had made love last night for the first time in many months. Even before she had become ill, their intimate moments had dwindled to an occasional and cursory kiss before turning their backs on each other for sleep. It was not anything they had planned or discussed and there had been no row to spark off any resentful or punitive treatment of each other.

He wondered now how it had happened. Perhaps, as he grew into his new role at work, he had unconsciously substituted the adrenalin rush of power, heady stuff when tasted for the first time, for the pleasure of sexual desire fulfilled. Perhaps he had mentally pigeon-holed his wife as belonging to his old life and she had not seemed to belong in the new. She had become no more than background in his world, part of the furniture at best, and certainly useful for solving his dilemma over his old mother's increasing frailty and need for care. And once his mother had moved in, he had felt too inhibited and Kate had simply been too tired, often going off to bed before him and being fast asleep by the time he joined her.

He heard Dr Kenny's pronouncement again. *Your wife is exhausted. She is not a machine.* He felt a familiar, sharp flick from the remorse that had plagued him for the past month.

He had been doubtful when she had begun to make her ideas known to him as they settled down for the night. 'Ye're surely no ready for this yet, are ye, bonnie lass? We dinnae want ye tired out an havin' a setback – no with the party tomorrow night.'

But the very thought of the next day's events seemed to act like an aphrodisiac spur. Her eyes brightened, moist lips parted, little excited giggles escaping between each rapid breath.

He demurred again although he could not help responding to her allure. 'Are ye sure ye're able for this, darlin'? What if..?'

But when her hand had stolen to his enlarged manhood and she murmured, 'Weel! It looks like *someone's* interested even if you're no!' he had given up the fight and taken her in his arms, surprising himself by the tide of passion and delight that engulfed him.

312

Even so, he was tentative, worried about her fragility, and this expressed itself in a gentle tenderness that brought its own rewards. Neither of their climaxes had been full-blown or exhaustive but they had been left with the delicious sense that there was a lot more where that came from, that the future was bright.

Thinking of it now, he felt a tell-tale tightness in his winter drawers and hastily moved his thoughts on, glancing down to check that his suit jacket was still lying quite flat.

It had been during their post-coital pillow-talk that Kate had told him all about Aggie's secret doings over the past few months and the forthcoming concert her sister was starring in. His reaction was similar to that of Kate and Jeannie: delighted for Aggie; not surprised she had been chosen as the soloist; scorn for the Novello show director. Kate's account of the taming of Father O'Malley was not as racy and rib-tickling as Jeannie's had been but the story was good enough to stand up for itself and Johnnie hooted appreciatively, causing Old Maggie to start awake and rap irritably on the floor with her stick. They guiltily stifled their laughter, snuggling down still further in the bed to smother it.

Johnnie had never liked the priest and had resented his interference in their marriage in the early days – he, too, had had the 'wasting seed' talk which led to Eck's cavalier treatment of the young trainee priest. Since he had gone back to his Protestant faith, Johnnie had avoided Father O'Malley at all costs, though he knew that the priest had stopped Kate in the street one day and lambasted her about it, a fact which had endeared the priest to Johnnie still less.

'That Jeannie Gilhooley!' he applauded. 'She should be in that United Nations. She's unstoppable.'

'Ye can say that again!'

They talked too about Aggie's fear of Eck's reaction. It had been some ten years since Agnes and Maisie had come crying to their Aunty Kate's house with the sad tales of what they had to witness and endure at home. Johnnie had not seen the girls since they had emigrated five years ago but he was not likely to forget their sobbed-out stories and how often he had wanted to go round and punch Eck's lights out. Kate had always restrained him: *Ye'll only mak it worse fur Aggie and the bairns.*

These past years he had seen the change from violent bullying to sneering denigration and he had accepted, like them all, that this was an improvement and life was now easier for Aggie. When Kate described how terrified her sister had been of Eck's knowing about her lovely secret, of his acid derision being poured upon it, Johnnie had at first struggled to understand, having always assumed that Aggie was more than a match for her abusive husband, that she barely noticed his sneers and cared even less about them. But Kate had persisted with her tale and explained how Jeannie had discovered from Bob that Eck had a soft spot for his sister-in-law.

'So, it wis a' doon tae me!' Kate exclaimed dramatically, rolling her eyes and making him laugh. 'An it'll be doon tae *you* tae get him a day aff tae go and see her singin' at the concert.'

'So, *that's* why I got banished through to ma mother's room when I brought him home from the park last Sunday? Well, are you no the wee clever clogs? I could do wi you at some o' these damned union meetings, I'm thinkin'. Ye'd likely get better results than me and Chic do when we meet wi Eck an Bob.'

They had settled down to sleep eventually, drifting out on a receding tide of murmured half-remarks half-answered, close, companionable and loving. It was not until he opened his eyes next morning and turned to look happily at his wife that the thought struck him like a wet slap in the face: Kate had wound Eck round her little finger quite easily because Eck was in love with her. The thought that continued to disturb him as the day progressed was not that he had anything to fear from Eck – the chances of Kate having any romantic feelings for him were so unlikely as to be laughable - but rather that, if Eck found her so irresistible, so might other men. Who else might be casting covetous eyes on his precious wife? Just how blind had he been these past years?

The van-man rattled the metal shutter down over the back of the van and, whistling tunelessly, prepared to make the return journey to Leven. He had already opened the driver's door when he was accosted by a shout – well, more of a strangled, wheezing yelp. A plump woman was charging down the street towards him and emitting as much sound as her over-stressed lungs would permit. '*That'll be number 361*,' he thought, '*and aboot bloody time tae!*'

The 'Ne'erday trifles' were ordered through the bakery, which made a nice wee fee for being the agency for The Store in Leven at this time of year. Aggie took the orders from each woman and noted

314

each woman's 'store number'. The Store was a co-operative shop and each customer had a number so that, each time they purchased goods, the amount was noted against their number. Annually, the profits were divided among the customers according to the amount they had spent.

The van had started the day full of trifle-bowls, each with a numbered paper ticket stuck to it, and, by half-past-twelve, all but one of the bowls had been collected. Only number 361 forlornly remained and he had waited the best part of an hour, eating his dinner-time piece, smoking several Senior Service and browsing through an old copy of the *Dundee Courier* which had found its way on to the floor of the van. But he had finally lost patience and decided that number 361 was not coming.

He watched the woman running towards him and reflected that perhaps the time spent waiting had not all been wasted. Her full breasts were jiggling up and down delightfully and her skirt was riding above her knees as she lengthened her stride, showing a fetching glimpse of stocking top. Senga panted up to him and, not quite braking in time, almost fell into his arms.

'Fur peety's sake,' she gasped, 'ye were never drivin' awa wi ma trifle? Whit wis Ah goin' tae gie Kate and Johnnie the morn?'

She had invited her next door neighbours in for Ne'erday dinner, knowing Kate would not be able to go far and that they would be tired, their house in a turmoil after the Hogmanay party. Kate had demurred, saying that Senga had enough on her plate with her job at Annie's shop, her own family and the Get-together on the second. But Senga was giving Jeannie a run for her money in the 'unstoppable' stakes, energised by her new business success. 'It's nae bather at a'. We're eatin' onyway. An there's aye plenty.'

The metal shutter was noisily rolled up again and the enormous trifle duly found its rightful owner at last. The van-man finally drove off whistling cheerfully and Senga moved up the street to the other van which had also been doing brisk business all morning: Terry's butcher-meat.

This would be positively its last appearance, he had been telling them all. Mr. Smillie would be back in his shop on Monday morning and he, Terry, would be there with him, as the new assistant. The never-ending queue had been buzzing with the news – news which, if she had been the woman she used to be, Jeannie could have told them days ago.

Senga was one of the last to hear it, having been in the draper shop all morning and only now getting time to collect her Ne'erday steak pies – three large ones which would easily feed the six adults and five children who would be squeezing round her table tomorrow. She acknowledged the information vaguely, having a great many other things on her mind, not least juggling the basket with the trifle in it and the string bag with the three pies, only just managing to drum up enough polite concentration to reply when he asked her what she was doing tonight for Hogmanay.

'Ma neibour's havin' a party frae nine o'clock the nicht. We're a' stayin' tae bring in the New Year wi her an then goin' first-footin' frae there. She's been no weel an cannae get oot hersel so…'

'Fancy that!' Terry marveled. 'That's exactly the same as me. I've been invited to one just like that as well – and here in Methil too.'

'Well, that's maybe whaur ma neibour got the idea.' Senga was lapsing into vagueness again, her mind dwelling on all she had to do before presenting herself at eight o'clock tonight as promised, to help with the party preparations.

Jim Kenny scanned the waiting room before his late afternoon surgery. It was half-empty as was usual. Funny how people just didn't have time to be ill on Hogmanay! But there would be a waiting-room full of woebegone survivors on Friday all declaring that their upset stomachs and splitting headaches had nothing to do with the amount of alcohol consumed in the past two days and that their hacking, spluttering coughs had likewise nothing to do with the number of cigarettes smoked.

Self- abuse was rife at this time of year and he was resigned to the impossibility of persuading his patients to behave wisely. Besides, they lived hard lives and this was their annual escape, these two crazy days of over-indulgence and frenzied enjoyment. He could not find it in his heart – however much his professional instincts winced at the implications for their health – to condemn them.

He dispatched the dozen patients easily in an hour-and-a-half and was on the point of shutting up shop half-an-hour early when there came a hesitant tap on his door and a woman's scarf-covered head appeared round it. It was Kate Cruikshanks.

He had suggested to her at his last visit several days ago that, if she felt up to it and the weather was not too bad, she might come to the surgery for her next check-up. He rose to greet her delighted.

'It's good to see you in the land of the living again, my dear.' He examined her bright eyes and rosy cheeks approvingly. 'And looking very well.'

He paused to snatch his handkerchief out of his pocket and sneeze into it – he was nursing a cold. 'Forgive me. Maybe *I* should be consulting *you*!'

They both laughed as they moved to sit on opposite sides of his desk. Over the past month, they had somehow become like friends, discovering something of a shared worldview and an appreciation of each other's character. He had often lingered for *a wee blether*, making time in his busy schedule, counting it as a treat, a well-earned break in his day.

The medical formalities concluded and Kate's improving condition applauded, albeit with the ever-cautious rider, 'But don't overdo it. One step at a time', he walked her through to the empty waiting-room. Daylight was fading rapidly now.

'The auld year's dyin',' she said whimsically as they looked out through the glass of the door. Then she gave a sudden, intense shiver and a little gasp. He caught her barely contained excitement like a blast from a hot oven whose door has suddenly been yanked open.

She whirled round and smiled at him. 'Whit are ye doin' fur Hogmanay yersel?'

Surprised, he blinked uncertainly at her. 'Well, we don't really *do* anything much. The street we live in…well, the folks have grown old mainly. Eleanor and I are about the youngest ones there now. We sit up for a bit in case anyone calls after midnight but last year no-one did. So we may not bother this year.'

'That soonds like a richt damp squib!'

'You could say that!' he laughed. He loved the way she called a spade a shovel.

'Look, Doctor, jist tell me tae shove aff if Ah'm speakin' oot o' turn but wid ye like tae come tae ma Hogmanay party? Wi me havin' been ill…'and she explained the rationale for the party and its extensive, elastic guest list. 'Hauf o' Methil will likely be there. It's goin' tae be the berries! Och, why no come, you and yer wife?'

'Why not indeed?' he mused. Eleanor had always loved a party - they had met at one in their student days - and she loved new

experiences, having preserved a lot more youthful enthusiasm and willingness to take risks than he had. He felt suddenly light-hearted, devil-may-care, more like the daft medic student he had once been.

'I'll certainly give it serious thought,' he promised.

'Ach, dinnae dae that, fur ony's sake,' she parried. 'There's no goin' tae be onything serious aboot it. It's a pairty!'

They were both giggling like bairns as he let her out into the lamp-lit street.

The two men tramped cheerfully up the Avenue, quite unlike their usual end-of-shift progress. Of course, the shortened shift had helped and the five hours had flown by as the men sang, whistled, joked and teased their way through the afternoon. Everyone was in a fine mood, looking forward to good food, good drink, good company and a day off work tomorrow. Some of the men were planning to respond to the open invitation to Johnnie and Kate's party and there was talk of that; others had their own fish to fry in family or neighbourly groupings; all were in high good humour and the dreary, dirty pit had rung with the sound of their happy banter.

From time to time, one of the good singers had started up a well-known song and gradually they had all joined in, even the dour-faced foremen. Words describing Scottish scenes of great natural beauty – The Banks of Loch Lomond, Bonnie Strathyre and Rothesay Bay – had echoed through the gloomy caverns and tunnels.

Many of the men had been told by their wives about Aggie's concert and some of them had even been paying enough attention to remember being told. A few diehard Catholic types had voiced tight-lipped disapproval and doubt about the tales that Father O'Malley was in favour of it.

However, one particularly determined disapprover had actually brought the subject up with the priest after mass last Sunday. He had been able to report, with considerable disappointment, that it was all true. The priest had read him a lecture about prodigal sons and angels celebrating in heaven over sinners repenting - and had sent him on his way with a flea in his ear. There had been some head-shaking and confused murmuring but the authority of the priest had always been paramount and, although now severely challenged and even rocked a little, it was holding firm.

What was a great deal more interesting to most of the men was what *soor-faced Eck* was making of it. Bob and Eck had already had a discussion about it on their way to work. Bob had, of course, been told all about it the night before by Jeannie, once she was sure that the story was for public consumption, albeit not through *her* megaphone. She had got over that disappointment once she had completed her damage limitation exercise and, in any case, it had been superceded by the excitement of getting her new job.

Inevitably, the details were somewhat blurred in Bob's head, mixed up as they were in plans connected with broth and dumplings and Jeannie's arresting appearance at his bedside, fully dressed and perfectly groomed at eight o' clock in the morning. Not to mention a muddled background of wishes, commands, ladyships and chiels. However, he had managed to blunder cheerfully in where angels might fear to tread, saying, 'Ah heard yer Aggie's goin' tae be singing at some big do. Ye must be richt prood o' her.'

He was agreeably surprised by Eck's response. It said much for the miraculous effects of Kate's intervention that Bob did not get the response he expected. Something along the lines of 'Ah'll gie her prood! Bloody trollop! Dis she think onyone wants tae look at *her* up on a stage? Folk dinnae pay guid money tae look at ugly buggers like her' would certainly not have surprised Bob.

Unwittingly, Bob had struck exactly the right note, echoing Kate's *Do ye show that ye're prood o' her an interested in whit she sings?* Eck made a deep sound in his throat, as if releasing long-throttled emotion, a *harrumph* that startled Bob and made him stop in his tracks. Eck did not notice so that Bob had to hurry to catch up and was not sure he really had heard a-right.

'Ah'm thinkin' o' goin' tae see her masel.'

Bob was *dumfoonered*, as he later recounted to Jeannie. 'Goin' tae see her? You?' he burst out. If Eck had declared his intention of dressing up as Santa Claus and coming down the chimney with a sack of toys, Bob would not have been more astonished.

Eck fixed him with a beady glare. 'Whit's wrang wi that?' he asked belligerently. 'Ah'm goin' tae ask fur the day aff and high-an-michty Johnnie Cruikshanks had better gie me it or Ah'll ken the reason why!'

His response to the sly questions from the other men about Aggie's secret celebrity status was in the same vein and the men's curiosity and their hopes of goading the snarling beast – traditionally a popular game to enliven a dull shift – withered on the vine. Eck had indeed bearded Johnnie in his den at six o'clock when they came up to the surface and had come out of the deputy manager's office with a satisfied smirk on his face.

The walk home, therefore, was a follow-on from the earlier walk to work. Eck was positively triumphant. With unerring instinct, Kate had given Eck the very motivation he needed to go to the concert by hingeing it on Johnnie's capitulation.

'He didnae hae a leg tae stan on,' declared Eck, delightedly. 'Ah jist telt him:
ma wife has been knockin' her pan in seein' tae *his* wife fur weeks. He owes me! That pit his gas at a peep!'

In truth, primed by Kate, Johnnie had been glad to arrange for Eck to have the day off *on compassionate grounds*, though he did not use that phrase to Eck. That would go in his written report in Eck's personnel file and Eck would never know of it. Johnnie had been pleasant, accommodating and had even attempted familial solidarity, expressing his own pride in Aggie's success, which Eck had brushed aside. Eck preferred *his* version of the story, keeping his worldview of workers-against-management intact.

As they parted at number 22, with cheerful promises of seeing each other later that night at the party, Bob reflected that *'there's none sae queer as folk'*.

Aggie watched the two men from the upstairs bedroom window where she was dressing after a long, hot bath. The bakery shelves had been almost empty by four o' clock and she had thankfully closed up early, scooping the last few cakes and biscuits into a bag and hurrying over the road to Kate's house with them. There was already enough stored-up party food there to feed an army but still… Y*e can never hae too much on Hogmanay.*

She had found the house in silence as she slipped in through the open door, both ladies being asleep in the sitting-room, Old Maggie still in her chair by the dark window and Kate stretched out on the couch, only the glow of the fire illuminating the room. Aggie considered closing the curtains, banking up the fire and making their afternoon cup of tea but she decided against it. They all had a long

320

night ahead of them. *They* needed their afternoon nap and *she* needed to get home and ease her aching legs in a hot tub.

Wallowing in the delicious, scented foam – Kate had given her a bottle of gloriously flowery bubble-bath for Christmas, with sweet though misspelled expressions of gratitude on a sugary card that had made Aggie snort with mild, indulgent scorn - Aggie let her thoughts slide past the evening ahead, past the unwelcome prospect of an afternoon and evening in the company of Eck's sister Peggy and her very boring husband, where they were going for Ne'erday dinner, and on to the day of the concert.

In her mind, she re-played for the umpteenth time the anticipated sequence of events: an early morning bath and into her new underwear with an old skirt and cardigan on top; round to Mina's house to get her hair done; back home to change into her new skirt and blouse and powder her nose; up the road to the kirk to meet with the group of sopranos; a drive in one of their husbands' cars to Kirkcaldy; the famous light lunch in the café; picked up from there by the choir bus; on to Burntisland for the afternoon rehearsal; and, at last… The Concert!

The early events in the sequence she could easily picture. The later ones were uncharted territory and she could only imagine what they would be like. Her happy excitement exploded into unrestrained singing, the grimy, steamy bathroom amplifying it beautifully so that she felt wrapped in and transported by the music.

Thank God she did not have to think that it was all going to come to an end after the concert! Jeannie had been right: there was no way she could have just given one performance and then stopped. It had become the breath of life to her, bringing her alive as never before.

She left the bath water for Eck, adding a little more of the bubble-bath to it. *We'll be smellin' like a pair o' nancy-boys!* She thought of his hard, hairy body sinking into the silky, scented water. Oddly enough, the thought of that hard, hairy body did not fill her with the usual resigned revulsion. Indeed she even felt a flicker of… not exactly desire, but perhaps a kind of indulgent interest.

He had been unbelievably pleasant to her since Sunday. They had not spoken much about the choir and the concert beyond practical arrangements. He knew he was expected at Bob and Jeannie's for his noon-day dinner that day. But when it had cropped up, he had been casually accepting, as if this sort of thing had always been part of their lives. When she had talked a little of how she had seen the billboard

321

outside the church and gone along to the try-out, only to find herself immediately engaged as the soprano soloist, he had simply said:

'Weel, they had the sense tae ken a guid thing when they saw it.' And she had lit up inside just as if he had showered praises on her. After twenty years of being ignored and insulted, Aggie lapped up the scantiest crumbs of encouragement from him.

Now she finished dressing and gave herself a cursory glance in the full-length mirror on the wardrobe door. She had thought of wearing her new skirt with an old blouse for Hogmanay, keeping only the white blouse clean for the concert. But Annie had persuaded her otherwise. It had been one of the many things they had talked about in the Ladies' Bar on Monday evening.

'Dinnae chance it,' Annie had counselled. 'Some drunken bugger'll likely spew his guts up a' ower ye.'

It was a fair risk assessment. Two years ago Aggie had had to consign a frock to the bin after just such inconsiderate, deplorable behaviour from Chic Carswell, one of Johnnie's fancy management pals, who had unwisely mixed his drinks and ended up lying in a heap in a corner, not looking very fancy at all.

Annie had come up trumps and found a frock that had managed to escape Senga's clutches. It was not exactly the latest fashion, being of pre-war vintage, but it was new up to a point and it fitted Aggie's slender figure well, even giving it a little grace.

She heard Eck's foot on the stair and came out on to the landing. 'Ah've left the bath water fur ye,' she said, as she passed him and he caught a strong whiff from her of the soapy, jammy smell that was also emanating from the open bathroom door.

'Is it the bubble-bath again, then? We'll be smellin' like twa posies frae the flooer shop.' He was echoing her own thoughts.

Was he joking? Was he complaining? She did not wait to find out but went on towards the kitchen, calling: 'Ah'm goin' tae mak us a wee somethin' tae keep us goin' till we go tae the pairty. There's that much food at Kate's that we'll be eatin' a' nicht so Ah didnae think we needed a meal.'

He heaved a sigh of relief. He had been rather despondent at the sight of the bare kitchen table. Half-an-hour later, as they worked their way through a mound of sardines on toast, he said: 'Some of the lads at the pit were talking aboot yer concert an whit Father O'Malley's sayin' aboot it.'

She stopped eating. 'An?'

'Wee Kevin Reilly wis shootin' his mooth aff. He'd even been tae the priest an asked him aboot it.'

'An whit did Father Brian say tae him?' Aggie held her breath.

'Och the wee shite wis bletherin' bits o' the bible at us aboot prodigal sons and angels. Seems he got it frae the priest. Onyway, he got a flea in his ear an the rest o' them calmed doon when they heard that Father O'Malley's on yer side.'

Aggie let out her breath in a fishy puff. 'Ye ken whit, Eck? Ah think Ah'll gang tae confession the nicht afore Ah gang tae Kate's.'

'Oh, aye? Whit fur?'

'Tae confess ma sins, of coorse. An Ah micht jist gang roon the ither side of the confession box and gie that bonnie auld mannie a cuddle!'

Father O'Malley was tiring. It had been a long session. The Hogmanay queue of slate-cleaners seemed never-ending and the repetitious catalogues of sins were running through his weary brain like a broken record. And he was bursting for a pee.

As yet another absolved sinner left the box, he rose and came out into the church. Raising his hand in vague acknowledgement to the waiting penitents, he headed for the lavatory in the vestry at the side of the altar.

When he returned, he saw that his next customer was none other than his prodigal, Mrs Fairweather, the very cause of all the current angelic glee. He felt a renewed sense of calling that was not simply the result of relieving his bladder. He could not, of course, acknowledge her, the secrecy of the confessional being absolute.

Aggie slipped easily into the formula of childhood. 'Bless me, Father, for I have sinned…' But, to his relief, she did not waste her time in a diatribe of pointless peccadilloes but characteristically came straight to the point. 'Ah've no been at mass fur years. An Ah've often felt like murderin' that bugger Ah'm married tae!'

He was thoughtful, soothing even. 'Just feeling like doing something is not at all the same as doing it. That's just temptation and we all have it. The fact that you've resisted doing it is to your credit. God will reward you for that.'

She was surprised, her memories of confessional experiences not having in the past included this sort of leniency. 'But whit aboot no comin' tae mass?' she demanded, determined to make a clean breast of it now that she was here.

'Well, if you make up your mind to become a regular attender from now on … You have been in the wilderness but God's arms are always open to welcome back a sinner. That's why Christ died.'

He hesitated, skating round the boundaries of confessional confidentiality. Then, taking the bull by the horns, 'But is it strictly true you've not been at mass for two years? Not even at Christmas? Maybe midnight mass?'

He's rumbled me! Ach, God bless the auld soul! She felt an urge to burst into a rousing chorus of *I know that my redeemer liveth*, but she contained herself with difficulty and, bowing her head submissively, murmured such a heartfelt Act of Contrition that he felt sure he could hear those angels whooping it up in heaven.

Aggie came out of the church ten minutes later, having duly parroted the decade of the rosary that had been her penance. *'Ah made the auld soul's nicht,'* she thought with satisfaction. *'That's us a' square.'*

Then she set her course for Kate's house, light of heart and conscience, ready to plunge into party preparations.

A blast of heat met Aggie on the stairs. The door at the top of them was wide open and through it came some cheerful noise and a great deal of warmth. One thing, at least, that miners were never short of was coal and on Hogmanay the home fires were always blazing. Aggie thought of the old song her father had always sung when midnight came:

The fire was burning brightly
'Twas a night that would banish all sin
For the bells were ringing the old year out
And the New Year in!

She let the memory flood over her, a wave of rare nostalgia. *Och, Ah'm gettin' maudlin' afore Ah've even had a drink!*

As she moved into the house, she saw that the first door on the right was closed: formerly Maureen's girlish bedroom and now Kate and Johnnie's. She could hear voices in it, women's voices, and she could not help lingering to eavesdrop. It was Kate and Jeannie murmuring, frustratingly low, the aura of secrecy and complicity seeping out under the door like gas.

Aggie was about to concede defeat when Jeannie raised her voice: 'She's nothin' like Ah imagined. Nothin' like Angus. Kinda prissy and school-marmy but with a richt fiery glint in her ee. Pits me in mind o' a book Ah read aince aboot a schoolteacher in Edinburgh. Miss Jean Brodie she wis ca'd. It wis a gran story.'

Who could Jeannie be talking about? And who was Angus? Aggie had forgotten about the Windygates mystery and had never known about Kate's alleged links with the butcher. Aggie had been much too wrapped up in her own problems and their recent happy resolution to maintain an interest. Kate's voice suddenly sounded alarmingly close to the door and the handle rattled. Aggie started back.

'Come on, Jeannie,' Kate was saying. We'd better get on wi the work or folk'll be arrivin' an no a bit o' food or drink oot fur them.' The bedroom door was opening. Aggie dodged hastily across the lobby into Old Maggie's room.

Here an arresting sight met her eyes. The old woman was sitting fully-dressed on top of her bed staring fixedly at the wall opposite. Aggie could hear what she took to be a wireless broadcasting loudly.

Whit's she starin' at? Has she lost her marbles? Going to the side of the bed she followed the old woman's gaze. *In the name o' the wee man! Whit's that?*

A polished wooden box sat on a small table. Its small screen was showing rather blurry moving pictures and the broadcasting was coming from this box. Aggie tapped Maggie on the shoulder and the old woman unwillingly dragged her gaze away from the screen.

'Whit the hell is that?' Aggie mouthed. She approached the box fearfully and tentatively turned one of the knobs on the front of it. The noise level abated, to her relief, and it did not blow up in her face, which she counted as a lucky escape.

'It's a *tell-lay-viz-ee-on*,' enunciated Maggie with pride. 'Johnnie bought it for me. It's like the wireless and the pictures combined in yer own house.'

The old woman returned her attention to the magic box and Aggie realised it would be a waste of time trying to re-engage her. Instead, she sat down on the side of the bed and, for the next ten minutes, the two women stared at a ventriloquist with a dummy on his knee, magically making the dummy, which was called Lord Somebody and sported a monocle, talk. They were mesmerised that the ventriloquist could talk in his own voice one second and in the dummy's the next, without moving his lips as the dummy talked.

'That's amazin'. Yon's a clever wee mannie,' declared Aggie as the show ended. 'An whit a gran thing that is! Jist like the picters an the wireless a' rolled intae ane, as ye say.' She collected her wits and rose: 'Ah'll better go though an see if Ah'm needed tae help wi getting ready fur the pairty.'

'Well, I'll no be through till the programmes have a' finished,' Maggie was definite. 'Whenever *that* is. Mind ye keep some o' the food fur me.'

Aggie laughed. 'Ah dinnae think there's ony danger o' it runnin' oot!'

She marveled at how much easier Maggie was to deal with these days and this new-fangled box of tricks would keep her more contented still. *An that can only be good news fur Kate. Ah'm glad.*

She thought with some shame of how she used to think of her sister: that *Kate had had a damn soft life up till now, compared with the rest of them, and it was her turn to suffer a wee bit. Maybe help her appreciate what other folk had had to put up with while she lived in the lap of luxury.* Now Aggie no more wanted to identify with that old mean-spirited mindset than she wanted Maggie to backslide into the implacable *greetin'-faced auld bugger* she had been.

'The auld soul wis likely jist missin' her ain hame an her independence an took it oot on Kate,' she thought, with a flash of insight.

She moved towards the sitting-room, meeting Jim, Senga's husband, coming out with an empty coal-scuttle, bent on re-filling it from the bunker outside. The room had been transformed: the gate-leg table had been moved into the bay window, extended to its full length and covered in a beautiful, embroidered tablecloth (on loan from Senga); every chair and stool in the house had been gathered up and squeezed around the room in a tight, ill-assorted circle; and by the kitchen door stood a table sporting a promising array of bottles and glasses.

Annie was sitting at the table in the window, absorbed in the task of folding paper serviettes and interleaving them with plates. Her bulk had been proving difficult to accommodate in the bustle of furniture arrangement and Kate had tactfully found her this sedentary task. Senga was on her hunkers sweeping the grate, her back to Aggie, skirt stretched so tight over her rotund backside that the outline of her knickers and suspender belt showed. From the kitchen, came the sound of Kate and Jeannie still in conversation, though no longer of a secret content, with the clatter of cutlery and crockery and the *whoosh* of a tap being turned on.

Of Johnnie, there was no sign. The working-lunchers were having a non-working Hogmanay supper party and would be all sitting in *The Cross Keys* in St Andrews at this moment, wreathed in cigar smoke and satisfied contemplation. It had been a good year for yield and profit.

She moved into the kitchen doorway and surveyed the scene. Every available surface was covered in food. Jeannie was putting the finishing touches to an impressive mound of sandwiches, buttering the open end of the loaf first before cutting the slice off, in the old style. None of them had quite accepted the new 'sliced bread' that was beginning to appear and Aggie had had difficulty selling the few loaves she had tried in the shop. No-one really trusted that it could be as fresh as a traditional whole loaf that you cut yourself slice by slice as you needed it.

The sparse remains of a beef roast, a ham knuckle and a hunk of red cheddar, along with a large jar of mustard and a big pot of home-made chutney gave clues to the fillings. Kate was delicately cutting thin slices of black bun, her tip of her tongue protruding as she concentrated on achieving uniformity of size and shape in each slice.

On the rest of the work-tops: plates of sultana cake, cherry cake, Madeira cake and shortbread; bags of dolly mixtures and jelly babies, tubes of Smarties and wee iced fairy cakes for the children; bowls of pickled onions and soused herring; oatcakes spread with strong green-veined cheese – Kate had remembered that Eck liked this; and smart little chocolate wafer triangles, Johnnie's favourite - he could afford some expensive tastes these days.

'God bless the work!' Aggie sang out on a deep monotone, giving her voice the timbre of a solemn, churchy AMEN. The two women whirled round, catching the allusion to Aggie's successful wooing of Father O'Malley, and they all laughed together, sharing the in-joke.

Aggie felt an instant, heart-warming sense of inclusion. Kate and Jeannie might be the best of friends and obviously well into some plot together, but they now happily parted ranks and opened their charmed circle to her. The recent teamwork to overcome the difficulties around the concert had given her the entrée.

'Ah've jist cam' frae havin' a wee chat wi Maggie,' said Aggie. 'Weel, no much o' a chat. We maistly jist sat on her bed and goggled at that wee box wi the screen. She's fair enamoured o' it, is she no?'

'Telly-vision.' Kate nodded happily. 'It wis Johnnie's idea. It a' started when Ah sent him through tae have his tea and cake wi his mither last Sunday whilst Ah spoke tae Eck aboot yer concert. Mind Ah telt ye hoo Ah managed tae get him on his ain?'

'We mind fine.' Aggie and Jeannie spoke in admiring unison. They were both still in a little awe of Kate's courage and cleverness in this matter and Aggie had begun reluctantly to toy with the idea of actually taking an encouraging interest in his union work as Kate had instructed her. *It's got tae be a twa-wiy stretch, Ag, if ye're wantin' him tae keep it up an let ye cairry on wi yer choir after yer concert.*

'Weel, she wis tellin' him that afternoon aboot a' the wireless programmes she listens tae an hoo much she enjoys them - that wis *you* that got her started on them, Jeannie, ye wee smartie – an then, the verra next day, his boss wis tellin' him hoo he'd bocht his wife a telly-vision fur her Christmas an she didnae like it, didnae even want it in the hoose. She's the nervous type, Ah think, an she watched somethin' on it that pit her aff her sleep. So, Johnnie – he's never ane tae let the grass grow under his feet – he made him an offer fur it, richt there an then. The boss wis that pleased tae get rid o' it sae easily that he paid fur the electrical mannie tae come an pit up the aerial and connect it up early this afternoon. Did ye no see the aerial on the roof? It looks like we're goin' tae tak aff tae the moon!'

'Ah never noticed it. It wis dark when Ah cam' ower on ma way hame frae the shop. An Ah never looked up, onyway.'

'The programmes dinnae start till aboot four in the afternoon – and that's jist Andy-Pandy fur the bairns - and they finish at half-past-nine. But it'll fill in the hoors between tea-time and bed-time jist gran fur her. She gets awfy fed up then sometimes.'

Kate actually sounded sympathetically glad for the old woman rather than just *awfy fed up* herself as she had in the dismal, recent past and the change was not lost on the other two women who exchanged mutually gratified glances. They might not put it into words but they both knew they had done a lot more for Kate than just looking after her household whilst she was ill.

'Weel . . . ' - Aggie glanced at the kitchen clock - 'that's a quarter-tae-nine. Ah'll better start gettin' this stuff through tae the table. That doorbell will be startin' tae ring ony time noo.'

328

Kate and Jeannie squeaked in panic and began frantically to finish their tasks and clear up.

And so, at last, all was ready: the fire burning brightly with a replenishing bucket of coal ready in the clean-swept grate; the food table groaning with goodies and the drinks table buckling with bottles; the kitchen neat and tidy; Kate and her helpers seated demurely round the room, enjoying a well-deserved first drink.

Johnnie arrived home just in time to play mine host, a role he always excelled in, provided he did not have to do any of the preparatory work that preceded the event.

The first half-an-hour was not encouraging. Only two people came and they were Bob and Eck, so that the four couples and Annie sat round the room, the women listening to Senga prattling on about January sales, embroidery and the food she was planning for the Get-together, the men talking football and gardening, doggedly avoiding politics, unions, mines and anything else likely to ignite a Johnnie-Eck confrontation.

Kate was beginning to think that the idea of visiting a house *before* midnight on Hogmanay was just too radical for this community and the fear of failure, combined with her barely suppressed excitement every time she caught Jeannie's eye, was making her feel rather sick.

But, at last, at twenty-to-ten, the doorbell rang and Johnnie leapt up in relief and rushed down the stairs. He was delighted to find Dr Jim Kenny and his wife. Kate had told him, when he had popped home to change his shirt before heading to St Andrews, that she had invited them and they had speculated on whether the doctor would come.

'He's no much o' a lad for fraternising with his patients,' Johnnie had warned her. 'He's a good doctor and he's looked after ye right well these past weeks but he likes to keep his professional an private lives separate.' But Kate had discounted this *high-falutin' management-speak* and remained optimistic.

Behind the doctor, loomed the tall figure of Graham from the pub. The bar had been busy until eight o'clock with back-shift men celebrating their early escape from the pit, but the last hour it had been almost empty as they went home to snatch a wee sleep and then get spruced up for the impending jollifications. Graham had been able to complete his nightly tidy-up routine even before half-nine, close up as soon as it came and stroll across the road.

After that, it was as if everyone else had been watching to see if anyone was really going to go to the party for, as soon as these three arrived, people came streaming out of their houses to join in the fun. The doorbell rang constantly, though many people simply came straight in on the noisy tide.

By half-past-ten every room was occupied, even the smallest bedroom – Robbie's old room – where people simply pushed the packets of 'continental pads' aside and sat on the floor using them as backrests. Kate had worried as to how they could make space in the sitting-room for Maggie's wheelchair but, in the event, it was not necessary. Maggie did not need to come to the party. It came to her and her room was full of people, sitting on the bed, leaning against the walls, perched on the window sill, even sitting on the commode with its lid closed. She was happily holding court, telling them all about the wonders of television and giving a minute-by-minute account of all she had watched that evening.

Chic Carswell, when not mixing his drinks, - he had a regrettable tendency to experiment, usually with disastrous results – was a *dab-hand wi the squeeze-box* and soon the house was full of lilting accordion music with several people taking turns at the piano to follow his lead. Terry, the butcher-van lad, had brought his fiddle, Tam-from-the-Offie produced a surprisingly tuneful sound from a comb with a sheet of paper over it and Jimmy, the brewery-man, contributed the percussion by means of rapping two spoons up and down his arm. It was a grand noise.

Senga's oldest son boldly asked Nellie's oldest daughter up to dance. She consented, blushing but delighted, and, in the tiny space left in the middle of the sitting-room, they swung round on each other's arm, knocking over plates and glasses as the lassie's skirt billowed out.

Many of the tunes they played were Jimmy Shand numbers and Graham felt himself becoming sorrowful. When Chic struck up the *High Level Hornpipe*, which had been his granny's favourite, he rose quietly and began unobtrusively to make his way out of the house. '*It was a mistake to come,*' he thought. '*I can't bear it.*'

Bob had spotted him and moved to catch him on the stairs. For a moment, the two men did not speak. Then Graham made a helpless gesture and sank down on one of the stairs. Bob discreetly closed the inside door, sat down beside him and offered him a cigarette. They smoked in silence for a few minutes then Graham began to talk about his beloved Granny: about his childhood memories; about her funny wee ways; about the time they fell out about something – he could not now remember what - and didn't speak for a whole week; about the trips to Broughty Ferry beach and the funny old bathing costume with matching hat that she always wore; about the presents she always gave him, totally predictable and unvarying – he had more ties and socks than any man he knew; and so on and so on.

Bob listened and sighed, nodded, shook his head or chuckled, whatever the memory merited. At last, after half-an-hour, Graham simply stopped talking and sat with the tears running down his cheeks. Bob handed him his handkerchief in silence and waited, conveying no sense of hurry, no idea of judging, no feeling of need to utter comforting platitudes. At last, Graham took his own cigarettes out of his pocket and, after offering Bob one, shakily lit up his own.

'You're a treasure, Bob,' he said quietly. 'I can't think of anyone else I could have done that with.'

Bob beamed modestly. 'Ye were needin' it, son,' he said simply. 'Ye were needin' it.' And they rose and went, arm in arm, back into the busy throng.

Jeannie accosted Bob as he surveyed the drinks table and set about pouring himself another dram. 'Whaur hae ye been? Ah wis lookin' fur ye.'

He patted the side of his nose with a forefinger. 'Wid *you* no jist like tae ken, Miss Nosey-Knickers. Mind yer ain business!'

She looked askance. *Miss Nosey-Knickers* was a regular character in several of their fantasy games. She glanced furtively round the room, afraid others might have heard, but no-one was paying them any attention. She moved a little closer and inclined her head, encouraging him to lean down into earshot. Then she whispered 'Ah'll be mindin' yours, lad, later, dinnae think ye'll get awa wi that!'

Then she turned her back and moved away so quickly that he was left standing alone with a remarkably fatuous grin on his florid face.

By quarter-past-eleven, the musicians were in need of a break and the cry went up for Aggie to sing. To everyone's surprise, she called for requests. Usually she sang exactly what she wanted, disdainfully ignoring requests, and they had simply to be grateful for what she gave them.

But tonight this was a new, happy Aggie: she was jovial and accommodating, only protesting that, if she sang all the many songs they were clamouring for, she would run into the bells at midnight.

It was a new Eck too, they could not help noticing. There were none of his usual snide comments and feigned boredom at the thought of his wife singing. He even put in a suggestion for a song and helped her struggle to her feet, out of the tight corner into which she was wedged. Only Jeannie noticed how he darted a glance under his beetle-brows to see if Kate had noticed this unprecedented courtesy to his wife and she saw the approving smile and almost imperceptible wink that Kate flashed him.

'Go'an yersel, Katy,' thought Jeannie. 'Ye've got that man eating oot o' yer haun.' She had never liked Eck, particularly hating the way he spoke so disparagingly of Bob as a *brainless big saftie* but still used him as a sounding board and mental prop. It gave her no small satisfaction to see Eck behaving like an infatuated puppy, pleading for approval.

'Richt,' Aggie composed herself. 'Ah'll gie ye ane Scottish, ane Irish and ane Novello an that'll hae tae dae ye the noo.' She took a deep breath, fleetingly imagining herself on The Alhambra stage and feeling her heart-beat quicken. After *My Love is like a Red, Red Rose* and *Danny Boy,* she ended with Novello's *I can give you the starlight,* and an appreciative sigh, worth ten times more than facile applause, rippled round the house as tears were wiped and noses blown.

Amid the murmurs of 'Jist lovely, Aggie' and 'Ye get better every year', Jeannie leapt up.

'Holy Moses! It's nearly quarter-tae-twelve an wid ye look at the mess in here!'

For the next ten minutes, the house resembled a scene from an old silent film, as they raced about jerkily, the women clearing plates and half-eaten food away, the men straightening furniture, opening all the windows to let the Old Year out and the New Year in, charging everyone's glass ready for the midnight toast.

Only Kate did nothing. She sat very still, her face ashen and her breathing rapid. No-one noticed until Johnnie turned to ask what she wanted in her glass for the midnight toast. Then he let out a shout of horror and rushed over to her, calling out for Dr Kenny.

'Dinnae fash yersel!' she muttered shakily. 'Ah'm a' richt.'

332

Dr Kenny looked keenly at her and felt her pulse. 'You're just a bit over-excited and over-heated.' He raised his voice. 'Get this lady a large glass of cold water.'

He turned back to Kate. 'Drink it all before you have any more alcohol, my dear. And calm down. It's only Hogmanay. There's one every year.'

She smiled tremulously at him. 'Ah ken, silly o' me…' but he could see she was trembling and he remembered the sudden blast of palpable excitement that afternoon when she had begun talking about the Old Year passing. *'There's something else afoot here,'* he thought.

By the time Kate had been given her glass of water and the panic had subsided, there were only three minutes to go and the cry went up: 'Wha's goin' tae be the first-foot? Turn on the wireless quick, fur ony's sake, we dinnae want tae miss The Bells!'

Johnnie snatched a lump of coal from the bucket in the grate; Senga ran to the kitchen and found a new packet of tea in a cupboard; Graham, who had been standing in the lobby, bemused, watching all the frantic activity, found himself press-ganged into service.

'Ye're tall, dark and handsome, that's a' that matters,' declared Senga as she put the tea in his left hand.

'Listen for the bells on the wireless – ye'll hear them out the window. Mind ye come in before the last bell.' Johnnie put the lump of coal in his right hand and Graham found himself bundled down the stair and out of the house.

It was a clear, starry night with a breathless hush over the world. He stamped up and down the short path towards the gate. No-one had thought to give him a coat and, after the over-heated house, he felt the frosty cold keenly. He could hear the wireless bellowing out its last minute of broadcasting before the big moment. Otherwise all was silent. You might have thought the house was empty of people, so quiet were they all as they waited.

Then, suddenly, a big black car drew up at the gate and, to Graham's surprise, people started to pour out of it. He recognised one of the Gilhooley twins – they were frequent customers in his bar – jumping out of the driving seat. He did not know the large, beefy man coming more slowly out of the front passenger seat.

Graham moved to the gate and saw three others coming out of the back of the car: the other Gilhooley twin; an unknown, neatly dressed woman; and another young man, with a full head of black curly hair, whom Graham did not recognise. All five of them began to stream towards the gate just as the bells began to peal out.

He half-turned to speak to them; then he remembered Johnnie's admonition: *Mind ye come in before the last bell.*

Recalled to his duties, he hurried up the two outside steps. As he pushed open the front door and began to enter, he felt a heavy, restraining hand on his shoulder. Turning, he saw the big man who had been the front seat passenger.

'Who are *you?* Sorry, but I've got to get in there before...'

He was pulled gently but inexorably aside. The young man with the black curly hair slipped past him and began mounting the stair. He too was carrying a lump of coal and a packet of tea. He turned briefly on the second stair and gave Graham a broad, charming grin.

'Sorry, pal,' - the voice was Scottish but overlaid with a Canadian drawl - 'but my mother would never forgive me.'

Graham followed him upstairs wonderingly. The young man walked confidently into the house, holding up his hand for continuing silence from the people crowding in the doorways of the lobby. And he got it: other than few amazed gasps, the crowd was dumbstruck. *'It's like the second coming,'* thought Graham.

The man pushed open the sitting-room door and paused. He stood, framed in the doorway, looking across the room at Kate.

'Happy New Year!' the Scottish-Canadian voice rang out. She rose. Eyes closed, holding out her arms, she stumbled blindly towards him. Around her, frozen in disbelief, her party guests stared open-mouthed.

'Robbie! Oh, son!' she cried and fainted clean into his arms.

CHAPTER SEVENTEEN

NEW YEAR

Of course, it was pandemonium. All the people who had been crowded into the other rooms had surged out in Robbie's wake and there was now a solid press of bodies in the doorway and in the lobby. Information was passed down the line right out on to the stairs: 'It's young Robbie. He musta cam' hame frae Canada. Kate's passed oot. She wis surely no expectin' him.'

For the second time in five minutes, Johnnie called for Dr Kenny, this time more frantically. The cry was taken up and eventually found its target: Jim Kenny had slipped into Maggie's bedroom just before midnight to get out of the way of the frantic tidying-up and had to be winkled out from a crowded corner and passed through the mob in the lobby like a parcel in a children's party game. By the time he reached the sitting-room, Kate had been laid out on the floor with Johnnie and Robbie kneeling anxiously on either side of her.

The doctor took command. The belt round Kate's waist was unbuckled, the tie neck of the pretty dress was loosened and he bade everyone step back and give her air. He took her pulse and bent down to put his ear to her chest. Then he called for two glasses of cold water. When these came, he dipped his fingers into one of them and sprinkled her face and neck liberally several times. This brought a reaction, to everyone's relief, and he motioned to her husband and son to lift her up and sit her in the armchair. Johnnie put his hands under her armpits and Robbie lifted her legs under the knees.

'On the count of three, son. Ups-a-daisy...'

Reversing towards the chair, Johnnie caught his foot on the edge of the hearth rug and stumbled backwards, plunking himself heavily into the chair and ending up with Kate on his knee. Robbie, still hanging on to her knees, fell on top of them both.

Kate came to with a vengeance. 'In the name o' God,' she gasped. 'Whit are you twa tryin' tae dae tae me?' Then she began to giggle, sob and hiccup all at once, her hands clutching at Robbie's thick black head of hair as it lay in her lap, kneading her fingers in it as if her life depended on it.

Dr Kenny insisted on her sitting down properly and putting her head down between her knees but there was no need really. The faintness had gone, now that the unbearable moment of climax had passed, and she was unwilling to waste time staring at the floor when she could be feasting her eyes on her son. So changed, so strange, so dear, so familiar.

By the time descriptions of the unfolding drama had been conveyed throughout the house and marveled over, people had quite forgotten to wish each other *Happy New Year* and it was only when Chic seized his accordion and began to hammer out a rousing chorus of *A Guid New Year tae yin an a'* that they actually remembered the occasion.

Then the joy of having a homecoming prodigal as a surprise first-foot – *and* from so faraway – gave an air of heightened excitement, even abandonment, to the party. No-one wanted to leave and go first-footing though some regretfully dragged themselves off to answer the call of duty and fulfill promises to elderly, housebound relatives who would be sitting alone, waiting for the first doorbell of the year to ring.

Once he had been through to greet his old grandmother and laughingly evade her demands, just as he had always been able to do, Robbie sat on the floor at his mother's feet for the first hour whilst a queue of well-wishers streamed past them.

Of course, there were questions to be answered: Had she been expecting him? How had he got here and when? Where had he been hiding till midnight? Why had he arrived with Angus Smillie, the butcher who had been away being ill for months? And who was that strange woman with the butcher? What was the Gilhooley twins' part in all this? Why had they all arrived at once? And so on.

Johnnie, standing behind Kate's chair, seemed too dazed and delighted to frame any questions as such but his entire body and facial expression conveyed his bafflement. When Angus came over to wish the little family group a rather formal *Happy New Year*, Johnnie stiffened.

It was not lost on him that the butcher had arrived with Robbie and, as Kate recovered her composure and began to talk to Robbie, he soon picked up from the snatches he could hear and that they could fit in between dealing with the queue that she had indeed been expecting him, that this 'surprise' had been long in the planning.

He was in a considerable state of shock, having gone from concern for Kate's health just before midnight, to the shock of seeing his son – whom he had thought on the other side of the ocean – standing in his sitting-room doorway, to the drama of Kate fainting, to tripping and falling backwards with her in his arms. Even so, his befogged brain could just work out that there was some kind of connection between Kate and Angus Smillie that he had known nothing about.

An unwelcome bell tolled in his head and he was reminded of his thoughts as he drifted off to sleep last night. *If Eck found her so irresistible, who else might be casting covetous eyes? Just how blind had he been?*

From his vantage point, standing behind Kate's chair, he was also able to observe the demeanour and reactions of everyone else to the dramatic turn of events. Particularly interesting were those of the now-obsolete *Holy Trinity*, as he had dubbed them when the rescue package for Kate had been in full swing.

Aggie was frankly and unreservedly delighted and asked no questions, awkward or otherwise. Not one to pry or gossip, she now struck Johnnie as someone living on a different and joyful plain from the rest of them, so that the fine details of other folks' lives concerned her even less than before.

Annie, manoeuvering her bulk with difficulty out of the window corner where she had been squashed for the past three hours and fighting her way across the crowded room to where Kate was holding court, had a triumphant air.

'Ah kent a' alang that you twa were up tae somethin',' she declared loudly, anxious to establish her superior status above the ignorant and amazed mob in the lobby.

Johnnie wanted to ask her 'Which *two* are you talking about?' Did she mean Kate and Robbie or Kate and Angus Smillie or Kate and someone else?? But he did not get the chance nor did he need to.

Jeannie had hung back observing it all with a huge, satisfied smile on her face, contenting herself with a nod of approval to her twins and a complicit grin and wink to Angus, which went unnoticed in the general melee. But at last, it was her turn to come to the throne and offer her New Year wishes. Johnnie saw that her eyes were dancing

337

mischievously and that she was merely play-acting demure and delighted surprise.

Kate leapt to her feet. She had been able to contain herself when Angus had come up, although she had longed to be more demonstrative of her gratitude and her pleasure at seeing him again. But she knew that she must talk in private to Johnnie first and explain it all to him: the last thing she wanted was him getting the wrong idea about her and Angus, not now that she and Johnnie were so close again. When Jeannie stepped forward, she entertained no such qualms. Indeed she probably put all her gratitude for all of them who had played a part in pulling it off, Gilhooley twins included, into the enveloping hug she gave Jeannie.

'Ah'd never hae done it withoot ye. God bless ye, Jeannie, and a Happy New Year tae ye!'

The party was almost ready to break up. It was two o'clock, much later than most people had intended to stay.

Dr Kenny was making meaningful faces at Johnnie who was still standing sentinel behind Kate's chair. Robbie had risen from his worshipful position at Kate's feet and had been moving around the company, greeting old friends, recounting tales of his new life, showing photos of his children and the house where they lived in Montreal, passing on messages and good wishes from his wife, Janet, to *her* family and old friends.

He suddenly came back into the centre of the sitting-room and called for silence. Everyone assumed he was about to propose yet another toast – there had been many – but he only said 'Give me five minutes before y'all leave. Wait here!'

Then he went into the lobby and took a bulky package out of the pocket of the overcoat he had been wearing and which was now hanging up on the row of pegs. He disappeared with it into the bathroom and there was some speculation as to what he could be doing, speculation which turned to excited cries of surprise when he emerged. It said much for their fortitude that they were able to sustain yet another bruising surprise that night.

Robbie was barely recognisable: he had blacked his face completely and painted on enormous white lips and white rings round his eyes, which were snapping with glee. On his hands, he wore huge, dazzlingly white gloves.

'It's Al Jolson!' cried someone and they all laughed. This was a well-known Deep South Black American singer from the twenties whose songs were known and loved on both sides of the Atlantic.

'Ah bet Ah ken whit he's goin' tae sing as weel,' someone else said.

With a fine sense of drama, Robbie walked across the room and dropped to one knee in front of Kate, white-gloved hands clasped on his heart.

'Maaaammy! Maaaaammy!' he sang. He had obviously been practicing, honing the act for this very moment, and he gave it all he had. When he came to the lines, *'I'd walk a million miles; For one of your smiles'*, it is fair to say there was not a dry eye in the house.

And so, at last, it was time for explanations.

Dr Kenny and his wife lingered till nearly three. *She* had had a wonderful time and knew she would never again settle for the dreary, non-event Hogmanays in their salubrious cul-de-sac. *He* insisted on giving Kate a final check-up and advising her that she should get herself off to bed and rest now. She barely heard him or even noticed his ministrations, only just managing a polite farewell to the couple as they left.

Her attention was all upon this final stage in her great plan and she felt surprisingly calm and determined. Apart from the regrettable exhibition she had made of herself – *fancy me passin' oot an fallin' doon like an auld drunk jist at the best bit!* – she felt it had all gone swimmingly. And Robbie, in his inimitable fashion, oozing his boyish brand of effortless charm and loving his mother too much to allow her worry about it, had soon made her feel that her faint did not matter, indeed had even added to the dramatic glamour of the occasion.

'It was just like the movies, Ma,' he reassured her. 'Something like that always happens to the leading lady. It's the best bit in the film. We couldn't have done it better if we'd rehearsed it. We gave them all a great show!'

Now only thirteen people remained in the house: Old Maggie, Annie, Aggie, Eck, Jeannie, Bob, Angus, Terry, the unknown woman, Graham, Kate, Johnnie and, of course - the star of the show – Robbie.

The old woman had been settled down to sleep by Jeannie and Annie. It had taken two of them because she had been incoherent with over-tiredness and enervated by hours of company, making her alternately voluble and unable to pay attention to the simplest command or virtually comatose, a dead weight, and beyond one person's strength to handle.

'We'll no see much o' her 'til denner-time, thank God,' said Jeannie as they joined the meeting which was being convened in the sitting-room.

Graham had been about to slip away when Jeannie had detained him. 'Ye got dragged intae it at the start,' she said somewhat shamefacedly. 'Ye've a richt tae hear hoo it a' ties up.'

By tacit consent, chairs had been rearranged in the disordered room to form a meaningful circle. The women had made a big pot of tea and prepared a tray. The men mainly helped themselves to bottles of beer and lamented the end of the whisky although Angus, who had not had strong drink for several months on doctor's orders, now felt he had had more than enough alcohol for a first re-acquaintance and weighed in with the women for a nice cup of tea. Behaviour which made Johnnie regard him with even more suspicion.

Looking round the circle, Kate reflected on all the different levels of knowledge and understanding. She and Angus had been in it from the beginning, when it was just a tantalising idea; then there was Robbie himself who had come happily on board after several Wednesday afternoon telephone calls; next had been Jeannie in the Anstruther tea-room, whose role in the plot had dramatically expanded during the weeks of Kate's illness. It had been necessary to enrol Ethel Morrison, Angus's long-lost cousin, to tie up loose ends in Canada – the unknown woman was none other than his hospital visitor and most people had, by now, been politely, if puzzlingly, introduced to her by Angus. The Gilhooley twins, who had been last to be let in on the big secret, had left some time ago to do some serious Hogmanay business of their own.

The middle layer – it was like three concentric circles – comprised those who had hovered on the edges from an early stage, knowing something was afoot but with no idea what it was: Aggie, who had first spotted Kate setting off for Windygates and had been suspicious; Jeannie, who had been in this circle but had moved into the inner one after the Antruther tearoom episode; Annie, who had been so close to the centre at the very beginning, with her offer of granny-sitting on

Wednesdays, but who had never quite, despite her best efforts, penetrated the inner circle; and Bob who had started out very much *in* on early efforts to fathom out Kate's strange behaviour but who had drifted to the edges once Jeannie assumed her new persona and became Kate's confidante and accomplice.

On the outer ring were: Terry, who had simply been asked to come to the party and use his van as the taxi home to Windygates for Angus and Ethel; and finally Eck, Maggie and Johnnie, who had had no inkling of any surprise drama about to unfold.

It was time to bring everyone – except for the now-snoring Maggie – on to a level playing field, time for cards on the table, time to clear the air and any other metaphor that applied in this confused gathering.

Kate had one thing on her side at least, in this endeavour: you might have expected most people to be befuddled with drink by this stage. However, the series of shocks which Kate and Robbie had provided in the space of a few short minutes, and the ensuing babble of discussion and good-natured jostling to see the two stars, had sobered everyone up and focused their minds.

So it was a surprisingly alert group that met in Kate's sitting-room for the *denouement* at three o'clock on New Year's morning.

Johnnie and Robbie talked in low voices so as not to disturb the two sleeping women in the house. Robbie was tucked up in a makeshift bed on the sitting-room couch with only his underwear on. The Gilhooley boys, characteristically, had gone jaunting off to fry their own fish at about half-past-one, completely forgetting to take Robbie's suitcase out of their boot, so he would have to wait till later today to retrieve it. The fire had been banked up for what remained of the night and only a faint glow showed in one corner of the mound of smoking dross. Johnnie wore striped, flannelette pyjamas, a woolen cardigan and the battered old slippers he was much attached to.

When the last visitor had finally departed at almost four o'clock, Kate had suddenly drooped alarmingly, like a puppet, which one moment is dancing and sprightly, and the next, as its strings are cut, becomes floppy and lifeless.

All the colour drained out of her cheeks and she had difficulty framing or finishing the simplest sentence. Though longing for time alone with her to talk out his own private reactions and questions, now that he understood exactly the sequence of events, Johnnie recognised the danger signs and recalled Jim Kenny's last words as he had seen the doctor and his wife out the door at ten to three: 'She's had more than enough, Johnnie. Get her away to bed and no more excitement tomorrow.'

But that was easier said than done. Kate appeared very wide-awake as the group had gathered. She took the reins of the meeting into her hands with surprising firmness and orchestrated a blow-by-blow account of how it had all been planned and accomplished.

She called upon each of the principal players to recount his or her part in it. She began right at the beginning with her own feelings of remorse at having been so bad-tempered and unsympathetic to Angus the day he was taken ill in his shop, though she was discreetly ladylike about the nature of the symptoms of his illness.

She went on to describe her decision to pay a hospital visit to him to apologise, once she saw her way to getting an afternoon off her household duties, thanks to Johnnie's working lunch in St Andrews and Annie's kindness in offering to take over Maggie's care.

She flashed Annie a warm smile: 'If it hadnae been fur Annie that day, the hale thing wid never have got started.' Annie glowed and cast a triumphant look at Jeannie.

She then called upon Angus to explain how things had developed. This was the tricky bit – one which Kate and Jeannie had chewed over several times and which Jeannie had then discussed with Angus. After several of Jeannie's visits to Windygates, they had, between the three of them, agreed exactly what Angus would say and how he would say it.

The crucial thing was to nip in the bud any idea that there was anything immoral, salacious or even romantic between Kate and Angus. He was to make it clear that she had been invited to his home in Windygates for one purpose only: to help her get in touch with Robbie and Maureen by means of his telephone.

He described how, during two hospital visits, she had talked sadly and longingly of her children, so faraway, so dearly missed for five long years, and of her growing despair of ever seeing them again now that she had her old mother-in-law to look after. Angus did not dwell on just what the care of old Maggie had entailed at that time – quite apart from the veto it placed on any hopes of going to join or even visit the emigrants. There were enough people in the room with a keen

342

understanding of what Kate had been struggling with and how ill she had become as a result.

Angus's tentative offer of the use of his telephone so that she could, at least, talk to her children had been grasped gratefully. Trying to make such long-distance calls from the public phone-box was hopeless and the cost prohibitive. Indeed, she had never even thought to try. And so had begun the Wednesday visits and the phone calls to Canada.

Kate took up the tale from there, picking her way delicately through the minefield of suspicion and speculation from Annie and Aggie, flickering jealousy from Eck and affronted resentment from Johnnie.

The first time they had managed to book a transatlantic call and actually get through had been wonderful but it had been tantalisingly short and Kate had wept in frustration when they had been cut off. Angus had begun to wonder if he was only making matters worse for her.

Then he had hit on the idea of suggesting that they ask Robbie to come home for a visit. Maureen could not leave her young family but Robbie thought he could manage three weeks away at the end of December as he was changing jobs from the retail trade to a new post in a printing and publishing company. The surprise first-foot idea had been *his* brainwave. Of course, money was a problem but Angus had kindly offered to pay for his passage.

Angus coughed modestly and explained that his parents had left him quite comfortable. He was a bachelor with no family responsibilities and a lucrative business. It had been his pleasure to help out and was his way of thanking Kate for her kindness in visiting him in hospital.

At this point, he bravely admitted to the company how low in spirits he had been, both in hospital and in the early weeks after he returned home to convalesce. Apart from Canadian Cousin Ethel's visit, which he had been too ill to benefit from, he had had no other visitors and Kate's visits had been a godsend.

'I was in her debt,' he said simply. 'She was my Good Samaritan.'

He had baulked at so baring his soul when Kate and Jeannie had first conveyed the idea to him. But he understood well how important it was to prove that Kate had acted out of initial remorse and subsequent good-heartedness and that he had responded out of gratitude and compassion. There was to be no whiff of anything else.

It said much for his fondness for Kate and concern for her welfare that he had agreed, not only to expose his vulnerability and loneliness to such a large group, but also to hide and deny his real feelings for her. *She* might be quite sure that, on her part, there were no romantic longings in their liaison; *he* was well aware that, on his part, there were plenty, though they remained unspoken.

Kate explained how there had been difficulties some weeks getting to talk to Robbie at his work – it was mid-morning across the Atlantic when she phoned, lines were always busy at that time and booking a call could be difficult and hazardous. Then she had fallen ill, anyway, just as they had been about to finalise plans for getting the money to him to book a passage home in time for Hogmanay. Her hopes and plans might all have foundered but luckily, the day she was taken so badly, she had met Jeannie on the bus. They had agreed to gloss over the details of Jeannie's attempt to play Mata Hari.

Jeannie took up the tale and explained how she had acted as the go-between for Kate and Angus for five weeks. It had been her idea to involve Cousin Ethel, who also lived in Montreal, after Angus had remembered about her and mentioned her to Jeannie. The two had spent an hour one day hunting for the scrap of paper with Ethel's address on it, which she had left on the top of Angus's hospital locker and which he felt sure was somewhere in the house.

Once it had finally been found at the back of a drawer – Jeannie now enjoyed a pleasantly extensive knowledge of Angus's wardrobe and possessions – there was, as he had been fairly sure he remembered seeing, a telephone number too. He had phoned her that day but got no answer. However, working out the time difference carefully, he had stayed up and telephoned her again at midnight – seven in the evening there. This time she had answered.

Ethel was now invited to tell her tale. Of course, she had been delighted to hear from Angus. It had been so many months since her unexpected and unfruitful visit to him in hospital that she had almost given up. She had been unable to wait in Scotland any longer last May as she was due back at work after her holiday – she was a librarian in Montreal.

They had talked Morrison – Smillie family stuff for a while and then he had put her in the picture about what he and Kate were trying to achieve and the difficulties they were encountering because of being unable to talk for any reliable length of time on the phone to Robbie, and time being too short to rely on letters if they were to pull off the Hogmanay surprise.

She had readily agreed to act as their agent. She would go and introduce herself to Robbie and Janet and then arrangements could be made through her. Evening calls to her home were much easier than the daytime calls to Robbie at his work.

'Then, when I was helping Robbie to get the money Angus sent over, to book his passage and to make the arrangements with Angus to pass on to Jeannie and Kate, I just thought: *'Why don't I go too?'* I had got quite excited hearing about the wonderful surprise that was being planned. I felt I couldn't bear to be the only person not here to see it happen! And to be in the Old Country for Hogmanay again...and Robbie said he'd be glad of the company...' Her Canadian drawl petered out and she glanced a little uncertainly round the group.

'An richt welcome ye are, hen!' Kate beamed at Ethel whose rather severe countenance softened as she smiled back. 'Ah wis delighted when Ah heard ye were comin'. If it hadnae been fur you at the Canada end, we'd hae been strugglin'. An it'll gie you an Angus a chance tae hae a richt guid chinwag aboot yer auld aunties an grannies an a' that.'

The easy, familiar way she said *'Angus'* was not lost on Johnnie. He had been watching them both closely as the tale unfolded.

The conspirators went on to explain how things had been managed at this end, how Jeannie had roped her twins in to drive her to Windygates on Hogmanay morning, to pick up Angus and drive on to Greenock to meet the ship as it docked. It had been a bit of a squeeze getting all six of them in the car but fortunately the twins were lanky fellows and neither Jeannie nor Ethel took up much room. Angus's bulk had been accommodated in the front passenger seat and the other four had somehow stuffed themselves into the back.

No-one asked why *both* twins had felt it necessary to go: it had long been accepted by all that where one twin was, there would be the other. Indeed, the joke in the pub was that *if one of them ever gets married, he'll need a right big bed – for three!*

Of course, strictly speaking, Jeannie did not have to be there either but they had decided that it would be nice for Ethel to have another woman in the welcoming party and, in any case, it was just too delicious a moment to miss out on after the weeks of machinations to accomplish it. Kate had insisted on her going, seeing it as Jeannie's reward, and knowing that nothing could have been a better thank-you present for her.

Then it had been back to Angus's house and a lovely meal round his big dining-table for them all. Time to congratulate themselves on pulling it off. Time to remember and recount some of the false starts, blind alleys and frustrations of the past three months as the big idea was born and grew and finally reached fruition. And time, too, to look excitedly forward to midnight and the climax of all their plans.

At last, in the late afternoon, Jeannie had been escorted down the hill to the bus by the twins and Robbie, while Angus and Ethel had cleared the meal and chatted on towards firm friendship. Ethel had expressed gratifying delight over the carefully prepared guest room whilst, next door, old Mrs Clancy's eyes had been almost falling out of her head as she watched all the comings and goings. She was to be further scandalised over the next week when she realised that yet *another* woman was not only on the scene but was actually living in his house. In her eyes, that would make a count of *four*!

And, finally, they had all driven over in time for the bells and the rest was history. Terry, who was going to be Angus's new assistant when the butcher shop opened again next week, had agreed to come to the party, wait till Angus and Ethel were ready to go home and then be their taxi to Windygates.

'Well, son,' Johnnie said now as they sat over a last nightcap dram – he had unearthed a secret supply, having kept a bottle back to take in to Senga and Jim's that day when they went for their Ne'erday dinner. 'It fair took my breath away when ye all explained how it had been managed. Messages going back and forward like that from Kate to Jeannie Gilhooley to Angus Smillie to his cousin Ethel over there and finally to yerself... an then all the way back again... an nobody else here kennin' a thing about it! It must have been like Chinese Whispers. Did things no get a bit mixed up sometimes?'

Robbie grinned sleepily: it had been a long and very exciting day and he was exhausted. He had also drunk more whisky in the past five hours than he normally did in five weeks. Money was tight at home with a young family to provide for and 'Scotch' was expensive in Canada.

'Can we talk about it tomorrow, Dad? I just gotta get some shut-eye...' His words were slurring and his eyes were drooping.

Johnnie sighed as he looked down fondly but in some exasperation on his son. He felt wide-awake, buzzing with questions, needing to process a whole gamut of emotions and reactions. But the two people in the house who could help him do that were now both fast asleep.

He went over to the window and, skirting round the table - now a messy muddle of dirty plates, smeary glasses and stale food - he pulled aside the curtain and stared out at the deserted street. He was reminded of the last time he had felt like this - like the only person in the world awake. It had been the first night when Kate took ill and he had been up yet again, seeing to his mother's intimate and unsavoury needs, panicking about how on earth he was going to manage without Kate.

'Kate...' he thought now. Why had she kept it all such a secret? Why had she felt it necessary to go all the way to Windygates to make the phone calls? He could have perhaps arranged for her to use the phone in his office if she had told him what she wanted to do? But she had obviously felt it necessary to keep even her initial hospital visit to 'Angus' a secret and – no! – he would not have been at all happy at the thought of her going to that man's house in Windygates. No husband would be happy that his wife was visiting another man, and an unmarried man in his own home at that.

Johnnie replayed the concert of explanations over in his mind. The bottom line was that Kate had talked to Angus about her deep unhappiness, how much she missed her children and had been longing for five years to see them again and how impossible that had become now that she had the care of her old mother-in-law. And Angus, listening to a woman who had been on the point of drowning in misery, had cared enough to throw her a lifeline.

Johnnie frowned as he tried to recall whether, in the five years since Robbie and Maureen emigrated, Kate had ever talked to *him* about her unhappiness or about her growing, desperate need to see them again. He realised with shame that he really did not know.

He had no memory of such a conversation but then, how often had he listened to her? How aware had he been of her feelings, of the signals she had been sending out? Jim Kenny had been the one to ask the question: *Have you been listening to what she has been saying? Have you been aware of how she has been looking?* And, of course, he had not and had had no idea – even when it must have been staring him in the face - that Kate had been on the point of physical collapse. Little wonder that he had no recollection of whether or not she had tried to talk to him over the years about her feelings and her misery.

What must she have felt when – on top of her own sadness and longing and *his* indifference to it – he had moved his incontinent, demanding old mother in and simply left her with the punishing task of setting up a care routine. He knew now what that entailed and still blushed when he thought of his own mercifully brief experience and startlingly incompetent efforts. And he was not blind or deaf either to the way Maggie treated Kate although that seemed a lot less vicious since Kate had been ill, thank God.

As he watched a few staggering first-footers determinedly wend their way over the crossroads and on to the last house on their list, he felt his simmering, jealous anger towards Kate and his suspicious resentment towards Angus begin to abate. He did not really think there had been anything improper in their relationship. He had watched both of them intently, employing all his people management insight.

He knew Kate well enough, he felt sure: he would *know* if she was being unfaithful, surely? True, she had kept the Hogmanay secret amazingly well but that had been a conspiracy of several people, all supporting each other in the secrecy. That was a very different matter from concealing an illicit, romantic liaison. And Jeannie would have soon guessed if anything improper was going on: if ever a woman was good at picking up on hints and nuances, it was that wee woman. Acting as first point of contact between Kate and Angus for weeks, she could hardly have failed to know – if there *was* anything to know.

And yet, there was *something*. Johnnie felt sure, that underneath all this squeaky-clean exterior, there lurked a hidden, murky streak - and if not in Kate, then it must be in Angus.

*She's still **my** Katy but **there's** a man bears watchin'*, he thought as he finally let the curtain drop and made his way through the silent house to slip in beside his sleeping wife.

THE END